PRAISE FOR LEONARD GOLDB

"Imaginative, murderous . . . . captures the top shelf in the mystery world."—*Kansas City Star*

"Rushes along at a brisk clip."—*Chicago Tribune*

"A medical thriller . . . with uniquely ghastly murders."—*Los Angeles Times Book Review*

"A page-turner with medical realism and characters who command our sympathies."—*Charleston Post and Courier*

"Fascinating . . . devilish."—*People Magazine*

"Outstanding specimens of suspense."—*Knoxville News-Sentinel*

"Diabolical."—*The Virginian-Pilot*

"Bone-chilling and provocative."—*Tulsa World*

"The stuff of nightmares."—*Library Journal*

PATIENT
ONE

OTHER BOOKS BY THIS AUTHOR

LEONARD GOLDBERG

PATIENT ONE

MiDNIGHT INK
WOODBURY, MINNESOTA

FIRST EDITION
First Printing, 2012

Book design and format by Donna Burch
Cover design by Ellen Lawson
Cover art © Blood: iStockphoto.com/Renee Keith; Caduceus medical symbol: iStockphoto.com/jgroup

Midnight Ink, an imprint of Llewellyn Worldwide Ltd.

Library of Congress Cataloging-in-Publication Data
Goldberg, Leonard S.
  Patient one : a novel / Leonard Goldberg. — 1st ed.
    p. cm.
  ISBN 978-0-7387-3046-2
1. Emergency physicians—Fiction. 2. Presidents—United States—Fiction.
3. Presidents—Russia (Federation)—Fiction. 4. Terrorism—Fiction. I. Title.
  PS3557.O35775P38 2012
  813'.54—dc23
                            2011041375

Midnight Ink
Llewellyn Worldwide Ltd.
2143 Wooddale Drive
Woodbury, MN 55125-2989
www.midnightinkbooks.com

Printed in the United States of America

For Mia and Jackson

Attack him where he is unprepared,
appear where you are not expected.
—Sun Tzu, *The Art of War*

PROLOGUE

They had no idea they were being poisoned.

The elegantly dressed guests swallowed the concealed toxin without tasting it and washed it down with expensive wine and champagne. The toxin traveled past the pharynx, through the esophagus, and into the stomach, causing no ill effects or damage because it was encased in a thick, lipid coat. But once it entered the small intestines, the protective coat dissolved away and slowly released its contents. The toxin, floating freely at first, was unaffected by the alkaline pH and proteolytic enzymes of the intestinal juice. But gradually individual molecules of the toxin found their way to receptors lining the intestinal wall. There they attached themselves firmly, then swept into the intestinal cells and quickly overwhelmed their defense mechanisms. From that moment on, the outcome was inevitable. With pinpoint accuracy, the toxic molecules began disrupting metabolic pathways that were crucial for the cells' survival. The killing process was underway.

The two hundred and fifty distinguished guests, having no symptoms yet, continued to ingest the hidden toxin. Some went back for second and even third helpings of the delicious delicacy. They would suffer the most.

ONE

THE MORGUE ATTENDANT PULLED back the sheet covering the body on the gurney. "Extra crispy, huh?"

José Hernandez nodded and averted his eyes from the charred remains of a firefighter sent down from the hospital's ICU. *Holy Mother of Mercy! What a terrible way to die!* He winced at the thought of the pain this man must have endured, and felt nauseous from the sweet, greasy smell that rose from underneath the sheet.

"You okay?" the attendant asked as he transferred the corpse to a refrigerated unit in the wall.

"Just tired," José replied. "They have me working a double shift."

"That'll wear you out," the attendant said, then rapped on the railing of the gurney. "We're all done here."

José guided the empty gurney out of the morgue and into the basement of University Hospital. He paused briefly to gather himself, then stretched his weary legs and tried to bring life back into them. The stretching helped, but only a little. José continued down the dim corridor, leaning heavily on his gurney. It had been a very busy night, with a seemingly endless line of patients that needed to be rushed to radiology and the ICU and the OR. He hadn't stopped—not even for a moment—since the beginning of his first shift. But the hectic activity was slowing at last, and he would shortly take a break in the room where orderlies could relax and refresh themselves.

As he passed a bank of elevators, his cell phone chirped loudly in the stillness. The caller ID said that it was his pregnant wife. Instantly, he sensed bad news. She never phoned him at work, except for emergencies. He quickly answered. "*¿Ana, está todo bien?*"— Ana, is everything all right?

"I'm fine," she replied in English. "I'm just calling to tell you that the dizziness I had earlier is gone. So now you do not need to keep worrying about me." Ana always spoke in English to him when she talked about "serious matters," a legacy of her more assimilated second-generation Angeleno family.

"You should still rest," José said, breathing a sigh of relief. "The baby will need all of your strength."

"I'll rest more," she promised.

"And I'll see you tomorrow morning, after I get off. I will stop at the market, and make a special breakfast for us."

"You spoil me."

"It is easy to spoil a beautiful woman."

His wife laughed that sweet little-girl laugh he loved. "Stop your nonsense, and go back to work."

"Sleep well, *ángelita*."

José put his cell phone away and pushed the gurney along the vacant corridor. Now he had a bounce to his step. His wife's voice had reinvigorated him. *Nothing could go wrong today*, he thought contentedly. The past two weeks had been the best in his life. The

4

very best. It started with his wife informing him that she was pregnant with their first child. She was certain it would be a girl, and they would name her Maria. What a blessing! A gift from God, after years of trying. Then came the second major event, the one he'd awaited even longer: just the previous week, he had finally been sworn in as a citizen of the United States at a public ceremony at the Convention Center on Figueroa Street. Finally he had become an American. His unborn daughter would automatically become one, anyway, but now she would have two American parents—and that would assure her a good life. And to top everything off, he had been elevated to his new position as an orderly at the medical center. He was no longer just part of a cleaning crew that mopped floors and scrubbed bathrooms. And his modest salary would be almost doubled.

José made the sign of the cross and thanked God and his patron saint for the good fortune that had come his way.

Ahead he saw two fellow orderlies who, like himself, were dressed in white. One was thin and pale, the other stocky and balding. Both were Anglos. José wondered how he should address them. Certainly not with too much respect, now that they were equals. *You are no longer a cleaner,* he reminded himself, pulling his shoulders back slightly. *You are a hospital orderly.*

The thin man waved cordially.

José waved back and greeted them, "Good evening. I am José Hernandez."

"I am Aliev," the thin man said, not bothering to introduce his co-worker. "Very busy tonight, eh?"

"Yes. It's been nonstop."

"Too bad these new gurneys are not functioning well."

"What do you mean?" José asked.

"Some of the wheels have been breaking. Two patients have fallen off their gurneys already today," Aliev informed him.

"My wheels are working fine," José said.

"You had better check them," Aliev advised. "You don't want yours to malfunction with a patient on it."

"Yes, I'll take a look," José agreed, and leaned over to examine the wheels.

He never saw the blow coming.

The balding man slammed the back of his clenched fist into José's neck, with the force of a sledgehammer. The Hispanic orderly dropped to the floor, stunned and unaware of what had happened. Before José could regain his senses, the balding man looped a string of piano wire around his throat. Betraying no emotion at all, he tightened the garrote and shut off the orderly's air supply. Once his legs stopped kicking, it took José Hernandez less than a minute to die.

"Hurry," the man who called himself Aliev urged.

The balding man dragged the body into a nearby room, then forcefully stuffed it into a narrow metal locker. Before closing the door, he ripped off the orderly's ID card and tossed it to Aliev.

"You want other ID, like wallet?" the balding man asked in broken English.

"No, just the card."

Aliev studied the plastic card briefly. The photograph on it bore no resemblance to him, but that was of little concern. No one closely checked ID cards on orderlies late at night. He pinned it onto his shirt.

Stepping out into the corridor, Aliev said, "Now, quickly, get onto the gurney beneath the sheet."

The balding man stared back at him uncomprehendingly. The word *sheet* was unfamiliar to him. "*Soh tsa khaet*"—I don't understand, he said in Chechen.

Aliev repeated the order in his native Chechen, then switched back to English. "While we are in the halls of the hospital, speak only as the Americans do. Understand?"

"Y-yes," the balding man said haltingly and climbed onto the gurney. "Only American."

"Good." Aliev nodded his approval. He had demanded that his Chechens speak proficient Russian and rudimentary English. Some understanding of the latter two languages could prove to be critical for the success of their mission. "Your shoes are showing. Draw them back."

Again the balding man did as he was ordered. "Can you see them now?"

"No."

Aliev pushed the gurney down the deserted corridor, peering into each room he passed. All were quiet and empty, except one. Its door was closed, with music playing behind it. Aliev ignored the sound and glanced at his watch. It was 9:10 p.m. The security guard would begin making his rounds soon. The guard was old, with a noticeable limp. But he carried a two-way radio, and that could cause trouble. Aliev moved on, picking up the pace.

As he turned the gurney into a waiting elevator, Aliev asked, "Is your silencer attached?"

Under the sheet the balding man fingered the silencer on his 9mm Glock, then answered, "Yes."

"Be ready," Aliev said, and punched the button for the ninth floor of the medical center.

TWO

THE PRESIDENT'S PAIN STARTED halfway through the official dinner. It was a deep, burning sensation in his upper abdomen that radiated into his chest. He reached for a glass of water and took a sip. The burning eased.

"What a lovely banquet, Mr. President," said Ivana Suslev. "So *many* movie stars."

"Well, this is where they all live," the President said to the wife of the visiting Russian leader.

"I see Tom and Jennifer and Nicole," she stargazed at the tables below. "Do you think I might meet them?"

"I think we can arrange that." The President smiled to himself. He'd been briefed that Ivana Suslev was fascinated with American film stars, and the protocol officers had seen to it that several major stars sat in her line of sight, directly in front of her.

They were seated on the dais in a large banquet hall at the Beverly Hills Wilshire Hotel. In attendance were two hundred and fifty members of Los Angeles' wealthy elite. Mostly bankers and builders and financiers, with just enough Hollywood stars and entertainment moguls. They were invited to the gala to honor the President of the United States and the President of Russia, who would soon sign a friendship pact that had heavy economic overtones. Although the pact made no mention of petroleum, every sentence was dripping with it. Russia now controlled the largest of the world's untapped oil reserves, and had promised to supply the United States with every gallon it needed. America's dependency on Middle Eastern oil was about to end.

This sea change had taken place during the past year. Using advanced American technology, a giant oil field containing 220 billion barrels had been discovered in the Western Siberian Plain, increasing Russia's known oil deposits to 360 billion barrels. And another smaller field to the north was being actively explored. The total reserves of Russia would soon exceed 400 billion barrels, second only to the oil reserves of all OPEC countries combined. With these new discoveries, the world had undergone a massive power shift. The economic influence of OPEC in general and the political importance of the Arab states were diminishing daily. And with their oil reserves dwindling, the situation could only worsen for them.

The two presidents had convened this formal official dinner to proclaim the increased friendship and joint economic interests that existed between America and Russia. Their more subtle motive was to let the world know that OPEC would no longer control the market and dictate the price of American oil.

Ivana Suslev was now talking about Rodeo Drive and its wonderful shops. Bally. Hermès. Bottega Veneta. The President nodded, but he really wasn't listening. His gastric pain had returned, bringing with it a twinge of nausea. He was tempted to take one of the antacid pills he always carried in his coat pocket. But he knew he couldn't. Not here, not with hundreds of people and a powerful head of state watching. Any pill, any sign of illness, would be interpreted as a weakness. And weaknesses could be exploited.

John Merrill, at forty-five the youngest American president since John F. Kennedy, was assumed to be in excellent health. His annual physical examination revealed a resting pulse of sixty beats per minute, a blood pressure of 110/70, and a normal stress test. His personal physician officially reported that the President had a mild case of acid reflux with esophagitis, which was well controlled with Prilosec. But in fact the esophagitis wasn't mild and wasn't well controlled with Prilosec, and the indigestion that came with it was bothering him more and more. The annual press release also glossed over the discomfort in his right knee, the result of an old football injury incurred while he was a star quarterback at Stanford. That too was nagging him now.

Merrill stretched out his leg under the table, and the knee joint cracked pleasantly. The ache he had been experiencing disappeared. *Too bad I can't do the same thing for my stomach*, he thought sourly, and wondered what had set off his acid reflux this time. It was probably the lemon-cured salmon that followed the lightly seasoned soup. Or maybe the beluga caviar he'd consumed at the Russian reception earlier in the evening. *Goddamn it! I've got to watch what I eat.*

Out of the corner of his eye Merrill saw his wife, who was four seats away, push her chair back and stand. She smiled and spoke briefly to Dimitri Suslev, then hurried off to a side door that led to a guarded corridor. A Secret Service agent followed her out.

"Excuse me," Merrill said to Ivana Suslev, and signaled to the Secret Service agent behind him.

Aaron Wells, the President's lead agent, quickly stepped over and leaned in close. "Yes, sir, Mr. President?"

"See if the First Lady is all right," Merrill whispered.

Wells moved away and spoke into the microphone that was inside his sleeve next to his wrist. After a short conversation he came back to the President. "Her stomach is a little queasy, sir."

"Goddamn lemon-cured salmon," Merrill muttered under his breath.

"What's that, Mr. President?" Wells asked at once.

"Nothing," Merrill replied and glanced over to his wife's empty chair. "Dr. Warren should take a look at her."

"The agent assigned to the First Lady suggested that we have her seen by your personal physician, but she refused, Mr. President."

"Have Warren check her anyway."

"Yes, sir."

As the agent moved back, Ivana Suslev asked Merrill, "Is there anything wrong, Mr. President?"

"Everything is fine," Merrill assured her, wondering if the combination of lemon-cured salmon and beluga caviar had set off his wife's stomach, too.

Lucy Merrill, like her husband, was sensitive to spicy foods and did her best to avoid them. On state occasions, however, she sometimes indulged a bit, but only after taking a double dose of Prilosec. The drug usually controlled things. *But not tonight*, Merrill thought unhappily as a second wave of burning nausea came up into his throat. He took another sip of water, but this time it didn't help much.

Dimitri Suslev, a short, squat man with a large head and thick black eyebrows, stood and bellowed out, "Mr. President, I propose a toast to you and the people of your great country."

Merrill got to his feet and raised his glass. He liked Suslev, but he did not trust him. Russian leaders had a long history of making alliances and pacts, only to break them later when they no longer served their purposes. And Suslev was no different. He had pledged to give exclusive drilling and distribution rights to the three American oil companies that had played a crucial role in the discovery of Russia's new oil fields. Yet he was currently negotiating a clandestine compact with the Chinese government that included a multibillion-dollar oil and gas pipeline that ran from the Siberian Plain to northern China. Suslev had seen the opening and taken it, despite the promise he'd made months earlier.

The Russian concept of diplomacy, Merrill thought darkly. *To them, treaties are meant to be used, not adhered to. So I'll watch him. And I'll keep in mind that America is racing ahead with a new internal combustion–based technology that could release the one and a half trillion barrels of oil trapped in the massive shale beds of Wyoming, Montana, and Utah.*

Currently, the oil in shale was being extracted by a process called fracking, which consisted of blasting water, sand, and chemicals into the oil-soaked rock. But fracking was far more expensive and considerably less effective than the newly discovered process. Once the internal-combustion method was perfected, it was estimated that oil could be produced from shale at a cost of $75 a barrel. *Just imagine that! Over a trillion barrels of oil, all belonging to America! We would be energy independent for hundreds of years, and with oil at $75 a barrel our nation's economy would boom.* But perfection and implementation of the new technique was thought to be at least eight to ten years away. Until then, America needed Russia. But Russia also desperately needed American investment and know-how to rebuild its massive infrastructure. *And that*, Merrill thought, *would keep Suslev partially honest. For now.*

The toast went on and on.

Merrill held up his glass of water and wished Suslev's long-windedness would come to a close. But the Russian president rambled on, now saluting the American Secretary of State and his wife, who were seated beside him. Suslev paused, then began extolling the natural beauty of California. *Goddamn it! Wrap it up!* Merrill growled under his breath.

Another wave of nausea traveled up Merrill's esophagus and he swallowed it back. But it left a sour, bilious taste in his mouth. Again he considered reaching for an antacid pill but resisted the urge. He pasted a smile on his face and gazed down at those assembled, many of whom had their glasses raised. But something was wrong. Some of the people appeared to be hurrying out. A dozen or so. Mostly women, with their hands covering their mouths. One of the seated movie stars was bent over, with her head between her knees. The man next to her appeared to be retching.

An intense surge of nausea caused Merrill to gag. He tasted vomit coming up. Quickly he turned to Wells, stood, and said, "Get me to the john. Now!"

"Liberty is on the move!" Wells barked into his microphone. "Clear the head!"

He took the President's arm and led him past the startled guests on the dais. They raced out the side door and down a long corridor, now joined by four more Secret Service agents, two to each side of the President. A maid standing beside a laundry cart was roughly shoved into a linen closet. A nearby elevator door opened, and an agent peeled off to stop the passengers from exiting.

"Secure the entire hall!" Wells shouted. "Nobody in or out!"

Merrill dashed into the men's room and entered a stall just in time. Kneeling down, he put his face over the toilet bowl and brought up a torrent of vomit. Then another mouthful, then another, until his stomach was empty. Finally he opened his eyes and took a deep breath. Perspiration was pouring off his forehead in big droplets. A wave of dizziness came and went. He tried to stand but felt lightheaded, and sank back to his knees. Then he vomited again. Now the vomit tasted peculiar, more sweet than bitter. Once more he attempted to get to his feet and, as he did, he stared down into the toilet bowl. It was filled with blood. Bright red blood!

Merrill felt as if he was about to pass out. Desperately gathering his strength, he reached up for the handle to the stall door and slowly pulled his body to a standing position. He paused a moment and steadied himself before staggering toward the door of the men's room. Again he threw up bright red blood, with most of it splattering over his shirt and coat. He reached for the door and opened it, then collapsed into the arms of Aaron Wells.

"Liberty is down!" Wells cried out into his microphone. "Liberty is down!"

The corridor suddenly seemed filled by men in suits, with wires from earphones snaking down their collars. The President was lifted by four agents. Two had his legs, two his upper torso. Wells grabbed a large towel from the laundry cart and draped it over the President's blood-soaked shirt and coat. The group ran down the corridor with four more agents joining in, their weapons drawn. They formed a phalanx as they entered the lobby and rushed for the rear entrance, knocking over everybody and everything in their way. A man in a wheelchair was pushed into a sofa, a large potted plant alongside him sent flying. Two chatting women were bowled over. A bellman at the door was slammed into the ground. In the driveway the presidential limousine was waiting, motor running.

The President was quickly placed in the back seat, with Aaron Wells at his side. Another agent was in front on the right, a third in the driver's seat. A black Chevy Suburban pulled up in the rear, carrying another team of heavily armed Secret Service agents.

"Go! Go!" Wells yelled.

The LAPD motorcycle escorts gunned their engines, and with lights flashing led the way out of the drive.

The presidential motorcade sped out onto Wilshire Boulevard, sirens blaring.

THREE

In a light drizzle, Dr. David Ballineau hurried up the lawn to his West Los Angeles home, a step behind his eleven-year-old daughter who was still wearing her Harry Potter costume.

"Did you really like the play, Dad?" Kit asked, her wizard's hat tilted to one side.

"It was wonderful," David enthused. "And you were great."

"I think I messed up one of my lines."

"I didn't notice, and I doubt that anyone else did either."

"Good," Kit said, and smiled. "I didn't want to embarrass myself in front of a lot of people."

As he opened the front door, David glanced back at the dark, misty night and sampled the air. The humidity was heavy, a consequence of the big winter storm that was lingering off the Southern California coast. It would bring plenty of rain, David thought. That would make the freeways slick and cause cars to hydroplane, setting the stage for gruesome accidents, similar to the one he'd seen earlier that day. For emergency room physicians like David

Ballineau, rain was unwelcome, particularly when accompanied by thick mist.

"Dad, is that woman in the audience who got sick going to be all right?" Kit asked, wiping her feet on the doormat.

"She'll be fine, honey," David assured her.

"She's lucky you were there."

"Yeah. Very lucky." He watched Kit scamper up the stairs and called after her, "Don't forget our agreement, Kitten. No late night phone calls. Right?"

"Just one to Susie," she said over her shoulder. "And it'll be a quickie."

"How quick?"

"B-Y-K-I."

It took him a moment to decipher her spoken text message. BYKI stood for Before You Know It. She's growing up so fast, David mused with that combination of pleasure and terror peculiar to fathers of daughters. One day she was a toddler, the next a beautiful, spirited young girl who could steal his heart without even trying.

"Okay, Dad?" she yelled down to him.

"Okay."

Kicking off his loafers, David stopped in the kitchen for a cold beer, then strode into the small library and, propping his feet up on his desk, began to relax for the first time in fourteen hours. *Christ! What a monster of a day!* he murmured wearily to himself, thinking back to the events that began at 7 a.m. and never ceased. From the moment he stepped into the emergency room at University Hospital, all hell seemed to have broken loose. It started with the burned firefighters who had gotten trapped in a wind-blown inferno just north of Los Angeles. Most were suffering from smoke inhalation and second-degree burns. But a few had been charred beyond recognition and were now fighting for their lives in the hospital's ICU. Then came the victims from a high-speed, multi-car accident on the San Diego Freeway that left two dead and a dozen seriously injured. The injuries were horrific. Amputated limbs. Open tibial fractures. Ruptured spleens. Torn aortas. A museum of bloody horrors.

David rocked back absently in his swivel chair, still seeing the charred and severely injured patients in his mind's eye and knowing most wouldn't survive.

There was one life he was certain he'd saved. But that came later on, when his twelve-hour shift in the ER was over.

After giving a report to the incoming physician, David had dashed out of the hospital and hurried over to Kit's private school, where she had one of the leading roles in a play based on a Harry Potter book. Arriving late, David had been in his seat only a few minutes when the woman behind him sucked too hard on a breath mint and aspirated it deep into her posterior pharynx. Despite numerous Heimlich maneuvers, the mint remained lodged in place and compromised the woman's air supply. She started to panic and dashed out of the auditorium, which only made matters worse. When David caught up with her, she was gasping for air and beginning to turn cyanotic. He was forced to do a tracheotomy, using a knife from the school cafeteria. By the time the paramedics arrived and David returned to his seat, the play was nearly over. He never got to see his daughter on stage.

David swallowed a sip of cold beer and thought about how many more special moments he might miss in Kit's life because of his profession. *I have to plan better*, he vowed determinedly. *Yeah. Better planning. Right!* he scoffed at himself, now recalling the age-old adage—*If you want to make God laugh, tell Him your plans.* David had learned the wisdom in that proverb the hard way, a long time ago.

"Wooooo!" Kit said, prancing into the room. She had a wool blanket draped over herself from head to toe.

"Why the blanket?" David asked, smiling at his daughter and loving her more than anybody could love anyone.

Kit pulled the quilt away from her face and looked at him quizzically. "Don't you remember that part in the play, Dad? When Harry Potter wore his special blanket, no one could see him."

"Oh yeah," David said, reacting quickly because he'd missed that section of the play. "But I thought the blanket worked only for Harry."

"Uh-uh," Kit corrected him. "It does magic on anyone who wears it."

"Got it," David told her, nodding. "So I can't see you, but I can still hear you. Correct?"

"Of course you can hear me," Kit replied, placing the blanket back over her head. "We're having a conversation, aren't we?"

David grinned broadly. "Good point."

"You've got to put a lot of feeling into your voice, Dad," Kit urged. "You have to make people believe you really can't see me."

David had to bite his lip to keep himself from laughing. "Okay."

"And you have to sound like something is spooky."

"I can do that."

"Excellent," Kit approved. "Now we'll start again."

Just then Juanita Cruz, their live-in housekeeper, entered the library and said, "*Tomorrow* you will start again." She removed the blanket from Kit's head and gently stroked the child's raven hair back into place. "That is enough play-acting for tonight, Little One. Now you must do your homework."

"Can't I do it later?" Kit tried to beg off.

"Now!" Juanita insisted.

"Dad!" Kit pleaded, looking to her father for support.

David shrugged. "Homework is important."

"Five more minutes," Kit bargained with Juanita.

Juanita ignored the girl's plea and pointed to the door of the library with her index finger. "Are you going to embarrass us by making me say it a third time?"

"Phooey!" Kit protested, and headed out of the room.

Juanita followed her to the door, then turned back to David. "Have you had your dinner yet, Dr. Ballineau?"

David shook his head. "I'm not very hungry. Maybe I'll have something later."

"There is cold chicken and pasta in the refrigerator."

David watched her leave, grateful as always that he had such a wonderful housekeeper to help him raise Kit. *What in the world would I do without her?* he wondered, but he already knew the answer. *Somehow I'd manage. I'd muddle through, just as I did when Marianne died.* His gaze drifted over to the picture on his desk of his wife, dead just over eight years. Sometimes it seemed like the tragedy happened only yesterday, other times like it occurred an eon ago. He sighed deeply, recalling that the pain had slowly and finally subsided. But the emptiness was still there, and all the joy in the world couldn't remove it. He could forget about the emptiness for a while, but it never really left him. And never would.

His eyes went to the calendar on his desk. Kit had circled Sunday's date with a thick red crayon. It marked the anniversary of Marianne's death. On that day Juanita would take Kit to her church and light candles in memory of Marianne. And David would tag along. But he would refuse to sing and recite prayers about a good and merciful God, again asking himself the same questions in church. Where was this good and merciful God when

Marianne was dying a slow and painful death from leukemia? And where was God when a three-year-old child cried every night for her mommy?

David shook his head at the sad memories, still wondering how a merciful God could let all that happen. A young minister once told David that God sometimes tested people in harsh ways. Well, David thought somberly, he had no use or belief for that kind of God. Not then. Not now. Not—

The phone beside the calendar rang. It was his private line, which meant it had to be the hospital. No one else called this late at night.

David reached for the phone. "Yes?"

"Dr. Ballineau, this is Betsy in the ER. We've got a big problem on our hands."

"What?"

"A hundred cases of severe gastroenteritis, and even more coming in. We're overflowing and way understaffed."

"Get all the interns and residents to come down to the ER," David instructed. "They should be able to handle straightforward gastroenteritis."

"They're already here, but it may not be straightforward gastroenteritis," the nurse went on. "And we're dealing with some very, very important people."

"Such as?"

"The President of the United States."

"I'm on my way in," David said, hanging up.

———

It was like talking to a statue, and hoping it would respond.

Carolyn Ross sat across from her mother in the living room of their Santa Monica home and tried to make conversation. But her mother just stared into space, lost in the deep haze that came with Alzheimer's disease.

"Mom," Carolyn asked softly, "Can I get you something to drink?"

The woman stayed silent.

"Are you thirsty?"

Again, nothing. Saliva drooled out of the woman's mouth and down onto her chin.

Carolyn reached over for a Kleenex and dabbed it away. Her mother didn't seem to notice as more saliva dripped out, now spilling onto the woman's bib.

Carolyn continued to clean the drool, remembering back to a time when her mother was so neat and tidy she wouldn't tolerate even a speck of dirt or dust. And she'd been so independent, never wanting to need anyone for anything. But now the poor woman was totally dependent, Carolyn thought sadly. Her mother had to be fed and bathed like a baby, and had to wear diaper-panties that required changing every few hours. It was a living nightmare.

At least I know how to care for Mother and keep her comfortable, Carolyn told herself. *And my salary as a nurse means I can afford to hire a sitter to look after Mother during the day while I'm away. Thank goodness for that.*

Carolyn discarded the saliva-laden Kleenex into a nearby trash can, now wondering how the poor and those with modest incomes managed to care for family members afflicted with Alzheimer's disease. How do they afford it? How? Between the sitters and medicines and doctor visits, the expenses never stopped mounting. For these families, Alzheimer's must be an overwhelming burden. A double living nightmare.

Carolyn's cell phone chirped. She stared at the phone, then at her mother, hoping the high-pitched sound would register in the woman's mind. It didn't. The costly drugs her mother was taking weren't helping at all.

Sighing resignedly, Carolyn reached for the phone. "Hello."

"Carolyn, this is Kate Blanchard on the Pavilion," said the junior nurse. "The head nurse had to leave for a family emergency and we've going to be really shorthanded. According to the doctors in the ER, we're about to be swamped up here with acutely ill patients that have severe gastroenteritis. Apparently they'll be coming in droves."

"To the Beaumont Pavilion?" Carolyn asked. The Pavilion's plush suites were always reserved for the rich and famous. "When I left this evening, all fourteen rooms were occupied."

"They still are. But since most of our patients are here for diagnostic workups, they can temporarily be transferred to the Intermediate Care Facility. That will make room for some of the terribly ill patients who also happen to be dignitaries." The junior nurse paused as if to catch her breath. "It's bad, Carolyn. It sounds like they'll be needing every bed they can free up."

Carolyn groaned inwardly. She had no choice but to go in. It would be impossible for one nurse to handle a ward overflowing with really sick patients.

"I'll be there in fifteen minutes."

"Don't come through the ER," Kate warned. "It's a madhouse down there."

Carolyn clicked the cell phone off and quickly thought of the essential things she had to do. First, she had to call the sitter and hope the neighbor could come and spend the night. Hastily, she punched in a phone number. The sitter answered on the second ring. "Dolly, I've got an emergency at the hospital. I need you to look after my mother tonight." She listened for a response, then said, "Of course you can bring your dog. But you must come now."

Carolyn placed the phone down and turned to her mother. "Mom, I've got to go back to the hospital. But Dolly will be here soon to stay with you. Okay?"

The woman continued to stare ahead with a blank expression.

"I love you," Carolyn whispered and kissed her mother's forehead.

Her mother showed no response.

"I have to go upstairs and change," Carolyn said and hurried to the door. Halfway there, she stopped abruptly. Behind her, her mother was making some sort of sound. Carolyn spun around. Her mother had her lips pursed and was sending Carolyn kisses. There even seemed to be a hint of a smile on the woman's face. Then, in an instant, the expression disappeared and the woman went back to staring into nothingness.

"Oh, Mom!" Carolyn whispered, her tears welling up as she ran for the stairs.

FOUR

THE EMERGENCY ROOM AT University Hospital was in turmoil. Doctors and nurses were racing back and forth in the corridors, clearly overwhelmed by the influx of sick people. And more were coming through the front entrance. The noise they made was deafening, with shouts and yells and cries for help mixed in with moans and groans and the sounds of individuals retching. Every room was taken, every bed and gurney occupied by nauseated patients. Even the space on the floor was filled with elegantly dressed people throwing up into handheld basins. The overcrowding was made worse by the Secret Service, which had closed off an entire section of the ER for the President of the United States. Two agents were hurriedly placing waist-high wooden barricades across a corridor to discourage the curious.

Aaron Wells pointed to the barricade, saying, "I want another row of those things about ten feet back, and line them up so you can knock over one without knocking over all the others." He waited for the additional barricades to be put in position, then added, "And I want two agents behind each row. Nobody in, nobody out, without my say-so."

Wells quickly surveyed the interior of the ER again, looking for weak spots. The two examining rooms in the middle of the section, which held the President and the First Lady, had no windows or exits except for their closed doors, and those were being guarded by a pair of agents. There was no staircase or fire escape to be concerned with. At the end of the corridor was an elevator on hold, its door open and guarded by two more agents. Secure enough, Wells told himself, but he was still worried about the mass of sick people, which could provide cover for an attack on the President. If the crowd, for any reason, suddenly rushed the barricades, they would rapidly overrun the agents guarding the President. Or terrorists could jump out of the crowd with automatic weapons or grenades, and kill everybody in the section.

"The crowd!" Wells grumbled to himself. "The goddamn crowd!" He couldn't throw them into the street, and there was no way to check them all out. The President was in a dangerous position and had to be moved.

Wells saw Agent Dan Morris, the second in command, coming through the barricade and waved him over. In a low voice he asked, "Did you locate the President's daughter?"

Morris shook his head. "We're still looking."

"Look harder," Wells urged. The first thing on the President's mind would be the well-being of the First Lady and their daughter. "Did you check the hotel?"

"She's not there," Morris said. "And she's not here. I've got men posted at the entrance to all the ERs in the vicinity. As soon as she and her date are found, they'll be brought here."

"What about Suslev and his wife?"

"They're in another part of the ER, with their own security."

"Are they as exposed as we are?"

"More so."

"Shit!"

"Yeah."

Morris asked, "What caused all this? Food poisoning?"

Wells shrugged. "I guess."

Morris moved in closer and quietly inquired, "How's Liberty?"

"Not good."

A middle-aged man just beyond the barricades began retching loudly, then threw up a stream of brownish liquid. The vomit gushed from his mouth, like a projectile. The patients around him ducked and brought up their arms to cover themselves from the spray. A few were so ill they barely moved. The stench of vomit filled the air and made the patients nearby even more nauseated. Wells looked away and over to a set of swinging doors that led to the outer waiting area. It was another weak point. He considered having an agent circulate beyond the doors, but decided against it. All the agent would see was a swarm of people throwing up over each other.

Wells cursed to himself. He wished the President had taken the Secret Service's advice and had his meeting with the Russian leader in Washington, where everything could be tightly controlled. But Liberty insisted on having the official dinner in Los Angeles. It was a gesture of goodwill to the President of Russia, who would later fly to San Francisco, where world leaders were gathering for a celebration of the United Nations Charter. To hold the official dinner in Los Angeles, with its generous political donors, would be convenient for everyone, the President had said. It would also be much more dangerous, the Secret Service had argued. But the President had insisted. And the end result was a nightmare in the making, Wells thought grimly. Nothing in the ER was under control. Everything was in a maddening state of flux, and this left the President vulnerable. Very vulnerable.

"Aaron," an agent by the barricade called out, "the ER doc wants to talk with you."

Wells signaled the young resident over and asked, "What?"

"We're having trouble finding a ward we can empty out," the resident answered.

"Don't tell me your problems. Just get it done." Wells was a big man, with broad shoulders and a square jaw. His balding blond hair had been shaved off down to the skin, leaving his steely gray eyes as the most prominent feature of his face. He gave the resident a hard stare, then said, "And do it now."

The resident wasn't accustomed to being intimidated, but the agent's glare caused him to look away. "Maybe we could clear out the special unit."

"What's that?" Wells asked.

"It's a restricted ward that's used for patients receiving experimental drugs," the resident replied. "But it may not be possible to evacuate—"

"Just do it!" Wells cut him off. "I don't care how you do it. Just do it!"

The door to the trauma room holding the President opened, and his personal physician, William Warren, stepped out. There was blood on his hands and on the sleeves of his coat. Glancing over to Wells, he immediately sensed the agent's worry. "The President is stable."

Wells breathed a sigh of relief inwardly. *Thank sweet Jesus in heaven above!* he thought, but said only, "Good."

"Do we have a ward cleared for the President?" Warren asked.

"Not yet," Wells replied unhappily.

"What's the holdup?"

Wells gestured with his thumb to the young resident. "He's a little slow following orders."

"Well, let's see if we can speed him up," Warren said in a neutral tone, but his temper was rising. He turned to the resident. "I want you to listen carefully because I'm only going to say this once. We need a safe ward for the President and we need it now. If necessary I can have a fleet of ambulances outside this hospital in a half-hour with a doctor in each one. We'll pick a floor and have the chief of service meet us there. Then we'll roll out the patients and put them in ambulances which will take them to other hospitals. And we'll end up with a safe ward for President Merrill. So the choice is as follows—either you do it or we'll do it for you."

The resident swallowed nervously. "But, sir, I can't just…"

"Let's get those ambulances," Warren instructed Wells. "Twenty-five should do."

"What about the doctors?" Wells asked.

"Get a list of all the physicians who live within a ten-mile radius of the hospital and have the police…"

"Aaron," an agent at the first row of barricades yelled out, "there's another doctor who wants to see you."

The resident peered over and said hurriedly, "That's the director of the emergency room. Maybe he can do what you want."

"An ER specialist isn't going to be of much help," Warren groused.

"He's also a senior staff member at the medical center," the resident informed him. "When he gives an order, people jump."

Warren briefly studied the doctor by the barricades. "So he has a lot of pull, eh?"

"And a lot of push," the resident added. "He runs a tight ship down here, and knows how to move patients out. Nobody stays for long."

Warren looked over to Wells and nodded. "Let's see what he has to say."

Wells waved the doctor in and watched him approach, keeping his eyes on the new arrival's hands and making sure they were always in sight. "Are you in charge of any of the wards?"

The doctor shook his head. "Just the ER."

Wells groaned to himself. *Shit! This guy isn't going to be any help.* "Who's in charge of the beds?"

"No one person," the doctor replied. "Each specialty controls its own ward."

Shit! Wells thought again.

Warren stepped forward and introduced himself. "I'm William Warren, the President's physician."

"And I'm David Ballineau, the staff physician on call tonight." He was tall and lean, in his mid-forties, with an angular face, close-cropped salt-and-pepper hair, and pale blue eyes that seemed to be fixed in place. His clean-cut good looks were marred by a jagged scar across his chin. "The nurse notified me that you need a special area for the President."

"I need more than an area," Warren told him. "I need an entire ward cleared so that the President can be protected. Can you help us with that?"

"I can certainly try," David said. "But first, I have to know the President's diagnosis."

"That's not your concern," Wells blurted out.

"Yes, it is," David answered, standing up to the powerfully built agent. "We have special wards for specific illnesses. If he has just food poisoning, he can go to a general medicine ward. If he's had a myocardial infarction on top of it, he'll need to be in the ICU."

"He has straightforward food poisoning," Warren said. "He's got nausea and vomiting, and is throwing up some blood."

David looked at Warren oddly. "People with garden-variety food poisoning don't throw up blood. Never. You'd better look for another diagnosis."

Warren hesitated. He did not want to discuss the President's medical history with anyone, not even with another doctor—who might turn out to be loose-tongued. But he knew there was no getting around this conversation, if they were to make the necessary arrangements for protecting the President. Warren took David's arm and guided him away from the Secret Service agent.

"What I say to you goes no further than this hospital corridor. Understood?"

"Understood," David replied.

"The President has acid reflux disease with moderately severe esophagitis," Warren described, keeping his voice low. "I believe his esophageal mucosa is already thinned out, and the toxins from the food poisoning must have eroded through it. That's why he's bleeding."

David nodded slowly. That combination *could* be responsible for the bleeding. But bacterial toxins rarely caused upper gastrointestinal hemorrhaging, even under extreme circumstances. In all likelihood, there was another reason for the President to be vomiting blood. "How much blood has he lost?"

"Enough to drop his hematocrit to 40 percent."

David knitted his brow and did a quick mental calculation. The hematocrit was the ratio of packed red cells to a given volume of plasma, expressed as a percentage. The normal value was 46 to 50 percent. David estimated the President had lost at least 500 ccs of blood.

"Is he still bleeding?"

"Not actively," Warren answered, then corrected himself. "At least, he's not throwing up red blood any more."

"We should scope him as soon as possible," David recommended.

Warren hesitated again. The quickest way to make an accurate diagnosis was to pass an endoscope into the President's stomach and search for the bleeding site. But the procedure required anesthesia, and the President had had a severe allergic reaction to the anesthetic when he was endoscoped a year ago.

"We'll hold that for the present."

"If he's still bleeding, now would be the time to check him endoscopically," David urged.

"But he may no longer be bleeding."

"Let's pass a nasogastric tube and find out."

Warren considered the suggestion carefully before asking, "Are you experienced at that?"

"I've done it easily a hundred times," David said. "And while we're doing that we should have him typed and cross-matched for four units of whole blood."

"I've already ordered two units."

"That's not enough." David reached for his cell phone and called the blood bank. After speaking briefly, he came back to Warren. "If the President starts gushing blood, we'll need at least four units to hold him."

"That's not likely," Warren said.

"Maybe not," David said with a shrug. "But if he does, we don't want to get caught short, do we?"

"Lord, no," Warren concurred. This doctor was obviously experienced when it came to acute G.I. bleeding. *Excellent! I can use him until the specialists arrive. And they will tell me whether there's an urgent need to call in an endoscopist or some other expert. But wait a minute! Who were these specialists being called in to treat the*

President? I don't know them or how good they really are. This is a teaching hospital after all, and the most senior specialists could be academicians rather than active practitioners. Warren glanced back into the treatment room where the President lay. The cardiac monitors at his bedside showed a steady pulse and blood pressure, with no evidence of new hemorrhaging. "We could have the President helicoptered to Air Force One in fifteen minutes," Warren said, more to himself than to David, "then zoom like hell back to Washington."

"You may not have fifteen minutes," David cautioned. "If he starts to really spout blood aboard that helicopter, you could have a dead president on your hands. Then you'd be flying his corpse back to Washington on Air Force One."

"You've got a point," Warren agreed, and for a moment envisioned what a nightmare that would be. He hurriedly cleared his mind. "Dr. Ballineau, can you quickly get us the ward we require?"

"The best location for the President would be the Beaumont Pavilion," David proposed. "It's a closed-off floor with a single corridor and has a total of fourteen individual suites."

"Excellent," Warren approved immediately and beckoned Wells over, saying, "I think we've got a ward for the President."

David thought for a long moment before adding, "But I can only give you eleven of the suites."

"I need the entire floor."

"That's not possible," David said firmly. "Three of the patients are too ill to be moved off the floor. I know this for a fact, because I'm the attending physician up there."

Warren stared at David, not certain he understood. "They have an emergency room up on this pavilion?"

David shook his head. "It's a medicine ward for the rich and famous who have difficult diagnostic or therapeutic problems," he explained. "All staff members are required to teach on the wards or in the clinics for six weeks, and I spend my teaching time on the Beaumont Pavilion rather than down in the ER. It's a change of pace."

"And a little more perspective on the real world of everyday medicine, eh?"

A *lot* more perspective, David wanted to say. The Pavilion reminded him why he liked the ER so much. In contrast to the wards that moved along at a snail's pace and where most of the time was spent talking, the ER was action-packed and hectic, full of excitement and drama.

Warren tried to read David's expression, but couldn't. "Are you having second thoughts about using the Beaumont Pavilion?"

David shook his head again. "The Pavilion is fine, but those three patients must stay put."

"They'll have to be moved for security's sake," Warren insisted.

"Security won't be a problem with these three."

David described the three critically ill patients, highlighting the important features. The sickest was a movie star in her sixties with cirrhosis, who was drifting in and out of hepatic coma while she waited for a liver transplant. The second patient was a young college student with a lupus-induced pericardial effusion that was gradually impeding her heart's ability to pump blood. And the final patient was an eighty-year-old man with polymyositis, a rare inflammatory disease involving the large muscles.

"These people are so weak they can't get to the bathroom without help," David concluded.

"I still don't like it," Wells said.

"If you're worried about them, you could post agents outside their doors," David suggested.

Wells and Warren exchanged glances, a silent message passing between them.

"Okay," Wells consented reluctantly, now determining how the eleven suites would be used. The two presidents and their wives would occupy four rooms; four rooms would be needed for the Secretary of State and the Russian Foreign Minister and their wives; and two more would be held open for the President's daughter and her date. The final suite would be used for operations and communications. He turned to David and asked, "How many non-patient rooms are on the floor?"

"Four," David told him. "There's a nurses' lounge, a chart room, a treatment—"

A loud, coarse shriek came from the waiting area beyond the swinging doors into the ER. Then another shriek, even louder. It sounded like the cry of a wild man.

Instantly, the Secret Service agents drew their weapons and assumed firing positions, all aiming at the entrance. They waited, nerves taut, now hearing the sounds of tables and chairs being knocked over. A female voice screamed. Someone yelled for help. Then there was an eerie silence. Then thumping footsteps. Suddenly the swinging doors burst open, and a huge red-bearded man charged into the ER. Wide-eyed, he looked crazed and fierce.

"I'll kill you all!" he roared. "I'll tear your goddamn heads off!"

"Be careful!" David quickly warned the others. "He's a PCP user, and he's violent."

Wells asked in an even voice, "Does he come in a lot?"

"At least once a week," David said. "Everybody down here knows him."

"Has he ever been armed?"

"Never."

Wells rapidly studied the man, who was wearing a tight-fitting T-shirt and jeans. There were no bulges in his clothing, nothing to indicate he was concealing a weapon.

"Morris," Wells called over to his second in command. "Do you see anything in his back pockets?"

"*Nada*," Morris replied promptly. "He's not carrying."

The crazed man raised his arms and flexed his massive biceps. "I'll kill all of you sons of bitches."A metal pan dropped to the floor behind the barricade and rattled around noisily. The sound startled the heavily muscled man and he bolted straight ahead, making a beeline for the President's room. Two Secret Service agents jumped on the man and tried to tackle him, but were quickly thrown off. The PCP user shrieked again and charged onward.

"Stop or I'll shoot!" Wells yelled, but Warren was now partially blocking his line of vision.

The man ignored the warning and was almost to the President's door. David appeared to back away, but then in a flash he lunged forward and delivered a vicious chop to the man's trachea. The intruder dropped to the floor, grasping at his neck and sucking for air.

David stepped aside, and felt his pulse racing as adrenaline flowed through his system. It was an instinctive act, a maneuver drilled into him by special training years and years ago. It was an instinctive act, all right, and a stupid one too. It could have gotten him killed by the PCP-crazed intruder, or by a trigger-happy Secret Service agent. David took a long, deep breath and gathered himself.

"Je-sus!" one of the nearby agents muttered in wonderment, his eyes going from the doctor to the huge man on the floor who was still trying to catch his breath.

"Put restraints on him, hands and legs," David directed calmly. "Then take him to the holding room. The nurse will tell you where it's located."

Wells repeated the instructions to a trio of agents, then turned to David.

"Where did you learn how to do that?"

"I took a self-defense class," David said tonelessly.

Like hell, Wells was thinking. *The doc moved like a pro. And besides, the hit he put on the crazy guy wasn't defensive.* Wells glanced at the doctor's name tag and decided to run a quick security check on David Ballineau. "We need you to clear that floor for us now."

"First, I should place a nasogastric tube in the President," David advised. "We've got to know whether or not he's still bleeding."

Wells looked over to Warren, who nodded in agreement, then took David's arm and guided him past another agent and into the treatment room.

The President was lying motionless on an operating table under a set of kettledrum-shaped lights. His coat had been removed, but not his bloodstained shirt. One sleeve was rolled up to make room for an IV line that was slowly dripping saline into his arm. A nearby monitor showed the President's blood pressure to be 98/70, his pulse 90 beats per minute.

David stared at the President. The man projected an aura of power even when he was sick and on his back. He had chiseled, aristocratic features with a strong, jutting chin and graying brown hair. And he appeared to be larger, much larger, than he seemed on television. David did his best to maintain his professional composure, but his brain kept reminding him that he was about to treat the President of the United States, the most powerful man on the face of the earth.

David watched Warren increase the flow of saline into Merrill's arm, then brought his gaze back to the President. David's awe at the man's office was tempered by the fact that he was no fan of John Merrill, and had voted against him twice. Unlike his predecessor, who had fought like hell to stop terrorism, regardless of the cost or consequences, Merrill was more deliberate and cautious, always reaching out to backstabbing allies to form a consensus that never really worked. The end result was inaction that allowed terrorism to grow and flourish, and intimidate people around the globe. A perfect example was when Hezbollah opened fire on a U.S. naval vessel sailing for Haifa. Merrill decided to consult with the Arabs before bombing a lone Hezbollah encampment in Lebanon. One goddamn raid! A single bombing run on a base that had probably been vacated because the terrorists had been warned in advance by our so-called allies. It was a feeble response that only encouraged the terrorists more.

And Merrill's soft stance on immigration, and his unyielding opposition to stem cell research, also irked David to no end. If he could, he'd vote against Merrill a third time.

"Your blood pressure is up over a hundred," Warren commented. "That's a good sign, Mr. President."

David quickly cleared his mind and pushed his personal feelings aside. The Hippocratic Oath instructed him to treat, not judge. And so the President would be looked upon as just another patient, an important one to be sure, but nevertheless just another patient. David's mantra in the ER was *See 'em, fix 'em, and send 'em on their way*. That's exactly how he would deal with John Merrill.

"Mr. President," Warren asked quietly, "are you feeling any better now?"

Merrill waved away the question and inquired, "How's my wife?"

"She's doing fine, Mr. President," Warren reported.

"And my daughter?"

"We think she's gone to another hospital, Mr. President," Warren replied. "They'll notify us as soon as she's located."

"I want her brought here."

"It'll be done, Mr. President."

Merrill tried to sit up but was too weak. "Give me a hand here, Will."

Warren rushed over and helped the President up, then watched closely for any signs of hypotension caused by his blood loss. The President remained steady.

"Are you okay, sir?"

"I'm fine," Merrill said, sitting on the edge of the table and letting his legs dangle. In truth, he felt a little lightheaded. "So what do we do next?"

"You should stay here overnight for observation," Warren recommended.

"Why?" Merrill asked at once. "I'm not vomiting blood anymore."

"But you still may be bleeding, Mr. President," Warren cautioned. "It's in your best interest to remain under observation for the next twenty-four hours."

Merrill sighed resignedly. "All right. If you think I must."

"I do," Warren assured him. "And while they're clearing a ward for us, I'd like Dr. Ballineau to pass a tube into your stomach."

"What!" The President stiffened at the thought of a tube going into him. "What the hell is that for?"

"To determine if you're still bleeding," Warren answered.

"It's really necessary, eh?"

"It's really necessary," Warren replied. "And Dr. Ballineau here is an expert at doing it."

Merrill looked over at David, and studied him at length. "How'd you get that scar?"

"I jumped out of a helicopter and landed on my face rather than my feet," David answered flatly.

"Were you in the military?" Merrill asked.

David nodded. "A long time ago."

Merrill smiled thinly. "Well, let's hope you're better at passing tubes than jumping out of helicopters."

David smiled back wryly at the President's quick wit. "I am, Mr. President."

Warren interjected, "He's done the procedure a hundred times, Mr. President."

Merrill took a deep breath, readying himself, his eyes never leaving the expressionless doctor. "So tell me, how is this tube put in?"

"Through your nostril, into your throat, and down into your stomach," David detailed. "All you have to do is swallow, Mr. President. Done right, it'll take about ten seconds and you'll barely feel it."

Merrill glanced over to Warren, who nodded back reassuringly. "Okay, let's get it done."

David stepped over to a large basin and quickly washed his hands. After drying them, he put on latex gloves and reached for a cellophane packet containing the nasogastric tube. He slowly unwound the clear plastic tube. It was three feet long and the diameter of a pencil. From a distance it had the appearance of a long gray snake.

Merrill's eyes widened. "Don't tell me that whole damn thing is going into me!"

"No, sir," David told him. "Only about a foot's worth."

"Goddamn lemon-cured salmon," Merrill cursed under his breath.

"What?" David asked.

"Nothing," Merrill said and prepared himself for the worst. "Let's get this over with."

David lubricated the tip of the plastic tube with a clear jelly and brought it up to the President's nose. "Here we go," he said and gently threaded the tube in.

Merrill felt only a little discomfort as the tube passed through his nostril and into the back of his throat. But when the tube reached his hypopharynx, the President began to gag, and this caused the burning pain to return.

"Swallow, Mr. President." David encouraged him. "Swallow."

Merrill gulped and gagged, then gulped again. With a final swallow, the tube entered his stomach.

"Well done, Mr. President," David said, and taped the nasogastric tube in place. Next he used a large syringe to aspirate gastric juice from the President's stomach. The fluid was colored deep brown and had a few tiny clots floating in it. After capping the syringe, David connected the nasogastric tube to a suction bottle and watched the gastric juice flow into it.

"Why is it so brown?" the President asked. His voice was nasal-sounding because of the placement of the nasogastric tube, but he had no problem speaking since the tube went directly from his pharynx into his esophagus, bypassing the larynx.

"It's old blood," David explained. "The stomach's acid turns hemoglobin that color."

"Does that mean I'm not bleeding now?" the President asked hopefully.

"It tells us you aren't hemorrhaging," David said. "But you may still be oozing. We'll leave the tube down for a while and watch.

If the gastric juice becomes clear, it'll mean the bleeding has stopped."

Warren looked down at the peculiarly colored gastric fluid. It was so deep brown it resembled coffee grounds, and that made him wonder if the entire lining of the President's stomach had sloughed off. Warren considered the possibility that the President wasn't suffering from a simple gastroenteritis. He shuddered at the next thought that went through his mind. Maybe someone had tried to poison the President! Some poison might had eroded away the mucosal lining of his stomach. But the food served at the official dinner had been carefully scrutinized, and all the chefs, kitchen personnel, and waiters thoroughly checked. Still, the possibility of poisoning couldn't be excluded.

Keeping his expression even, Warren said, "We should send a sample of the gastric juice to the FBI laboratory for stat analysis."

"Better that we do it here," David advised. "We'll have the answer while the FBI is still filling out paperwork."

"And you'll check for corrosive toxins too, eh?" Warren asked in a low voice.

David nodded. "We'll do a comprehensive drug and toxin screen on his blood and gastric juice."

"How sensitive is this screen?" Warren asked. He wanted to be certain nothing was missed. "What type of test is it?"

"They use gas chromatography and mass spectrometry that can detect a few parts per million, and you can't get much more sensitive than that. The screen can clue us in to the presence of hundreds of different drugs and poisons."

Merrill's eyes darted back and forth between the two doctors. The phrases *gas chromatography* and *mass spectrometry* didn't bother him, but the mention of toxins and poisons did.

"What is this about poison? Has someone tried to poison me?"

"We have to check out all possibilities, Mr. President," Warren explained.

"But I wasn't the only one who became ill."

"They may have poisoned everyone just to get to you," Warren theorized. "Now, Mr. President, I don't want you to worry. This is probably going to turn out to be good old-fashioned food poisoning. But we have to cover all the bases."

Merrill felt a streak of fear go up his spine, but he kept his expression even. He remembered back to the last time he had food poisoning, and it was nothing like this. Quickly he turned to David and asked, "What do you think?"

"I'm thinking along the same lines as Dr. Warren," David hedged. "We're somewhat concerned because you've vomited blood, and that's not usually seen in people with food poisoning."

"Are the others throwing up blood?" Merrill asked.

"No, sir, they're not."

"So my diagnosis may not be the same as the others."

"It may not," David had to admit.

Merrill nodded slowly, the concern now showing on his face. The possibility of being poisoned gnawed at him. "Dr. Ballineau, I take it this hospital has some very fine specialists."

"They're among the best in the world, Mr. President," David said.

"I think we should call them in."

"I do, too," David agreed. "If it's all right with you, I'll clear the ward upstairs and get you situated. Then we can have our specialists evaluate you."

"Good."

David reached for his cell phone and called the Beaumont Pavilion. As the head nurse answered, David's gaze went back to the President's nasogastric tube. Red blood was beginning to flow through it.

———

Carolyn Ross reached for a pen in her nurse's uniform and began writing down David Ballineau's instructions. Eleven patients would have to be transferred. Six would go to the Intermediate Care Facility, the remaining five to private rooms on the general medicine ward. All rooms had to be thoroughly cleaned. All would be scrupulously searched by the Secret Service. The nurses on duty would remain on an extended shift. The interns were to be summoned to the Pavilion, where they would stay until further notice. All visitors would be asked to leave immediately.

Carolyn placed the phone down and promptly remembered something she should have asked. *What about the diet orders?* She realized that the patients coming up were suffering with gastroenteritis, but their symptoms would in all likelihood be short-lived. And not all would be on IVs.

She called David Ballineau's number and got his message service. "Shit!" Carolyn grumbled. She did not want to waste any more time. There were too many things to do. The diet orders would be put on hold.

Carolyn dialed the number of the Beaumont Pavilion's kitchen, which was located one floor down. It had its own crew of chefs who prepared meals that the patients ordered from menus. Its dishes were considered by some to be equal to those found in the better restaurants in Los Angeles.

The chef answered, "Yes?"

"This is Carolyn Ross, upstairs. You'll have to stay late," Carolyn directed. "We have some very distinguished patients being admitted, and they will require special diets."

"No problem," said the man pretending to be the chef. "I'll await your orders."

Kuri Aliev hung up and nodded to a heavyset man standing guard over two bound, blindfolded chefs. The man quickly tightened the silencer on the end of his pistol, and fired single shots into the eye sockets of the chefs, killing them instantly.

FIVE

Marci Matthews was frightened by the commotion going on around her. The head nurse was disconnecting all of her cardiac monitors, while a trio of housekeepers was rapidly cleaning her room on the Beaumont Pavilion. One was mopping the floor, a second scrubbed the bathroom, and a third was collecting all the cards and toys Marci's classmates had sent her. Nobody in the room was talking and they all had grim expressions, Marci noticed. *And it was night. Nine o'clock at night. Something bad was happening.*

"Can you tell me why I'm being moved?" Marci asked nervously.

"A patient with special needs has to come into your room," Carolyn Ross explained, then added a lie. "He has to be close to the nurses' station, in case of an emergency."

"He's real sick?" Marci inquired.

"Very sick."

"Sicker than me?"

"Yes."

Nobody can be sicker than I am, Marci thought miserably. *Nobody*. And for the hundredth time she asked silently, *Why me? Why me, dear God? What have I done to deserve this?* And again God didn't answer. Marci sighed sadly, wishing it was all a nightmare from which she'd awaken healthy, like she was six months ago. Her mind drifted back to the day her illness started and turned her life upside down. She was a junior at UCLA, a cheerleader, secretary of her sorority, and in love with the best-looking guy on campus, who loved her back even more. Then the rash started on her face and arms, and grew worse in the sunlight. Then came the joint aches and chest pain, and the diagnosis of systemic lupus erythematosus. And the final blow was a pericardial effusion—a collection of fluid around her heart—which made her feel weak and short of breath.

After treatment with cortisone and immunosuppressive drugs, her symptoms improved. But the effusion persisted. She was warned that if her symptoms worsened again, the doctors would have to remove the fluid from her heart with a needle. Marci shivered to herself, not wanting even to imagine what that would be like. They said it wouldn't hurt. But that's what they told her when they took fluid off her lungs. And it had hurt like hell.

"You're not taking me to remove the fluid from my heart, are you?" Marci asked at length.

"No," Carolyn assured her. "There's no need for that, not with your symptoms getting better."

"The drugs are really helping," Marci said, but she was being less than honest. The drugs had been working, making her feel stronger and stronger, until just after lunch. Then her symptoms of weakness and shortness of breath began to return. It wasn't as bad as before, and Marci kept hoping the beneficial effects of the drugs would kick in again. "Dr. Ballineau says that sometimes the drugs work even better with time."

"Dr. Ballineau is a straight shooter," Carolyn told her. "If he says it's so, it's so."

"And he said we could even increase the dose of my medicines if we need to," Marci went on, wondering if she should tell the nurse about her worsening symptoms.

"Let's hope that won't be necessary." Carolyn reached for a hand mirror on the night table and asked, "Do you want to carry this?"

"Yes."

Marci took the mirror and carefully studied her face. She still considered herself pretty, with her soft features, doe-like brown eyes, and blond ponytail. But the cortisone was making her cheeks puffy, and the red rash on her forehead was more obvious. And she knew deep down that it was just a matter of time before her illness caused her beauty to disappear altogether. Then people would stare at her rash and her bloated face, and feel sorry for her. And she would be ugly and never have another date or get married and have children. Tears welled up in her eyes, and she looked away to hide them.

"Do you have anything hidden away we should take with us?" Carolyn broke into Marci's thoughts.

"My Mickey Mouse slippers under the bed," Marci said, still looking away.

Carolyn reached for the slippers adorned with the Disney character and placed them on the bed. "Anything in the bathroom?"

"My curling iron and hair dryer are in the cabinet drawer."

Carolyn hurried into the oversized bathroom, with its marble fixtures and glass-enclosed shower, and fetched Marci's personal items. She gave the bath and bidet a final glance before returning to the sitting area, where a housekeeper was dusting off a 42-inch plasma television screen that was set into the wall. Another housekeeper was carefully arranging leather-upholstered chairs around a polished coffee table.

Although Carolyn had worked on the Beaumont Pavilion for over a year, she was still impressed by how luxurious the individual suites were. They looked like rooms you would expect to find in a Ritz-Carlton hotel. And that was the intent when the Pavilion was designed. The rooms were reserved for the privileged and wealthy, and particularly for those benefactors who contributed generously to the hospital. The house staff had aptly nicknamed the floor the Gold Coast. Tonight, Carolyn thought somberly, it would be called by another name—the Western White House.

"Will my parents be notified that I'm changing rooms?" Marci asked.

"We'll see to it," Carolyn replied.

"Maybe I should call my dad," Marci suggested.

"Let us take care of it," Carolyn said. Marci's father was a powerful entertainment lawyer who made demands every time he came onto the floor and, on a few occasions, when he was unhappy, ended up calling the dean's office. The last thing Carolyn needed this evening was an angry phone call from a pain in the ass like Bert Matthews.

"Done!" the head housekeeper called out.

"Grab the foot of the bed," Carolyn instructed, glancing around to make certain all the wires and monitors were disconnected. Then she quickly put the side rails up.

With care they guided the bed, Marci still in it, out the door and down the hall. Just past the nurses' station they stopped and waited while another bed was being wheeled out of a nearby room. It carried Diana Dunn, a movie actress in her early sixties who had once starred alongside some of Hollywood's most handsome leading men. But her beautiful face and body were now withered and wasted by progressive liver failure. As usual, her skin color was yellow, her breathing labored, and she was asleep. And she would sleep forever, Carolyn thought grimly, unless a donor for a liver transplant was found soon. Very, very soon.

Carolyn shouted over to Kate Blanchard, the junior nurse on the Pavilion who was pushing Diana Dunn's bed, "Kate, would you take Marci down to fourteen and get her set up?"

"I've got to connect Diana to her monitors," Kate shouted back as she repositioned an IV line. She was tall and young, with sharp features and jet-black hair. "It'll take a few minutes."

"Have one of the interns do it," Carolyn directed.

"Gotcha."

"Did you put Sol in his new room?" Carolyn asked.

Kate shook her head. "He won't move until he talks to you."

"Christ!" Carolyn grumbled under her breath. She put a confident smile on her face and squeezed Marci's hand. "Kate will take good care of you. You're going to do fine, kiddo."

"You promise?" Marci asked, trying to read the nurse's expression.

"Carolyn doesn't lie."

Marci waved with her fingers as her bed was wheeled away. She grinned almost enough to cover her fear.

Carolyn raced down the corridor and checked her wristwatch. She was already behind. The rooms should have been cleared out ten minutes earlier for the President. And it would take at least another ten minutes to get everything in order. But Carolyn loved the adrenaline surge and excitement of an emergent situation, where things had to be done quickly and correctly under pressure. That was what had attracted her to being a flight nurse for MedEvac, hopping into helicopters and flying to crash scenes, where life-and-death predicaments awaited her. And often she was the only trained medical person aboard, so she served more as a doctor than a nurse, starting IVs, administering drugs, and opening airways. Her schedule was hectic, twelve hours on and twelve hours off, with frequent double shifts.

But how she loved it, and she would still be doing it if her mother hadn't become ill. A couple of years earlier, her mother started becoming forgetful, and a few times wandered off and got lost. With her mom's diagnosis of Alzheimer's disease, Carolyn could no longer be away erratically and for prolonged periods of time. So a year and a half earlier, she gave up flight nursing and took the position of head nurse on the Beaumont Pavilion.

In this luxurious ward, which often felt to her like a boring prison, she worked a tedious eight hours a day, five days a week, on a regular schedule. The only good part was the generous salary that allowed her to hire a sitter to care for her mother during the time she was on duty at the hospital. That damned disease takes away so much from the patient and the patient's family. It changed everything for everybody, destroying hopes and dreams and lives. A wave of sadness came over Carolyn as she thought about her mother withering away, now only a shell of the person she used to be.

An alarm suddenly sounded behind Carolyn.

She spun around and saw an intern trying to reattach a monitor wire to Diana Dunn's chest. He was having a difficult time with it.

"Do that when you get her into a room," Carolyn called out. "Let's keep this corridor clear."

"Mrs. Dunn won't stop twisting and turning," the intern called back. "I don't think the wire will stay on."

"Then tape it down with double strips."

Carolyn hurried along as she turned for an open door, now thinking about the half-dozen things she still had to do before the President arrived on the ward. There just wasn't enough time to do everything. And only God knew what else the Secret Service would want done.

She entered Sol Simcha's room and gave the small, thin man a stern look. "Why won't you move?"

"Oh, I'll move," Simcha said pleasantly, looking up from his chair. "I just wanted to talk with you first."

"About what?" Carolyn asked impatiently.

"Anything," Simcha said with a shrug. "You're the only person who talks to me. And more importantly, you're the only one who listens."

"And that makes me special, huh?" Carolyn asked.

"Doubly special," Simcha replied sincerely. "And besides, it's not often that an old man like me gets to talk to a pretty girl like you. And there's something else you should know."

"What?"

"Whenever I see you, I automatically feel better."

Carolyn's heart melted, as it always did in the presence of Sol Simcha. She wasn't sure how he did it. Maybe it was his kind face, or maybe his gentle voice, or maybe the sweet disposition he had despite having lived through the hell of a Nazi concentration camp called Auschwitz. Her gaze drifted from his heavily lined face and thinning gray hair to his forearm, where a row of faded numbers were tattooed. "We'll talk as we go. Now let's get you in bed, and we'll wheel you to—"

"No," Simcha interrupted. "If I'm to move, I'll walk, like a *mensch*."

Carolyn groaned good-naturedly. Although she was in a hurry and short on time, she'd make time for Sol Simcha. She helped him up and waited while he steadied himself on legs damaged by an inflammatory muscle disease called polymyositis. "Okay, let's go nice and easy."

Simcha shifted his feet, barely able to lift them off the floor, but somehow he managed to get them moving forward. They made slow progress out of the room and into the hall, with Simcha holding on tightly to the nurse.

Carolyn noticed that the old man was breathing more heavily than usual. A progressive type of interstitial fibrosis was affecting his lungs. It was a rare complication seen in some patients with polymyositis. And it made the shopping mall magnate's condition even more miserable, but he never complained about it. He figured it was minuscule compared to what he had already been through in life.

"Your arms seem stronger," Carolyn said.

"They are," Simcha agreed. "But my legs are still weak as a kitten."

"Maybe the strength will come back to them soon, too."

"From your lips to God's ear."

Carolyn gently patted the old man's hand. "Somebody once told me that most Holocaust survivors had lost their faith in God."

"That's not true," Simcha said at once. "We just think He was looking the other way when it happened."

After a pause, Carolyn said, "You're a remarkable man, Sol Simcha."

"I like the way you say Simcha, with a hard *cha*," Simcha praised. "You say it pretty good for being an Episcopalian."

Carolyn smiled briefly. "Simcha sounds like an unusual name. Do you know its origin?"

"I picked it myself," Simcha told her. "When I was rescued from the concentration camp and brought to America, it was the happiest time of my life. So I said to hell with my Ukrainian name, which was filled with bad memories, and chose the word in Hebrew and Yiddish for happiness or celebration. Simcha."

"Nice," Carolyn said, warmed by the story. "And I think you're still a happy man, even with your illness."

"I am," Simcha told her. "And you should be happy too. You're a wonderful nurse, and you have such a handsome doctor for a boyfriend."

Carolyn looked at him strangely. "I don't have a boyfriend."

"The way you gaze at Dr. Ballineau says otherwise."

"God! Is it that obvious?"

"Yes."

Carolyn shrugged indifferently. "I don't think he even notices me."

"Then you're blind," Simcha said bluntly. "He looks at you the same way you look at him."

Just ahead, the elevator door opened and Aaron Wells stepped out, followed by two other agents. He hurried over to Carolyn and asked, "Are you the head nurse?"

"I am," Carolyn said.

"I'm Agent Wells," he introduced himself. "Have you got this ward cleared?"

"I'll need another ten minutes."

Wells frowned, unhappy with the report. "How many rooms have been vacated?"

Carolyn pointed to her left. "All those from the end of the corridor up to the nurses' station."

"And how many people work on this ward?" Wells asked. "Limit it to essential personnel."

Carolyn thought for a moment. "There would be five altogether. Two nurses, two interns, and a ward clerk."

"No resident?"

"He's out sick."

Wells motioned to the agents behind him. "Bill, Owen—check every room wall to wall, ceiling to floor. Throw out everything that's not furniture."

The agents dashed down the corridor as Wells spoke briefly into the microphone on his wrist. He was directing another agent to come up and run security checks on all the medical personnel.

Simcha's jaw dropped as he noticed the wire snaking down from the agent's earphone to his collar. He quickly turned to Carolyn and asked, "Are we being moved for the Pres—?"

Carolyn brought a finger to her lips, hushing him. She gestured to Kate Blanchard, who was behind the nurses' station. "Kate! Put Sol in room twelve for me, please."

Wells waited for the patient to shuffle away, then came back to Carolyn. "I need to look at all the rooms that won't be occupied by patients."

"Let's begin here," Carolyn said, heading for the chart room.

Two interns, wide-eyed, stepped aside as the powerfully built Secret Service agent entered. Wells quickly searched them, then turned his attention to the charts hanging on a metal rack and made certain they contained only medical records. Next he went through the drawers of two desks and the overhead shelves above them. Finally he opened the interns' doctor bags and poured their instruments on a tabletop. He rummaged through stethoscopes, ophthalmoscopes, and small reflex hammers, and found nothing that could be used as a weapon.

"Sorry for the inconvenience," Wells told the interns, then turned to Carolyn. "Lead on."

They walked through a door and into a large closet, which served as the medicine room. The shelves were stocked with bottles of tablets and liquids and plastic bags of IV fluids. A locked narcotics cabinet was off to the side. There were no windows or other connecting doors.

"Okay," Wells said, backing out.

Carolyn showed him the way into the nurses' station. A husky young African American man with very broad shoulders and hands the size of hams was sitting behind the desk. He quickly got to his feet and straightened his tie.

"This is Jarrin Smith, our ward clerk," Carolyn said.

"I've got to search you," Wells informed the clerk.

"No problem," Jarrin said, turning around with his hands held up high.

Wells frisked him and found only a small nail clipper. "Sorry for the inconvenience."

"No problem," Jarrin said again.

Carolyn led the way across the corridor and into the nearby nurses' lounge. It was spotless, with a refrigerator, microwave oven, coffeemaker, and two couches. The tall metal lockers were open and held only jackets and umbrellas. A bathroom at the rear had been recently scrubbed.

As they left the lounge, Wells asked, "The guy at the front desk is big as a tree. Is there a reason for having a clerk that large?"

"His size is irrelevant," Carolyn replied. "He's a sophomore in medical school, and works some of the night shifts because he needs the money."

They hurried on and came to the treatment room. In its center was an operating table with overhead lights. There were two metal stools around the table, and behind them a glass cabinet filled with medicines and supplies. Off to the side was a basin and, next to it, a countertop that held blood-drawing equipment. The walls were covered with white tiles, the ceiling with removable synthetic panels.

"Can they do emergency operations in here?" Wells inquired.

"Only minor procedures," Carolyn replied. "Things like tracheotomies and thoracenteses."

"What is the last thing you said?"

"Thoracentesis. It's the removal of fluid from the chest using a needle."

They continued on to the end of the corridor and entered a windowless room that had stacks of serving trays and gleaming silverware. A cabinet off to the side contained linen napkins, fine glassware, and colorful tablecloths.

"This is where we get our patients' meals," Carolyn said.

Wells glanced around, looking for ovens and stoves or adjoining rooms. There weren't any. "Where is the food prepared?"

"Down one level," Carolyn replied. "The Beaumont Pavilion has its own chefs, and all meals are ordered by the patients from a menu. The meals are sent up to us on the dumbwaiter next to the cabinet."

Wells went over and carefully examined the dumbwaiter. It was small, not more than three feet across and three feet in height, with four adjustable shelves. "Who controls it?"

Carolyn pointed to a switch beneath the small elevator. "We can send it down by pushing that button. The light next to it stays green while the dumbwaiter is up here. It turns red when we send it down."

"Can the people in the kitchen bring the dumbwaiter down?" Wells asked.

Carolyn shook her head. "They can only send it up. When it's on its way up, our light will turn green and begin to flash. When it reaches the Pavilion, the flashing stops."

Wells narrowed his eyes. "Why do you have all these precautions?"

"It's really not a precaution," Carolyn said with a shrug. "It just prevents the kitchen from sending up meals that could sit around and become cold."

Wells nodded and moved over to a metal crank on the side of the dumbwaiter. "And what's this for?"

"In an emergency we can manually operate the elevator," Carolyn told him. "But we almost never—"

Abruptly, Wells brought his hand up, interrupting her. He listened intently to the message coming in over his earphone, then turned for the door. "The President is on his way up."

They dashed into the corridor, which was now clear of beds and personnel. At the far end, Wells spotted the two agents and signaled them with a rapid rotary gesture to hurry up.

"Where do you want the President?" Carolyn asked.

"In the room farthest away from the elevator," Wells answered and listened to another message coming over his earphone. "And I want the First Lady directly across from him. Put the Secretary of State and his wife between the President and the Russians."

"Do you want the windows covered?"

"We'll take care of that."

They ran down the hall at full speed, racing past the treatment room and the lounge. At the nurses' station Kate Blanchard, the clerk, and two interns were seated around the desk, chatting with one another.

Carolyn yelled over, "Everybody on their feet for the President!"

The group quickly stood, their postures ramrod straight. The ward clerk placed his hand over his heart.

All eyes went to the elevator panel and watched the floor numbers flash by. 6 … 7 … 8 … 9 …

The elevator jerked to a stop and the door opened.

Two Secret Service agents quickly stepped out into the corridor and made sure the way was clear, then signaled back to David and Warren before moving aside.

David pulled the front of the gurney out of the elevator and swung it around. The fluid in the suction bottle draining the President's stomach was now colored bright red, and fresh blood was coming out of his nose and mouth.

"Call the blood bank and tell them we need two units of whole blood up here stat!" David cried out.

The President groaned and gagged.

More fresh blood poured out of his mouth and nose.

SIX

THE PRESIDENT CONTINUED TO ooze blood around his nasogastric tube. It was bright red and coming mainly from his mouth. With effort he turned on his side and hacked up enough blood to cover the bottom of a small basin.

"Why am I bleeding so much?" Merrill gasped.

"In all likelihood, whatever caused your food poisoning has eroded away some of your esophageal lining," Warren answered. "And we think the lining was already weakened by your acid reflux disease. That would explain why you bled and the others didn't. Dr. Ballineau has also raised the possibility that you might have Mallory-Weiss syndrome."

Merrill's eyebrows went up. "What the hell is that?"

"It's bleeding due to a tear in mucosa of the esophagus caused by strenuous retching," Warren described.

Merrill looked over to David. "Does it require surgery?"

"Not if it's a small tear, Mr. President," David said.

"You keep using the word *if*," Merrill complained.

"That's because I want to be totally forthright," David said. "Until we can confirm what's going on inside your gastrointestinal tract."

"So these are all mere guesses, aren't they?" Merrill asked irritably.

"Yes, Mr. President," Warren had to concede. "The only way to be sure of the diagnosis is for you to undergo endoscopy."

"I hate those damn things," Merrill growled his displeasure. He could still remember the last time an endoscope was passed into his stomach. His throat had stayed sore for a week and he had developed widespread hives from the anesthetic that lasted off and on for a month. "It's absolutely necessary?"

Warren nodded firmly. "Not only will it give us an accurate diagnosis, it might also reveal a localized bleeding site. And if that's the case, we can cauterize the area and stop the bleeding immediately."

Merrill thought for a moment, then slowly nodded back. "Where will it be done?"

"Here," Warren replied.

David stepped forward and suggested, "It might be best to do it in the endoscopy unit. They have the setup for it, with the necessary drugs and equipment and cameras."

Warren promptly shook his head. "We'll do it here on the Pavilion, where we can protect the President."

David considered the matter briefly before saying, "I guess we could do it in the treatment room. But it'll be awfully crowded. Of course, the final decision will be up to the gastroenterologist who will be performing the endoscopy."

"He'll do exactly what we tell him to do," Warren asserted. "We'll need the name of the gastroenterologist so the Secret Service can run a security check."

There was a quick rap on the door.

"Yes?" Warren called out.

Aaron Wells walked in and hurried over to the President. "Sir, we've located your daughter and her date. They had gone to the emergency room at Cedars-Sinai. We're having them transported over here by helicopter. They should be arriving shortly."

"Thanks, Aaron," Merrill said with genuine gratitude.

Wells nodded, trying not to stare at the bloodstained sheet covering the President. "Sir, your daughter will probably ask to see you as soon as she gets here."

"Check with Dr. Warren first," Merrill directed.

"Yes, sir."

Merrill waited for Wells to leave, then looked over to his personal physician. "Find out how ill she is."

"Yes, Mr. President," Warren said.

"And I want all the blood cleared off of me," Merrill ordered. "I don't want my daughter seeing me like this."

"It'll be done, Mr. President."

Merrill lay back on his pillow, feeling weak and lightheaded. Another wave of nausea came and went. "Let's get this endoscopy done ASAP."

Warren rapidly checked the cardiac monitors next to Merrill's bed. The President's blood pressure was 98/68, his pulse 96 beats per minute. The pulse rate was fast, but not that fast, considering how much blood had been lost. "Mr. President, Dr. Ballineau and I will be just outside if you need us."

As they headed for the door, Merrill called after them, "When can I have this damn tube removed from my nose?"

"As soon as the endoscopist arrives, Mr. President," Warren called back.

Out in the corridor Warren turned to David and asked, "Who is the best endoscopist at University Hospital?"

"Jonathan Bell," David replied. "He runs the endoscopy unit and is co-chairman of the gastroenterology department."

"Get him up here," Warren said, then signaled Wells over. "Aaron, the President will have to be seen by a specialist whose name is Jonathan Bell. Check him out."

Wells spoke hurriedly into the microphone on his lapel, fully aware there wasn't enough time to obtain a complete security profile on the specialist. But using the Secret Service's computerized system, which checks through all the national intelligence indices, they'd rapidly get whatever information was available quickly on Jonathan Bell, and his wife, his children, and his associates. If the specialist's background wasn't spotless, he wouldn't be allowed to come anywhere near the President.

Warren watched David click off his cell phone and asked, "Did you reach Dr. Bell?"

David nodded. "He's on his way in. He lives in Pacific Palisades, so it'll take him about twenty minutes to get here."

Warren asked, "How many people will be involved in the endoscopy?"

David thought briefly and replied, "Three altogether. There'll be the endoscopist, an anesthesiologist, and someone experienced in the treatment of shock in case the President has further complications."

"And who will that someone be?"

"Me."

David checked his watch. It was 10:10 p.m. He'd never make it home in time to tuck his daughter, Kit, in bed and kiss her goodnight and tell her to have sweet dreams. It was a reassuring ritual he did every night, without fail for eight years, since the death of

Kit's mother from leukemia. His kiss always brought a smile to the girl's face, and that made everything in the world seem right—at least for a moment. He reached for his cell phone and said, "I have to call home and tell them I'll be late."

"Don't mention the President," Warren said. It wasn't a request.

"I won't." David stepped away and punched in his home number. Juanita Cruz picked up on the first ring. In the background, David heard the sound of a television set tuned to a Spanish channel.

"The Ballineau residence," Juanita answered.

"Hey, Juanita," David said. "Is everything okay?"

"Everything is fine," Juanita replied. "Your daughter is hard at work on her homework." There was a pause before she asked, "Is something wrong, Dr. Ballineau?"

"Only that I will be home very late tonight," David told her. "We have an emergency at the hospital and it looks like I'll be here for the next two hours. There's no way I'll be able to tuck Kit in tonight."

Juanita waited before answering. "She will be disappointed."

"I know."

"And she will worry."

"I know that, too."

Juanita paused again, then said, "I will tell her that you will kiss her forehead while she is asleep."

"Good," David said, thinking how wise and caring Juanita was, and how fortunate they were to have her.

"Hold while I get the little one for you."

David grinned to himself. "The little one" was Juanita's pet name for Kit, and she never addressed her by any other title, even though Kit insisted she was almost a teenager and that Juanita would have to accept that fact.

"Fine," Juanita had said. "I will call you 'the little one who is now almost a teenager.'"

Juanita had come to work for them six months after Kit was born. The kind, strong woman had left an abusive husband in Costa Rica and had emigrated to America with a young daughter who became a registered nurse and currently worked at Grady Hospital in Atlanta. When David's wife died, he asked Juanita to move into the guest house and look after Kit full time. Juanita was delighted to do so, since she was living alone in an apartment then. And she loved Kit almost as much as she loved her own daughter.

"Hi, Dad," Kit said as she came on the phone.

"Hi, beautiful," David answered. "What are you doing?"

"Homework. We're studying the bees."

"Bees, eh?"

"Yeah. Did you know we'd all be dead in four years if the bees suddenly disappeared?"

"You don't say."

"Ah-huh," Kit went on. "Without bees there'd be no pollination and without pollination there'd be no plants and without plants there'd be no food and all the animals would die."

"Wow!" David enthused. "And we'd all be gone in four years, huh?"

"That's what the teacher said, but he was just quoting Albert Einstein."

David shook his head admiringly, now envisioning his daughter with her raven hair, cream-colored skin, and sky-blue eyes. She was just gorgeous. And smart as a whip, making all As and always on the honor roll. And she was starting to like boys almost as much as she liked soccer. *Oh, Marianne!* David thought sadly, now seeing his dead wife in his mind's eye. *You're missing so much.*

"Dad?" Kit broke the silence.

"Yeah?"

"Why the phone call?"

"I have an emergency at the hospital," he explained. "Someone very, very important is really sick, so I'll be getting home late and won't be able to tuck you in."

"Oh," Kit said, her voice barely audible.

David's heart sank. His daughter sounded so let down.

"I can stay up and wait for you," Kit offered.

"That's not a good idea," David said. "I won't be home until after one or two o'clock, and you need your sleep. Remember, you've got a big soccer game tomorrow afternoon."

"You're right," Kit agreed, brightening up a little. "You'll be there for the game, won't you?"

"I wouldn't miss it for the world," David promised. "Now you finish your homework and crawl under the covers and have sweet dreams."

"I love you, Dad."

"I love you too, Kitten."

David put his cell phone away, still feeling guilty about not being home with his daughter to kiss her goodnight. His absence would only remind Kit that, unlike most other children, she had only one living parent—and that, if something happened to him, there was no backup and she would be all alone in the world. Just the thought of it had to frighten her. But David was stuck, and he knew it. There was no way he could abandon the President—or any other sick patient, for that matter.

Warren stepped over and studied the expression on David's face. "Is there a problem?"

"No," David answered curtly. "No problem."

"Then our next step is to set up the endoscopic equipment," Warren said. "How do we go about doing that?"

"We don't," David told him. "We wait for Dr. Bell. It's his show."

Warren was about to ask another question about the procedure but held his tongue.

The Secretary of State and his wife were being wheeled on gurneys into nearby rooms. They were a handsome African American couple with light skin and silver-gray hair. Both looked very ill. Coming in behind them was the Russian president and his wife and two security guards. Ivana Suslev was in a wheelchair, her head drooped onto her chest and her blond hair in disarray.

When the corridor was finally cleared, Warren came back to David and kept his voice low. "With the drugs the President will receive for his endoscopy, how long will he be out of commission?"

"An hour and a half, maybe two hours," David estimated.

"Well, we won't have to worry about the Twenty-Fifth Amendment then."

"What's that?"

"It's the part of the Constitution that transfers presidential powers to the Vice President."

"On second thought," David backtracked quickly, "it might be best to check with the anesthesiologist. The President could be down a lot longer if something complicated is found."

"Who will be the anesthesiologist?"

David shrugged. "That will be up to Dr. Bell."

"We'll have to have him—"

"Will!" the President shouted from inside his room. "Will!"

Warren spun around on his heels and hurried into the suite, with David a step behind. The President had propped himself up on an elbow and was vomiting red blood into a small basin. He was retching so hard his body was bouncing off the mattress. He threw up again and again, then dropped back on his pillow exhausted.

"You'd better get that endoscopy fellow in here," Merrill said weakly.

"He's on his way, Mr. President." Warren's eyes went to the cardiac monitor. The President's blood pressure was 92/60, his pulse was 104 beats per minute. And he looked pale now. Warren turned to David and asked very quickly, "Do you have any suggestions?"

David studied the monitors, then glanced over to the basin that was brimming with blood. The President had filled the basin twice, and that alone amounted to nearly a quart of blood. *One more massive hemorrhage could kill him*, David thought, as he desperately searched his mind for an answer to the dilemma. Then he remembered back to a patient with erosive gastritis who was bleeding and wouldn't stop. Quickly David gazed over to a bucket of crushed ice on a night table. It was sitting next to a pitcher of water. He dashed across the room and poured the water into the bucket of ice chips, then swirled the slush until it was freezing cold. "Mr. President, I'm going to rinse your stomach with ice water through the tube in your nose. The name for the procedure is 'lavage.'"

Merrill swallowed back another wave of nausea. "What good will that do?"

"Very cold liquids will cause the blood vessels to constrict, and that might slow down the bleeding," David explained. "I think it's worth trying."

Merrill nodded quickly. "Do it."

David hurried over and filled a 50cc syringe with ice water, then attached it to the end of the nasogastric tube. Over and over, he lavaged the stomach with water so cold it burned his fingertips. At first, the gastric juice David retrieved was colored deep red. Then it turned light red, and finally pink. "It's working," David said.

"Do you have any idea how long it will last?"

"It's impossible to say," David replied. "If we're lucky, it'll hold until the gastroenterologist gets here."

"My stomach feels like it's frozen," Merrill complained.

"That'll pass, Mr. President," David assured him.

Merrill turned on his side and spat a mouthful of pink saliva into the basin.

"Do you know I had an uncle who bled to death this way? They said something was wrong with his blood."

David's eyebrows went up instantly. "Did he have a coagulation defect?"

Merrill nodded and looked over to Warren. "What was the name of that strange disease he had?"

"Von Willebrand's disease," Warren replied.

"Jesus Christ! You're a bleeder!" David blurted without thinking. "You've got an inherited defect."

"No, he doesn't," Warren disagreed immediately. "The President's father, who was a senator and the brother of the man with von Willebrand's disease, had no bleeding tendency. And the President has never shown any propensity to bleed. But to be on the safe side, the President was evaluated with a bleeding time and Factor VIII level. Both tests were within normal levels, excluding the diagnosis of von Willebrand's disease."

David asked the President, "Have you ever had major surgery or a tooth extracted?"

"I had a molar extraction years ago."

"How much blood did you lose?"

"It took almost a week for the bleeding to finally stop," Merrill recalled, then glanced over to his personal physician. "And, Will, the fact of the matter was that Father had the same bleeding disease as my uncle. They kept it quiet because it could have been politically damaging to him. He, too, once had presidential aspirations."

"And you knew you had the disease, as well?" Warren asked incredulously.

Merrill shook his head. "My blood tests were always negative. I thought the disease had skipped over my generation."

David gave the President a skeptical look. With Merrill's family history and his prolonged bleeding after a simple dental extraction, he must have known he had the disease and, like his father before him, was hiding it for political purposes. But then again, people believed what they wanted to believe. Maybe Merrill was actually convinced he didn't have the disease. After all, this was his first major hemorrhage.

Finally David said, "Mr. President, von Willebrand's disease is an inherited disorder of coagulation characterized by a prolonged bleeding time and a low level of a protein in the blood called Factor VIII, which is essential for clot formation. But these abnormalities can vary in a given patient, with the tests being normal one week and abnormal the next. So, even with normal tests you can still have the disorder, Mr. President. And this would explain why you're bleeding so much."

"Jesus Christ!" Merrill groaned sourly. "Am I going to just lie here and bleed?"

"No, sir," David answered at once. "The bleeding responds to injections of fresh plasma and to concentrates containing high levels of Factor VIII."

"Then inject me with them," Merrill said.

David hesitated, now in over his head. He sounded impressive, but his knowledge of von Willebrand's disease was limited to the single case he'd heard discussed at a Grand Rounds conference. He could define the disease, but treating it could be a tricky matter.

"Mr. President, I have no experience in the use of concentrates, which is the preferred treatment for this disorder. That requires a specialist in blood diseases. So what I'd like to do is give you fresh frozen plasma, which will stabilize your bleeding, and call in a hematologist to advise us on how to administer the Factor VIII–rich concentrates."

"Do it," Merrill directed.

David turned quickly to Warren. "If he starts bleeding again, lavage his stomach with more ice water."

Warren was about to ask what to do if the bleeding didn't stop, but David had already dashed out of the room. Warren sighed heavily to himself. He was out of his depth and knew it. *The President was a GI bleeder with a coagulation defect!* It was a rare, complex condition, and the President would need specialists in both hematology and gastroenterology to survive another major bleed. And even they might not be able to save him. The President suddenly gagged, and more stingy clots oozed from his nose. Warren could only hope it didn't signal the start of another bleeding episode.

David sped down the corridor, passing a cluster of Secret Service agents and two big, burly Russian security guards. All the doors were closed, but David could hear the occupants throwing up. The smell of vomit was everywhere.

At the nurses' station, David called over to the clerk. "Where's Carolyn?"

"In the treatment room."

David hurried on, deciding to order two units of fresh frozen plasma. That should hold the President for now, assuming the diagnosis of von Willebrand's disease was correct. It was, he told himself. It had to be. There was no other explanation for that much bleeding in a simple case of food poisoning. *Damn it! A coagulation defect! I should have thought of that early on, because I've seen it before. I've seen patients in the ER bleeding like hell from minor wounds because they had a coagulation deficiency that was either inherited or caused by blood-thinning drugs like Coumadin. And I almost missed the diagnosis in the President of the United States. Jesus Christ! Get your head out of your ass, and think!*

He entered the treatment room and found Carolyn rummaging through a drawer. She cursed under her breath.

"What are you looking for?" David asked.

"Pliers," Carolyn replied. "Kate broke off the key in the narcotics cabinet. Those Secret Service agents must have removed all the tools."

"That can wait," David said urgently. "We've got to clear this room except for the bare essentials."

"Why?"

"Because they're going to do the President's endoscopy in here. They don't trust any other place in the hospital."

"Those guys don't take any chances, do they?"

"Not when it comes to the President," David said, and walked over to the phone on the wall. "Has the blood bank sent up those units yet?"

Carolyn shook her head. "They're having trouble finding a match for the President."

"Damn it!" David groused and rubbed at his forehead, as he tried to think through the predicament. No matched blood was available, and none would be any time soon. Plasma alone wouldn't help the President's worsening anemia. "We may have to use O negative blood in him."

"Is it that bad?" Carolyn asked.

David nodded. "At the rate he's going, the President could bleed out on us."

"Oh, Jesus," Carolyn breathed in a whisper.

David rapidly dialed the number of the blood bank and spoke to the technician in pressing tones. "I need that blood up here now! ... I don't care! ... Get it up here!" David's jaw tightened, a vein on his temple bulged. "Put the director of the blood bank on!"

While he waited, David glanced over to Carolyn and said, "And to complicate matters, the President probably has a coagulation defect."

"This is getting worse by the minute."

"Tell me about it."

Carolyn watched David pace around the phone, pleased that he was there tonight rather than the other attending physician, Oliver Sims, who was brilliant but slow and hesitant. In contrast, David was sharp and quick and decisive, and at his best in emergency situations. Like now. She tried to pry her eyes away from him, but couldn't. Her gaze kept coming back to his uneven good looks that she found so captivating. She wondered if Sol Simcha was right about David watching her. If David was really interested, he was doing a good job of hiding it.

"I don't give a damn who he's talking to," David yelled into the phone. "If the director is not on this line in sixty seconds, I'm coming down to get the blood myself."

He listened intently, then added, "You just wasted five seconds. You've got fifty-five left."

David's eyes narrowed. "Now you've got fifty." He cursed under his breath and looked over to Carolyn. "Can you believe this?"

"They've only got the night crew on," Carolyn said. "I suspect they're overwhelmed."

"We're all overwhelmed," David grumbled. "We've got a bleeding President up here, and they can't shift it into high gear."

A large fly suddenly buzzed by Carolyn. She tried to swat it out of the air with her hand, but missed. "Damn flies!"

"You've got flies up here?" David asked, surprised.

Carolyn nodded. "A large colony somehow found their way up to the Pavilion and, even with pest control, we can't seem to get rid of them."

David brought his attention back to the phone. He pressed it to his ear and said, "Dr. Nelson, listen closely because I'm only going to go through this once. This is David Ballineau on the Beaumont Pavilion. I need two units of O negative blood and two units of fresh frozen plasma, and I need them now... No! Not twenty minutes! Now!... Then warm them quicker and have them up here within ten minutes or we're going to have a dead President on our hands... Good! Ten minutes then."

David hung up and growled, "I wonder what else is going to go wrong."

"Will they be able to eventually find a match for the President?" Carolyn asked.

"Probably. But in his case, eventually may be too late." David quickly glanced around the treatment room, then pointed to pieces of furniture that wouldn't be needed. "Let's move the supply cabinet and the metal stools into the hall, and the small table has to go too."

The ventilation system overhead switched on noisily and blew cool air down on them. Small black particles floated down as well.

"What the hell is that?" David asked, waving at the dust in front of his face.

"The air filter needs to be changed," Carolyn told him. "I've already called the maintenance people about it twice." She reached for the phone on the wall. "I'd better call them again."

"Don't bother," David said. "The Secret Service won't let them come up."

Carolyn studied the ventilation duct as more particles came down. "I know how to remove the filter, and that's where most of the dust is."

"Then let's get it out."

"Shouldn't you get back to the President?"

"His doctor is with him, and until the blood arrives there is not a whole lot I can do for him. And we can't do the endoscopy in here, with crap flying out of the air duct."

Carolyn pushed a metal stool over to the countertop. "Hold this for me, David."

"How are you going to unscrew the duct cover without tools?"

"Trust me," she said, reaching into her pocket and holding up a nickel. "It's a broad, flat screwhead, and sometimes a nickel is all you need."

David grabbed the legs of the stool and watched Carolyn climb up onto the countertop. She stepped over to the sink, then stretched up and used the nickel to unscrew the metal duct. David moved in closer to the countertop to catch her in case she slipped. He glanced up and studied the nurse he'd been attracted to from the first day he saw her. She was slender and shapely, with soft, patrician features and long, brown hair that curled at her shoulders. Not beautiful, he thought, but really pretty. And smart, too. *So why don't I ask her out? Am I worried it'll interfere with my duties as an attending physician? Is that it? Or is that just an excuse for not wanting to get involved again? And not wanting to get hurt again?* David shook his head at his stupid daydreaming. *Think about a sick President, not a pretty nurse.* "How's it going up there?"

"Just about done," Carolyn said, quickly turning the last screw. "One more—"

A screw fell out and dropped toward the floor. It hit the metal stool beside the counter and bounced up. Effortlessly and without thinking, David caught the screw in midair and gave it back to Carolyn.

"Good hands," she commented.

"I was born with them," David said.

"They must have been useful in athletics."

"And other things."

"Such as?"

"Such as catching screws."

Carolyn smiled. There was a lot more to David Ballineau than he let on. He was like a book she wanted to read. Her problem was opening it. She fastened the last screw into the frame, then tossed a round, dirty filter into a nearby trash can. "Want to help me down?"

"Sure."

"Be careful. My palms are covered with soot."

David reached up for her waist, which seemed almost small enough for his hands to wrap around. He slowly lowered her until they were face to face. A lock of her long brown hair fell across her temple and cheek. She didn't bother to tuck it back in place. Instead she just blew at it, and it returned to its original position. Then she smiled to herself as if she had performed some difficult task. David had a nearly irresistible urge to bring her closer, but he forced himself to lower her to the floor.

"Thanks," Carolyn said.

"No problem," David replied, now noticing a smudge of dirt on the end of her nose. He reached over and removed it with the tip of his index finger.

"What's that for?" Carolyn asked, smiling again.

David showed her his finger. "Cleaning service."

Carolyn smiled wider, wondering what it would feel like to run her hands through his salt-and-pepper hair. For starters. "Send me a bill."

"First chance I get."

He watched Carolyn lean over the sink and slowly soap her hands, fingers to palms, as if she was gently massaging them. Everything about her seemed to attract him. Her hair, her long legs, her slender waist, her soft features. But most of all it was her moves that enchanted him. Like the way she blew a strand of hair away from her face and soaped her hands. There was something very sensual about those moves. David continued to stare at her long legs and tight body. He felt himself stir and hastily looked away. *Ask her out to dinner, goddamn it! Just ask!* He cleared his throat and said, "Ah, Carolyn."

"Yes?" she said, reaching for a paper towel.

"I was wondering if—"

Jarrin Smith appeared at the door of the treatment room and knocked gently. "Dr. Ballineau, the anesthesiologist for the President's endoscopy is here."

"Have him come in," David said.

"*Her*," Jarrin corrected and stepped aside.

Karen Kellerman, wearing a stethoscope and a string of pearls around her neck, entered the room. She was strikingly attractive, in her late thirties, with ash-blond hair and eyes so blue they were almost violet. Her long, white laboratory coat was opened wide enough to reveal a curvaceous figure.

"Hello, David," she greeted him with a smile. "How have you been?"

"Good," David said icily. He stared at her for a long moment before continuing. "Are you aware the endoscopy will be done in here?"

"Yes."

"Good," David said again, then lowered his voice. "What you're not aware of is that the President is a bleeder."

Karen's brow went up. "What!"

David nodded. "He's got von Willebrand's disease, which we're in the process of bringing under control."

"How much—"

"That's all you need to know for now," David cut her off. He turned his back to her and spoke to Carolyn. "Once you get this room cleaned up, it might be worthwhile to spray the air with some disinfectant."

"And we should wipe down everything with an antiseptic," Carolyn added as she finished drying her hands. "Including the filthy ventilation duct."

David came back to Karen and said, "You can sit anywhere you like. Just don't get in the way of things."

"Perhaps I can help," Karen offered.

"Just stay the hell out of the way," David growled.

Karen looked down, stung by David's brusqueness. After an awkward pause, she asked quietly, "Can we talk in private for a moment, David?"

"About what?"

"The misunderstanding you and I had."

"There wasn't any misunderstanding," David snapped. "It was straightforward. I had a great idea, and you took it and profited from it. That's called stealing."

Karen's face closed. "You're oversimplifying what happened. You never gave me a chance to explain."

"Stealing is stealing, any way you cut it."

Carolyn cleared her throat loudly, not wanting to be caught in the middle of the hostile exchange. "I'll fetch Jarrin so we can get this room spic and span."

She hurried out into the corridor and quickly looked around the Pavilion. Everything was running smoothly. Patients were being placed in their rooms in an orderly fashion, with Kate directing traffic. Secret Service agents were scurrying about to make certain the President was secure. And Jarrin was on the phone, busily reading off a list as he ordered up more supplies. She gestured to him with her hand, signaling him to speed the conversation up.

Behind her Carolyn could hear the two doctors arguing. From what she could piece together, David had come up with an idea for a portable cooling blanket. It could rapidly decrease the body's temperature and be particularly valuable in patients with sky-high fever and those suffering from spinal cord injuries and cerebral anoxia. A portable cooling blanket was ideal for use in ambulances and MedEvac helicopters.

"You can't sugarcoat it," David was saying. "You stole my idea and sold it to the highest bidder."

"You didn't seem that interested in the blanket," Karen countered. "You made it sound like it was just a passing theory you had."

"That's bullshit!" David shot back. "I even drew sketches of the design and showed them to you."

"Those were crude outlines that didn't begin to resemble the final product," Karen argued.

"More BS!" David said, then asked, "Why did you do it? For the money?"

"Goodness, no! I make more money now than I know what to do with."

"Then why?"

"Because it was a notable achievement that would further my academic career," Karen explained. "That may not seem important to you because you're already at the top of academia and secure. But I was still a step away from a tenured professorship, and this invention got me promoted. Believe me, David, it wasn't for the money."

"Then why did you license it to a big medical supply corporation?" David demanded. "Those royalty checks come to you, don't they?"

"No," Karen answered at once. "They go to Doctors Without Borders, a group I've worked with closely since I was a resident."

There was a long pause before Karen spoke again. "Had I known I was going to lose you over this, I would have never done it—never in a million years."

"It's too late for words," David said with finality. His mind went back three years to a winter vacation they'd taken in Cancun. It was so good then. Now it was a sour memory. "What we had once together is long gone and never coming back."

"Don't be so sure," Karen said in a smug tone. "Time has a way of healing spats between lovers."

Carolyn groaned inwardly and cursed at the turn of events. She and David were just starting to get close. And suddenly an old flame shows up. A gorgeous old flame. Carolyn cursed again at her bad luck. She wondered if fate was going to screw her life up once more.

Off to her right Carolyn heard a sudden commotion. She glanced over to the elevators and saw gurneys and wheelchairs being moved out of the way. A male voice cried loudly, "The Russian Foreign Minister is on his way up!"

Carolyn raced over to the door of the treatment room and called in, "David, I have to help get the Foreign Minister set up.

You might want to start moving the medicine cabinets into the hall."

David nodded and reached for the phone. "As soon as I find out what's holding up the blood I ordered for the President."

Carolyn dashed back out into the corridor just as the elevator door opened, and the Foreign Minister was wheeled out on a gurney. Only the man's head was visible above the white sheet covering him. There was caked vomit around his nose and mouth. His wife was brought out of the elevator behind him. At the rear was a barrel-chested Russian security agent, hand inside his coat, his eyes quickly surveying the surroundings.

Carolyn pointed down the hall past the treatment room. "They go in suites ten and eleven."

As the gurneys were turned around, Carolyn touched the arm of the security agent. "Do you understand English?"

"Yes," the agent said.

"After you've checked the rooms, please stand outside in the corridor while we get the patients squared away," Carolyn requested. "It will only take a few minutes."

"Understood."

Vladimir Yudenko darted ahead and made certain the rooms were safe and secure. He paused briefly to marvel at the size of the suites, which were as large as some apartments in Moscow. Then he moved into the corridor and waited for the patients to be wheeled in and the doors closed behind them.

Yudenko glanced down to the far end of the hall, where most of the activity was. And where the presidents of Russia and the United States were no doubt located. He spat in the direction of both before making his way to the other end of the corridor. Glancing over his shoulder once more, he knocked on the door to the kitchen and entered. A Secret Service agent was standing by the open dumbwaiter.

"All clear?" Yudenko asked.

"All clear," the agent said.

"Good." Yudenko reached for the door, then suddenly spun around and drew his silenced revolver. He fired two shots into the Secret Service agent's chest, one ripping into the heart, the other into the aorta. The agent bled to death in seconds.

Yudenko moved quickly over to the dumbwaiter and pushed a switch. The green light beside it turned red. The dumbwaiter started on its way down.

Yudenko holstered his weapon and sprinted back to his post outside the Foreign Minister's room. Out of the corner of his eye he gazed down the corridor to see if anyone had noticed his brief absence. No one had. Everybody seemed to have their backs to him. Good, he thought, pleased that things had gone so smoothly and easily so far. Yudenko checked his watch. Now all they needed was another eighty seconds.

A young nurse came out of the room of the Foreign Minister's wife and paused to write herself a note. Then she turned, as if heading for the kitchen area. Yudenko reached for his revolver, but the nurse abruptly whirled around and raced off in the opposite direction. She barked out orders to someone before disappearing into a side room. Yudenko checked his watch again. Fifty seconds to go.

Yudenko's pulse quickened in anticipation. *So close to success! So very close!* Kuri Aliev's plan was working to perfection. Soon his name would be shouted from every rooftop and praised in every mosque, and forever enshrined in the hearts and minds of his countrymen.

"The President's daughter is coming up!" someone yelled out.

The door to the Foreign Minister's room flew open. Carolyn Ross rushed by Yudenko and ran for the nurses' station.

"Put the daughter in room three, across from the President," Carolyn ordered loudly. "And call down to the pharmacy. We're going to need more five-percent glucose in saline."

"How many bags?" the ward clerk asked.

"Twenty," Carolyn replied. "And get a dozen vials of potassium chloride."

Carolyn hurried on and reached the bank of elevators a second before the President's daughter was wheeled out. Anyone could tell that the new patient was the First Lady's daughter. Their resemblance was striking. Both had narrow faces, high-set cheekbones, and sandy blond hair. They could have passed for sisters. Next, the daughter's date came out of an adjacent elevator. It was impossible to tell what he looked like, because he was retching and his face was buried in a small basin.

As Carolyn backed away to give the gurneys more room, she spotted a group of chefs coming down the corridor. There were four of them, all dressed in white, with their chef's hats cocked off to one side. Carolyn stared at them, wondering what they were doing up on the Beaumont Pavilion. *They never came to the floor. Never. Not even to . . .* Then she saw the oversized weapons they were pointing at everyone. For a moment she was paralyzed by fear. But then she somehow managed to find her voice.

"Look out!" Carolyn yelled. But it was too late.

The sound of automatic gunfire filled the air, followed by screams and shrieks and cries for help. People tried to run, but stumbled and tripped over themselves in the mayhem and panic. Carolyn found herself on the floor, with heavy bodies atop her. There was more rapid fire. *Pop! Pop! Pop! Pop! Pop! Pop!* More people fell, screaming out in agony.

Carolyn pushed herself up and scurried on her hands and knees for the safety of the nurses' station. She banged into a female body lying spread-eagled, with its chest ripped open and gushing blood as its lungs and heart emptied onto the floor.

Carolyn heard more shots whizzing by overhead and moved faster. She reached the nurses' station and tried to wriggle under the desk. But the space was already taken by Jarrin Smith, who was grimacing and holding onto his arm. Blood was oozing between his fingers. Carolyn curled herself into a ball and, shaking with terror, started praying. *Oh, God! Don't let me die! Please don't let me die!*

There were more yells and shrieks, and more gunfire. Some of the bullets ricocheted into the medicine room and shattered glass and bottles. Two interns dashed from the chart room, blindly running for a way out. Carolyn saw the pair, but there wasn't enough time to warn them. A stream of bullets tore into their heads and necks. The interns were dead before they hit the floor.

Then there was quiet. Total quiet, except for the occasional weak groan. Someone yelled out something in a foreign language that Carolyn didn't recognize. Nearby another shot rang out, followed by another scream of pain. *Oh, God! Oh, God!* Carolyn cringed and pressed herself against the carpet, and prayed she wouldn't be the next to die.

SEVEN

THE TERRORISTS BEGAN DRAGGING bodies into the chart room, stacking them up like firewood. First in were the interns who were barely recognizable, with half their heads blown off. Then a pair of Russian security guards were piled on, one still gripping an ammunition clip. Carolyn Ross had to look away when the terrorists lifted the next corpse. It was Kate Blanchard, her chest torn open and dripping blood. Carolyn still couldn't believe this was really happening, not here, not in a prestigious teaching hospital. And she kept wondering through her fear who the gunmen were and why they were killing innocent people.

"*Sikha! Sikha!*"—Quickly! Quickly! Kuri Aliev urged his Chechens to rapidly remove all the bodies from the hallway.

Carolyn's eyes came back to the dead on the floor. Most were Secret Service agents, with the wires to their earphones visible on the backs of their necks. Just beyond them was a young messenger from the blood bank. The box-like container beside him, which usually held bags of blood and plasma, had bullet holes in it. Carolyn couldn't tell if its contents were intact.

Aliev yelled another set of orders down the corridor, still speaking Chechen. Carolyn had no idea what he was saying, but she could sense a change in his posture and voice. Now he looked even more menacing and cold-blooded. After a pause, Aliev shouted a spate of commands that included a few words Carolyn thought she could understand. *Telefon. Cell fon. Ifon.* Then he spun around and turned his attention to the remaining corpses. He barked out more orders and his men hurriedly cleared away the last of the dead. They quickly picked up the semiautomatic weapons lying in bloody pools on the floor, removed their ammunition, and threw them into a nearby linen closet. The door to the closet was then jammed shut using metal spikes.

Moments later a young, stocky gunman ran up to the group and deposited a large sack at Aliev's feet. It contained all the phone devices collected from the patients. It also held the room telephones that had been ripped from their wall sockets.

"*Dika*"—Good, Aliev said, then came back to the survivors and spoke in English. "All right. Who is the doctor in charge?" There were five people lined up against the wall next to the nurses' station: Carolyn Ross, with blood splattered across the front of her uniform; Jarrin Smith, pressing a towel on the wound in his arm; William Warren, holding his side where a bullet had torn through a muscle but had not entered the peritoneal cavity; Vladimir Yudenko, who had a split lip and a nasty bruise across his forehead; and the President's daughter, Jamie, badly shaken but unharmed.

"Who is the doctor in charge?" Aliev asked again. He was a short man at five and a half feet, with dark piercing eyes, black hair, and hollowed-out cheeks. When no one answered his question, he brought his submachine gun up and pointed it at Jarrin Smith's head. "You have five seconds to reply. One … two … three …"

Carolyn quickly stepped forward. "There is no doctor in charge now," she said. "The interns are dead, and the resident is out sick." She glanced in the chart room at the mound of corpses and tried to locate David Ballineau's body. Her heart dropped as she thought she saw his salt-and-pepper hair in the tangle of arms and legs. "And ... and you've killed the only staff physician who was here."

Aliev gazed down the line of survivors, then came back to William Warren. He briefly studied the bespectacled, slender man with silver-gray hair. "Who are you?"

"I'm the President's personal physician," Warren answered, still holding his side where a bullet had ripped through the outer edge of his latissimus dorsi. It hurt more than it bled.

"You will do," Aliev said. "My men are checking all the rooms. So far, we know where the presidents and the foreign ministers and their wives are located. But three of the rooms are occupied by civilians. I need to know who they are."

Warren shrugged. "I'm not familiar with them. I only look after the President."

Aliev stared at Warren dubiously. "But you will know what is wrong with them, and whether they are legitimate patients."

"Perhaps I'm not making myself clear," Warren said. "Without having seen and examined them, I can't—"

Aliev cut him off with a wave of his hand, then turned to Carolyn. "You are the major nurse here. Correct?"

"Right," Carolyn replied, trying not to look at his menacing weapon. She gazed away but could still feel the heat from its barrel. "I'm the head nurse."

"Which means you have a lot of contact with the patients. Yes?"

"Yes."

"Then you will tell me all about them," Aliev said, nudging her down the corridor with his submachine gun. "And you will come too, doctor. You will explain to me things the nurse cannot."

They walked down the corridor, which was now eerily quiet. All the doors were closed except for the one to the kitchen area. A fifth terrorist, with his arm in a bloody sling, stuck his head out and uttered a long sentence in Chechen.

Aliev turned and glared at him, then growled an order. The terrorist disappeared back into the room that held the dumbwaiter.

From a nearby suite came the sound of someone throwing up violently. Then there was a loud groan and more vomiting, followed by the noise of liquid splashing onto the floor.

Aliev ignored the sounds and looked over to Carolyn. "I will require a large room. Which is the largest room on this pavilion?"

Carolyn thought for a moment. "I guess the nurses' lounge. It's a little bigger than the suites."

"Good," Aliev said. "We can put all the hostages in there. That will make it easier to control their activities."

Carolyn looked at him incredulously and blurted out, "You can't! They'll never sit still for that."

Aliev's eyes narrowed into angry slits. "We will shoot those who resist and leave their bodies in the room as a warning to the others. Or perhaps we should begin by killing one of the hostages. That would remove all resistance, eh?"

Carolyn realized she had gone too far and softened the tone of her voice. "Sir," she said deferentially, "I didn't mean to imply that they would fight you. I was just trying to tell you that their physical condition would make it impossible to crowd them all into the lounge. Please keep in mind that these patients have terrible nausea and vomiting, and some have severe diarrhea as well. I don't think they could stand to stay in one room with only a single bathroom."

Aliev considered shoving all the hostages into a cramped lounge despite the vomit and fecal stench they'd be exposed to. He couldn't care less about their discomfort. But if the conditions became unbearable, the hostages might riot and try to break out. Then he'd have no choice but to shoot them. And for now he wanted them alive because they might be useful as bargaining tools later on. They could also serve as human shields. Finally Aliev nodded and said, "They may remain where they are. But they are to stay in their rooms, and if they so much as step into the corridor they will be shot. There will be no exceptions. Understood?"

"Understood," Carolyn said.

"And you and the doctor will limit yourselves to going only into the President's room," Aliev went on. "I want him kept alive. What happens to the other hostages is of no concern to me."

"But the President will ask about his wife and daughter," Warren interjected. "He'll insist on knowing that they're all right."

Aliev's face hardened. "He is in no position to insist on anything. Nor are you."

Warren held up a hand defensively. "I'm only trying to tell you that I know the President very well and—whatever your demands—he won't budge an inch unless he knows his family is being looked after."

"And the President's wife takes a diuretic medicine for her hypertension," Carolyn inserted. "Fluid loss in these instances can be life-threatening."

Aliev narrowed his eyes. "How do you know what medications the President's wife takes?"

"Because I asked when I checked her into her room and took her vital signs," Carolyn answered at once.

Aliev hesitated, then slowly nodded. He wanted the President's family alive. They could be used to manipulate John Merrill at a crucial moment. "You will be allowed to care for the President and his family, but no one else."

Carolyn gathered up her courage for a final request. "Sir, there's also a desperately ill—"

"No one else," Aliev snapped harshly. "Now let us move on."

As the trio approached Marci Matthews's room, Carolyn said to Aliev, "These patients are very sick. Is it really necessary to put them through this?"

"Yes," Aliev said and pushed the door open. "Now stop asking questions, and do as you're told."

Marci watched the group enter, her doe-like eyes darting back and forth between Carolyn and the large weapon Aliev was holding. She hurriedly pulled the sheet up to her chin and tried to push herself away. The pulse rate on her cardiac monitor suddenly jumped to 100 per minute. "What . . . what's going on?"

Carolyn walked over and took Marci's hand, then squeezed it gently. "Listen carefully to me, Marci. Some men with guns have taken over the floor and we're all now their prisoners. We have to follow their instructions. Do you understand?"

Marci nodded rapidly. She wanted to ask another question, but the words caught in her throat and wouldn't come out, so she just kept nodding.

Aliev asked, "What is wrong with her?"

"She has a disease called lupus," Carolyn answered.

Aliev looked over to Warren. "What is this lupus?"

"It's an inflammatory disease of the skin, muscles, and joints."

"And in her case it also involves the heart," Carolyn added.

Aliev studied the girl with the red rash on her face and asked, "Can you walk?"

"Only to the bathroom," Marci muttered in a weak voice. "And then I become really short of breath."

Carolyn said quickly, "I thought that was getting a lot better."

Marci shook her head. "It's coming back, just as bad as before."

"When did this start?"

"A little while ago."

Carolyn groaned silently. The Beaumont Pavilion was totally unprepared to deal with a rapidly developing pericardial effusion. She turned to Aliev and said, "If Marci gets worse, we'll have to send her down to a special ward."

Aliev waved away the idea with his weapon. "Nobody leaves or comes to this floor."

"But she—"

"Nobody!" Aliev said resolutely, and jerked Carolyn away from the bedside. "Let us go to the next patient."

As they were leaving, Aliev glanced back at Marci and warned, "You keep this door closed, and under no circumstances open it. If you try to leave, you will be shot."

Marci looked away and started sobbing.

In the corridor, Carolyn stepped in front of Aliev and said urgently, "You don't seem to understand how sick that girl is. If she develops more fluid around her heart she will die. The only way to save—"

"You are the one who doesn't understand," Aliev interrupted. "I don't care whether she lives or dies. She is irrelevant. Now let us proceed to the next patient."

Carolyn glared at the man, incredulous at his lack of humanity. But then she remembered he was a cold-blooded killer. One more death wasn't going to bother him.

Aliev shoved her across the hall and into the room of Diana Dunn. The first thing that struck them was a strong, pungent odor. It had a sour and metallic quality.

"What is that smell?" Aliev asked, wrinkling his nose.

"It's the odor given off by patients in liver failure," Carolyn told him. "It's called fetor hepaticus. I don't know what causes it."

Warren explained, "It's the result of backup of sulfur-containing compounds that the failing liver can no longer metabolize."

"Oh," Aliev said, as if he understood.

To Carolyn the question-and-answer drill now seemed similar to the teaching rounds that the house staff made every day. *Except this isn't an academic exercise*, she thought darkly. The leader of the terrorists was making certain that none of the patients posed a threat to him or his men.

Aliev was bending over the bed, studying the patient's face carefully.

"I have the feeling I have seen her before."

"She's Diana Dunn, the movie actress," Carolyn said.

Aliev was taken aback. He leaned closer and examined her face once more. "But she was beautiful. This is an old hag."

"Liver failure does that to a person," Carolyn said.

"Is she conscious?"

"Sometimes."

Aliev poked the actress's ribs with his weapon.

"Ohhh!" Diana moaned softly.

He poked her again. Harder this time.

Diana Dunn slowly opened her eyes and stared out into space.

"Ah!" Aliev said, pleased with himself. "So you are awake."

With effort Diana sat up and turned her eyes to Aliev. Her face took on a pained expression. Then she waved a hand theatrically and began acting. "I can't do that, Roger! I won't do that! I won't come to Paris and wait around like some toy to be used at your convenience."

"What?" Aliev asked, caught off balance.

"My God!" Diana went on. "At least leave me some dignity."

Aliev asked Carolyn, "What is this nonsense?"

"She's confused and disoriented," Carolyn explained. "She's reciting lines from a movie she made years ago. She does that a lot."

"Can she get out of bed?"

Carolyn nodded. "Sometimes she wanders around, but she's harmless."

"If she wanders into the hall, it will be her final performance," Aliev threatened, motioning Carolyn and Warren to the door with his weapon.

Back in the corridor Warren leaned against the wall and pressed a handkerchief to his wound, which was bleeding more heavily now. "I need to rest for a minute."

Aliev pushed him forward. "You can rest later."

Warren moved on, bothered more by the tightness he felt in his chest than by the wound in his side. He hoped it was musculoskeletal pain and not a return of his angina, which had been diagnosed a year earlier and was controlled so well with medication. Warren stretched his spine and took a deep breath, and the pain seemed to ease. But he was still worried about it being angina. *Christ! Not here. Not now.*

They entered Sol Simcha's room and found the elderly man sitting in his wheelchair reading from a Hebrew prayer book. He slowly raised his head.

"Sol," Carolyn said softly, "these people have taken over—"

"I heard the shots and screams," Simcha broke in with a nod. "And I knew exactly what it was. I heard those same sounds a long time ago," he said, looking Aliev in the eye, "at a place called Auschwitz."

Aliev stared down at Simcha and focused in on the faded numbers tattooed across his arm. "You are a Jew?"

"Yes," Simcha said, closing his prayer book and kissing it.

"The Holocaust was a hoax," Aliev jeered.

"It happened," Simcha said flatly.

"A myth," Aliev insisted.

"It happened," Simcha said again.

"It was an invention made up by the Jews so they could take Palestine away from the Arabs."

Simcha shrugged.

Aliev grinned widely. "So you agree, Jew?"

"I'm old and tired," Simcha said in a quiet voice. "I barely have enough strength to call you a Nazi piece of *dreck*."

"*Dreck*?" Aliev asked. "What is *dreck*?"

"It's a Yiddish word for *shit*."

Aliev's grin abruptly disappeared. He raised his weapon up to Simcha's head.

Carolyn quickly interceded. "He has a severe muscle disease. He can barely walk. And he is taking medications that make him say things he ordinarily wouldn't."

Aliev continued to point his weapon at Simcha, his finger tightening on the trigger.

"It's the medicine talking, not him," Carolyn pleaded. "Sometimes he just babbles on, not even knowing what he's saying."

"He knows," Aliev growled.

"Please!" Carolyn begged.

Aliev slowly lowered his submachine gun and gave Simcha a long, stern look. "I will make time for you later, old man."

"I'll be here," Simcha said with equanimity.

They walked out of the room and down the corridor. The smells of stale vomit and blood were everywhere. Two terrorists were rapidly moving in and out of suites, with handkerchiefs held up against their noses. A third terrorist was guarding the three other survivors. Vladimir Yudenko, Jarrin Smith, and Jamie Merrill were seated on the floor across from the nurses' station. The terrorist standing over them had taken off his chef's uniform and now was dressed in black pants and a black turtleneck sweater.

As Aliev approached the group, he spoke to Carolyn. "Place the President's daughter in a separate room. She is not to see the President, and her door is to be kept closed. Do you understand?"

"Yes," Carolyn said and helped the badly frightened girl to her feet.

"You are to rejoin us in two minutes," Aliev ordered. "Don't make me send someone to find you."

"I won't," Carolyn said, wishing that a rescue team of special agents would suddenly appear and engage the terrorists in a fierce gun battle. *Yeah. Right. And in the process we'd all be killed. Which is probably going to happen, regardless of what we do or don't do,* Carolyn thought dismally. Sol Simcha, who was an expert on facing terror, believed that too. That's why he unblinkingly called the lead terrorist a piece of shit.

Her gaze went into the chart room, where dead bodies were stacked one on top of the other. Noisy flies were already beginning to gather, attracted by the fresh blood. Carolyn knew they would soon find their way into the vomit-laden suites and become really bothersome to the patients. Somehow she'd have to get the chart room sprayed with an insecticide. But that wasn't high on her list of priorities at the moment. Staying alive was.

"What's the problem?" Aliev asked impatiently.

"The President's daughter is a little unsteady on her feet," Carolyn lied. "We don't want her to fall and hurt herself."

Aliev shrugged. "I have one more question. You said the old man was taking some type of medicine that made him brave. What is it?"

"High doses of prednisone," Carolyn answered. "It can make people very aggressive."

"And very dead if they don't watch what they say," Aliev said, then came back to Warren. "Let us go see the high and mighty President of the United States."

They continued down the corridor, passing the rooms of the Russian president and his wife. The door to the suite of the Secretary of State was cracked open, letting the strong odor of vomit seep out. From within came the sound of a man retching. Aliev closed the door tightly. The retching noise disappeared. The odor did not.

The way into the President's suite was blocked by Aaron Wells. The agent was sprawled out on the floor, eyes wide open, the bullet holes in his chest bubbling up frothy blood with each shallow breath. As Aliev stepped over him, Wells brought up a hand and feebly grabbed the terrorist's ankle. He strained to hold on, but the effort caused even more blood to spurt from his chest. Aliev glanced down and fired a round point blank into Wells's mouth. The back of the agent's head exploded, bone and brain flying out.

Warren looked away in disgust, detesting the terrorist and his savagery but helpless to do anything. And now he feared what the terrorist had in store for the President. The tightness in Warren's chest suddenly returned. He took another deep breath, but this time the pain didn't subside.

They entered the President's room without knocking. Merrill turned his head and looked over to them. His jaw dropped, his pulse abruptly racing at the sight of the heavily armed terrorist. For a moment his reasoning was a blur. But he quickly gathered himself. He realized that if they just wanted to kill him he would have been dead minutes ago. *No*, he thought darkly, *they have something else in mind.* Merrill's gaze went to William Warren and the bloody handkerchief he was holding against his side.

"Are you badly hurt, Will?" Merrill asked.

"I'm fine. It's only a superficial wound," Warren replied as he leaned against the wall to take his weight off his feet. "Mr. President, I'm afraid these men have taken over the Pavilion."

Merrill nodded knowingly. "So I figured, when I heard the shouts and screams. How are my wife and daughter?"

"They're unharmed, Mr. President."

"And my agents?"

Warren shook his head. "All dead, Mr. President."

Merrill sighed sadly, thinking about the Secret Service agents who were sworn to protect him and, if necessary, give their lives for him. All good, decent men who were so close to him they almost seemed like family. Merrill brought his gaze over to the terrorist, measuring him and trying to determine his ethnicity. Not Arab or Asian or Middle Eastern. The man appeared to have coarse Caucasian features. "What do you want?"

"Oh, we want a lot of things from you," Aliev answered.

"Then you're going to be disappointed," Merrill said bluntly. "The United States does not negotiate with terrorists."

"You'll negotiate," Aliev assured him. "I promise you that."

Merrill felt a wave of nausea and swallowed it away. "Don't bet on it!"

Aliev smirked. "Nor should one bet on a small group of fighters being able to take the President of the United States prisoner, eh?"

"Just because you have me as a hostage doesn't mean we'll meet your demands," Merrill rebutted.

"We will see."

Merrill tried to keep his expression even, but his jaws were tightening. *How did this happen? Goddamn it! How?* The Pavilion was supposedly closed off and heavily guarded by a dozen Secret Service agents. How did the terrorists get in so easily? And how did they put together a plan so rapidly?

"Do you mind telling me how you pulled this off?"

Aliev shrugged. "Later, perhaps."

"It had to be the illness," Merrill guessed, his mind working well now that the initial shock had worn off. "Somehow you induced the illness that caused us to come here, where we'd be vulnerable."

Aliev looked back, stone-faced.

"That had to be it," Merrill insisted.

"And University Hospital was the medical center closest to the hotel," Warren surmised. "You knew we'd use this facility."

Aliev remained silent.

"At least tell us the poison you used," Warren beseeched. When Aliev didn't answer, Warren added, "If it's something lethal, we won't even listen to your demands. Why should we bother?"

"It was a Russian toxin we placed in the caviar," Aliev replied finally. "It was the same gastrointestinal poison they used on us in Chechnya. The toxin is encapsulated in tiny pellets and is slowly released hours after it is ingested. Then the nausea and vomiting start and last for about six hours. And just like you, all the Chechens who swallowed the poison in their food were rushed to the hospital for treatment." Aliev's expression turned into a nasty scowl. "And that is when the Russians opened up with their heavy artillery, destroying the hospital and slaughtering hundreds of men, women, and children."

Aliev paused to glare at his listeners, his eyes now filled with rage. "Do you know that over the past twenty years Russian soldiers have killed a hundred thousand Chechens? A hundred thousand! And the world said nothing. Then we kill three hundred and eighty-five in a school at Beslan and the world screams at us. What kind of arithmetic is that?"

"It seems to me your grievance is with the Russians," Merrill said, his voice neutral.

"They will pay," Aliev said vengefully. "They will pay a much higher price than they ever imagined. But you also have Chechen blood on your hands. A lot of Chechen blood. So these are my demands. The United States will release all Chechen fighters it now has imprisoned at Guantanamo and at Bagram prison in Afghanistan. In addition you will release all Chechen prisoners now held by your CIA in its secret prisons in Poland and Romania. This will free over a hundred Chechen fighters who will be flown to destinations of our choosing. The Russians will do the same, releasing Chechens from their Siberian work camps and from their prisons outside Moscow. They have some of our most important leaders and generals, and we want them back."

"What you want and what you'll get are two different things," Merrill said defiantly.

"We will see what happens when the killing starts," Aliev threatened.

"What killing?" Merrill asked at once.

"You will be given four hours to free the prisoners and have them in planes on the way to safe destinations," Aliev replied. "If this is not done, we will begin killing hostages, one every half-hour, until our demands are met. And we'll begin with the patients."

From the doorway Carolyn blurted out involuntarily, "You can't do that! You can't just murder innocent people!"

"Oh, yes, I can and I will," Aliev said coldly, his eyes still fixed on Merrill. "Mr. President, we killed close to four hundred people at Beslan, over half of them children, and none of us shed a tear. So believe me when I say we will kill all the patients here and all the Russians, then your Secretary of State, then your wife and daughter, if we have to."

Merrill's face hardened. He wanted to get his hands on this man, tear his heart out and grab his weapon. But he knew that was wishful thinking. In his weakened condition, Merrill could barely stand, much less tangle with an armed terrorist. With effort he calmed himself, knowing that senseless anger was the last thing he needed. But Merrill's stomach kept churning and brought on another wave of nausea. He abruptly sat up and vomited enough red blood to half fill a small basin. Then he retched again and more blood came up.

Aliev jumped back, wide-eyed and revolted by the bloody vomit. "What is happening?"

"Your toxin has caused the President's stomach to bleed," Warren answered immediately. "This makes his condition very precarious."

Aliev thought for a moment before saying, "Then he will have to hurry and meet our demands, won't he?"

Merrill gagged and dry-heaved, then gagged again and spat out a mouthful of blood. Exhausted, he dropped back down on his pillow.

Warren rushed over to the bucket of ice chips, but they were all melted, the water now at room temperature. He needed fresh ice to make a slurry and repeat the frigid gastric lavage that had stemmed the bleeding earlier. And he needed a gastroenterologist stat, particularly one who was an expert endoscopist. Warren quickly turned to Aliev and urged, "We have to bring in a specialist for the President."

"No specialist."

"He could die," Warren pressed. "We've got to stop the hemorrhaging."

"You stop the hemorrhaging," Aliev ordered. "You are a doctor."

"But I'm not—" Warren clutched his chest and sank to his knees. His breathing became labored, his face ashen. "I … I think I'm having a heart attack!"

"Lie down!" Carolyn hurried over and eased him to the floor. She quickly took his pulse. It was 108 beats per minute, and irregular. She couldn't tell whether he was going into atrial fibrillation or having frequent premature ventricular contractions. "I think you've having a ventricular arrhythmia."

In a weak voice Warren muttered, "Use lidocaine."

Carolyn bolted for the door. In the hallway she yelled to the small group of survivors at the nurses' station. "Jarrin, grab a wheelchair and get down here stat!"

She dashed back into the room and again took Warren's pulse. It was even faster now, at 120 beats per minute, and still very irregular. Carefully she tried to pick up the rhythm. Was it completely irregular, as in atrial fibrillation, or was there some regularity as in multiple PVCs? Despite her experience as an emergency flight nurse, she was in over her head and knew it. She needed the patient hooked up to a cardiac monitor, and if the rhythm was bizarre she'd need a cardiologist looking over her shoulder. Warren's pulse jumped to 140 per minute, with some of the beats thready and difficult to feel.

"I can't tell the rhythm."

Warren tried to remain calm, but the tightness in his chest was worsening and he was certain he was having a myocardial infarction. And he could feel the erratic beat of his heart. Warren brought a hand up to his carotid artery and felt for a pulse. After a brief moment he said, "I think it's PVCs, but I can't be sure."

"If it's PVCs, lidocaine should work," Carolyn thought aloud.

Warren nodded, his eyes closing.

"Do you know the dose?" Carolyn asked hastily.

Warren shook his head.

Carolyn desperately tried to remember the correct dose of lidocaine to treat multiple premature ventricular contractions. She recalled that a patient had received the drug intravenously a week earlier on the Pavilion, and that it was given initially as a bolus. But the dose escaped her.

Jarrin barreled into the room, pushing a wheelchair in front of him. His wounded upper arm was now tightly wrapped in a strip of towel. Blood was still seeping through.

Aliev quickly moved in front of the wheelchair and stared down at Carolyn. "What do you think you are doing?" he demanded.

"We have to put him in a room and start treatment," Carolyn replied.

"You are to treat only the President and his family," Aliev snarled. "No one else. No exceptions."

"But he's having a heart attack," Carolyn pleaded.

"Too bad," Aliev said stonily.

What a bastard! Carolyn seethed to herself. She took Warren's pulse again. It was still irregular, maybe even more so than before. *Without lidocaine he'll go into ventricular tachycardia*, she thought. "He'll die if he's not given the necessary drugs."

Aliev shrugged. "So he dies."

Oh, God! *How do I get him into a room and start lidocaine? How?* A sudden idea came to Carolyn. Use the President's illness. "He's the only doctor we've got on the Pavilion. I'll need his instructions on how to keep the President and his family alive."

Aliev considered this proposal but still didn't appear to budge.

"And he's no threat to you," Carolyn added. "He's so weak he can barely stand."

Aliev hesitated a while longer, then reluctantly gave in. "Put him in a room, but your first priority is the President. Understood?"

"Understood," Carolyn said and rapidly turned to Jarrin. "You can draw blood, can't you?"

Jarrin nodded. "Do it all the time in the clinic."

"Good. Then you can insert an IV line for us," Carolyn said. "It looks like Dr. Warren is having a myocardial infarction. I want you to help him into your wheelchair and put him in the room where we'd planned to house the First Daughter's date. Then start an IV with five-percent glucose in water. After that, I want you to hustle down to the nurses' station and get out the cardiology handbook and find the dose of lidocaine for PVCs. Write it down for me."

"Got it." Jarrin gently lifted Warren off the floor and seated him in the wheelchair. He gave Warren a reassuring pat on the shoulder and said, "I'll have you set up before you know it, doctor."

Jarrin and the wheelchair were halfway to the door when the President retched and brought up another mouthful of blood. He spat it into the metal basin, which was now close to overflowing. Then more blood came up, most from his mouth, some from his nose.

Carolyn glanced over to the cardiac monitors. The President's pulse was 124 beats per minute, his blood pressure dropping to 88/50. *Oh, Christ! He's going out on us.* She hurriedly turned to Aliev. "We need a specialist for him, now!"

"No," Aliev said with a firm shake of his head.

"He's going to bleed to death!" Carolyn screamed at the terrorist.

"Then you had better give him some medicine to stop it," Aliev suggested, showing little concern.

What a bastard! Carolyn thought again. *What do I do? What can I do? The President is hemorrhaging, and he's got a coagulation defect. Oh, God! What can I do? He needs blood, and we don't …* Suddenly she remembered the dead messenger from the blood bank.

She dashed out of the room and down the corridor. *Maybe the plastic bags of blood in the messenger's container hadn't been punctured by bullets.* But Carolyn knew that was wishful thinking. *If the President continues to bleed and there's no blood to transfuse him, he'll die, right here, right in front of my eyes. And there's nothing I can do but watch.* Carolyn's heart was pounding so hard she thought it would jump out of her chest.

She came to the bank of elevators and went over to the messenger's container, which was laying on its side with two bullet holes in it. There was a puddle of dark red blood beneath it. "Oh, shit!" Carolyn groaned, as she turned the container right side up and removed its lid. Sticky red blood was everywhere. The two bags on top had been punctured by bullets, their contents emptied out. Carolyn threw them aside and dug deeper into the goo. Then she felt a fullness, then another. One bag of blood and one bag of fresh plasma were still intact.

As she was about to stand, her eyes went to the bank of elevators. The terrorists had driven metal spikes into the bases of the doors, jamming them shut and making a rescue attempt via the elevator shafts impossible. Carolyn quickly glanced over to the nurses' station. Jarrin and Yudenko were watching her every move. The terrorist guarding them had his back to her. She hurriedly tried to extract the spikes by hand, but they wouldn't budge. *Damn it!* she growled at her futile effort. Then her gaze focused in on the sturdy lid of the messenger's container.

The terrorist at the nurses' station yelled at her in Chechen.

Carolyn held up her hands and showed him her blood-covered palms, then reached into the container and pretended to search it further.

The terrorist uttered a few words and turned away.

Carolyn grabbed the lid of the container and forced it under a metal spike. Slowly she pried the spike up, but left it loosely in place so that just a shove on the door would cause it to fall out. Now one elevator door could be opened, giving the Secret Service a way in.

Carolyn picked up the bags of blood and plasma and sprinted back down the hall, passing Aliev, who was giving orders to another terrorist outside the President's suite. Once inside the room, she tried to close the door, out of habit, but Aliev kicked it open. "Watch her!" he instructed the other terrorist.

Carolyn ran into the bathroom and washed the blood off the sticky bags, then checked again to make sure they were intact. They were. Dashing back to the bedside, she glanced over to the President, who was retching up a bloody froth. His blood pressure was down to 85/50.

"Which do I give first?" she asked herself aloud. "The blood or the plasma?"

The terrorist at the door looked over his shoulder at her, then turned back and faced the corridor.

"Jesus, Carolyn!" she berated herself. "Make up your damn mind! Which? Or does it matter?"

"The blood first," she decided finally. "He needs the red blood cells most of all."

As she held up the bag of blood to check the name on the label, she saw a slip of paper floating down from the ceiling. It landed on the floor between her and the guard. Quietly, she tiptoed over to the slip and picked it up. It was a prescription blank from University Hospital. On it was written:

1) Administer plasma first, run in as fast as possible.
2) Give Warren aspirin 325 mg.
Get EKG
Hold lidocaine

DAVID

Carolyn jerked her head up to the ceiling just as one of the panels slid aside.

David looked down at her with a finger pressed over his lips.

Then the panel moved back into place.

EIGHT

"We're stuck up here with no way out," Karen Kellerman whispered into David's ear. "Like mice caught in a cage."

"Except mice don't have to worry about Uzi submachine guns being pointed at them," David whispered back.

"Do you think they're done shooting?" Karen asked nervously.

"For now," David said, his voice barely audible. "But it'll start again if someone does something stupid."

"But even then, they won't shoot up the ceiling."

"Don't count on it, particularly if they decide to fire over people's heads."

Karen gazed around the dim ceiling crawlspace, with its maze of metal pipes and electric wires. Even if the stray shots missed them, the bullets would shred pipes and wires and turn the crawlspace into an uninhabitable hell. "If we surrendered, they probably wouldn't hurt us," she suggested weakly. "After all, they'll need doctors to keep the President alive."

"Do you want to die?"

"No."

"Well, that's what will happen if we go down there. In all likelihood, nobody will leave the Beaumont Pavilion alive."

Karen swallowed hard. "They won't kill the President, will they?"

"Sure they will," David told her. "Our government is not going to negotiate with the terrorists. They'll stall for time, then attempt a rescue that will almost certainly fail. There'll be a big firefight and everybody on the Pavilion will end up dead, including the President."

"How do you know that?"

"Because I've been there," David said vaguely. "Now stop asking dumb questions."

"There's one more thing."

"What?" David asked, becoming annoyed.

"My asthma."

"Oh, Christ! I forgot."

David knew all about Karen's asthma. It was an acute asthma attack that brought Karen to the medical center's ER where she met and was treated by David. She had a moderately severe form of the disease that required therapy with both pills and inhalers. "Have you got your inhaler with you?"

"No. I left it in my purse."

"Shit," David muttered and glanced around the crawlspace. It was windowless with no discernible cross-ventilation. The stale air barely moved and was filled with particulate matter. It was an ideal environment to bring on an asthmatic attack. "The first thing we have to do is get you to a place where there's some circulation of the air from below."

"Is there such a place up here?"

"Yeah," he answered and pointed to his left. "At the far end of the space over the kitchen area. I felt a draft coming up between the panels. I want you to go over there and stay put. Try to actually breathe in the draft."

"That by itself is not going to work," Karen warned. "I can already feel my chest tightening. I'll need my inhaler soon."

"The next time I send a note down to Carolyn, I'll see if they have an inhaler in the Pavilion."

"And if they don't?"

"Then we've got double trouble," David said candidly. "Now scoot over to the place I told you about and remain there. Don't even twitch a muscle while I scout around and see how the other patients are doing."

"David," Karen said too loudly. "I'm—"

"Shhh!" He hushed her at once. "Talk only when you absolutely have to, and then do it in a whisper. Any wrong sound that comes from this space and we're both dead. You understand *dead*, don't you?"

"Y-yes," Karen gulped shakily.

"Then move out like a mouse on tiptoes and stay on the metal grid," David said and watched her disappear into the dimness. Slowly he glanced around the enclosed space, but his mind was still on Karen's asthma. One bad attack and she'd make enough noise to attract every terrorist on the floor below. And the two of them would be goners. The terrorists would shoot first and ask questions later. David grumbled under his breath, hoping against hope that the asthma attack wouldn't occur. But deep down he knew it would, and without an inhaler for Karen they would be dead ducks.

With care, David turned his body around and again studied the crawlspace between the Beaumont Pavilion and the roof of the hospital. It was slightly over four feet high, with a solid plaster ceiling and a floor that consisted of a thick metal grid upon which rested removable synthetic panels. Most of the space was taken up by rows of pipes and tubes and bundles of wires that were criss-crossed at varying distances by elevated tubes and pipes. Off to the right was a large metal container that David assumed was part of the ventilation system because it clicked off and on intermittently. There was no light except for the rays coming up through the openings for the ducts.

As he crawled away, David reached up and measured the height of the crawlspace once more. It stayed at just over four feet. There was plenty of room to crawl noiselessly over the grid, but not nearly enough to stand and move quickly, even in a severely crouched position.

David wriggled his way quietly along the metal grid in the ceiling above the Beaumont Pavilion. Peering down a ventilation duct, he saw the President's wife below. Lucy Merrill was stretched out on her bed, a damp washcloth over her forehead, an IV running into her arm. On a nightstand beside her was a basin filled with vomit. David could hear her soft moans as he moved on.

Now he was over the corridor. He paused to study the terrorist standing guard between the rooms of the President and the First Lady. The man was stocky and balding, and he carried his Uzi submachine gun like an experienced fighter—low and at his waist, both hands on it and ready to fire at a moment's notice. Tucked under his belt were two additional clips of ammunition, each holding thirty rounds. By himself, David thought grimly, the terrorist could fire ninety rounds in under a minute.

He moved on, squeezing past metal pipes and bundles of electrical wires, his mind still on the terrorist's weapon and the damage it could inflict. The Secret Service agents never stood a chance, he told himself. The terrorists had come out blasting, filling the air with so many rounds from their Uzis that anybody who even peeked out of a doorway was dead.

Long ago David had learned how to distinguish one automatic weapon from another by the sound it made. The noises produced by an Uzi and by an AK-47 were the same to most people, but they were like night and day to David. So when he heard the automatic gunfire while he was in the treatment room, he knew it was Uzis and he knew there were a lot of them. His initial instinct was to go out the window, but there was no outside fire escape and the ground was ten stories down. So he opted for the crawlspace above the ceiling. He jumped onto the countertop and climbed into the space, pulling Karen up after him—and found himself trapped. There was no obvious exit to the roof. The only way out was down through the Beaumont Pavilion.

David continued to crawl through the metal grid, passing over the Secretary of State's room and the room of the Russian president before coming to the suite where William Warren lay. A guard was outside the partially opened door, smoking a cigarette. David squirmed past him and peered down through a crack in the ceiling. Carolyn was slapping EKG leads on the bare-chested physician. A defibrillator was at the bedside, an IV line slowly dripping into his arm.

David nodded to himself. Getting an IV started was the first order of business, and Carolyn knew it. The line would be critical for administering drugs. If Warren had gone into shock initially, they would never have found a vein and the older physician would have certainly died. *Good for you, Carolyn*, David thought. She was smart as hell and twice as brave. Christ! The way she stood up to that terrorist to protect Sol Simcha! David kept his eyes on the attractive nurse, thinking that the only way to know what a person was really made of was to test that individual under the worst of conditions. A few people rose to the challenge. Most didn't. Carolyn was one of the few.

For a moment David felt a twinge of guilt for not staying down on the floor with the others. In retrospect he knew he could have waited for things to settle down and surrendered and probably survived. But then he would have ended up being another doctor-prisoner who might well have been kept away from everyone except the President. From up in the crawlspace he could treat all the hostages. And he could do other things, too.

His gaze went over to William Warren, who was beginning to sweat profusely. His skin color was worsening, his breathing now more rapid. *Hurry up, Carolyn!* David urged. *Hurry!*

Carolyn finished taking Warren's EKG and tried to decipher its unusual rhythm. The R waves, which represented contractions of the ventricles, should have been tall and narrow and peaked, like skinny triangles. But here they appeared broad and peculiarly shaped, with an obviously irregular rhythm that Carolyn didn't recognize. As a MedEvac nurse, she had been trained to read EKGs and had no problem diagnosing commonplace arrhythmias. But Warren's arrhythmia was so bizarre and complex that it was impossible to interpret. It was unlike anything she'd ever encountered. Carolyn looked out to the guard in the corridor who had his back to her. Then quickly she stared up at the ceiling and, with an exaggerated shrug, motioned to the EKG, indicating her quandary.

A panel in the ceiling slid open and David's face and hand appeared. He formed a circle with his thumb and index finger and gave her a *you're doing fine* sign. Next he pointed to the EKG, then over to the IV pole, and made a *wraparound* gesture.

Carolyn spread her hands apart, gesturing back. *What does that mean?*

David took a prescription slip and wrapped it around his finger, and again pointed to the IV pole. Then he signaled upward.

Carolyn nodded quickly and glanced over to the guard once more. He still had his back to her. She hurriedly wrapped the EKG strip around the top of the pole and lifted it toward the opening in the ceiling.

Just as David grabbed the strip, Warren opened his eyes and saw Carolyn holding the IV pole up. He didn't notice the opened panel behind his bed. "Is something wrong with my IV?"

"No," Carolyn lied easily. "I'm repositioning it so I can see the flow rate more clearly."

Warren suddenly felt his heartbeat becoming more erratic, the tightness in his chest more noticeable. "I … I think I'd better take a nitroglycerine tablet."

Carolyn looked up, as David nodded his approval. She searched for a nitroglycerine tablet from the crash cart and placed it under Warren's tongue. Warren's complexion was taking on a grayish hue. *A bad sign*, Carolyn thought. Death was coming.

David rapidly read the EKG. It showed an evolving myocardial infarction with a grossly abnormal rhythm. There were multifocal PVCs, which were occurring so frequently that in places the rhythm resembled a deadly ventricular tachycardia.

"I'm having trouble catching my breath," Warren gasped.

Carolyn glanced over to the cardiac monitor. Warren's blood pressure was bouncing around, the number changing by the moment. She wondered if the monitor was malfunctioning. Quickly, Carolyn reached for a stethoscope and placed a blood pressure cuff on Warren's arm, then took a manual reading. 92/64. Warren was straining to fill his lungs, and his skin color was turning ashen. Again Carolyn hurriedly inflated the blood pressure cuff.

Whiff! Whiff! Whiff! Then she slowly let the air out. The reading was 84/50 and barely audible. He was going into shock.

A gurgling noise came from Warren's throat. It sounded agonal. Now his lips were blue.

A prescription blank floated down onto the bed.

Carolyn snatched it up and quickly read David's orders.

- *Give IV bolus of lidocaine 80 mg, followed if necess. by 40 mg bolus every 8–10 mins. to total dose of 200 mg*
- *Maintenance dose 2 mg/min.*
- *If it doesn't work, use defibrillator set at 200 joules*

Carolyn reached for a needle and syringe and drew up 80 milligrams from a vial of lidocaine. She injected it directly into Warren's IV line. Then she waited. Seconds ticked off. Warren's color was still poor, his breathing shallow.

Carolyn looked up at the ceiling and silently mouthed the question: *Should I give another bolus?*

David held up an index finger, signaling her to wait.

Carolyn mouthed up, *defibrillator?*

David shook his head, then pointed to the EKG and made a *turn it on* gesture.

Carolyn switched the EKG machine back on. And waited again. The strip started moving. It still showed bizarre complexes, but not as many as before. Then the R waves narrowed into slender triangles and became more normal-appearing. Carolyn could now clearly see the heart rate slowing. Warren was reverting to a normal sinus rhythm. Carolyn hurriedly took his blood pressure again. It was 100/70. Then again. 108/74.

She let out a sigh of relief and asked, "How are you doing, Dr. Warren?"

"Better," Warren said softly. "I'm breathing much easier."

"Good," Carolyn told him, noticing that his facial complexion was turning pink. "You're back to a sinus rhythm, thanks to a big bolus of lidocaine."

"It's you I should thank," Warren said gratefully. "And I do."

"You're welcome," Carolyn replied and glanced up at the ceiling. David gave her a *thumbs up* signal and moved the panel back into place.

He squirmed his way around a metal partition and headed for the corridor. Warren needed to be in a CCU where he could be constantly monitored and anticoagulated, and perhaps receive a thrombolytic agent that could dissolve away the clot blocking one of his coronary arteries. But the terrorists would never let that happen. Nobody was going to leave the Pavilion, regardless of the gravity of their illness. It sounded heartless, but it was the smart move. The terrorists realized that in order to secure an area, it had to be done absolutely and completely. One breach, one small opening, and all could be lost. They knew that a few could hold off many in a given area as long as all the entrances and exits were sealed. It was a basic tenet of guerrilla warfare.

Below David heard the voices of the terrorists. They were speaking in Chechen, and sounded as if they were arguing. He peered down through a ventilation duct in the ceiling and studied the men in black. There were three of them—the leader; the balding, stocky one; and the wounded one. The leader was yelling at the wounded terrorist, shoving him into the room with the dumbwaiter and hollering out, "*Leela!*"

David didn't understand the word *leela*, but quickly figured out what the argument was about. Earlier he had seen the wounded terrorist standing in the room with the dumbwaiter and watching the others as they booby-trapped it. Now the man was wondering why he had to continue guarding the dumbwaiter. *Because it represents a way in*, David thought strategically. A possible passageway that, although mined, might still be circumvented. The leader knew it, the terrorist with the wounded arm didn't.

As David turned his body in the direction of the President's room, his knee banged against a metal duct. It made a metallic, ringing noise. David froze in place and held his breath. The terrorists went quiet, then began speaking in urgent tones. *Goddamn it! They know I'm here!* David's brain screamed. *I'm a dead man!*

Suddenly the air conditioning system clicked on and cool air blew down into the corridor. There was another pause. Then one of the terrorists laughed and spoke in a lighter tone. David pricked his ears, listening intently, and waited. The men continued talking, but now their voices seemed more distant. The terrorists were walking away.

David breathed a deep sigh of relief. They must have believed that the metallic sound they had heard was made by the air conditioning switching on. But David still didn't move. He remained absolutely motionless, wondering if two of the terrorists had walked away and left one behind to listen and see if the noise would recur. He let a full five minutes pass before he peered down through the duct again. The corridor was clear.

Carefully David started off again, moving slowly and staying well clear of the metal ducts. *You're rusty!* he berated himself. *You would have never made that mistake when you were in Special Forces! But that was a lot of years ago, and you're not the same person you once were. So be careful, and don't do anything stupid.*

He pushed on, now picking up the scent of death. Not just plain, ordinary death, but violent death that had its own peculiar odor. Maybe it was caused by gunfire mixed in with blood and fear and decay. But whatever caused it, the smell was distinctive to David and made his mind flash back to Somalia, and to the firefight, and to the dead piled up in heaps. *So many dead. Forty or more. Mostly Somalis, a few of ours. And for what? Nothing had changed there. All that death, and it hadn't mattered a damn.*

David came to another ventilation duct and looked down through it. He was over the chart room that was filled with dead bodies. Arms and legs were entangled into a bizarre patchwork. Heads were blown open, their brains oozing out and mixing with pools of blood. And now the smell of death became more intense. Then David saw a corpse with no head. It was gone. It was totally gone, leaving only the stump of a neck behind. David flinched as a gruesome flashback came into his mind. It was the horrifying image of his best friend in the Special Forces, a sharpshooter from Tennessee who hadn't returned with his comrades from the field of battle. They went back for him and found him outside a Somali village. Beheaded! The bastards had sawed his head off! The image grew sharper and sharper and now David could see the carotid arteries dangling down from his best friend's severed head.

Perspiration poured off David's brow as the full-blown panic attack began. *The head, the severed head with its eyes gouged out!* David's hands started to shake so violently he had to grab a nearby metal beam to steady them. Then the shortness of breath came. He strained frantically, gasping for air and feeling as if he was about to suffocate. With effort he forced himself to expand his lungs. He did this over and over until his respirations gradually returned to normal. But it took another full minute for the trembling to stop.

He lay back, drenched in sweat, and cursed at his post-traumatic stress disorder. Goddamn it! When will it end? When? The clinical psychologist at Walter Reed had told him the attacks would diminish with time, and they had. But they were always lurking near the surface, waiting for the right trigger to set them off. A trigger that reminded him of warfare. Like a missing head.

He took a deep breath, turned onto his stomach, and gazed down at the dead bodies again, avoiding the one that had been beheaded. Atop the stack was Aaron Wells, who was staring up at him with lifeless eyes. David was about to continue when he abruptly stopped.

Goddamn it! I'm going in the wrong direction! Think what you're doing or you'll get yourself caught and maybe killed!

He turned and headed back to the President's room at the far end of the corridor. He moved cautiously, brushing up against bundles of wires and staying clear of the metal ducts. Just ahead he heard a conversation going on in one of the rooms. He slowed even more, now inching his way toward the sound. It was a man's voice speaking English. There was no accent. Not a terrorist, David decided. He reached a ventilation duct and gazed down. He was over the First Daughter's room. She was watching a news program on television. The reporter was describing the illness that had befallen the President and all the guests at the official dinner. He said that President Merrill was now a patient at University Hospital, and was resting comfortably. There was no mention of a hostage situation. *They'll find out soon enough*, David through grimly, and moved on.

He approached the President's suite and stared down at the guard outside the door. David inched his way forward, pulling his body along rather than wriggling and squirming. Once over the room, he noiselessly removed a panel from the ceiling and looked down at the sleeping President. There was blood caked around his mouth, with no evidence of fresh bleeding. But Merrill's color was pale, very pale.

David's eyes darted over to the cardiac monitor. The monitor was adjacent to the bed over five feet away, but its large illuminated numbers made it easy to read. The President still had a tachycardia of 120/minute, and was borderline hypotensive with a blood pressure of 94/60. That was a high enough pressure to perfuse his brain and kidneys. But one more big bleed and the bottom would drop out, and the President would die.

David's gaze went to the bag of fresh plasma that was dripping into Merrill's arm. The bag was half empty. Maybe that would be enough plasma to stem the hemorrhaging, David hoped. At least for a while. But for how long?

Merrill coughed and gagged and was suddenly awake. He retched and blood gushed out of his mouth and onto the sheet covering him.

David groaned silently and quickly replaced the panel in the ceiling. Maybe the President had no time left at all! He hurriedly reached for his cell phone and dialed 411. Then, in a voice barely above a whisper, he asked the directory-assistance operator to connect him with the Secret Service office in Los Angeles.

NINE

THE NATIONAL SECURITY COUNCIL listened in stunned silence to the demands of Kuri Aliev coming over the speakerphone.

"The prisoners are to be dressed in civilian clothes and placed on military transport planes, with a crew of only pilot and co-pilot. Once they are airborne, you will be given instructions on their final destinations. The list of prisoners will be faxed to you and to your counterparts in Moscow. There are two hundred and eighty-six names in all. Everything must be done within four hours. If the deadline is not met, we will kill a hostage every half-hour until it is."

The council could discern Aliev's voice resonating in the background. He was speaking on a phone connected to a PA system, so that all the hostages on the pavilion could hear his threats. "You have exactly four hours."

Ellen Halloway, the first female Vice President of the United States, leaned toward the speakerphone and said, "Even if we wished to comply, that's not enough time."

"Ha!" Aliev scoffed. "You could mobilize your entire fleet of stealth bombers and have them halfway to Iraq in four hours. So stop talking foolishness."

"But those aircraft are on standby and ready to—"

"If you want to waste time arguing, that is your business," Aliev cut in. "But the clock is running. You now have three hours and fifty-nine minutes."

Ellen Halloway ran a hand through her sandy blond hair, which was pulled back and held severely in place by a silver clip. In her mid-fifties, she was tall and attractive, with high cheek bones and deep brown eyes. "I need to talk to the President."

"Why?"

"To make certain he's still alive."

There was a long pause before Aliev said, "Hold."

Halloway leaned over to Arthur Alderman, the Director of National Intelligence, and asked in a barely audible voice, "Any ideas?"

"Keep the conversation going," Alderman whispered back. "Perhaps that will give the President a chance to send us some sort of message."

Martin Toliver, the Secretary of Defense, was seated to the Vice President's left. He moved his chair in closer, and hissed, "Tell that Chechen bastard we don't negotiate with terrorists!"

"That's up to the President, not us," Halloway said, keeping her voice low.

"But he's got a gun pointed at his head," Toliver argued.

"He's still the Commander in Chief," Halloway said.

An Air Force colonel with a small suitcase handcuffed to his wrist entered the Situation Room in the White House and saluted sharply. "Madam Vice President, the nuclear codes have been changed. New launch codes have been activated."

Halloway nodded. That was one less thing to worry about. They had to assume that the military officer, who carried the nuclear football and followed the President wherever he went, had also been taken hostage or killed. "Thank you, Colonel."

The Air Force officer stepped off to the side.

"What the hell is taking him so long?" Toliver growled.

Halloway held her palm out, urging patience, as she tried to think through the nightmarish dilemma they were facing. Not only was the President being held hostage by the terrorists, but so were his family and the Secretary of—

"Ellen?" John Merrill's voice came over the speakerphone. There was some static as the call was being transmitted to Washington from the Beaumont Pavilion via a Secret Service line. "Ellen?"

"Yes, Mr. President," Halloway replied. "I'm here with the Security Council."

"Good," the President went on. "I want all of you to know that I have complete confidence in Vice President Halloway. I'm sure that she, together with the Council, will find a way to resolve this matter."

"Thank you, Mr. President," Halloway said, keeping her voice even and assuming the terrorists could hear her. "Now, first off, how are you feeling?"

"I've had better days," Merrill answered.

The council members gathered around the oval conference table nodded to one another. The President sounded strong and in control of himself.

"You of course know that we've been taken hostage by these terrorists," Merrill told her.

"We know."

"And you should also know any rescue attempt would be very dangerous, even if carried out by a highly specialized team," Merrill went on. "Very dangerous and very difficult."

"We're aware of that, Mr. President."

"A lot of people would die," Merrill warned, but not too strongly. "Your military advisors will tell you how much damage three submachine guns can—"

There was a sudden rustling noise, then a grunt. The line went quiet.

The council members stared at the speakerphone and waited anxiously. Seconds ticked off.

"Very clever, Mr. President," Aliev came back on. "You were trying to tell your people that you saw three terrorists outside your door, so that is how many there must be. Well, I hope you govern better than you count."

"I was simply warning them not to do anything foolish," Merrill said evenly.

"If they do try, Mr. President, I can assure you that you and your family will be the first to die," Aliev threatened, then paused a long moment before speaking to the council again. "Lady Vice President, you now have three hours and fifty-four minutes to release the prisoners."

"We need more time," Halloway said urgently. "We're asking you to reconsider and give us an additional hour."

There was no reply.

The Situation Room remained silent. No one uttered a sound. The staff and military aides standing behind the council stayed motionless, their ears pricked. Everyone waited for Aliev's voice to come back on the line. Half a minute passed. Still there was no response.

Abruptly the silence was broken by a loud dial tone.

Ellen Halloway exhaled loudly and pushed the speakerphone away. "The President told us he wants us to try a rescue mission."

"That's what it sounded like to me." Toliver was a lean man, in his early sixties, with a narrow, cold face and black hair that was graying at the temples. "And he wants it done ASAP."

Halloway looked over to Alderman. "What do you think?"

"I think he wants us to keep our options open," Alderman said thoughtfully. "He mentioned the rescue attempt twice, but he also told us how desperate it would be. Perhaps he was saying to plan a rescue but be prepared to negotiate."

"Goddamn it!" Toliver blurted out. "We don't negotiate with terrorists. That's our policy."

"That's the Israelis' policy, too," Alderman retorted. "But when push comes to shove, they do it. Then cover it with some humane rationale."

Toliver's face hardened. "Are you saying, give in?"

Alderman shook his head. "I'm saying we should cover all the bases. We should make plans for a rescue and for giving in to their demands. Then use whichever one we think serves the President and our country best."

"Good," Halloway agreed immediately. "Any dissenters?"

No one at the table raised a hand, although Toliver obviously had to strain not to do so.

"Good," Halloway said again. "Now, giving in is easy. Trying to rescue the President is doubly difficult. How do we go about it?"

All eyes went to General Walter Pierce, Chairman of the Joint Chiefs of Staff. A Medal of Honor winner in Vietnam, he was tall and ramrod straight, with a square jaw and a craggy handsome face that never seemed to smile. Without hesitation he said, "We're going to need a Special Ops team."

"Which branch?" Halloway asked.

"Either Navy SEAL Team Six or the Army's Delta Force," Pierce answered promptly. "They are the elite of the elite, and either gives us the best chance to rescue the President."

"Pick one."

Pierce hesitated briefly. He favored Delta Force because they, like him, were Army. And besides the Navy SEALs had already had their moment in the sun with the killing of bin Laden. But Pierce pushed his bias aside and said, "Whichever one is closest to Los Angeles."

Toliver interrupted. "Ellen, if this is to be a military operation, I'll be the one in charge."

Halloway narrowed her eyes at Toliver. She did not trust the word or judgment of the Secretary of Defense. The man was experienced, but too far to the right for the Vice President's liking. And he tended to shoot from the hip. "In the President's absence, I sit in his chair."

"Not when it comes to military action," Toliver countered. "Check the regulations."

"But the President is not just absent," Alderman pointed out. "He literally has a gun aimed at his head, which brings up the question of whether he's capable of discharging the functions of his office."

Toliver bristled at the Director of National Intelligence, whom he knew was both friend and confidant to the Vice President. A close friend and confidant who could control her. "Are you suggesting that we invoke the Twenty-Fifth Amendment?"

A hush fell over the room, everyone sensing the enormous significance of the moment. The Twenty-Fifth Amendment to the Constitution allowed the transfer of powers from an incapacitated President to the Vice President.

"What I'm suggesting is that we get the Attorney General over here to tell us what is constitutionally correct," Alderman replied evenly. "In the meantime, let's come up with some sort of rescue plan that we may or may not implement." He turned to the Chairman of the Joint Chiefs of Staff. "You've got the floor, Walter."

"Hold on a second while we locate the whereabouts of our Special Forces teams," Pierce said.

He turned to the other Chiefs of Staff and issued a quick set of orders. The orders were immediately passed on to aides standing by, all of whom rushed off to a nearby communications room.

"We can't make any decisions until we hear from the Attorney General," Toliver persisted.

"We're just exploring options," Halloway said, thinking that if—God forbid!—she were to become the permanent President, Toliver would be gone from the Cabinet within three months. It wasn't that he was inept. Far from it. But she considered him an ideologue, and dangerous. "The clock is ticking," she warned, "so let's concentrate on solutions, not our relative positions."

Alderman took out his pipe, but he left it unlighted. He nibbled on the stem, convinced they were going to end up with a dead President, regardless of whether or not the terrorist's demands were met. That was how Muslim terrorists worked and thought. Death in a jihad meant martyrdom, which guaranteed eternal paradise. Dying with their victims was usually part of the plan. He made a mental note to instruct the Attorney General to stay close by, in the event a new President had to be sworn in.

"I can tell you this," Toliver said with conviction. "No matter what we do, the Russians will never negotiate with these terrorists, even if we beg them on bended knees."

Halloway asked, "How can you be so sure?"

"Because I know that some of their Chechen prisoners participated in the massacre at Beslan," Toliver answered. "They'll never let them out. Never in a million years."

Halloway had to nod at Toliver's assessment. Russia continued to mourn the loss of the little children slaughtered in their schoolhouse at Beslan, even though the event had taken place years ago. It was Russia's 9/11, and they would never forget it. The Chechen prisoners involved were still alive only because Russia had abolished the death sentence.

"And even if we give in to their demands," Toliver added on, "we all know there's little chance they'll release the President. They'll just keep using him over and over until he's of no more use."

"We have to leave the option to negotiate on the table," Halloway argued. "If only to buy ourselves more time."

"More time for what?" Toliver argued back. "The Chechens aren't going to budge off their deadline. So if we delay just an hour, it'll cost two innocent hostages their lives. Is it worth it?"

The Vice President stared at him for a long moment but didn't reply. She had no answer.

Suddenly a wooden panel on the wall slid open and revealed a large video screen with maps of the United States, Asia, and Africa. Military emblems were flashing on all three continents.

"Bad news," Pierce reported as he walked over to the screen and began pointing. "There are currently four units of Navy SEAL Team Six. One is now on a training mission in the Okefenokee Swamp in Georgia, another is participating in war games off the Florida Keys. The remaining two are in Africa. They're dealing with pirates in Somalia and hostage takers in Nigeria. They're all more than five hours away."

"What about Delta Force?" Halloway asked.

"They have two elite units and both are in the mountains between Pakistan and Afghanistan, hunting down Al-Qaeda terrorists."

Halloway nervously played with a loose strand of her hair. "What about other Special Ops teams here in America? Aren't some in or close to California?"

"A number are," Pierce replied, nodding. "But you asked for the elite of the elite. The others are very good, but they don't have the expertise and experience of the Navy SEAL Team Six or Delta Force."

"Which would decrease our chance for success even further."

"I'm afraid so."

"What about the 82nd Airborne?" Toliver proposed.

"Won't work," Pierce said immediately. "First, they're located in Kentucky, and it will take them almost five hours to reach Los Angeles, not counting the time it would take to get things set up. Secondly, this operation will require teamwork and split-second timing that has been practiced over and over. One mistake and we've got a lot of dead people on our hands. The 82nd just doesn't have the necessary experience."

Halloway suggested, "What about a local SWAT team?"

"They're not up to it," Pierce said and took his seat. "They're good when it comes to bank thieves holding hostages or a bomb threat, but not when it comes to cold-blooded terrorists. They'd be out of their league."

"The CIA?" Halloway asked.

"You can't use a CIA team on American soil," Alderman answered.

"Why not?" Toliver asked brusquely. "Because it might upset the FBI?"

"Because there's a law that says you can't." Alderman puffed on his smokeless pipe, trying to find a solution to their problem. The military Special Ops teams, the CIA, and local SWAT teams were out of the question. The FBI had a Hostage Rescue Team, but they were stationed at Quantico, more than five hours away. And besides, they weren't really killers. That's what was required here. Stone-cold killers who moved quickly and stealthily, like black cats in the night.

Alderman searched his mind, with its near-encyclopedic memory, for an answer. A highly trained team, he thought. One that could go anywhere any time and do pinpoint kills. One that could get in and out with clockwork precision. Alderman's brain suddenly clicked. He now recalled a plan he'd been recently briefed on in which a special team was to be sent into Mexico to settle a score with a heavily guarded drug lord who had captured and mutilated two DEA agents.

Alderman shifted his considerable frame in his seat. At two hundred and fifty pounds, his weight caused the chair to squeak. He rubbed his double chin thoughtfully, then ran a hand through his thinning hair. It was an involuntary ritual he performed every time he came up with an answer to a difficult problem. "Madam Vice President, there is a Secret Service Special Operations team that is used in sensitive presidential-threat cases. This team was recently called on to deal with a vicious drug lord."

Toliver looked at him quizzically. "What does a drug lord have to do with protecting the President?"

"On the surface, not much," Alderman explained. "But when the drug lord executes two DEA agents and then threatens to kill the President of the United States, it becomes a threat to national security. As you know, after 9/11 Congress passed an anti-terrorism statute that empowers the Secret Service to assume control over any felony involving possible terrorism. When it comes to fighting terrorism, this team is authorized to go anywhere in the world."

"Are they good?" Halloway asked. "I mean, as good as our military Special Ops teams?"

"Oh, yes," Alderman assured her. "And every bit as experienced, too. They know how to grab and kill, and improvise if necessary. They were the ones who brought the Bali incident to a successful conclusion."

"I thought that was done by military Special Ops," Toliver interjected.

Alderman shook his head. "It was the Secret Service team."

Halloway remembered back to the near-tragic event that took place on the island of Bali. Months earlier, two Under Secretaries of State, Jack and Valerie Traynor, had traveled to Indonesia to do the groundwork for an upcoming presidential visit. After completing the preparations, the couple decided to vacation at a posh resort on Bali, where they were taken hostage by terrorists who threatened to kill them if the President didn't cancel his trip. The terrorists also threatened to assassinate the President if he insisted on visiting. Within days, the Secret Service team entered the resort on stealth helicopters, rescued the hostages, and killed five terrorists. And they did it without so much as breaking a window.

"Where is the team located?" Halloway asked at length.

"Beltsville, Maryland. But they may not be there," Alderman said. "They travel all over the globe. Their last mission was scheduled in Mexico. I recently signed off on the plan."

Halloway perked up. "How far from the California border?"

"That's what we have to determine." Alderman turned to an aide and snapped his fingers rapidly. "Find out where they are!"

The aide placed a call on his cell phone and spoke in staccato sentences. Then he waited, anxiously tapping his foot against the floor. Abruptly he pressed the phone to his ear and listened intently before firing off a string of questions. He turned back to Alderman and reported. "Sir, the Secret Service Special Ops team is just outside Manzanillo, Mexico."

"Get Manzanillo up on the screen," Alderman ordered.

The directive was issued. Almost instantly a map of Mexico appeared on the video screen. A red arrow zeroed in on Manzanillo, a city on the western coast north of Acapulco.

"What's the flying time to Los Angeles?" Alderman asked at once.

"Three hours and twenty minutes," the aide replied.

"Get them out!"

"Sir, they're in the middle of a firefight."

"Get them out and airborne now!" Alderman demanded.

The aide hurriedly passed on the order.

Halloway strummed her fingers on the conference table, calculating how much time the team would have to rescue the President. She checked the digital clock on the wall that was set to Los Angeles time. They had three hours and forty minutes until the deadline. "It's going to be close. They'll have barely twenty minutes to land and execute a rescue."

"I think even less than that," Alderman estimated. "It all depends on how fast they can fight their way out and get to the airstrip."

Halloway stopped strumming the tabletop. "Are you saying they won't make it back in time?"

"That's what I'm saying," Alderman answered gloomily. "We must come up with other options."

"Including the military," Toliver insisted.

"Including the military," Alderman conceded, thinking what a disaster it would be to have Toliver in command. He puffed on his pipe and again concentrated on the problem at hand. But now his mind kept drawing blanks.

————

Kuri Aliev hurried up the steps of the fire stairs and onto the roof of the hospital. The night was very dark and misty, with a dense fog rolling in from the sea. Good, he thought, knowing that the poor visibility would render a rescue attempt by helicopter difficult. Aliev made sure the door to the roof was closed and then, with his satellite phone, placed a call to a cargo plane sitting on the tarmac at Guadalajara International Airport. His second-in-command, Akhmad Basagev, answered on the first ring.

"*Mar-shal du hög*"—Greetings to you, Aliev said.

"*Mar-shal du hög*," Basagev replied.

After greeting each other, they began as planned, speaking in an unusual Middle Eastern dialect of Chechen that they learned while training with Hezbollah along the Syrian-Lebanese border. It contained so many Arabic words that even a native Chechen had difficulty understanding it. Aliev was using this strange dialect in case the Secret Service and their translators were listening in on the call.

"I have good news," Aliev informed him. "Our plan has been set in motion. We have the hostages, and our demands are known to both governments."

"Do we have any indication they will comply?"

"I can tell you the Russians won't," Aliev predicted confidently. "But the Americans will. They have no stomach for this kind of thing."

"But what if the Americans refuse to negotiate? What if they do not allow us to fly on to Chechnya with our hostages?"

"Then we will detonate our nuclear bomb over Los Angeles rather than over the oil fields of Siberia," Aliev said, now thinking about the special nuclear device that had been heavily salted with cobalt. In addition to a massive blast wave, the bomb was designed to spew out a huge cloud of radioactive cobalt that would contaminate a vast area and make it uninhabitable for decades and decades to come. The detonation would turn Russia's oil fields into a worthless desert of death. It would do the same to America's second-largest city.

Basagev broke the silence, saying, "Destroying Los Angeles would not be nearly as meaningful to our cause."

"True," Aliev admitted. "But it would kill two presidents and their foreign ministers, and bring the Great Satan to its knees."

"And send millions of infidels to hell."

"That too," Aliev went on. "Now tell me, is your cargo plane ready?"

"All is in order," Basagev said. "The bomb is aboard—ready to be armed. Our flight plan and manifest have been approved. And the appropriate officials have been bribed."

"Well done," Aliev praised. "You are to request permission to take off immediately."

There was a long pause before Basagev asked, "My brother, forgive me for bringing up this evil thought. But what if the Americans mount a successful rescue operation and you are killed?"

"Then, with my last breath, I will activate the homing device on my satellite phone, which will pinpoint the exact location for you to detonate the bomb over Los Angeles."

"In that event, I should fly in low to maximize the blast effect."

"Exactly."

"Peace be unto you, Aliev."

"*Miyarsh Noxchi Che*"—Long live free Chechnya, Aliev replied, reverting back to the common form of the Chechen language. "*Miyarsh Noxchi Che.*"

Moments later the large cargo plane taxied out onto the runway. Basagev quickly ordered his crew to arm the nuclear bomb once they were in flight—in case Los Angeles was the chosen site. Not a bad second choice, Basagev thought on, now envisioning a giant ball of fire engulfing the entire metropolitan area and turning it into ashes. Of course the blast would also kill him and his crew. But he was unafraid, because he knew there was no higher honor in this world or in the world to come than to die in a glorious jihad.

"You are cleared for takeoff," the control tower notified him.

With a roar of its engines, the cargo plane sped down the runway and lifted off into the pitch-black Mexican night.

TEN

DAVID PEERED DOWN AT the cardiac monitor behind the President's bed. Merrill's blood pressure had stabilized at 104/80, but his pulse continued to race at 122 beats per minute. *Not good*, David thought, now envisioning the pathophysiology going on inside the President's vascular system. The transfusion of plasma had expanded Merrill's depleted intravascular volume, allowing his blood pressure to return to near normal. But it hadn't replaced the red blood cells he'd lost, so his hemoglobin remained low and unable to carry adequate amounts of oxygen. To make up for this deficit, his heart had to pump faster and faster to send out more and more oxygen-poor blood to his peripheral tissues. *Not good*, David thought again. A continuously overworked heart could lead to arrhythmias and even cardiac failure.

His attention went to the plastic bag of plasma dripping rapidly into Merrill's arm. There was only a small amount remaining, not more than 25 ccs. David lowered his head through the ceiling and carefully studied the sleeping President's face. Merrill was even paler than before, with caked blood around his nose and mouth. The basin on the nightstand was half filled with blood, but David couldn't tell if it was old or new.

His eyes drifted over to the suction bottle containing Merrill's gastric juice. It was colored light brown. Maybe there was still a little bleeding, David surmised. Maybe the plasma transfusion had partially corrected the coagulation defect. And maybe it hadn't. Maybe the President was still bleeding internally and the blood was traveling down through his colon rather than up through his gastric tube. That would cause a black, tarry diarrhea that gave off an awful smell. David lowered his head farther to sniff at the air above the President's bed.

Suddenly the door opened and the guard peeked in. David jerked his head back through the opening in the ceiling, but didn't have enough time to replace the panel. He stayed motionless, holding his breath. For some reason the guard walked over to the President's bed and stared down at him for a long moment. The guard was so close to the opened panel that David could see the early bald spot on the crown of his head. If the terrorist looked up, David knew he was a goner. The guard continued to stare down, as if contemplating some action. Then he abruptly spun around and left the room, closing the door behind him.

David started breathing again. He wiped the perspiration from his brow and, steadying his nerves, gazed down at the President. Once more he was struck by how pale Merrill appeared. The President's complexion was more white than pink. *He desperately needs a blood transfusion*, David thought, as his eyes went to the bag of plasma that was nearly empty now. It had to be replaced by the bag of blood or the IV line would become dry and clogged. *Where's Carolyn? Where the hell is she?* Then, with a sigh, he answered his own question. *She's busy being doctor and nurse to a dozen patients, some so ill they belong in an ICU. And she's holding up like a real trooper. She is some woman.*

David put the panel back in place and crawled away on the metal grid, heading for the large bathroom that adjoined the suite. He stayed well clear of the metal piping and moved noiselessly past bundles of wires. On reaching the bathroom, he made sure he was over the marble countertop and then, grasping a bar of the grid, lowered himself six feet down. He paused on the countertop, listening for any sound, then climbed off and tiptoed into the President's suite. Again he hesitated, his eyes now on the door that was cracked open. He took a deep breath and made himself wait while listening for motion in the corridor. The only noise he heard was the thumping of his own heart.

Quickly he went to the bedside and took down the empty plasma bag, then replaced it with a bag of packed red blood cells. After adjusting the flow rate to two ccs per minute, David hurriedly examined the President without touching him. Most of the blood on and around Merrill was old, and David didn't detect the awful odor of a tarry stool, which would have indicated ongoing gastrointestinal bleeding. *So maybe I bought some time. But how much? Not a lot*, David guessed. *Not with just one bag of plasma.*

Abruptly David pricked up his ears. There were approaching footsteps in the corridor. The guard began to open the door. In an instant David dashed across the suite and into the bathroom. He heard the door open wide and someone walking in. With a single bound he was on the marble countertop. But the footsteps were closer now. Much closer. He didn't have time to climb up into the crawlspace. Silently he eased himself down from the countertop and moved behind the door to the bathroom. He crouched low and scanned the room for a weapon. Any weapon. He didn't see any. There was a roll of toilet tissue, a big plastic cup, and a box of Kleenex. His eyes came back to the plastic cup. *Maybe the cup*, David thought. Yes, maybe the cup would do. He crept over to it.

Suddenly the loud, pinging alarm of the monitor sounded. David froze in place, thinking the President had gone into shock. *He's bleeding out. The plasma didn't hold. I've got to get back to him. But what about the guard?* David hurriedly reached for the plastic cup, put it on the floor, and crushed it with his shoe. The cup split into pieces, one of which was long and slender with a sharp point. David knew exactly how to use it on the terrorist.

The guard was yelling in rudimentary English above the loud pinging noise. "What wrong?"

"It's nothing," Carolyn yelled back, shutting off the alarm. "One of the attachments dropped off the President."

Carolyn! It was Carolyn. David lowered his makeshift dagger and gathered himself, not daring to peek out. The guard was either with her or watching her through an open door. Better to stay put, he thought. David pressed up against the wall and waited.

"Well, Mr. President, I see you're awake," Carolyn was saying. "It's time to start your blood transfusion."

"Do I need another needle stick?" Merrill asked weakly.

"Oh, no. We'll use the IV line that is already—" Carolyn stopped in mid-sentence. She saw the bag of blood running into the President. *David*, she realized immediately. She quickly looked up at the ceiling, then into the empty bathroom. He'd come and gone with a guard at the door. How did he manage that? How ...?

The guard blurted out something in Chechen, breaking into her train of thought.

"Goddamn it! If you want to speak to me, do it in English!" Carolyn said sharply. She wasn't being overly brave. She knew they weren't going to shoot her, at least not now. They needed her to keep the President alive—or so they believed.

Out of habit she checked the label on the bag of blood to make certain it had the President's name on it. It did. He was AB negative, a rare blood type that was hard to come by, even under normal circumstances. Bringing her hands down, she noticed blood on them. A shiver went through her as she wondered if the bag had been damaged by the terrorists' bullets that had shot up the messenger's box. She quickly examined the plastic bag and found it intact. The blood was old and had probably come from the bags in the box that had ruptured. Thank goodness!

She headed for the bathroom to wash her hands. At the basin she gazed in the mirror and studied her face. Her lipstick was gone, her hair a mess, and there was a blood smear on her cheek. *I look like hell—* Suddenly her eyes bulged. David was standing beside the door behind her. He had his index finger on his lips. He signaled for her to turn on the faucets.

Peering around the doorway, he made certain the way was clear, then rushed over and pressed himself against the wall.

"Where's the guard?" David asked quickly.

"By the door," Carolyn replied.

"Facing in or out?"

"Out."

"Good," David said. "Now run the water faster."

Carolyn turned the faucets up to full force, then looked over to him. Her lower lip began to quiver and she had to bite down to calm it. Then she flew into his arms. "Oh, David! I'm so frightened!"

"You're doing fine," he whispered, holding her close. "You're saving lives, left and right."

"But for how long?" Carolyn asked, her voice trembling. "We're all going to end up dead. None of us will leave this floor alive."

"Don't be so sure."

She stared up at his face. "Are you saying there's a way out?"

"We'll see," David said, although he knew their chances for escape were slim. "But we've got to play it very smart."

Carolyn nodded, trying to read his face and decide if there really was a glimmer of hope. "What do you want me to do?"

"Leave everything to me," David said, keeping his voice low. "First off, you should know that Karen Kellerman also got out alive. She's in the ceiling crawlspace with me."

"Is she wounded?" Carolyn asked at once.

"No, but she has asthma and doesn't have an inhaler with her," David said rapidly. "Do you have any inhalers in the Pavilion?"

Carolyn shook her head. "Not that I know of."

"Check and see," David went on. "If not, I want you to prepare some small syringes with a cc of 1:1000 epinephrine in them."

"That won't help much in a bad asthma attack."

"It's better than nothing," David said. "Now tell me about our patients."

"Dr. Warren is starting to have PVCs again despite the increased dose of lidocaine," she reported.

"If they become frequent, give him bretylium, ten milligrams IV, then maintain him at one milligram per minute," David said automatically. "And keep the defibrillator at hand. What about Marci?"

"Not good," Carolyn told him. "She's having trouble breathing."

"Is she leaning forward to get a full breath?"

Carolyn nodded again. "Just like before."

"Shit!"

"Yeah." Carolyn stared up at his pale blue eyes and studied them. "Aren't you frightened?"

"Some," David admitted.

"You don't show it."

"That's because you're not looking closely enough."

"I'm looking plenty close enough," Carolyn whispered, standing on her tiptoes and kissing him firmly on the lips.

"What was that for?"

"Good luck," she lied.

David kissed her back, even harder. "Let's make it double good luck."

They heard footsteps coming toward them, the guard grumbling to himself.

David quickly disengaged and stepped away. He positioned himself against the wall beside the door and whispered. "If he starts to come in, scream at him."

"What?" Carolyn asked, not certain she'd heard him correctly.

"Scream at him," David instructed. "Like you would if he walked in while you were sitting on the john."

Carolyn took a deep breath and readied herself.

David reached for his handkerchief and wrapped it around the flat end of the plastic sliver, converting it into a dagger. He held it up high and waited, his heart pounding in his chest.

Carolyn summoned up all of her courage and turned to face the approaching guard. She tried to appear surprised, then screamed at the top of her voice, "Get out of here, you perverted son of a bitch!"

The guard stopped in his tracks, caught off balance.

"Out!" Carolyn yelled and pointed to the corridor.

The terrorist gave Carolyn a long, menacing look and spat on the floor, then mumbled something in Chechen and walked away.

"And stay the hell outside!" Carolyn called after him.

David nodded to himself. She was so damn smart! She was telling him the guard was on his way out of the room. And what a performance she put on with her scream. It was perfect, just perfect. *Jesus*, he thought again, *she is some woman!*

He waited another ten seconds and moved over to the marble countertop, now noticing how tightly he continued to grip the makeshift dagger. And the dagger was trembling in his hand. For a brief moment he wondered if he could have really used it. Did he still have the nerve and skill to kill? Would he have sliced into the man's carotid artery, giving it about as much thought as opening a can of tomatoes? *Yeah. I guess so. I guess I could have done it to save Carolyn and myself.* But he knew that was just talk. And talking about killing a man was a lot different from actually doing it.

Before putting the makeshift dagger in his pocket, David re-wrapped it with his handkerchief to protect himself from its pointed end. But the increased pressure caused the plastic sliver to crack and crumble. Shit! David growled at his stupid blunder. Now he was weaponless again. *Mistakes! I'm making too many mistakes!* Fuming at himself, he threw the pieces of plastic into a trash can. Quickly he mounted the countertop and reached for the metal grid, then pulled himself up through the opening in the ceiling.

David hurriedly put the panel back in place and made certain it fit snugly. His heart was still racing and skipping beats from the narrow escape. Gathering his nerves, he remained motionless and waited for his pulse to slow, all the while listening to see if the terrorist was going to return for a second look.

Karen came up alongside him and whispered in his ear, "Jesus Christ! You almost got yourself killed."

"What the hell are you doing over here?" David whispered back harshly. "I told you to stay by the far wall."

"It got really musty in that area and I started to wheeze," Karen explained. "So when I saw the opening in the ceiling, I crawled over to breathe some fresh air."

"How's your asthma doing?"

"So-so," Karen reported and coughed mildly. "But I'm more worried about you than me. Had that terrorist taken one more step, you would have been a dead man."

"But Carolyn saved the day, didn't she?" David asked with a crooked grin. "She put on quite a show, eh?"

"I guess."

"There's no guessing to it. She stared that terrorist in the face and didn't back up an inch," David said admiringly. "That takes something special."

"I didn't know you two were so close," Karen remarked, keeping the jealousy out of her voice.

"We aren't."

"That's not what I saw going on down in the bathroom," Karen said. "I think you've got yourself a new girlfriend."

"We'll see after all this is said and done."

"For being as clever as you are, David, sometimes you're awfully blind to the obvious."

"That's one of my flaws," David said gruffly. "Now I want you to return to your space by the far wall without making a sound. Do you think you can manage that?"

"I can try." Karen nestled up against him and kissed his neck before backing away to her hiding place.

ELEVEN

DAVID FELT THE VIBRATION of his cell phone through his pants pocket. He moved quickly and quietly over the nurses' station. Jarrin Smith and the Russian security agent were seated at the desk, a terrorist standing guard over them. The floor around them was littered with trash and soaked with blood. The stale odor of decay was everywhere, and triggered a flashback in David's mind, but he pushed it aside and crawled on until he was close to the treatment room, where there was little chance he'd be overheard.

He reached for his cell phone and answered in a whisper. "Yes?"

"Dr. Ballineau, this is Special Agent Cassidy. Are you still in the crawlspace?"

"Yes."

"Good. Now we have to talk fast, because we don't know how much power is left in your phone's battery."

"Fire away."

"We finally got the floor plans for the Beaumont Pavilion and the floor beneath it," Cassidy said hurriedly. "Let's start with who is in which rooms. Begin with the President and his family."

"Do you have numbers for the suites?"

"Yes."

"The President is in suite one, the First Lady is in two, their daughter in three." David rapidly went through all the rooms and the patients they contained. Then he described the nurses' station, treatment room, nurses' lounge, and kitchen area.

"Where is the First Daughter's date?" Cassidy asked.

"Dead."

"Is the President still hanging on?"

"Just barely," David reported. "The plasma seems to have slowed his bleeding, and he's receiving a blood transfusion now."

"Hold on," Cassidy said. "I want you to speak with a hematology specialist."

David heard background noise. Then a voice came on. "David, this is Bill Gershon. Can you hear me?"

"I hear you," David said, pleased to be talking with the medical center's expert on coagulation defects. "We've got a big problem up here, Billy."

"Are you certain it's von Willebrand's disease?" Gershon asked.

"Not positively," David replied. "But the disorder runs in his family."

"That's good enough for now," Gershon said. "What have you treated him with so far?"

"One unit of fresh frozen plasma and one unit of packed red cells."

"In all likelihood that's not going to hold him long."

"I know."

"He needs Factor VIII–rich concentrates."

"I'm aware of that, but the terrorists won't let anything or anybody come up to the Pavilion."

"The concentrates may well be his only hope."

"Then you'd better think of a way to get those bags of concentrates up here."

There was a long silence.

"Put Agent Cassidy back on while you're thinking," David directed.

There was another pause before Cassidy returned to the line. "I'm here," he said.

"We have to talk about the terrorists and what you're up against," David urged.

"Okay, let's begin with—"

"Just listen!" David cut him off. "There are five terrorists, all Chechens, all experienced, all cold-blooded killers. One has an arm wound, but it's minor and won't stop him from fighting. They're all armed with Uzis, clips in and ready to fire. All are carrying extra clips of ammunition under their belts. In addition, two have long knives, and two have grenades."

"Stun grenades?" Cassidy asked quickly.

"I don't think so," David replied. "From high up they look like the explosive type."

"And side arms?"

"Their leader is carrying a Sig Sauer automatic pistol, which he probably took from one of your dead agents."

Cassidy cleared his throat. "How do you know so much about weapons?"

"I was in the military a long time ago."

"Army?"

"A branch of it."

"Ah-huh," Cassidy said, like a man making a mental note. "A second ago you mentioned dead agents. Did any survive?"

"None that I know of."

"What about Wells? Did you actually see his body?"

"He was the last to go," David replied. "He went down at the President's door, fighting until his last breath."

There was a long pause before Cassidy spoke again. "Let's go back to the terrorists. Do they tend to congregate in one place?"

"They're constantly moving in the corridor and in and out of rooms," David answered. "They're obviously experienced. They know what they're doing."

"So they don't have anyone standing guard at the elevator or fire stairs?"

"They don't need permanent guards there," David told him. "The elevator doors are jammed shut, and they've got some type of metal chain device locking the fire door. I think they've also planted some explosives in the fire stairs. If you tried to blow your way in, they'd kill everybody before the smoke cleared."

"What about the dumbwaiter?"

"It's up here, so you can't get it back down to the kitchen," David informed him. "And in addition, they've booby-trapped it with something that looks like C-4. But to be doubly sure, they always have a guard in or close by that room."

"Clever bastards."

"And some."

Cassidy grumbled a profanity under his breath. "I need to know precisely how closely the President is being guarded."

"There is always someone in the corridor just outside his room. And the door is kept partially open."

"So if we placed someone in the crawlspace he could take the guard out," Cassidy thought aloud.

"There's no opening from the crawlspace to the roof," David pointed out.

"We could make one," Cassidy proposed.

"They'd hear you," David warned. "But even if you could, then what?"

"Then we'd neutralize the guard and help the President up and out."

"Forget it!" David told him. "The President is so weak he can barely stand, much less hoist himself up. He'd be two hundred pounds of dead weight. There's no way you could lift him ten feet and get him up and out through this crawlspace, which is partially blocked by a metal grid. Everyone would be killed, including the President."

"Have they planted explosives at the presidential end of the corridor?" Cassidy asked.

"Not yet," David answered. "But I wouldn't put it past them. If they think they're going to die, they'll want to take the President with them."

Cassidy grunted unhappily under his breath before saying, "We've got a gastroenterologist here who needs to speak with you."

He doesn't need to speak with me, David thought miserably. *He needs to be up on the Pavilion passing an endoscope that could stop the President's bleeding.*

"David? This is Jonathan Bell down here. Am I coming through?"

"Loud and clear," David said to the co-chief of gastroenterology at University Hospital.

"This doesn't sound like garden variety food poisoning."

"It's not," David answered. "The terrorists somehow managed to put a toxin in the caviar served at the state dinner. That's why the symptoms started so quickly."

"What type of toxin?" Bell asked.

"I can't be sure," David replied. "I overheard Aliev say that it was encapsulated in tiny pellets for slow release, but he didn't mention a specific name. The symptoms last for four to six hours, if you can believe what Aliev told the President."

"It sounds like a bacterial enterotoxin."

"Or its first cousin."

"Well, that can be treated with simple fluid replacement."

"Except for the President, who may be bleeding to death right under my nose."

"I know, I know," Bell said. "What have you done so far from a G.I. standpoint to stem the hemorrhaging?"

"I've got a nasogastric tube down to monitor the bleeding and suck out his gastric juice."

"Good."

"And I had to lavage his stomach with ice water early on."

"You can do that again if needed and continue doing it for ten minutes. With a little ingenuity, you might be able to hook the suction apparatus—"

"I'm up in a crawlspace between the Pavilion and the roof," David interrupted sharply. "Not down on the damn floor."

"Sorry," Bell apologized. "I forgot for a moment."

"Do you have any other suggestions?"

"I'd give the President twenty milligrams of Pepcid IV," Bell advised. "That'll stop his acid production and might slow down his bleeding. You repeat that in—" He stopped in mid-sentence to berate himself. "Oh, Christ! I keep forgetting you're not down on the floor."

"I'll try to get a message to the nurse."

"Good show!" Bell said, then added, "Our prayers are with you, David."

"Save them for the President," David said hoarsely. "He's the one who needs them."

Cassidy came back on the line. "We're going to sign off now, Dr. Ballineau. Hold tight while we figure a way to get those bags of Factor VIII up to you."

"Be very, very careful," David cautioned. "The ceiling is paper-thin. One slipup and I'm dead, and so is any chance you have to save the President."

TWELVE

MARCI LEANED FORWARD IN bed and strained to inhale air into her lungs. "Am I going to die?" she gasped.

"No," Carolyn replied evenly. "It's just pressure from your pericardial effusion."

"But my symptoms have never been this bad." Marci was now breathing rapidly through her nose and mouth. "I feel like I'm dying!"

"Let me increase your oxygen," Carolyn said, adjusting the plastic cannula in Marci's nose and raising the oxygen flow to four liters per minute. "Is that better?"

Marci nodded, but she was still sucking for air and her vital signs on the monitor were worsening. Her pulse was up to 112 beats per minute, her blood pressure dropping to 96/70. "Is Dr. Ballineau coming up to see me?"

"We're trying to reach him now," Carolyn lied and looked up at the ceiling, hoping that a sheet of instructions from David would come floating down. But none did.

"Maybe you should call him again," Marci said weakly.

"Let's give him another minute or two."

Carolyn gazed over to the closed door and prayed Aliev wouldn't open it and find her in Marci's room. If he did he'd be furious, and only God knew what he might do. Despite Aliev's warning, Carolyn had little choice but to be with Marci. It was as if some invisible force was making sure Marci wouldn't suffer by herself.

Carolyn had been hurrying into the medicine room to fetch more drugs for Dr. Warren when she happened to notice a flashing light at the nurses' station, indicating someone needed help. It was Marci. So Carolyn waited patiently for the guard in the corridor to move away, then crept into Marci's suite, all the while holding her breath. Jesus! It was so dangerous! So risky! But she had to do it. She couldn't just leave the desperately ill college student to die alone. Maybe she could help. But deep down Carolyn had the awful feeling Marci was going to die regardless of what she did. *Poor thing*, she thought sadly and turned her attention back to the patient who was struggling even more to breathe.

Marci had her mouth pursed like an *O* so she could draw in more air. Her lips turned to a dusky color as she bent over even farther in an effort to force more air into her lungs.

She's dying, Carolyn thought desperately. *And I don't know what to do next. Do I increase the dose of prednisone and Imuran? And, if so, how much? Or should I give her morphine, like they do to patients having a myocardial infarction? No, no! This wasn't an M.I. Don't do something that could make her even worse.*

Carolyn gazed over to the cardiac monitor. Marci's vital signs were deteriorating, and would continue to do so without appropriate therapy. There was a treatment sure to save Marci's life, but one Carolyn didn't dare perform. Carolyn moaned to herself. *Without the right equipment, I couldn't even think about doing a pericardiocentesis*. A pericardiocentesis! Sticking a big, long needle through the chest wall and into the heart, then aspirating the fluid that had accumulated in the pericardial space. It was a dangerous procedure, even when done by an experienced cardiologist. The last pericardiocentesis Carolyn had seen ended up with a terrible complication. The needle had sliced open a coronary artery, killing the patient.

She looked up at the ceiling again, with all its panels in place, and whispered loudly, "Damn it, David! Where are you?"

There was no response. The panels didn't move.

Marci's systolic blood pressure was down to 92, her pulse up to 118 per minute. And her respirations were growing weaker, the effort required to breathe exhausting her.

In the stillness Carolyn closed her eyes and prayed for guidance. *Tell me what to do, God! Tell me how I can help this poor girl! Do I try—?*

Suddenly the silence was broken by the sound of a gunshot coming from the corridor. Then another shot. Then the sound of running footsteps.

Carolyn shuddered. *They've killed somebody else!*

She hesitated, not sure what to do. Racing into the corridor could get her shot. But then again, somebody might be badly hurt. Gathering up her courage, Carolyn slowly moved to the doorway and peeked out. Two terrorists were standing over a body outside Sol Simcha's room. Carolyn's heart dropped as she stepped into the hallway.

"Stupid old man!" Aliev was saying. "I warned him not to leave his room."

Simcha was lying face down on the floor, not moving.

All he's been through, Carolyn thought sadly, *only to die like this.* It wasn't right and it wasn't fair. She went to his side and gently turned him over. There was no blood on his hospital gown, no sign of a wound.

Simcha smiled up at her weakly. "I think I slipped."

"Are you all right?" Carolyn asked.

"Yes," Simcha said and reached a hand out. "Could you help me sit up, please?"

Carolyn gently pulled the elderly man up to a sitting position. "Sol, you must stay in your room. It's very dangerous to step out into the corridor."

Aliev glared down at Simcha. "If it happens again, old man, the bullets will end up in your head rather than in the wall."

"Come on, Sol," Carolyn said, raising him to his feet. "Let's get you back into your bed."

Simcha resisted her pull. "I'm not going back in that room. The ceiling is falling."

"What?" Aliev asked. "What are you talking about?"

Simcha gestured with his withered arms. "The panels were coming down from the ceiling. I could see the openings where they once were."

Aliev dashed into the room and looked up, pointing his Uzi at the ceiling. All the panels were in place. There were no open spaces. He glanced back to Simcha in the doorway. "Where was this opening?"

"Above my pillow," Simcha replied.

Again Aliev studied the ceiling, now focusing in on the panels above the bed. He climbed up on the mattress to see if any of the panels were loose.

Carolyn immediately surmised what Sol had seen. It was David, peering down from an opened panel as he made rounds on his patients. The old man had seen a space without a panel and assumed the panel had fallen off. Quickly she thought of a way to explain

Sol's sighting. She turned to Aliev, who was jumping down from the bed. "It was probably the medication he's taking. High doses of prednisone can cause hallucinations."

"Well, he had better stay in his room while he is having hallucinations," Aliev warned. "Because if he steps out again, my men will have orders to kill him."

"I'll make sure he stays in bed," Carolyn said, then thought of a way to return to Marci's side. "Perhaps I should remind all the patients to do likewise, if of course you agree."

"Do it," Aliev ordered. "Then you are to—" He stopped in mid-sentence and narrowed his eyes. "What are you doing in this area? You were told to remain near the President and his family."

"I ... I had to fetch some drugs from the medicine room," Carolyn explained hesitantly.

Aliev gave her a long skeptical look. "Obtain all the drugs you will need, because you will not be returning to this end of the corridor again."

"But some of the patients require—"

"You will not be returning," Aliev reiterated. "And anyone caught in the corridor who shouldn't be there will be shot. That includes you, major nurse."

Carolyn swallowed hard as a chill ran down her spine. "May I have permission to go for drugs for the President again, if needed?"

"No, you may not," Aliev replied icily.

You bastard, Carolyn thought. *You merciless, cold-blooded bastard.*

"Now finish up in here and return to your station," Aliev directed. "And stay there!"

Carolyn waited for Aliev to leave, then helped Simcha back into bed. Once he was comfortably situated, she leaned in close and said in a stern voice, "Don't mention the ceiling again to anyone."

"But it was falling down, and I wasn't hallucinating," Simcha argued.

Carolyn took his hand and squeezed it tightly, making sure she had his full attention. "Listen carefully to me, Sol. Regardless of what you see or don't see, never mention the ceiling to anyone. Our lives may depend on it."

Simcha stared at her, mystified. "I don't understand."

"Just do what I tell you to do," Carolyn urged.

The cardiac monitor's alarm suddenly sounded in Marci's room. *Ping! Ping! Ping!*

Carolyn sprinted out across the corridor and rushed to Marci's bedside. The young woman was wide-eyed and gasping for breath, her color even worse than before. Her pulse was 128 per minute, her blood pressure down to 86/64.

Marci feebly reached out a hand. "Help me, Carolyn! Please!"

A panel directly above opened.

David stuck out his arm and pointed to the nightstand. On it was a folded prescription blank. Carolyn grabbed it and quickly read the instructions.

Give Solu-Medrol 1000 mg IV push.

Carolyn ran for the medicine room.

————

David crawled away, cursing under his breath for not being more careful when he peered down into Sol Simcha's room. The old man had seen the ceiling panel move and thought it was about to fall on him. And he almost divulged David's position in the crawlspace. *Damn it! Watch your step or you'll get yourself killed.*

David pulled on the collar of his shirt, which was drenched with perspiration. The space above the ceiling was becoming uncomfortably warm, causing him to sweat heavily. And now he was aware of his parched throat and growing thirst. He knew that would only get worse as he lost more body fluids in the heat. Then dehydration would set in and lead to weakness and mental slowing, he thought miserably. *Somehow I've got to find water. But where?* He passed alongside a very warm metal pipe, and that caused him to sweat even more profusely. Again he pulled at his soaked collar. *Where the hell was water available?*

He couldn't use the faucets in the bathrooms because of the noise they made. The sound of running water might attract the attention of one of the terrorists who were continually sticking their heads into the suites to check on patients. And the water fountains were all in the corridor. There was no way to get to them unseen. Just the thought of water intensified David's thirst. He concentrated on finding a place where liquids might be located, going from room to room in his mind. Then it came to him. The kitchen! The refrigerator in the kitchen! They kept cartons of bottled water in there. He crawled along the metal grid more rapidly, heading for the kitchen and hoping it wasn't being guarded at the moment. Coming to the end of the corridor, he peered through a slit in the ceiling and searched the area. There were no guards and no sounds. Silently he crept over the kitchen and again looked down. No guard! The door closed! All clear!

Suddenly there was a noise. It was a noise like rubbing, and it wasn't far off.

David stayed motionless as the sound grew closer and closer. Peering into the dimness, he couldn't make out any moving shadows or figures. He held his breath and prepared to lash out at the sound. Then Karen appeared.

David exhaled at length and wriggled alongside her. "Next time warn me when you're crawling around."

"You told me to be quiet," Karen whispered.

"Then warn me quietly."

"I'll try," Karen said and loosened the collar of her Oxford blouse. "David, it's getting really hot in this area."

"The whole ceiling space is heating up and we're rapidly becoming dehydrated," David told her. "Without some replacement fluids soon, we're going to be in deep trouble."

"We—we won't have to give up, will we?" Karen asked hesitantly.

"Not while there's bottled water down in the kitchen."

"How will we get to it?"

"Watch."

David removed a ceiling panel and, holding onto the metal grid, lowered himself onto the sink. He paused briefly and listened for sounds. There weren't any. He jumped to the floor and hurried over to the refrigerator. In a flash he had the door open and the top off a bottle of ice-cold water. He gulped down a pint and was reaching for a second bottle when he heard footsteps approaching. Quickly he grabbed the second bottle and tossed it up to Karen's outstretched hands. In a split second, he closed the refrigerator door and discharged his empty bottle onto a nearby counter. Then he leaped up onto the sink and climbed into the crawlspace.

As he replaced the ceiling panel, the door opened and a terrorist entered. David slowly backed away, thinking the terrorist might see the discarded bottle and become suspicious. Quietly wiggling backwards, he was unaware that his stethoscope was slipping out of his side pocket. It dropped down onto a steel grid and made a loud, metallic ping. David froze in place. The terrorist must have heard the noise.

David heard the terrorist grumble, then grunt. Then everything became quiet. The silence lasted for several seconds before the terrorist grunted again. The man sounded closer now. David remained absolutely still, barely breathing. Slowly the ceiling panel directly in front of him slid away. David saw the terrorist's large hands reaching up through the opening.

A moment later the terrorist's head appeared in the crawlspace, his eyes staring straight into David's.

"Ali—," the terrorist began to yell.

But before he could utter a complete word, David grabbed the terrorist by the throat and, placing his thumbs over the Adam's apple, crushed the man's larynx and shut off his airway completely.

The terrorist struggled to free himself, but David lifted him up so his feet dangled in the air. The Chechen could make only a gurgling sound, with his larynx shattered and caved in. He twisted and turned as he suffocated to death.

David released his hold and the terrorist fell heavily to the floor, bouncing up once before settling. Then all was quiet again.

David hurriedly climbed down, trying to think where he could hide the body. There were no closets in the kitchen, and the space under the sink wasn't large enough to contain the terrorist. His gaze went over to the dumbwaiter, but then David recalled it was booby-trapped. Suddenly there were voices in the corridor. Two voices! Maybe three! David reached for the terrorist's Uzi, but it was attached to a sling and crammed under the man's body. The voices came even closer.

Thinking quickly, David picked up the terrorist's head and slammed it against the tile floor, causing an obvious depressed fracture over the temporal area. Then he scrambled up into the crawlspace and slid the ceiling panel back into place. Motionless, he waited and watched through a narrow slit in the ceiling. He barely noticed Karen moving up beside him.

"My God, David!" Karen hissed, stunned by the ruthlessness she'd just witnessed. "You killed that man!"

"I sure hope so," David said tonelessly.

"It was so cold-blooded."

"Killing usually is," David retorted. "Now be quiet. More of those bastards are coming." He peered down through the slit in the ceiling once again before adding, "And don't move an inch."

Aliev and the terrorist with the injured arm entered the kitchen and saw the body on the floor. Both men instantly had their Uzis at the ready. They spread apart and carefully searched the room, even looking into the dumbwaiter but not touching it. Aliev grumbled loudly as he checked the area under the sink.

"*Vella*"—Dead, the other terrorist said in Chechen as he leaned over the body to feel for a carotid pulse. "And look at his head! He must have tripped and hit his skull on the floor."

In the crawlspace above, Karen pressed her ear against a panel and tried to hear the conversation. "Do you understand anything they're saying?" she asked in a barely audible whisper.

"Not a word," David whispered back. "Now be double quiet. Don't even breathe hard."

Below in the kitchen, David heard Aliev and the other terrorist exchanging angry utterances. They kept raising their voices. David couldn't comprehend what they were shouting about, but he surmised they weren't convinced the man's death was an accident. Soon they would conclude that there was a Secret Service agent still alive on the Pavilion, and they would scour the entire area looking for him.

Aliev was growling in Chechen. "The man was a fantastic soccer player. Athletes do not trip over themselves and smash their heads in."

"What would account for it then?"

Aliev's eyes narrowed suspiciously. "Maybe there is an American agent still on the Pavilion."

"But we searched and …"

"Then search again!" Aliev cut him off. "Search everywhere! Every room! Every closet! Under every bed! Make certain we didn't leave an enemy agent alive."

"And if we find one?"

"Kill him," Aliev said, and stormed out of the room.

THIRTEEN

"Madam Vice President, we're in contact with *Eagle Two*," a communications officer called out.

"Put them on the speakerphone," Halloway said, hurrying back to the conference table in the Situation Room.

The other members of the National Security Council quickly took their seats and leaned forward. *Eagle Two* was the code name of the Gulfstream turbojet carrying the Secret Service Special Ops team out of Mexico.

"This is the Vice President," Halloway said into the phone, her voice firm and even. "To whom am I speaking?"

"Special Agent Joe Geary, ma'am."

"Are you the agent in charge?"

"Yes, ma'am. I'm commander of the Special Ops team."

"Have you been briefed on the crisis we're facing?" Halloway asked.

"Pretty much," Geary replied. "We're still getting some details from our agents on the ground in Los Angeles."

"How far are you from Los Angeles?" Halloway asked the key question.

"Two hours and forty-two minutes," Geary answered.

Halloway groaned to herself. The deadline for meeting the terrorist's demands was two hours and thirty minutes away. One hostage in the Pavilion was sure to be executed, and a second probably to follow. "I assume you're traveling at full speed."

"Yes, ma'am," Geary confirmed. "We are at 586 miles per hour, which is top speed for this aircraft."

"And you're on the shortest possible route back to Los Angeles?"

"Yes, ma'am."

There was a brief silence at the conference table as all members of the council were now certain the Secret Service team could not be back in time to meet the deadline. To a person, they wondered which individual the terrorists would choose to execute first. In their heart of hearts, they hoped it would be one of the Russian officials.

Halloway gestured to Arthur Alderman and pushed the speakerphone over to him.

"Agent Geary, this is Director Alderman," he began.

"Yes, sir," Geary said, his voice more crisp.

"First off, did you get your team out intact?"

"Yes, sir."

"Is our Mexican problem solved?"

"Well, sir," Geary said flatly, "we won't be hearing from Miguel Estrada again. But there were some difficulties."

"What difficulties?" Alderman asked promptly.

"The local Mexican police decided to protect Estrada and took some hits."

"How many?"

"A half-dozen or more," Geary replied. "And there was trouble at the airstrip outside Manzanillo as well. The authorities on the ground insisted on an additional bribe."

"And?"

"And it was a poor decision on their part, sir."

"How many casualties?"

"I can't be sure, but I'd estimate another half-dozen or so."

Alderman stared at the speakerphone, digesting the new information and not liking it. "Stand by, Commander."

"Roger that."

Alderman put the phone on hold and turned to the other council members. "We're looking at a diplomatic disaster."

"Why?" Halloway asked.

"Because that plane is carrying personnel who shot and perhaps killed a dozen Mexican policemen, and it's still in Mexican airspace," Alderman explained. "Their authorities will track it and no doubt send up fighters to intercept it."

Halloway narrowed her eyes. "Are you telling us they'd actually fire at our plane?"

Alderman nodded grimly. "That's what I'm telling you."

"No way!" Toliver blurted. "They wouldn't dare attack a clearly marked American plane."

"And therein lies our problem," Alderman went on. "The plane is unmarked except for a tail number that will show it's registered to Executive Transport Services, Incorporated. The corporation has a list of directors and executives that exist only on paper. All have recently issued Social Security numbers and addresses consisting of a post office box. None of the names have a residence, telephone, or work history."

Toliver's expression suddenly turned worried. "Do the Mexicans know this?"

"If they don't, they will shortly," Alderman told him. "Our plane had to file a flight plan into Mexico and give its identification number. In addition, it was on the ground in Manzanillo for a goodly length of time. You can bet the authorities there have the plane's ID number and have relayed the information to Mexico City." He paused to let the information sink in, then predicted, "They'll send up their fighter-interceptors and try to force the plane down."

"We can't let that happen," Halloway said resolutely. "We desperately need that team if we hope to save the President and the hostages."

"From the standpoint of international law, the Mexicans have every right to shoot our plane down." Alderman spoke in a low, deliberate voice. He already had a solution to the problem, but he thought it best to let the military advance the idea. "And of course Eagle Two is unarmed."

"Could we have our plane change course so it's over international waters?" Halloway suggested.

"We could," Alderman said unenthusiastically. "But we'll waste valuable time doing it. And the Mexicans would no doubt continue to pursue it because it's a rogue plane that in their minds committed a criminal act."

Halloway slammed her hand on the conference table so hard it vibrated. "They're not going to shoot that plane down! Not while I'm sitting in this chair."

"Maybe we should have them fly low enough to avoid detection by Mexican radar," Toliver proposed.

Alderman shook his head. "That would significantly reduce their air speed. And flying under four hundred feet can be very dangerous, particularly over mountainous terrain. Then there's the problem of fuel consumption, which is substantially increased at low altitudes."

"How do you know so much about this plane?" Toliver asked.

Alderman pushed a thin folder across the table. "I had my aide obtain the specifications for the Gulfstream turbojet."

Toliver glanced through the folder, searching for misstatements Alderman might have made. There weren't any. He slid the folder over to the Vice President, who ignored it.

"I need workable ideas," Halloway urged. "And I need them now."

An awkward silence fell over the room. No one seemed to have an answer to the dilemma. Their collective gazes went to the giant video screen. A small, pulsating figure of a plane was very slowly moving northward along the Mexican coastline. The screen was pinpointing the position of Eagle Two.

"There are ways to protect that plane," Walter Pierce said tonelessly.

"How?" Halloway asked.

"With our planes," Pierce said and turned to the Navy Chief of Staff. "Do you have any carriers nearby, Emmett?"

"I'll find out." Emmett Sanders was the first black full admiral, the first black naval chief of staff. He gestured over to an aide, who hurried into the communications room.

"This is becoming a military operation," Toliver proclaimed. "Which means I should be in charge."

Halloway turned to him, her expression now cold as steel. "You'll be in charge when the Attorney General says you're in charge."

"The regulations state otherwise," Toliver insisted again.

"I don't care about your damn regulations," Halloway snapped. "I only care about the Constitution, and that's what we'll follow—to the letter. So let's stop wasting time on protocol and start coming up with ideas that could save one of the best presidents this country has ever known."

"Amen!" someone in the background muttered unintentionally.

Before Toliver could turn around to see who had uttered the remark, two small silhouettes of naval ships appeared on the video screen. One was in port at San Diego, the other at sea well off the coast of northern Mexico.

Sanders reached for a phone and spoke briefly, then walked over to the video screen. He was a big man, broad-shouldered and balding, with a thick mustache. He produced a pointer and drew the council's attention to the aircraft carrier at sea. "This is the USS *Ronald Reagan*, steaming westward to Pearl Harbor, now four hundred and forty miles off the Mexican coast. With your permission, Madam Vice President, I can have her turn about and head due east, with a squadron of her fighter jets good to go."

Halloway hesitated only a fraction of a second before saying, "Do it!"

There was a sudden flurry of activity. People began moving back and forth, the air now filled with a dozen conversations going on at once. Everyone felt the excitement. Something was finally being done. A plan was being put into motion.

Alderman gestured subtly to the Vice President, letting her know he agreed with her decision. Inwardly he smiled to himself. The military minds were only five minutes behind his in coming up with the answer to their problem. But things would move more quickly now, particularly with Emmett Sanders at the wheel. The admiral was a superb tactician who had designed the plan that destroyed all of the Iraqi coastal defenses and naval installations during the First Gulf War, and he did it without losing a single man or plane.

Sanders was still standing by the large video screen, his eyes glued to the silhouette of the USS *Ronald Reagan*, which was slowly turning about. "Madam Vice President, we should plot a course that will allow our fighter jets to intersect with the Secret Service plane in the shortest possible time."

Halloway nodded. "Order it to be done."

"And our pilots should be on high alert, and suited up in full flight gear," Sanders advised.

"Agreed," Halloway said, nodding again. "How many planes can we put up on short notice?"

"A dozen F-18 Hornets at the rate of two every thirty-seven seconds," Sanders answered. "They can fly escort and, if necessary, take out the entire Mexican Air Force."

Which would be interpreted as an out-and-out act of war, Halloway thought miserably. At minimum it would provoke a diplomatic nightmare that would sour relations between the United States and Mexico for years to come.

Her gaze drifted to the only empty chair at the table, the one that should have been occupied by Mitchell Kaye, the President's National Security Advisor. Kaye was also an excellent diplomat who was fluent in Spanish and had close contacts high up in the Mexican government. He would have been the ideal person to deal with this crisis, but Kaye was currently a patient at Bethesda Naval Hospital, his body and mind ravaged by widespread pancreatic cancer. Halloway had visited him a week ago and barely recognized the man. *A tragedy*, she thought sadly, for Mitchell's family and for the country. With effort she cleared her mind and looked over to Alderman. "Perhaps we should call the President of Mexico and explain our situation to him."

"That won't do any good and could cause a lot of harm," Alderman told her. "First, the Mexican government is like a sieve. Within an hour of you telling their president of our predicament, the word would be leaked out and the entire world would know.

Terrorists would be emboldened, all American interests abroad threatened, more hostages elsewhere taken, and stock markets around the globe would start crashing, and on and on. Second, under no circumstances would the Mexican president allow that plane to leave Mexico. Remember, we just executed one of their high-profile citizens, shot up an airport, and killed a dozen or more of their police. Can you begin to imagine what would happen to the Mexican president if he simply let that Secret Service plane go? He'd be seen as a weakling, a coward, and a puppet of the United States, and no doubt would be run out of office. There is no way he's going to let that plane out of Mexican airspace."

Pierce nodded his agreement with Alderman's assessment. "If the tables were reversed, we'd never allow a rogue Mexican plane to get away. And if they tried, we'd shoot it down in the blink of an eye."

"So everything depends on Eagle Two evading those Mexican interceptors," Halloway concluded. Then she added in a firm voice, "But let's get that Navy SEAL Team Six in Florida airborne and on their way to California, in case the worst happens."

"Perhaps we should choose a backup Special Ops team that's closer to Los Angeles," Alderman suggested.

"And settle for a second-best unit?" Halloway countered. "Remember, we'll only have one chance to rescue the President."

Alderman nodded slowly. "I'm aware of that. But we must keep in mind the Navy SEAL team is over five hours away. That translates into at least four dead hostages."

"I know, I know," Halloway said softly, again wondering who the terrorists would kill first. A Russian in the initial round, she decided, then an American. "We'd better hope that Secret Service team has some luck to go along with their skills."

"I think we're putting all of our marbles in one basket," Toliver groused. "We're banking on this Secret Service team to save the President, and they can't even take out a Mexican drug lord efficiently."

"That was primarily my fault, not theirs," Alderman said, trying to keep his dislike for Toliver out of his voice. "I had the operation aborted in the middle of a firefight, which no doubt complicated matters. They were fortunate to get out unscathed. And remember, they did complete their mission."

Toliver shrugged, unconvinced. "They even screwed up at the airport."

"But when all is said and done, the drug king was killed and our men are alive," Alderman countered.

"But at what cost? Look at how many people they—"

"Enough!" Halloway glared at Toliver. "The Secret Service Special Ops is our best bet, and we're going to use them. Now if you want me to put it to a vote, I will."

Toliver sulked in his chair. He knew the vote would go against him. And where the hell was the Attorney General, who would almost certainly agree that the Secretary of Defense should be in charge, since the operation now involved the military? "I was just pointing out flaws."

Oh, yes, Halloway thought disgustedly, aware that Toliver was covering his own ass. If the rescue attempt failed, he would make sure the world knew that he alone had been against the plan to use the Secret Service team from the very start.

"All right," Halloway said, nodding to Alderman. "Let's get back to the Secret Service Special Ops team and see what they have in mind."

Alderman switched on the speakerphone. "This is Director Alderman."

"Yes, sir," Geary responded immediately.

"We know you're still receiving information, but we want plans for a rescue ASAP."

"Yes, sir."

"How soon can we expect to have those plans?"

"Within minutes of us obtaining the final pieces of critical information."

"Which are?"

"The thickness and construction of the walls, ceiling, and floor in the Beaumont Pavilion," Geary answered. "We also need a detailed diagram of the crawlspace in the ceiling where there is a complex of metal grids and pipes."

"The latter should be readily available," Alderman told him.

"It's not," Geary said. "And we have to have it so we can coordinate our activities with the man we now have in the crawlspace."

The Vice President sat up abruptly and pulled the speakerphone to her. "Did you say you have an agent in the crawlspace?"

"He's not an agent, ma'am," Geary replied. "He's a staff doctor on the Pavilion who managed to escape during the firefight."

Halloway's spirits sank. "A doctor won't be of much use in a rescue attempt."

"This one will," Geary informed her. "Before he went to medical school, he was in Special Ops."

Everyone in the Situation Room jerked their heads forward, their eyes and ears focused on the speakerphone. "Just how good is this man?" Halloway asked pointedly.

"Very," Geary reported. "If one goes by his past record, he is one tough *hombre*, ma'am."

"Give me an example," Halloway ordered.

Geary hesitated, then said, "His Special Ops team was sent into Somalia to take out a terrorist warlord. Nobody knew his whereabouts or would talk about it. So our man captured the warlord's top lieutenant and persuaded him to give us his boss's location."

Halloway asked, "How did he manage to do that?"

Geary hesitated again, longer this time. "He stuffed a stick of C-4 up the lieutenant's rectum and threatened to detonate it."

The room went silent again as people tried to envision the horror of having a powerful explosive stuffed inside one's body. With a cold-blooded warrior holding the detonator and glowering at you. It had to cause nightmares.

"What happened to the lieutenant?" Halloway inquired.

"After the information was obtained and verified, the C-4 was detonated."

Alderman nodded to himself, thinking that was a smart move. The lieutenant would have replaced the soon-to-be-killed warlord. And besides, he thought on, the lieutenant had no further value as a prisoner. Alderman leaned toward the speakerphone. "How long ago was this?"

"In the early nineties, sir," Geary answered. "So he may be a little rusty, but he'll be very useful for reconnaissance."

"Is he able to look after the President?" Alderman asked.

"Apparently so," Geary replied. "He sends down messages to a nurse on the floor."

"And he can keep us informed on the President's condition as well," Alderman noted.

"And relay other pieces of useful information via his cell phone," Geary continued on. "For example, we now know that the President and all the others became ill because of a toxin that was placed in the caviar."

Alderman and Halloway exchanged knowing glances. So that was how they did it! They poisoned the caviar, accurately predicting that the President would be rushed to the nearby University Hospital. And there they had killed the innocent chefs and waited for the moment to come up the dumbwaiter.

Alderman kept his expression even, but his mind was racing, digesting all the facts and putting them together. Everything had to be planned far in advance. The terrorists had to know every detail of the banquet. They had to know who would eat the caviar and where and when it would be served, and how the hospital would handle the President and send him to the Beaumont Pavilion, and a hundred other things. They had to have somebody on the inside. And it had to be a Russian who was a Chechen sympathizer. It was *their* caviar, which they'd insisted on including at the cocktail party.

"There's a goddamn Russian traitor behind this!" Toliver blurted out. "There's a leak on their side!"

"Obviously," Alderman agreed. "And it has to be high level."

"Please repeat," Geary requested.

"That was just side conversation, Agent Geary," Halloway told him.

"Yes, ma'am," Geary said. "And there's something else you should know. We have a second individual in the crawlspace. A female physician named Karen Kellerman."

"Does she have military experience, too?" Halloway asked.

"No, ma'am," Geary answered. "It looks like she's always been a civilian, but we may have a problem here. She spent three months in Chechnya with Doctors Without Borders, working as an anesthesiologist."

"When was this?" Halloway asked immediately.

"Two years ago," Geary replied. "And last year she wrote a generous check for the Chechen Hospital Fund. We're trying to determine if the fund is a front for Chechen terror groups."

"Christ!" Halloway muttered under her breath, then said, "I'm going to put you on hold for a moment." She hurriedly pressed a button on the speakerphone and looked over to Alderman. "What do you think, Arthur?"

Alderman held up a hand, as if in the midst of deep thought. But he was silently berating himself. *Stupid! Stupid! I ignored the obvious.* The Chechens no doubt arranged for the caviar to be poisoned and that required a Russian on the inside. But the details of the hospital would best be provided by an employee of the medical center. A staff member would be the perfect mole.

Alderman glanced down at a thick dossier before him. It held all the pertinent information on the Beaumont Pavilion that had been gathered by the Secret Service agents on site. He didn't bother opening the dossier because he'd already memorized its contents.

Finally Alderman said, "It would make sense for the terrorists to have a collaborator in the hospital. They would greatly value someone who has intimate knowledge of the Beaumont Pavilion, with its private kitchen one floor down and the elevator that connected the two. And they had to know the size of the elevator and how it worked and a dozen other small but important details."

Halloway considered Alderman's conclusion at length before saying, "They could have gotten all that information by careful reconnaissance."

"True," Alderman agreed. "That's why it is so critical to determine if this charity Karen Kellerman donated to is a terrorist front. And we should also check to see if she was originally scheduled to be on call tonight, or whether she asked someone to switch so she could be in the hospital at the time of the attack—in case the terrorists required more information."

"Good," Halloway approved. "And we should alert Dr. Ballineau of our suspicions. She may have been waiting for the chance to give away his location to the terrorists."

Alderman nodded, but his thoughts were far more sinister. If the woman was proven to be part of the terror group, Ballineau would have no choice but to kill her. "She could also pass on to the terrorists all the information we're transmitting to Dr. Ballineau. This of course would give the Chechens advance warning of what's about to come their way."

"So the terrorists would love to have her stay in the ceiling space with Dr. Ballineau as long as possible," Halloway reasoned.

Alderman nodded again. "It would be like the Chechens having a seat at this table."

Halloway quickly reached for the speakerphone. "Agent Geary, let us know the moment you learn more about this Kellerman woman."

"Yes, ma'am."

"Now let's get back to the rescue plan," Halloway went on, refocusing her mind. "Within the next hour I want two options on how we should go about rescuing the President. And with each option we need to know relative risk and predicted casualty counts."

"Roger that."

"And remember, rescuing the President and his family is priority one," Halloway said, then added a grim reminder before clicking off. "Everybody else is expendable."

FOURTEEN

From the crawlspace in the ceiling, David crooked his neck but still couldn't clearly see the cardiac monitor in Marci's room. In the dimness he could hear her struggling to breathe. David quickly moved to the area over the bathroom and climbed down onto the marble countertop. He paused a moment to detect any sounds before tiptoeing to her bedside. Hurriedly he glanced at the cardiac monitor, then at Marci. Although her vital signs had stabilized, she continued to have a tachycardia of 104 per minute and her respirations were noisy and labored. And she had the dusky color of someone not receiving enough oxygen.

David reached for his stethoscope and placed it softly on Marci's chest, then listened carefully. Her heart sounds were so faint they were difficult to hear. It was the classic sign of a large pericardial effusion. A wall of fluid was now trapped between the outer lining of the heart and the heart muscle itself. This would blunt any sound the heart made. And, as the fluid increased, it would constrict the heart and press down on it, like a tight grip squeezing on a partially inflated balloon. Unless treated promptly, it would kill her.

Marci's eyes fluttered open. She stared at David for a moment, then said between gasps, "Hi, Dr. Ballineau."

"Hey, Marci," David said quietly. "How are you feeling?"

"Not so good," Marci panted. "I think the effusion is coming back."

"I think so, too."

"Wi… will you have to take it out with a needle?"

"Probably," David replied.

Marci nodded weakly. "Anything is better than not being able to breathe."

"But first we'll give the medicine a little more time to work. Okay?"

Marci nodded again. "Are the terrorists still here?"

"Yes," David said, keeping his voice low. "I had to sneak up the back way, and I don't think they saw me. Now it's very important they *not* know I was here. Because if they capture me, they may not let me treat you. Got it?"

"Got it."

"So it has to be our secret."

"Can I tell Carolyn?"

"No," David said firmly. "Now go back to sleep."

"I'll try."

David adjusted the position of the nasal prongs to make sure the flow of oxygen into Marci's airway was unimpeded. Her breathing now seemed a little less labored. He waited for her to close her eyes, then hurried into the bathroom and jumped up on the marble countertop. He glanced back at Marci and watched her again straining to breathe. *She's going to die*, he thought glumly, *and there's not a damn thing I can do about it. The IV Solu-Medrol helped, but not much and not for long. Soon her effusion will in-crease and her symptoms will worsen drastically. Only a pericardio-centesis would give her relief, and we have neither the equipment nor facilities to do it on the Pavilion. Marci is already as good as dead, and her struggle with death is sure to be slow and agonizing.* David glanced at his wristwatch. It was nearly 11 p.m. In all likelihood, Marci Matthews would not live to see midnight.

David shook his head sadly, then climbed up into the crawl-space and headed for the presidential end of the corridor. Once more he concentrated on avoiding the metal pipes, knowing that if he made another metallic noise it would tip the terrorists off to his presence. And this time they wouldn't walk away.

As he came to Diana Dunn's room he heard the actress's de-manding voice. She was arguing with Carolyn.

"I will not be confined to my room," Diana was saying.

"You don't have any choice," Carolyn told her. "Because if you walk out into the corridor, they'll shoot you."

"Who will shoot me?"

"Terrorists."

"Terrorists! What is this, some kind of joke?"

"It's not a joke," Carolyn informed her. "A group of Chechen terrorists have taken over this floor, and everyone on the Pavilion is now a hostage. If you stick your head out of the door, it may be the last thing you do on the face of this earth."

"Do they know who I am?" Diana huffed.

"They know and they couldn't care less," Carolyn went on. "Their main interest is a patient at the end of the corridor. His name is John Merrill, and he happens to be the President of the United States."

Diana's eyes bulged. "Holy shit!"

"So if you value your life, stay put!" Carolyn ordered.

David moved on. Diana Dunn had picked a bad time to come out of her hepatic coma and become rational. She would have been better off staying slumberous and confused. But then again, she had no control over her hepatic encephalopathy, which came and went unpredictably—and would continue to do so until she received a new liver.

A ghoulish thought suddenly came to David's mind. Suppose—just suppose—a rescue attempt was successful and all the terrorists were killed except for one, who was barely alive and brain-dead. And suppose his liver was a perfect match for Diana Dunn. Could they grab his liver for transplant? Of course. The paperwork would be tricky, since removing a brain-dead patient's organs without permission was a criminal act—an honest-to-God felony—even if the patient was a terrorist. But there were ways around that. And it would be poetic justice. The terrorist bastard would end up actually saving a life. *Yeah, right*, David brought his mind back to reality. The chance of a rescue mission succeeding was poor at best. In all likelihood, any rescue attempt would fail and result in everyone being killed, including Diana Dunn.

David abruptly came to a dead end. Directly in front of him were intersecting pipes that were hot to the touch and radiated their heat into the crawlspace. As he backed away, beads of perspiration broke out on his brow and forearms, reminding him that he was already losing the fluid he had consumed in the kitchen. Soon he would need water again. And obtaining it would be doubly dangerous now. The terrorists were looking everywhere for him, even unexpectedly sticking their heads and shoulders up through the ceiling panels and scanning the crawlspace with powerful flashlights. On one occasion, a beam of light came within a foot of David's head as he was tucking himself under a large pipe. *It's becoming a game of cat and mouse,* he thought gloomily, *and the cats are closing in.*

David felt the vibration of his cell phone. He quickly reached for the phone, but it began to slip from his sweaty hand. In the dimness he tightened his grip, but one of his fingers accidentally pressed on the button that switched the vibration off. The cell phone suddenly chirped. David hurriedly returned the phone to vibration mode and silenced it, then held his breath and listened for a reaction to the sound from below. Everything stayed quiet. No yells, no footsteps. The only thing he heard was the pounding of his heart in his ears. *Jesus Christ!* he grumbled, breathing a sigh of relief. He brought the cell phone up and spoke in a barely audible voice. "Yes?"

"Hi, Dad," Kit said. "I'm under the covers and wanted to say goodnight."

"Oh, thank you, sweetheart," David whispered.

"Why are you talking so low, Dad?" Kit asked. "Is something wrong?"

"No, no," David lied. "I'm in a surgery room and I've got to be quiet."

"Are you coming home soon?"

"It'll be a while," David told her. He knew, in all likelihood, he wouldn't be home when she awakened, and that would frighten her. And if she learned he was trapped on the Beaumont Pavilion with the President, it would terrify her. She would be consumed by the thought that she was losing the only parent she had left. For an eleven-year-old, that was beyond horror. *Goddamn terrorists!* David fumed. He wished they'd all be slowly hanged at the end of a very long rope.

"Dad? Are you still there?"

"Yeah, but I've got to scoot now. They're coming to an important part of the operation."

"I love you, Dad."

"I love you, too, Kitten. Sleep tight."

David switched off the cell phone and crawled on, now picturing Kit pulling the covers up to her chin with her favorite teddy bear beside her. *I won't take any chances. I've got a young daughter who depends on me for everything, and I'm all she has. I have to get out of here alive. No matter what, I have to stay alive.*

David moved by a stack of multicolored wires, taking extra care to avoid the metal piping and be as silent as possible. He turned his mind to William Warren, and decided to check him next. All of the old physician's signs were bad, his recurrent arrhythmias were only the most ominous. Without Carolyn at his side he would almost surely have been dead by now. But even with her, chances are he'd never—

David abruptly stopped. Outside he heard the sound of an approaching helicopter. He concentrated on the noise of the engine and its loudness. *Put-put! Put-put! Put-put! Put-put!* Too small to be an Apache or Blackhawk, he thought. Way too small. The sound grew closer and closer, then gradually began to fade until it disappeared altogether. David nodded to himself. It was probably a Cobra, a two-seat MedEvac helicopter that was landing on the heliport behind the emergency room.

David continued on, now coming to the suite of William Warren. The silver-haired physician was moving around fitfully in his bed, clutching at the wound on his side, which was now bleeding more heavily. That was probably caused by the anticoagulant effect of the aspirin he'd been given to minimize the size of his coronary clot, David decided. But the bleeding wasn't serious. A pressure dressing would take care of that.

David's gaze went to the EKG leads on Warren's chest, then to the IV bag slowly dripping into his arm. The label on the bag read *BRETYLIUM*. David grumbled to himself. So the PVCs had returned despite treatment with lidocaine. A bad sign. It indicated there was a lot of ventricular irritability, which was a perfect setup for ventricular tachycardia. Warren needed to be in a CCU where he could be continuously monitored. An elevator ride down four floors could save two lives, Warren's and Marci's. But the terrorists weren't going to let that happen. Two more deaths wouldn't bother them in the least.

David squeezed past a metal grid and approached the chart room, with its stacked-up bodies. But now the smell had an acrid quality, like burning rubber. No. No, he quickly correctly himself. It was more like an electrical fire. But where was it coming from? He sniffed the air carefully, sampling it in all directions, but was unable to pinpoint the source of the odor. So he sniffed again, holding his nose up to the top of the crawlspace. The smell was coming from the presidential end of the corridor! Something was on fire! And the terrorists would pick up the odor soon. Then they'd remove all the panels to search the crawlspace to see what was on fire. And they'd find him.

David hesitated a moment, then moved quickly toward the source of the smell. He knew it was a risky maneuver, but he had no choice. *Maybe I can reach the fire and put it out before the terrorists pick up the acrid odor. Maybe the smell of vomit and blood below will dull their olfactory senses. Yeah. Maybe.* The odor was stronger now, and David thought he could see something flashing in the dimness ahead.

In the corridor beneath him, David heard a terrorist yelling, "Aliev! Aliev!"

Then David heard the sound of running footsteps. *Oh, shit! They've detected the fire! Now they'll start removing all the ceiling panels!*

But the footsteps stopped directly under him.

"*Hazha!*"—Look! the terrorist cried out. "*T'ye televizor!*"—On the television!

David gazed down through a crack and saw Aliev rush into the First Daughter's room, another terrorist a step behind him. Now they were speaking frantically in Chechen, their voices becoming louder and louder. David crawled slowly and quietly until he was directly behind them. Then he slid a panel back an inch and peered down.

Aliev began shouting at the large plasma television screen.

David moved the panel back another inch and saw what Aliev was yelling at.

A news helicopter was transmitting a live picture that showed the roof of University Hospital. It was from a distance, but one could still make out two small figures near the middle of the roof using what appeared to be an acetylene torch to cut their way through. And a reporter was describing it!

The news helicopter was unintentionally showing a rescue attempt. *Get out of there!* David's brain hollered. *Get your damn camera out of there!*

"Dr. Ballineau," a voice said in the dimness, "we're going to hand down some medicine for the President."

It took David a moment to realize the voice was coming through a hole in the roof that was made by the Secret Service agents using an acetylene blowtorch. "How large is the opening?" David asked hurriedly, now wondering if the hole was big enough for a man to squeeze his way in.

"Approximately eight inches," the agent answered in a low voice. "An arm can pass through without any problem. Are you ready to receive?"

Before David could answer, a spray of automatic gunfire came up through the ceiling. He curled himself up into a tight ball as bullets whizzed by, coming closer and closer.

FIFTEEN

CAROLYN HEARD THE GUNSHOTS and dashed to the open door of the First Daughter's room. She watched in horror as Aliev and another terrorist fired round after round into the ceiling. *Oh, my God! David! They know he's up there!*

"Stop!" she cried out. "Please stop!"

The terrorists paused, but only to place fresh clips of ammunition in their Uzis.

"The bullets you shoot up will come down," Carolyn pleaded, quickly thinking up a reason for them to hold their fire. "You could kill someone."

"That is the idea," Aliev said and pointed his Uzi upward. "Somebody is up there and should not be."

"Nobody is up there," Carolyn argued desperately. "It's only a crawlspace with wires and pipes."

"Someone is on the roof," Aliev growled and squeezed the trigger on his submachine run. Another burst of bullets tore into the ceiling. "We saw it on television."

Carolyn turned to the television screen, but now it only showed a news reporter. *Why would they televise someone on the hospital's roof?* she wondered. *Was it just part of a program that the terrorists misinterpreted as happening in real time? Maybe. But what about David? Was he in the area of the shots? Or was he watching over the critically ill patients? Please, God, let him have been away from this room.*

Aliev exhausted his second clip and tossed it aside. "They will think twice before they try another rescue."

Carolyn's eyes widened. A rescue attempt. That's what it was! They were going to come in through the roof. She suddenly shuddered to herself, wondering if David had crawled over to the area to assist the would-be rescuers.

Aliev barked out an order in Chechen. The other terrorist handed him his Uzi, then pulled Jamie Merrill out of her bed and onto the floor. He climbed up on the mattress, knocked a ceiling panel out, and hoisted the upper part of his body into the crawl-space. Using a flashlight, he carefully searched the area. After a few moments he came down and reported to Aliev. He pointed to his arm and made a dangling gesture, then babbled on, repeating the word *elektrichestvo* several times.

Aliev walked over to Carolyn and said, "Whoever was there is now dead. He will no longer be a problem to us."

Carolyn swallowed hard. She took a deep breath and forced her voice to remain even. "Was the dead man wearing a white coat?"

Aliev looked at her oddly. "Why is that important?"

"They may have been trying to send a doctor down to treat the President," Carolyn said.

"The only thing my man saw was an arm covered with blood, and it wasn't moving," Aliev said with a shrug.

It might not be David, Carolyn thought, holding on to the slimmest of hopes. She and the patients desperately needed David's expertise. And he was their only chance of escape. She had to know if he was still alive.

"We should bring the body down," she suggested. "It's very warm in that crawlspace and the body will decompose rapidly."

"The smell of death will not bother me or my men," Aliev said, unconcerned. "Now we are faced with another problem. Do you have any electrical tape?"

"Yes. At the front desk," Carolyn replied. She was talking to Aliev, but her hearing was concentrated on the ceiling, listening for any signs of life. "The ward clerk knows where it's located."

"The black man?"

"Yes."

Aliev gave another order using the term "electrical tape" and waited for his associate to leave, then came back to Carolyn.

"One of the wires is giving off sparks and making a burning smell. Tell your patient to ignore the odor. It is not dangerous."

"Did you hear what he said, Jamie?" Carolyn asked.

The First Daughter nodded rapidly, still badly rattled by the gunfire and the presence of terrorists. She had to bite down on her lip to keep it from quivering.

"You are scared, no?" Aliev asked her, a sympathetic tone to his voice.

Jamie Merrill nodded again, avoiding the terrorist's dark eyes.

"So was my daughter when the Russians bombed our house and killed her mother," Aliev went on. "Can you imagine a ten-year-old child holding her dead mother, trying to bring her back to life?"

Jamie shook her head.

"I see it all the time, over and over in my dreams," Aliev said softly. "I see my wife's mangled body. I see the terrified look on my daughter's face. It is a living nightmare. Can you understand that?"

Jamie tried to speak, but the words wouldn't come.

"No," Aliev answered for her. "I don't think you can. Because it wasn't your family that was destroyed."

Collecting all of her courage, Jamie requested, "I'd like to see my father."

"And I would like to see my daughter," Aliev responded. "Let us hope both of our wishes come true."

The second terrorist returned with a roll of black electrical tape. He spoke quickly to Aliev, repeatedly gesturing with his hands.

"Idiot!" Aliev muttered under his breath. He then asked Carolyn, "Would the black man know how to use the tape to stop the sparks?"

"No, but I do," Carolyn replied.

Aliev reached for the roll of tape and handed it to Carolyn. "Fix the wire."

Carolyn grabbed a chair and placed it on the bed, then said to Aliev, "Tell your man to hold its legs."

Aliev gave the order.

Carolyn climbed up on the chair and, standing on her tiptoes, was able to put her head and shoulders into the crawlspace. It was dark, with only dim light coming up through the ventilation ducts. Directly in front of her she saw the sparking wire. It was loose, with its insulation partially torn away. It wasn't really dangerous, and would be easy to repair.

Carolyn began coughing as she tried to clear her throat. The gunfire through the ceiling panels had stirred up the particulate matter in the crawlspace and caused the air to become foul and irritating.

"What is the matter?" Aliev called to her.

"The air is dirty up here," Carolyn called out loudly. She hoped and prayed David was still alive and had heard her voice and would send a signal that he was all right. As the seconds ticked off, Carolyn prayed even harder that David would respond. But everything remained dead quiet. Her spirits sank even further.

"Is there a problem?" Aliev asked impatiently.

"I've got to separate the damaged wires from the others," Carolyn lied. She gave thought to inducing a short circuit that might black out the entire Pavilion. That would confuse the terrorists, but only briefly since the auxiliary generators would kick in within a minute and restore electric power. But then again, a momentary blackout would give a rescue team the edge, particularly if they were wearing night-vision goggles, like the SWAT units Carolyn had witnessed when she was a flight nurse.

"What is the delay?" Aliev groused up at her. "It should not be taking this long."

"Do you want the damn thing done right or not?" Carolyn snapped, now using her fingernail to dig an indentation in the ceiling panel so she could recognize it when the next rescue attempt began.

"You had better not be trying anything foolish," Aliev warned.

"I'm almost finished." Carolyn tore off a strip of tape and expertly wrapped it around the exposed wire. The sparks disappeared. She climbed down and said, "It's fixed."

Aliev looked at her skeptically. He ordered the other terrorist to check and make certain the wire had been repaired.

The second terrorist climbed back up into the crawlspace, and a moment later came down, nodding.

Carolyn put the chair away and helped Jamie back into bed. The IV in her arm had become dislodged and would have to be restarted. "Is your arm hurting?"

"A little," Jamie replied.

Carolyn stopped the IV, which was now infiltrating into the subcutaneous tissue. "I'll get this squared away in a little while."

"Why won't they let me see my dad?" Jamie asked in a barely audible voice. "Is he okay?"

"He's fine," Carolyn assured her.

"Then why won't they let me see him?"

"Because it's easier to control families if you keep them in separate rooms."

Aliev had a cell phone pressed to his ear. "Put me through," he demanded.

After a moment's pause, he spoke again. "That was stupid, Lady Vice President … What was stupid? Your clumsy rescue attempt! … If you try it again, I will execute a hostage. That I promise you."

Aliev listened to the response, then stared at the cell phone incredulously. His face suddenly hardened. "What do you take me for? A fool? … Of course it was your people. Who else would have been up on the roof with a blowtorch? … Then you had better control them, or you will have a dead hostage on your hands."

Again he listened closely to the Vice President's voice. The corner of his lips curled up into a cruel smile. "So you don't think that killing a hostage would accomplish anything, eh? Would you be convinced of our seriousness if we tied an old Jew into his wheelchair and dropped him out of a window ten stories down? Of course we would alert the press beforehand, so the whole world could see what your stupidity brought on."

Carolyn's face lost color. They'd actually do it, and laugh while they did it! And *Al Jazeera* would be delighted to show the replay. Out of desperation she said, "If you do that, I won't do anything more for you."

Aliev placed his hand over the cell phone and glared at her. "Be careful!" he warned icily. "You may not be as valuable as you think you are."

"Leave him alone," Carolyn begged. "He's suffered enough."

Aliev cocked his head, as if reconsidering, then went back to his cell phone. "Lady Vice President, the major nurse here does not think it would be a good idea to throw the old Jew out the window. So I must come up with an alternative. If another rescue is attempted—any rescue at all—I will execute the President's daughter. I will put a gun to her head and pull the trigger while you and all your people in Washington listen in."

Jamie started kicking at her sheet and screaming hysterically, her voice high-pitched and filled with horror.

"As you can hear, Lady Vice President," Aliev continued on, "the President's daughter is not in favor of that option."

Jamie was still screaming when Aliev switched the cell phone off. But not at the prospect of being killed. She was pointing up at a narrow slit between the ceiling panels. A steady stream of red blood was dripping down on her.

———

David saw a ceiling panel come up, then another. The area above Jamie Merrill's room was abruptly flooded with light. He could hear the urgency in the voices below and knew the terrorists were on their way up into the crawlspace. Rapidly turning his body around, he wriggled away from the light and toward the eastern-most wall of the enclosure. Behind him, the voices were becoming louder. The orders were being spoken in Chechen, but David deduced what was about to happen. The terrorists would search every inch of the crawlspace, looking for the source of the blood that had spilled down into Jamie Merrill's room.

Up ahead he saw Karen's figure in the darkness and moved over to her.

"What's happening?" Karen asked anxiously.

"The terrorists are coming up," David said in a hurry. "We've got to hide."

"Where?"

"In the area between the large pipe and the wall."

"There's not enough room for both of us."

"Just do what I tell you," David directed. "Now crawl over the damn pipe and lie on your back, with your arms and legs spread apart as much as possible."

"What?"

"Just do it!"

David watched Karen climb over the large pipe and squeeze into the space between it and the wall. She made too much noise settling in, but the sound was muted by the loudness of the terrorists' voices. There were two of them in the crawlspace, David estimated, maybe three. The far end of the area suddenly lit up as more ceiling panels were removed.

David grabbed the top of the warm pipe and hoisted himself up, then rolled over on top of Karen. Involuntarily her arms went around his neck, her legs spreading wide enough to accommodate his lower torso. They were squeezed into the narrow space, face to face, body to body, with barely inches to spare.

"You're crushing me," Karen complained.

"Shut up if you want to live!"

The terrorists were moving toward them, shining their flashlights in sweeping arcs. A beam of light passed over the large pipe and illuminated the wall behind it. David pressed himself even closer to Karen as the light came to a stop directly over their heads. They could hear a terrorist grunting while he crawled closer and closer to the pipe. He seemed to be almost next to them.

Karen let out a soft wheeze.

There wasn't enough room for David to move his hand and place it over her mouth, so he kissed her instead. His lips sealed hers and stopped the sound. He continued the kiss until the terrorist backed away and the beam of light began to fade. It took another full minute before the terrorists left and darkness returned to the crawlspace.

"Damn, that was close!" Karen whispered as David lifted himself up off her.

"We were lucky," he whispered back, then helped her over the large pipe and onto the floor beside him. "Just plain lucky."

"I don't think it was luck," she said softly. "I think you're pretty good at this."

"I've had some practice."

"So I gathered." Karen took several long, deep breaths, as if testing her airway, then came back to David. "And you still kiss good, too."

"That was to shut off your wheeze."

She pecked his cheek in the darkness and stayed close to him. "Oh, I believe it was much more than that."

"Believe whatever you want," David said sharply, but he had to admit to himself that it turned out to be more than just a way to stop her wheeze. Goddamn it! He had tasted her warmth and it felt—

Abruptly a ceiling panel was pushed aside and a stream of light shot up into the crawlspace.

"They're coming back!" David said and pushed her toward the pipe. "Squeeze into that hiding place and lie on your side perfectly still."

"What about you?"

"Just do what I tell you," David urged in a hushed voice, now convinced that pressing against Karen in a tight space could put them in ever greater danger. As before, it would partially block off her nose and mouth and set off another attack of asthma, which could get them both killed. "Now go!"

Wriggling away from her, he moved in a northerly direction, keeping close to the pipe until he reached an even larger, intersecting pipe. *I'm halfway there*, David told himself, then rotated to his left. Suddenly a barrage of flashlights pierced the darkness. Aliev's voice barked out orders in Chechen. Two other voices answered. A moment later powerful beams of light began crisscrossing the musty air of the crawlspace.

One of the terrorists opened fire at something he saw. He sprayed shots erratically at the eastern wall of the enclosure until Aliev's grating voice stopped him. David stayed motionless and gritted his teeth against the stinging pain in his thigh. He wasn't sure how deeply the bullet had penetrated his quadriceps muscle, but it hurt like hell to move his leg. The bright beams of light came back to his area and were now directly overhead.

David tried desperately to squeeze himself under the giant pipe, but there wasn't enough room and part of his body remained exposed. He pushed even harder, but to no avail. An arm and a leg were still out in the open. *Shit! Oh, shit! I'm a dead man!* David's brain wailed as the beams of light dipped, coming closer and closer to him.

SIXTEEN

THE VICE PRESIDENT COULD barely contain her anger. She was yelling into the speakerphone. "Who the hell ordered that rescue attempt? Who?"

"It wasn't a rescue attempt, ma'am," Agent Cassidy answered from Los Angeles. "We were trying to get the blood concentrate the President needs to the doctor in the crawlspace."

"Is the President bleeding again?" Halloway asked hurriedly.

"We can't be sure, ma'am," Cassidy replied. "But if he's not bleeding now he will be very shortly, according to our blood specialist. That's why the attempt was made."

Halloway took a deep breath, calming herself. "Was the blood concentrate received by our man in the ceiling?"

"We don't know, ma'am," Cassidy said. "We've lost contact with the two agents we sent up."

"Do you know where those agents are now?" Halloway asked.

There was a pause before Cassidy answered. "They're still up there, ma'am. One of our helicopters flying above the hospital has an infrared camera that showed two figures lying motionless on the roof. They haven't moved for over five minutes—and there was a lot of gunfire earlier."

"Are you telling me they're dead?"

"That's our best assessment, ma'am."

Shit! Halloway grumbled to herself. Now there were two more dead, and the terrorists were on an even higher state of alert. "What about our people in the crawlspace?"

"No response there, either."

"Which indicates that Ballineau and Kellerman are probably dead too."

"Most likely, ma'am," Cassidy said. "But Kellerman is no loss. Our European contacts confirm that the Chechen Hospital Fund is a terrorist front and everybody who works over there knows it. And Dr. Kellerman's contribution to the front wasn't a one-time event. She's written multiple checks to them over the past two years, including an electronic transfer of five thousand dollars. We've also learned from the scheduling secretary at University Hospital that Dr. Kellerman switched on-call dates with a colleague so she would be on-call tonight. It surely looks like she's an integral part of the terrorist group, ma'am."

"Bloody traitor!" Halloway growled under the breath. "I take it that all this information has been double-checked."

"Yes, ma'am."

"Is there any chance that Dr. Ballineau survived?"

"I don't think so, ma'am. Before we had to pull our helicopters out, we tried repeatedly to contact Dr. Ballineau. There was no response."

Halloway kept her expression level, but she groaned inwardly. Things were going from bad to worse. She glanced over to Alderman, who was fiddling with his pipe, lost in thought. Her gaze drifted across to Martin Toliver. He had an *I told you so* look on his face. The Vice President cleared her throat and came back to the speakerphone.

"Agent Cassidy, listen carefully. There are to be no further attempts to enter or invade the Pavilion without the express consent of the National Security Council. Do you understand?"

"Roger that."

Halloway switched the speakerphone off and sank down in her seat. "For every step we take forward, we go back two."

"This is turning into a boondoggle," Toliver complained bitterly. "It's one mistake after another. We couldn't look more inept if we tried."

"It was a worthwhile attempt," Alderman said.

"Ha!" Toliver forced a laugh. "Two agents are dead with nothing accomplished, and you call that worthwhile?"

"A lot of men will die before this is over," Alderman said darkly. "And most of them will die in a noble cause."

Toliver shrugged. "I don't take much solace from that. Those two men died for no reason."

"They died for a good reason," Alderman snapped. "Those men were Secret Service agents who vowed to protect and, if necessary, give their lives for the President. And that's what they were doing."

"We don't know if the President was bleeding again," Toliver argued. "He may not have needed that blood concentrate at that very moment."

"I didn't know that you were an expert in these medical matters," Alderman jabbed.

Toliver's face colored. A vein over his temple bulged. "What I'm saying is that two men gave their lives and we have nothing to show for it. It would have been better to wait until we knew the President needed the blood concentrate. Our doctor in the crawlspace could have alerted us to that. And now he's probably dead, too. So, Mr. Director," he said directly to Alderman, "if you wish to call the attempt noble and worthwhile, go ahead. But it's cost three men their lives, and we no longer have the advantage of a man in the crawlspace."

Halloway had to agree with Toliver's grim summary of the situation. The death of two agents was bad enough, but the loss of the doctor in the crawlspace was a huge setback. Now they no longer had a way to check on the President and, more importantly, the Secret Service Special Ops team had lost a critical source of information on the movements and whereabouts of the terrorists. The chances of rescuing the President were rapidly approaching zero.

Halloway glanced up at the wall where a digital clock was ticking off the time remaining until the deadline. They had one hour and fifty-two minutes left.

The door to the Situation Room opened, and the Attorney General of the United States walked in. Benjamin Weir was a tall, lean man with sharp features and crew-cut gray hair. He was dressed in a tuxedo. A former professor of law at Yale, he was known for two things—his impressive knowledge of the Constitution, and the polka-dot bow ties he wore even with his formal attire.

"Sorry for not getting here sooner," Weir apologized. "I was at a dinner in Philadelphia."

Halloway motioned him to the empty chair usually occupied by Mitchell Kaye. "Ben, have you heard about the President?"

"I heard he was ill on the way over," Weir replied. "Some sort of food poisoning, I was told."

"Oh, it's more than that," Halloway said gravely. "Much more."

For the next few minutes she carefully detailed the events that had befallen the President. She emphasized his illness and hemorrhaging, and the fact that he and his family were being held hostage by Chechen terrorists. Halloway gave the Attorney General time to assimilate the information before saying, "We are currently in the midst of putting together a rescue plan that involves the Secret Service. What we need to know from a constitutional standpoint is this: in the President's absence, who takes command?"

Toliver quickly interjected, "You should also know, Ben, that this plan also involves the use of the military. In particular, the aircraft carrier USS *Ronald Reagan*, which is heading for the coast of Mexico."

Weir rubbed his chin thoughtfully. "Who gave the orders?"

"I did," Halloway answered.

"With no real authority," Toliver added, then hurriedly went on before anyone else could speak. "Now the regulations are straightforward on this matter. In the absence of the President, the Secretary of Defense takes command on all military actions."

"I'm aware of that," Weir said.

"So, it's settled," Toliver asserted. "I'm in command. And my first order—"

"Not so fast!" Weir interrupted. "The President is not only absent, he's a hostage. And this places him in a state of incapacitation and unable to discharge the duties of his office."

Toliver looked at Weir sternly. "Are you suggesting we invoke the Twenty-Fifth Amendment?"

Weir nodded. "The Constitution is very clear on this. If the President is incapacitated, the Vice President assumes the office. Of course, the majority of the President's Cabinet, as well as those here, will have to sign a document attesting to the incapacitation." All eyes stayed on Benjamin Weir, waiting for his next utterance. Everyone felt the gravity of the moment. The transfer of power was about to take place, and in all likelihood it would be permanent.

"Shall I have the document prepared?" Weir asked.

Without hesitation, Halloway said, "Have it drawn up."

Weir got to his feet and bowed formally to the next President of the United States. "You'll excuse me, ma'am."

Halloway waited for Weir to leave, then turned to the members of the council. "We don't sign the document. Not yet."

"Why not?" Toliver asked. "Why not get it over with?"

"Because we'd have to inform the country and the rest of the world," Halloway replied at once. "As Arthur explained to us earlier, news that the President is a hostage would cause panic and unfounded rumors, and a crash on the markets, and a dozen other things we don't need. And some of our enemies would take this to be a fine opportunity to stir up trouble and cause a crisis or two. They would consider our guard down, and they just might be right. So for now, the document will remain unsigned."

Smart, Alderman thought, *very smart*. Why bother with a document and its disadvantages when she was already in command? And now Toliver had been pushed aside, although he would remain an irritant. But no matter. He would always be outvoted. The Joint Chiefs would happily vote against the man who tried to downsize the military services, using his bureaucrats as hatchet men. Alderman's eyes went to the clock on the wall. They were down to an hour and forty-six minutes. He cleared his throat and said, "Madam Vice President, the time you gave the Special Ops team to devise a plan is almost up."

"Get them on the line," Halloway directed.

Alderman signaled an aide. A moment later, Special Agent Geary's voice came over the speakerphone. "Yes, ma'am?"

"Have you got a plan for us?" Halloway asked.

"Almost," Geary reported. "We now know what materials were used in the construction of the walls and floor of the Pavilion. And we've pinpointed the location of the President and his family."

"How accurate can you be?"

"Very, ma'am," Geary told her. "We used infrared imaging on their assigned rooms."

"How could you distinguish between the President and the terrorist guarding him?"

"The President was lying down, ma'am."

Halloway nodded at the explanation. "You've got ten minutes to get those plans to us."

"Roger that."

"And be very careful if you devise a plan using the roof of the hospital," Halloway counseled. "The terrorists will be watching the area now."

"We're aware of that, ma'am," Geary said.

Halloway drummed her fingers on the tabletop and thought further about the roof. "Do we know how they were able to discover our men up there?"

"A news helicopter entered the no-fly zone we had set up," Geary answered. "They inadvertently transmitted a picture of our men on the roof. The news people misinterpreted the images and reported that the men on the roof were probably Secret Service agents who were setting up some sort of special communications device. The terrorists no doubt saw it on TV as well, but unfortunately didn't misinterpret what our agents were really doing."

"I see," Halloway said through her teeth. *Goddamn it! Three dead men because of a fucking news helicopter that served no purpose except to put the hostages in even greater jeopardy.* She waited a moment for her anger to pass, then asked, "What steps are being taken to ensure this doesn't happen again?"

"We've informed all television stations that any aircraft that enters the no-fly zone will be shot out of the sky."

"Do you have the firepower to do that?"

"Yes, ma'am. We now have two Apache helicopters securing the perimeter."

"Get back to me in ten minutes with those plans."

"Roger that."

Halloway leaned back and gathered her thoughts, trying not to feel overwhelmed. It wasn't only the power of the office she had assumed that weighed so heavily on her. It was the responsibility of trying to save the life of a President she adored and the world needed. He was such an exceptional leader, who always seemed to make time for those around him. Particularly for her. She had been the senior senator from Ohio when he chose her to be his running mate. And all along the way he included her in his major decisions, showing her the ins and outs of the office, and grooming her to become the first female President of the United States. And she wanted the position so badly, but not this way. Not by signing some document.

"Madam Vice President," a communications officer cried out, "you've got an urgent call from the President of Mexico."

Halloway jerked her head around and stared at the row of wall clocks. It was midnight California time, 2 a.m. in Mexico City! "He knows! He knows about the Secret Service plane, and what the people on it did."

Alderman nodded and asked the officer, "Did they specifically request the Vice President?"

"Yes, sir."

"He knows," Alderman agreed. "And he knows the President is ill, so he assumes you must be in command."

Halloway again strummed her fingers on the conference table, concentrating, and tried to think through the problem. "I've got to buy us some time."

"He won't give you much," Alderman cautioned.

"I don't need much," Halloway said and turned to the communications officer. "Tell him we'll return his call."

"Should I give him a time, ma'am?" the officer asked.

"No. Just tell him ASAP," Halloway replied and quickly came back to Alderman. "Do we have satellites that will show us real-time pictures of all Mexican Air Force facilities?"

"I'm certain we do."

"Get them up on the video screen," Halloway ordered, then looked over to the Navy Chief of Staff. "Does the *Reagan* have to do anything special to launch its aircraft?"

"Just turn into the wind, Madam Vice President," Sanders told her.

"Which way are they sailing now?"

"With the wind, ma'am."

"Have them ready to turn about on my command."

SEVENTEEN

DAVID REMAINED PARTIALLY HIDDEN, with half his body squeezed under the large pipe. He held his breath as another strong beam of light passed by. For the past ten minutes the terrorists had been continually talking and searching the crawlspace, looking for the source of the blood that had dripped down into Jamie Merrill's room. Nearby, David heard two voices jabbering and complaining about something. It sounded as if their patience was growing thin.

The shaft of light came by once again, now pointing up to the metal grid and wires above David's head. His fear was mounting, and the closeness of the beam made it worse. He stayed perfectly still, trying to ignore the pain in his leg. There was more conversation between the terrorists, then an order. Suddenly, the light disappeared and the crawlspace became dark and silent.

Only then did David reach down and feel the wound in his lower thigh. It was bleeding profusely, despite the makeshift dressing he'd made by placing a handkerchief over the site and wrapping his tie around it. He couldn't determine if the bullet had nicked an artery, but if it had he could bleed to death there and then. Somehow he had to stop it.

Carefully he pushed himself away from the pipe and moved over to a ventilation duct that allowed a sliver of light to come through. He positioned his leg so he could examine the wound. It was a deep, inch-long gash above his knee. The bullet had torn out a piece of the lateral quadriceps muscle and blood was flowing from it, but not spurting. Good! It wasn't arterial bleeding. He pushed his handkerchief deeper into the wound and bound it tightly in place with his tie. The bleeding slowed.

Some distance behind him he heard a soft, prolonged wheeze. At least Karen was alive, he thought, although she too might be wounded. David pricked his ears and listened for cries of pain or distress, but all he heard was quiet. To make certain she was all right, he planned to check on her after seeing what the terrorists were doing in Jamie Merrill's room. Hopefully they weren't preparing for another search of the crawlspace.

He glanced down through the ventilation duct into the First Daughter's room. Carolyn was changing the blood-soaked sheets. Jamie Merrill sat off to the side, a blank stare on her face. A terrorist stood guard just outside the door, his back to the people in the room.

David considered climbing down into the suite and taking the guard out and grabbing his Uzi. He was sure he could do it, even with his injured leg. And he was sure he could herd Carolyn and the President's wife and daughter into the presidential suite, taking out a second guard in the process. But then what? There would still be three heavily armed terrorists remaining and David would be no match for them. He and the President's family would end up trapped in a single room with no way out. They'd still be hostages.

David lay back for a moment, the wound in his leg throbbing. He pushed down on the dressing and reorganized his thoughts. First, contact the Secret Service. Give them a fast update, and see if a rescue attempt was imminent. *It damn well better be*, David thought grimly. Time was running out for the President and Marci and Warren and everyone else.

He reached for his cell phone, but it wasn't there. Frantically, he checked all of his pockets. The cell phone was missing. *Jesus H. Christ! My only link to the outside is gone. I had it in my pocket so I could feel the vibration of an incoming call, and now it's gone. It must have slipped out while I was curling myself into a ball to avoid the bullets.*

He hurriedly oriented himself in the dimness, and crawled back to the spot where he thought he'd heard the voice of the agent on the roof. The metal grid around him was sticky with blood, but he didn't know if it was his or the agent's. Or maybe it was both of theirs. This was the spot, he told himself. He began groping the area for the cell phone, then abruptly stopped. Something hit his head. It wasn't metal. It was too soft for that. He reached up for the object. It was a human arm dangling down through the hole in the roof. It belonged to the dead agent overhead. It was cold and pulseless, and covered with blood.

David nodded to himself. The terrorists had probably seen the arm and believed it was the source of the blood dripping down. And maybe the hand on that arm was delivering the medication the President needed. David quickly felt around for the packs of Factor VIII, but all he detected was clotted blood. *Shit!* As he turned to backtrack, he noticed a small, faint light off to his right. He moved over to it. The light was coming from his cell phone. *I must have pressed the Talk button when I turned over on it. Lucky I did! But then again, maybe not so lucky. The lighted screen would be using up valuable battery power.* He quickly pushed the redial button. A moment later a voice came on.

"Special Agent Cassidy here."

"This is Ballineau," David whispered.

"You made it!"

"Most of me did," David said, keeping his voice very low. "Now this phone has been on for a while and will give out soon. We have to talk fast, so don't ask, just answer. Got it?"

"Got it," Cassidy replied, then hurriedly went on. "But first, there's some critical information I have to pass on to you."

"Go."

"Is Karen Kellerman alive?"

"I think so."

"Well, if she is, you'd better watch your back." Cassidy rapidly transmitted the information indicating that Karen Kellerman was a crucial part of the terrorist group. "The evidence has been confirmed by reliable sources."

"Son of a bitch!" David seethed, thinking that duplicity must be ingrained in Karen's DNA. She was a liar and a thief and now a goddamned turncoat! "They probably turned her while she was working over there."

"That's what we figure," Cassidy said. "We also figure that her existence up there threatens yours—if you get my drift."

"I got it," David muttered as his hatred for Karen boiled over. *She was a goddamn traitor!* he thought bitterly. An American traitor who would be responsible for the death of her President and dozens of others. Killing her wouldn't be a problem. Now she was just another terrorist.

"Ballineau?"

"Yeah," David said and quickly refocused his mind. "To begin with, your man on the roof is dead."

"We know."

"And the President's medicine wasn't delivered."

"We figured."

"The terrorists are getting nervous, and it won't take much for them to start killing people," David went on. "And the President is almost certain to start hemorrhaging again. So whatever plans you have, you'd better put them into high gear."

"We have a rescue team on the way."

"Patch me through to them."

Cassidy hesitated. "It might be best for me to relay your information."

"Patch me through!" David demanded. "Before this goddamn phone gives out."

"Hold."

David's thigh began to throb painfully again. He reached down to rearrange the makeshift dressing. The bandage loosened, the discomfort eased. But the bleeding started again, dripping down from his thigh onto the metal grid below.

"Are you there, Ballineau?" Special Agent Geary asked.

"Yeah," David replied in a hoarse whisper.

"I hear you're in a tough place."

"Not as tough as the place you're going to be in."

"Oh?"

"If you're thinking about coming in from above, you'd better think again," David advised. "That misadventure on the roof has the terrorists spooked. They keep looking up into the crawlspace every five minutes or so. They'll hear you coming a block away."

"What about blowing our way through the floor?" Geary asked.

"Where?"

"Away from the President."

"How far away from the President?"

"The nurses' lounge."

"Too far," David said immediately. "The terrorists will have an Uzi at the President's head before you can climb up through the hole."

Geary paused for a long moment. "Maybe we'll be able to tip-toe across to the President's bathroom and blow an opening in the ceiling."

"What about falling debris?" David cautioned. "The President could end up crushed under a mass of metal girders and wooden beams."

"It's just an option we're considering," Geary downplayed the idea.

"You're going to have to come up with a lot better plan than that," David told him. "Everything you've mentioned so far ends up with a dead President."

"You got any suggestions?"

Not even one, David grumbled to himself, knowing he wouldn't be of much help. His days in Special Ops were almost twenty years ago. A lifetime had passed since then, the memories vague except for the killing and the sounds and smells of death. Still, he searched back in his mind for the clandestine operations he'd once participated in. They'd never had to go into a city with a skyscraper or modern hospital. Never. It had always been some shitty place like Mogadishu or Basra. Places where indoor plumbing was considered a luxury. Mogadishu was the worst. It was a—

Suddenly David's memory clicked in. *Mogadishu. Oh, yeah!* His mind flashed back to the last mission he'd been on. A terrorist warlord was holed up in the penthouse of a crummy apartment building. The three floors beneath him were occupied by his guards, all heavily armed. Yet the Special Ops team got to him, killing him and his mistress and his personal sentries. Then they blew the building to hell, and made it back to a waiting helicopter. "You still there, Geary?" David asked urgently.

"Still here."

"Look up my military records," David went on hurriedly. "The operation in Mogadishu is the ..."

"*Where*?" Geary asked.

There was a sudden burst of gunfire around David. Bullets tore up through the ceiling and whizzed by him. Another burst came up through the panels near the giant pipes, filling the air with sparks and smoke.

"We see your blood dripping down," Aliev called up. "You have ten seconds to surrender or we will fill the crawlspace with so many bullets a mouse could not survive. One ... two ... three ..."

"Mogadishu!" David yelled into the cell phone. "The operation in Mogadishu! Do you read me?"

There was no response.

David looked at the screen on his cell phone. It was now totally black. *Oh, Christ! My cell phone is dead. The message never got through!*

"Six ... seven ... eight," Aliev was counting.

"Hold your fire!" David cried out. "Hold your fire! I'm coming down."

EIGHTEEN

DAVID CAREFULLY LOWERED HIMSELF from the ceiling, trying to contain his fear and wondering if they were going to shoot him for causing so much trouble. They would know he was the hidden enemy agent and blame him for the death of the terrorist in the kitchen. And, in all likelihood, they would execute him for doing it. Somehow he had to talk his way out of the bind he was in. Play dumb, he decided. Real dumb. He gingerly stepped onto the countertop in the bathroom, then eased his feet onto the floor. Blood was flowing freely from his thigh wound and soaking through to his pants.

Aliev pointed his Uzi at David, watching his every move. "So it was you who killed one of my men."

David looked at him strangely, feigning ignorance. "What are you talking about?"

"I'm talking about my cousin on the floor in the kitchen," Aliev snapped.

David shook his head. "I wasn't in the kitchen area. I was too busy trying to look after all the sick patients."

"And you came down into the rooms to do this?" Aliev probed. "To give medicines to everyone?"

David nodded slowly. "To check on the IVs and administer drugs when I could."

David immediately saw the trap he'd fallen into. He shouldn't have mentioned the drugs. Goddamn it!

"Where did you obtain the drugs?" Aliev asked pointedly. "The medicine room is guarded at all times. So who provided the drugs?"

"No one," David said, thinking rapidly. "I got the medicines from the cardiac cart in Dr. Warren's room."

Aliev stared at him, not sure whether to believe him. "All by yourself, eh?"

"All by myself," David replied, submissively averting Aliev's hard stare. "I had to try to help."

Aliev lowered his weapon, but kept his eyes glued suspiciously on David. "One man doing all these things?" he asked, then answered himself. "I don't think so. There must be others in the crawlspace."

"There are no more except for the dead agent," David insisted, thinking briefly about Karen Kellerman. If she had managed to dodge the barrage of bullets, she'd stay in place, scared shitless, until all the shooting was over. Then she'd climb down, get herself a good lawyer, and walk away scot-free. The treasonous bitch! If, on the other hand, the terrorists discovered her wounded, she'd talk and they would kill him.

"You have something more to say?" Aliev broke the silence. The tone of his voice indicated he didn't believe David's answer. "Yes?"

"No," David said evenly. "I have nothing to add. I've told you everything I know."

"You had better be telling the truth, or you will be the next to die," Aliev threatened. He barked out a set of orders to a terrorist at the door and waited for the man to leave before coming back to David. "How long have you been in the ceiling?"

"From the beginning." David limped over to a chair and sat down heavily. "While your men were taking over the ward, I climbed up into the crawlspace."

"So you made contact with the people on the outside," Aliev guessed correctly. "You guided the men on the roof."

David shook his head, knowing the direction the conversation was about to take. The leader of the terrorists was trying to determine how much information about him and his men had been passed on. "I attempted to contact the police," David said innocently, "but my cell phone was dead."

Aliev quickly snapped his fingers. "Let me have it."

David handed over the cell phone and watched while the terrorist checked it out. He turned to Carolyn and asked, "How are you doing?"

"Terrible."

"Welcome to the club."

Carolyn reached for a clean pillowcase. She ripped it apart and wrapped it around his thigh. "You're bleeding over everything."

"We'll take care of that in a minute," David said, pondering how much blood he'd lost and whether it would leave him weakened. He gently stretched out his leg, and the pain in his quadriceps intensified. Fresh blood came through the new dressing.

Aliev tossed the cell phone aside and studied David's white laboratory coat. "You are a doctor, yes?"

"Yes."

"Then you will take care of the President. We need him alive for now."

"First, I want to treat my leg wound and stop the bleeding."

Aliev came over and gazed down at the blood-soaked dressing. "How will you do this?"

"With the nurse's help, I'll close the wound with sutures," David said and got to his feet. "You can have one of your men watch if you'd like."

"Oh, I plan to," Aliev assured him. "I plan to watch everything you do."

David limped out of the room, leaving a trail of blood behind. Carolyn was at his side, Aliev close behind them. Some of the patients' doors were open, and David could see terrorists climbing onto beds to look into the crawlspace above the ceiling. *They'd take no chances now*, he thought grimly. The crawlspace was their only weak spot, and they knew it. They would secure the space and make certain it was no longer a viable point of entry.

Carolyn glanced over and saw the strained look on David's face. "What's wrong?"

"Everything."

Speaking sotto voce and barely moving her lips, Carolyn said, "If they find Karen up there, you'll be in big trouble."

"I hope she's dead," David whispered back.

"You don't mean that."

"The hell I don't," David hissed and quickly gave Carolyn all the details the Secret Service had gathered on Karen Kellerman. "She's a goddamn traitor!"

"But why?" Carolyn asked, with a stunned expression.

"Who knows?"

"Quiet!" Aliev demanded and nudged them on with the barrel of his Uzi.

Just ahead, the balding terrorist was having an animated conversation with another terrorist. He was speaking loudly and gesturing with his hands held wide apart.

"Boom! Boom!" he said excitedly, now practicing his poor English. "Big bomb! Many die!"

"*Hah! Hah!*"—Yes! Yes!" the other terrorist agreed. "Boom! Big *bomba*!"

Aliev rushed over to the pair and began screaming at them. He pushed the balding terrorist against the wall and pointed his submachine gun at him, all the while yelling angrily in his face. "Idiot! Idiot!" Then he started shrieking in Chechen.

David's complexion went ashen as he put the pieces of the conversation together. "Jesus Christ!" he whispered to Carolyn out of the side of his mouth. "They've planted a huge bomb somewhere up here!"

"Are they going to blow us all up?" Carolyn asked apprehensively. "You know, just after they leave?"

David shook his head. "More likely it's a safeguard against an attack. If the rescue attempt looks as if it's succeeding, they'll detonate the bomb by remote control and kill everybody, including the President."

"So we're all going to die, no matter what," Carolyn moaned.

Not if the Secret Service was warned, David thought. Maybe they could avert the disaster. But first they'd have to find the explosive device. Where would the terrorists place a bomb to implode the entire Pavilion? Not on the Pavilion itself. They'd probably plant it in the crawlspace between the ninth and tenth floors. And there might well be more than one bomb. Somehow they had to be disarmed. But how?

Aliev barked a string of orders to the balding terrorist, then shoved him over to David and Carolyn.

To David, Aliev said, "Fix your wound and be quick about it."

They moved down the corridor, the balding terrorist one step in back of them and muttering to himself in Chechen. The smell of feces and vomit permeated the air. Someone close by was throwing up noisily. David ignored the odors and sounds, still concentrating on warning the Secret Service. If the detonators weren't deactivated, they'd all die.

They came to the nurses' station, where Jarrin Smith and the Russian security agent were being guarded by a terrorist standing near the elevator. David noticed the bloodstained towel on Jarrin's upper arm. Then his gaze went to the large telephone on the desk in front of the ward clerk.

David wondered why the terrorists hadn't ripped out the phone, as they'd done all the others. *Because they wanted a secure landline in case their cell phones malfunctioned*, he reasoned. The Chechen guard nudged him on with the barrel of his Uzi, but David held up a hand, as if to request a brief stop, then began rearranging the bandage on his thigh. But his peripheral vision stayed on the telephone. During his entire time in the crawlspace he hadn't heard the phone ring. Not once. But there should have been an avalanche of incoming calls since the news was now out that the President was a patient on the Beaumont Pavilion. Why no calls?

Then the answer came to him. Hospital officials would have anticipated the deluge and had all the incoming patient-related calls diverted to an information officer. And what about outgoing calls? Every word would be monitored by the Secret Service! Every word!

David rapidly turned to Carolyn and said in a whisper, "When I tell you, go into the treatment room and get a roll of sterile gauze and some tape. And take your time getting them."

Carolyn nervously licked her lips. "Okay."

David turned to the balding terrorist and motioned to the wound, then to the treatment room.

The guard stared back quizzically, not understanding.

"Go," David said to Carolyn, then knelt down to examine Jarrin's wound. It was superficial and mostly clotted over. Moving even closer to Jarrin, he whispered, "When you see the chance, dislodge the receiver off its hook, but make sure it stays on the phone. Then, with your elbow, punch 0 for the hospital operator. Eventually she'll answer. When you hear her voice, tell her there's a bomb in the crawlspace between the ninth and tenth floors."

Jarrin's brow went up. "What!"

"Just do it," David urged.

Carolyn returned with a roll of gauze and handed it to David. He carefully dressed Jarrin's wound and repeated, "Bomb in the crawlspace between the ninth and tenth floors!" Then he turned to the Russian security agent, Yudenko, and asked quietly, "Do you speak English?"

The Russian agent nodded.

"And you heard what I just said?"

The agent nodded again.

"After I leave, do something to divert the guard's attention so Jarrin can dislodge the phone."

The balding terrorist yelled impatiently at David and gestured with his Uzi. "Move! And do it now!"

So the little bastard speaks good English after all, David thought to himself. "We're almost done," he said and quickly turned to Carolyn. "Tape the dressing in place and hurry it up."

Carolyn tore off a strip of tape and applied it firmly to the edge of the bandage, then asked the ward clerk, "Is this causing you any pain?"

"No," Jarrin replied before lowering his voice to a whisper so the terrorist couldn't hear him. "They found the loosened metal spike in the elevator door and drove it back in."

Carolyn swallowed anxiously and whispered back, "Did they see me pry it up?"

"I don't know, but they sure discovered it real fast," Jarrin answered.

"Oh, shit," Carolyn muttered under her breath.

The balding terrorist poked her ribs with his Uzi. "Move now or I shoot!"

As they walked down the corridor, Carolyn was still wondering if the terrorists had seen her loosening the metal spike. Probably not, she reasoned. If they had, she'd now be dead. Carolyn took a deep breath and calmed her nerves. *Be smart*, she told herself. *Don't take risky chances.*

They entered the treatment room and switched on the bright overhead lights. David sat on the side of the operating table and ripped his pants leg open, exposing the entire wound. It was a deep gash with ragged edges that had been torn away by the passing bullet. Much of the wound was located laterally, and was difficult for David to see.

"I'm going to have trouble putting the sutures in," he said.

"I can do it," Carolyn volunteered, grabbing a metal stool and pulling it over. "How would you like it cleaned?"

"Flush it with sterile saline, then pour some alcohol and peroxide into it," David instructed.

The guard stood outside the door with his back to them, but David was sure the man had his ears pricked, listening to every word.

"This is going to sting," Carolyn warned.

"Don't worry about it."

Carolyn poured a liter of saline into the wound, cleaning out the old blood and debris as well as the dirt on the margins. Then she began flooding the area with the mixture of alcohol and peroxide. "Here comes the sting."

David looked over to the door, then dropped his head and lowered his voice, "Be careful what you say. The guard understands English and he's listening."

"I know," Carolyn said quietly. "What was the purpose of telling me to be slow in getting the gauze from the treatment room?"

"I needed time to tell Jarrin to dislodge the receiver on the phone and attempt to reach the hospital operator," David answered in a low voice. "And tell her about the bomb."

"He's not going to be able to do that with the guard watching him."

"He might, if the Russian security agent can cause a diversion."

"Do you really think they can do it?"

"Probably not. But it's worth a try."

The guard at the door turned to study them. David feigned a grimace at the fluid in his wound, then murmured to Carolyn, "Get busy with the wound. Our guard is watching us."

Carolyn sponged away clotted blood and waited for the guard to look away before she spoke again. "My God, you had me worried! I thought you were dead."

"I came pretty close," David said, his voice very low. "Those bullets kept whizzing by my head. One was so near to my nose I swear I could smell it."

Carolyn quickly peeked over to the guard, then came back to David. "Was all that blood dripping down from the ceiling yours?"

David shook his head. "The first batch came from the agent. I think he caught one in the neck."

"Or head," Carolyn added softly.

"Or in his head," David agreed. "Whatever the source, he bled enough to give away his position and mine."

Carolyn poured more peroxide into the wound. "Are they going to try another rescue?"

"Probably," David said, hoping against hope that his message about the Mogadishu operation got through to the Secret Service. "And soon, I think."

"What are our chances?"

"Not good."

Carolyn raised her voice intentionally and spoke in a professional tone. "There's one area that's bleeding fairly briskly."

"Is the blood red or maroon?" David asked.

"Maroon."

"Then it's coming from a vein. See if you can put an absorbable suture around it."

Carolyn opened up a suture kit and placed it on the bed. After donning a pair of surgical gloves, she spread the wound apart to better expose the bleeding site. "Do you want some Xylocaine?"

David shook his head. "Just do it."

Carolyn expertly ran a suture around the bleeding vein and tied it off. The blood flow stopped immediately. "How would you like me to handle the rest of the wound?"

"Use absorbable sutures on the deeper layers and metal clips on the skin."

"Are you sure you don't want me to inject some Xylocaine?"

David stared straight ahead without answering. He blanked out the discomfort by thinking about Somalia and the helicopter crash, the pain in his jaw so terrible he wanted to scream and cry and tear his hair out. But he bore the awful pain in silence as they fought their way back to the base. And later, aboard a destroyer, they wouldn't let him look at himself in the mirror. The disfigurement was that bad. And that was only the beginning of the nightmare.

"All done," Carolyn said, painting the area with an antiseptic before covering the wound with a thick gauze.

"You're pretty good at this," David complimented.

"Six years as an ER nurse does wonders for one's ability to suture."

"At University's ER?"

"No. At L.A. County."

"What made you come over here?"

"It was closer to home," she said without going into details.

Carolyn used an alcohol sponge to clean off the blood and dirt high above the sutured wound. There she noticed another large wound at least two inches long, but this one was old and scarred over. She ran her finger along it and felt some nodularity deep within. "God! Where did this one come from?"

"From long ago," David said vaguely.

"Big secret, eh?"

David hesitated before muttering, "I was in the military."

Carolyn stared up at him. "Is that how you got the scar on your chin, too?"

David stood and stretched his leg. It hurt like hell, but no blood came through the dressing. He gave Carolyn a long look. He did not want to talk about his past. Moreover, he was raised with the dictum that real men didn't discuss their pain. They just endured it. Yet he found himself talking about the events that he had hidden away almost twenty years ago.

"It was a helicopter crash in Somalia," he was saying. "The enemy opened up just as we were taking off. The aircraft caught on fire and we had to jump. I hit the tarmac and shattered my anterior jaw, among other things."

Carolyn studied his chin and the old scar that ran along it. "They did a pretty fair job of putting it back together."

"It's not my chin you see," David told her. "It's a plastic one. I had some good people looking after me."

For a moment Carolyn saw sadness in David's eyes, but it quickly vanished. "When did all this—?"

David raised a hand, stopping the questions. "Enough about me," he said, walking around the treatment room and testing his leg. "Let's talk about you. How did you get to be so good with your hands?"

"I learned to suture in the ER at—"

"No, no," David interrupted. "Not the suturing. I was referring to the way you removed the clogged filter from the ceiling duct, and the way you repaired the wire that was giving off sparks in the crawlspace. How did you learn to do those things?"

"Out of necessity," Carolyn answered quietly. "My dad died when I was a teenager, so my mom and I had to fend for ourselves. She was a schoolteacher and didn't make much, so we had to learn how to fix things around the house. She was all thumbs, and I ended up doing most of the work." Carolyn looked away and sighed sadly. "Now I have to do everything for her. My mother used to be so bright and active, but all that's changed. Now she's slowly withering away with Alzheimer's. Sometimes she recognizes me and smiles. Other times, she just stares out into space."

"A nightmare," David remarked quietly.

"And it'll be even more of a nightmare if I don't make it out of here," Carolyn went on. "Because I'm the only person left in the family to look after her."

"We've all got people on the outside to worry about," David said in a somber voice, thinking about Kit, his concern for her almost unbearable. *What will my little girl do without me?* he wondered miserably. *Who will be there to protect her?* David thought briefly about the safeguards he had provided for his daughter. There was a two-million-dollar life insurance policy, and Juanita had agreed to serve as her legal guardian. But Kit would still be parentless, all alone in many ways, and scarred for the rest of her life.

Carolyn tried to read his expression and thought she saw a hint of sadness. "Are your parents still alive?"

"Both gone," David said, coming out of his reverie. "Both killed by terrorists."

Carolyn's brow went up. "What!"

David nodded slowly. "My father was a military attaché at the American embassy in Nairobi. My mother was the program director. They were out on a Sunday drive when terrorists blew up their car and killed them instantly. I was a junior in college at the time."

"You must have been shattered."

David nodded again. "And angry as hell. I applied for Special Forces the day after I was notified of their deaths."

"Do you have any family at all?" Carolyn asked.

"A young daughter," David replied. "And she has nobody in the world but me."

"How old is she?"

"Eleven."

Carolyn groaned sympathetically.

"Yeah," David said, his face closing. *Enough small talk*, he told himself and tested his leg again. He was still limping, but not as much. And the pain seemed less severe.

"How's the leg?"

"Good," David said, glancing down and seeing no blood on the dressing. "Let's hope your sutures hold."

"They will," Carolyn assured him. "But it still might be best to wrap an elastic bandage around the dressing."

David walked over to the supply cabinet and opened the top drawer. On one side were elastic wraps, on the other sterile instruments wrapped in cellophane. There were neat stacks of forceps and hemostats and scalpels. David's eyes focused in on the scalpels. He casually turned to Carolyn. "Could you step over here for a moment?"

Carolyn came to his side. "What?"

In a barely audible voice, David told her, "I want you to come in closer and block the guard's line of vision."

"No problem," Carolyn said quietly, her body now touching his. She felt the electricity running through her, and knew he sensed it too. They stayed close together, neither wanting to move apart.

"Sometimes, David," she murmured ever so softly, "you take my breath away."

"You've been doing that to me for a long time," David murmured back.

"Jesus! What a hell of a time for us to find out!"

"Some people never do."

Carolyn sighed sadly and rested her head on his shoulder. "'Better late than never' sounds kind of empty right now."

"Don't give up yet," David encouraged, touching her left hand. "Slowly drop this arm so the guard can't see the drawer." He waited for her to perform the maneuver and added, "Perfect! Hold it there."

With a single motion, David reached for the scalpel and tried to slip it between the tongue blades and pocket flashlight in the upper pocket of his white coat. But something was blocking its way.

The terrorist at the doorway was suddenly suspicious of what they were doing at the cabinet. He moved in for a closer look.

"Start talking about the patients," David whispered out of the corner of his mouth. He turned away from the guard and let the scalpel fall into the side pocket of his coat.

"I see where you had to start bretylium in Dr. Warren."

Carolyn nodded. "He began having a lot of PVCs again, despite the lidocaine."

"But he still has a normal sinus rhythm. Right?"

Carolyn nodded once more. "Yeah, but I have the awful feeling he's going to die on us. His color is really bad."

The guard studied them briefly, then grunted to himself and went back into the doorway. But he stood sideways, so he could keep an eye on them.

"Warren couldn't look any worse than Marci," David said. "Her pericardial effusion is getting bigger and bigger, and it'll soon reduce her cardiac output to zilch."

"Is there any way to remove some of that fluid?" Carolyn asked.

"Not without a pericardiocentesis," David replied. "You wouldn't happen to have a pericardiocentesis tray on the Pavilion, would you?"

Carolyn shook her head. "We've had no need for one."

"Until now."

They abruptly jerked their heads around, both startled by the sounds of a loud commotion in the corridor. Someone was frantically crying out in Chechen. Then there were return shouts and yells. The terrorist at the door turned and pointed his Uzi at them.

"Stay!" he bellowed.

Carolyn moved in closer to David and whispered, "Do you think it's a rescue?"

"I don't know," David whispered back. "But if you hear shots or an explosion, drop to the floor behind the operating table."

Now they heard footsteps in the corridor, running toward them. And more yelling.

David took Carolyn's hand and said, "Be ready to hit the deck."

Suddenly Aliev appeared in the doorway and waved his weapon at them. "You had better come quickly. Your President is bleeding to death."

NINETEEN

The Vice President closely studied the diagram of the Beaumont Pavilion projected onto a large wall screen. It showed precise measurements and details of every suite, including the positions of the beds, furniture, and fixtures.

"I don't like either plan," Halloway said. "Both place the President at too much risk."

"Particularly the one that blows a hole in the roof above the President's suite," Alderman concurred. "God knows how much debris could come down and crush him."

"And the plan to come up through the President's bathroom isn't a whole lot better," Halloway went on. "They'd have to blast their way up through thick marble tile."

"And all those heavy fixtures would probably drop to the floor below," Alderman added. "The entire bathroom could crash down and clutter up everything. Can you imagine the Secret Service team having to climb up through all that mess? They'd never reach the President in time."

"They claim they can control the blast and the size of hole it makes," Halloway argued mildly.

"Are you willing to bet the President's life on that?" Alderman asked.

"We may have no choice." Halloway's gaze went back to the diagram of the President's suite. There was a distance of twenty feet from the bed to the far side of the bathroom. If the blast hole was small enough, and if half the bedroom didn't come crashing down, the team would have a chance to get to the President. But not much of a chance, she had to admit. And what about Merrill's family? *They would probably die, and the President would never forgive us for saving him at the expense of his wife and daughter.*

At length she said, "I think we might be forced to go with the second plan."

There were loud murmurs and some grumbling at the conference table. Several members of the council were shaking their heads.

"If anyone has a better idea, let's have it," Halloway said sharply and waited for a response.

The room quieted. No one offered an alternative way to rescue the President. All eyes went to Ellen Halloway as the council members awaited her final decision. The digital clock clicked off another minute.

"Madam Vice President, you must leave the option to negotiate open," Alderman counseled. "If we move quickly we can send out orders to have those Chechen prisoners on transport planes within the hour."

Halloway shook her head. "The terrorists will just keep asking for more and more, and you know it. Releasing those prisoners will not save John Merrill's life."

"But it will buy us time to think our way out of this dreadful mess," Alderman argued.

Halloway hesitated, feeling caught between a rock and a hard place. All of her options were faulty and dangerous, with far-reaching consequences that would go on and on. Terrible consequences! *What would you do, John Merrill? What would you do if you were in my place?* She could sense the council's eyes on her, waiting for a decision. Clearing her throat, she asked, "Is Prime Minister Sergei Roskovich in charge of Russia now?"

"Yes," Alderman answered. "In the absence of their President, the Prime Minister assumes power."

"A tough customer," Halloway said, more to herself than to the others. She recalled Roskovich from a state visit to Moscow a few years back. He was a short, slender man with tight lips and cold, dark eyes. Before the breakup of the Soviet Union, he was reputed to be the second most powerful person in the KGB.

"Double tough," Alderman emphasized. "Roskovich is a real hard-liner."

"He won't budge an inch," Toliver agreed with a firm nod. "Not even a millimeter."

"We'll see," Halloway said, undeterred. "Get Roskovich on the line."

Alderman signaled to an aide standing near the communications room, then said to Halloway, "I know it's bitter medicine to negotiate, but it may be the best road to take for now."

"Negotiation is appeasement," Toliver said harshly.

"It may be the only way to save the President," Alderman argued.

"There may be another way." Toliver quickly stood to address the group. "I have a suggestion for us to consider."

"Let's hear it," the Vice President said.

Toliver went over to the diagram on the screen and pointed to the rooms adjoining the suites of the First Family. "The Secretary of State and his wife are situated in suites next to the President and his daughter. We could blast our way into the rooms of the Secretary and his wife, get our team in, and isolate the President and his family from the terrorists. And we wouldn't have to worry about the size of the hole the explosives made in the floor."

Halloway considered the proposal, carefully weighing the risks involved. The chance of killing the President was less, but it still existed, no matter how cautious they were. Yet the new plan did move the President farther away from the blasts, and that was its main advantage. She nodded to herself, thinking that Toliver's plan was the best one offered so far, or at least seemed so on the surface. Finally, Halloway said, "Of course, the Secretary of State and his wife may well end up dead."

Toliver shrugged, showing little concern. "That would be regrettable. But as you yourself acknowledged earlier, everyone except the President is expendable."

Halloway nodded slowly. She had said it and she had meant it. There would be no exceptions. She looked over to Alderman and asked, "Arthur, what do you think?"

Alderman thought for a moment, then said, "We're still talking about a double explosion that could bring down the entire wing, and that would be an unmitigated disaster. But that aside, Martin's plan has merit."

"It just might be workable," Halloway said cautiously. "Workable, but still very dangerous. All it takes is one terrorist near John Merrill, and our President is dead."

Her eyes went to the digital clock on the wall. The deadline was fifty-eight minutes away.

The communications officer called out, "Madam Vice President, we have the Russian Prime Minister on the line."

Halloway turned to Alderman. "As I recall, his English is reasonably good."

"It is when he wants it to be," Alderman replied.

Halloway pushed a button on the speakerphone. "Prime Minister Roskovich, this is Vice President Halloway. Can you hear me clearly?"

"Yes, Madam Vice President," he replied in an accented voice.

"I'm calling to inform you that we are doing everything possible to free all the hostages, including your President and Foreign Minister."

"We know you are, Madam Vice President. Can we offer you any assistance?"

"No, not at this time, thank you."

There was a pause. Halloway could hear some Russian chatter in the background. The only word she understood was *Moscow*.

Roskovich returned to the line. "If you wish, we can send you some of the sleeping gas we used on terrorists in the Moscow theater. It is much better—how shall I say?—is better perfected than before."

Halloway recalled the incident. Chechen terrorists had taken over a theater in Moscow and threatened to kill all the hostages unless their demands were met. The Russians responded by releasing sleeping gas into the ventilation system of the theater. But they apparently used too much or misjudged the potency of the gas. In the end all the terrorists were killed, but so were over a hundred innocent people. "Not for now, thank you," Halloway said.

"Well then, good luck to you and your forces," Roskovich concluded. "Like you, we will never negotiate with the Chechen terrorists, even if it means losing our President. After all, Madam Vice President, the office of the Presidency is much larger than any one man. Or any one woman," he added darkly. "We all realize that, don't we?"

"Yes," Halloway replied, her voice softer than she wanted. "Much larger."

"Please keep us informed."

The phone clicked off.

Halloway leaned back. "He didn't seem too upset at the prospect of losing his President."

"You can never read those ex-KGB people," Alderman told her. "They're as stone-faced as they come."

"And he's not going to budge when it comes to releasing prisoners," Halloway went on. "That's why he offered us the sleeping gas, which he knew we'd refuse. He was telling us that no matter how many deaths it takes, they won't give in to the terrorists."

"And for good reason," Toliver said. "They know damn well the terrorists will just use Suslev until he's of no more use. They realize they can never save their President by negotiating. And negotiation won't save ours either."

Halloway reached for a cup of lukewarm coffee and sipped it, thinking about advice that John Merrill gave when it came to making difficult decisions. *Find the core question and answer it. Everything else will fall into place.* There was currently one major question that kept gnawing at her over and over. *Should I negotiate with the Chechen terrorists? Should I exclude the Russians and try to cut a deal? After all, Chechnya's quest for independence wasn't really our problem. Why not let the—?*

"Madam Vice President," the communications officer called out as he hurried into the room, "we're picking up activity at an air base in northern Mexico. Our infrared satellites are detecting heat flares."

"Which means?" Halloway asked, quickly clearing her mind.

"Their jets are preparing to take off," the officer replied.

"How many?"

"Four."

All eyes went to the large video screen. Four red dots were pulsating in an area well north of Mexico City. Gradually the dots began to fade, the images becoming blurry.

"Our radar should pick them up shortly," the officer said.

A moment later another picture appeared on the screen. It clearly showed the silhouettes of four aircraft heading northward in formation.

"That will be their interceptor fighters," Toliver said, watching the jets beginning to take a more westerly course. As he continued to study the screen, a shadow of worry crossed his face. "Perhaps we should reconsider calling the President of Mexico."

Halloway strummed her fingers on the conference table, weighing the advantages and disadvantages of a phone conversation with the President of Mexico. She would have to admit that the U.S. government had sanctioned the killing of Mexican citizens, and he would be furious, regardless of the reason. He would demand the plane land immediately and surrender to Mexican authorities. She wasn't about to let that happen, and she wasn't going to tell him about the hostage situation, either. The only advantage of the call would be to try to smooth things over with Mexico, and at this moment that wasn't very important.

"What do you want to do?" Alderman pressed.

"Plot the course of the Mexican jets and see where they're headed," Halloway ordered briskly.

"And what about the *Reagan*, Madam Vice President?" Sanders asked. "They're still steaming due west with the wind."

"Have them turn about."

"And our Hornets?"

"On deck and ready to launch."

TWENTY

THEY WEREN'T ABLE TO stem the President's bleeding. Blood kept gushing up around his nasogastric tube and into the back of his throat. He spat out one mouthful after another.

David hurriedly aspirated Merrill's gastric juice into a large syringe. It was colored deep red. The hemorrhaging was not letting up, not even a little. He quickly filled the syringe with ice water and again lavaged the President's stomach.

"David," Carolyn said urgently. "His pressure is down to ninety over sixty, and dropping."

"I know, I know." David wiped the beads of perspiration from his forehead with the back of his hand, and tried to think of a way to raise the President's systolic pressure. *I've got to replenish his intravascular volume or he'll go into shock, and I've got to do it without any blood or plasma. But how? How the hell do I do that?* His gaze went up to the IV bag above Merrill's bed. "Open up the albumin drip all the way."

"It *is* open all the way." Carolyn called back.

"Then put your hands around the plastic bag and squeeze it," David directed. "That'll push in more albumin faster."

Carolyn reached up and applied firm pressure to the plastic bag, using both hands. The albumin-saline solution began running into the President's arm in a steady stream. Carolyn looked down at Merrill, with his ghostly white color. His gown and sheet and pillowcase were heavily soaked in red. She glanced over to the cardiac monitor and reported, "His pressure is up to eighty-eight."

"Keep squeezing," David urged. "You've got to maintain his systolic pressure above ninety."

"I'll try," Carolyn said, her eyes still on the monitor. "Oh, hell. He's dropping again."

"Squeeze the bag harder!"

Merrill started gagging and choking as more blood accumulated in the back of his throat. He now had trouble catching his breath. Gasping, he hawked up maroon-colored phlegm and asked, "Dr. Ballineau, am … am I dying?"

"Not yet," David replied calmly, beginning another ice-water lavage.

"I'll want to know," Merrill gulped. "I'll want to say goodbye to my wife."

"I understand," David acknowledged.

Carolyn sighed to herself, moved by the President's words. The man was looking at death, and the only thing on his mind was saying goodbye to his wife. *I'd like to be loved like that*, she thought wistfully. *And love someone back the same way.* The President suddenly groaned. Carolyn jerked her head down.

"What's that, Mr. President?"

"I've got a pain in my side," Merrill complained.

"Where?"

"By my right hip."

Carolyn quickly examined the area. Merrill was lying on the sharp edge of a used, wrinkled plastic bag of albumin in saline. She reached for the bag and tossed it aside. "Better?"

"Much," Merrill replied, inhaling deeply, his throat now clear. "I think I'm breathing easier, too."

"And I think we're making some progress with the ice-water lavage," David informed him. He held up the syringe containing the gastric contents he'd just aspirated. Its color was halfway between pink and red.

"Has the bleeding stopped?" Merrill asked.

"No," David answered honestly. "But it's slowed, and that's a good start."

"Will it begin again?" Merrill asked anxiously.

"Let's hope not," David said. But he knew it was just a matter of time before the hemorrhaging returned. And the next time they wouldn't be able to stop it, or even slow it. The simple fact was that whatever Factor VIII the President still had in his blood was quickly being used up by his continued bleeding and poor clot formation. It wouldn't take much of a bleed to kill him now.

David lavaged Merrill's stomach once more. The gastric contents were pink, with no clots present. He glanced over to the monitor. Merrill's blood pressure was 95/60 and climbing.

"Good news, Mr. President," David told him. "I think we've got a handle on it now."

"Thank you," Merrill said gratefully, and closed his eyes.

David motioned for Carolyn to follow him into the bathroom, well out of earshot from the President. The terrorist at the door stepped in so he could keep an eye on them. "One more big bleed and the President is dead," David said quietly. "And there's nothing we can do about it."

"Won't the ice-water lavage hold him?" Carolyn asked.

"Not for long," David answered. "He could break loose again in a matter of minutes."

"Shit!"

"Yeah."

"We're going to be famous," Carolyn said disgustedly. "We'll be known as the people who let the President die while we just stood by and watched."

"I guess." David tried to think through the dilemma, but knew there was no answer to the problem. Without blood or plasma transfusions or Factor VIII replacement, the President was as good as dead.

"I think you should speak with the head terrorist again," Carolyn suggested. "If you stress how desperate the situation is, maybe he'll let them send up more blood for the President."

David shook his head. "He won't change his mind. Never in a million years."

"Why not?"

"Because he's got a secure situation, and he plans to keep it that way."

"But how can he be threatened by a couple of units of blood?" Carolyn asked.

"You'd be surprised," David said. He, like Aliev, knew that all it would take was one little breach, one small opening, and the enemy would find a way to use it to his advantage. "It's similar to asking how a dumbwaiter can end up threatening the life of the President of the United States. On the surface, a dumbwaiter sounds innocuous, but here it turned out to be deadly, didn't it?"

"But surely they don't want the President to die," Carolyn argued. "A dead President is of no use to them."

"Sure he is," David countered. "They just won't let the outside world know. And after their demands are met, they'll load his body into a helicopter and fly off, promising to release him later."

"Jesus!" Carolyn cringed. "How can people be so cold-blooded?"

David gestured with his hands, but he knew the answer. Just instill enough hatred in them, then train them how to kill. That's all it took. Like the terrorists in Mogadishu who had known nothing but dire poverty and felt they had little to live for, but plenty to die for—particularly if they could kill infidels in the process. Death in battle held no fear for them because it promised eternal happiness in paradise. And so they killed and died eagerly, yelling with their last breath that "God is great."

And the Chechen terrorists were no different from the ones in Mogadishu. They were ruthless and cold-blooded, longing to kill and not afraid to die. They were perfect soldiers. And perfect bastards who were more than willing to blow up a hospital and murder a lot of innocent people. *With a bomb! A goddamn bomb!*

"We've got to do something," Carolyn said, breaking into his thoughts.

"Yeah," David agreed. "But what?"

Carolyn shrugged helplessly. "I don't know."

"The only thing that will really help is a unit of fresh whole blood," David said. "With anything else we're wasting our time."

Carolyn nodded dejectedly. "And even if the terrorists agreed to let the blood come up, we'd still have a problem finding a match for Merrill. Remember how difficult he was to cross match earlier. And to make matters even worse, he's got a rare blood type, very rare. He's AB negative."

David's eyes suddenly lit up. "Are you absolutely certain about his blood type?"

"Yes," Carolyn said, trying to read his face. "Why?"

"Are you doubly sure?"

"Yes," Carolyn said and headed for the bedside. "Apparently, the blood bank was able to get a match for him after all. Come on and I'll show you."

At the foot of the bed she reached into a trash can and extracted an empty plastic bag that had been used to transfuse the President. She held it up and pointed to the label. "See? It's AB negative."

"That's my blood type."

"So?"

"So we can use my blood to transfuse the President," David explained rapidly. "It'll be risky, but it's all we have to offer. And it just might work."

Carolyn hesitated, a look of concern coming across her face. "What if he has a bad transfusion reaction?"

"That's a risk we'll have to take," David said at once. "This is his only chance, Carolyn. It's either do or die."

Carolyn nodded slowly. David was right. But she also realized that a severe transfusion reaction could be fatal, particularly in a patient whose condition was already so fragile. "We could give the President a small amount of your blood as a test dose."

"Right," David agreed immediately.

"But there's a problem," Carolyn warned.

"What?"

"We don't have the setup to draw your blood and put it in a plastic bag to transfuse the President. Only the blood bank has that."

"There's a way to get around that."

"How?"

"Come on," David said, taking her hand. "I'll show you."

They ran out of the suite and down the corridor, the terrorist guarding them close behind. Aliev came alongside, running hard to keep up. Two more terrorists appeared out of doorways, their Uzis at the ready.

"Where are you going?" Aliev huffed.

"To the treatment room," David told him.

"Why?"

"For medicine to stop the President's bleeding."

Aliev moved aside and yelled out orders in Chechen. The other terrorists peeled off and went back to their duties. Except for the balding one. He remained close to David, even entering the treatment room with him.

David ignored the terrorist and asked Carolyn, "How many heparinized test tubes have you got?"

"Let me count." Carolyn hurriedly opened a drawer and removed two cartons of test tubes that were coated with the anticoagulant heparin. "I've got forty-two tubes, each ten ccs."

David calculated rapidly. "That's a total volume of over four hundred ccs we can use for transfusion."

"But how do we pool forty-two tubes of blood into a transfusable unit?" Carolyn said.

"That's easy," David explained. "And this is how we'll do it. Using a Vacutainer, I want you to draw my blood into all forty-two tubes. The blood won't clot because it'll be heparinized. We'll then take big 50-cc syringes and aspirate up the blood from the test tubes. In the end we'll have over eight large syringes filled with my blood."

Carolyn nodded quickly, now catching on. "And we'll connect those syringes to the President's IV line and slowly inject your blood. It'll be like giving him eight mini-transfusions."

"You got it," David said, nodding back. "Grab a tourniquet and get started."

Carolyn reached for a Velcro tourniquet and placed it tightly around David's arm, then waited for a vein to pop up. "We'd better keep in mind that you've already lost a lot of blood, David. You may not have much to spare."

"I've got a hell of a lot more than the President does, and I'm not the one dying," David said. "So let's get on with it."

Carolyn found a vein in David's antecubital fossa and expertly slid the needle in. As blood began to drip out, she pushed a test tube into the Vacutainer and watched it fill up with blood. Quickly she went through one test tube after another, loading each to the brim. Within minutes she had filled twenty tubes. "If you start to feel weak, let me know."

"I'm fine," David said, taking a deep breath. Suddenly he was aware of the perfume she was wearing. It was a fragrance he was familiar with. His late wife had used it. "Is that Arpège you have on?"

"It is." Carolyn looked up at him and smiled. "How did you know?"

"Can I tell you another time?" David asked evasively.

"You sure can," Carolyn said, removing a filled test tube from the Vacutainer and pushing in a fresh one. "If we ever get out of here, you're going to have a lot of stories to tell me, aren't you?"

"Just a few."

"Liar," she said, still smiling.

The terrorist guarding them moved in for a closer look. He obviously didn't understand what was going on. He muttered something in Chechen and pointed to the thirty-two test tubes filled with David's blood.

The smile vanished from Carolyn's face. "What do you think he wants?"

"Nothing important," David replied. "Otherwise he'd speak in English."

The terrorist's expression tightened. "Why blood?"

"For the President," David answered.

"Oh," the terrorist said and backed off.

Carolyn continued filling test tubes, one after another. David's blood seemed to be flowing much faster now. "Three more to go," she announced. "Do you want to aspirate the blood into the large syringes in here?"

"No," David said after a brief pause. "We'll do it in the President's suite. That way one of us can be aspirating the blood into a syringe while the other is injecting the blood into the President's IV line."

Carolyn shook her head in admiration. "Is there anything you haven't thought of?"

"I haven't thought of a way to get us out of here."

"But you will, won't you?"

"We'll see."

Carolyn watched the last test tube fill, then removed the tourniquet and needle from David's arm. Quickly she gathered up all the test tubes as well as a carton of 50-cc syringes and a handful of #16 gauge needles. "All set!"

David jumped off the operating table and headed for the door. Abruptly he stopped and put his hand on Carolyn's shoulder to steady himself. The room started to spin.

"Are you all right?"

"Just getting my sea legs," David said and waited for the wooziness to pass. Gradually the spinning sensation stopped and his balance returned. "Okay, let's go."

They walked quickly down the corridor, David keeping his arm hooked into Carolyn's. He tried not to lean on her, but found himself doing it anyway. And now his legs felt heavy as lead.

"You're not all right," Carolyn hissed, becoming alarmed.

"It'll pass," David attempted to reassure her.

"No, it won't. And you know it."

"Once we get the President squared away, we'll infuse a liter of saline into me. That'll expand my intravascular volume and I'll be fine."

"You'd better not get sick and leave me here all alone, David Ballineau."

"I don't plan to," he said, gritting his teeth together and willing his body to remain steady.

As they approached the President's suite, the alarm on his cardiac monitor suddenly sounded. *Ping! Ping! Ping!* They dashed into the room and found Merrill draped over the edge of the bed, head down, with blood pouring out of his mouth and onto the floor.

"Oh, my God," Carolyn gasped.

"Start filling the syringes!" David yelled and rushed to the President's side.

The cardiac monitor showed that John Merrill had no blood pressure.

TWENTY-ONE

"WHAT DO YOU THINK?" Halloway asked Joe Geary over the speakerphone.

"That was our first and best option," Geary answered without hesitation. "Unfortunately, ma'am, there's a problem with any plan that goes through the adjacent rooms. A big problem. We discovered that the main support for that wing passes under the floor of the suites where the Secretary of State and his wife are located. If we set off our blasts there, the entire side of the Pavilion would collapse."

Halloway shook her head despairingly. "Are you sure of that?"

"Yes, ma'am," Geary replied. "We had it checked by a structural engineer."

"So you've settled on the plan to blast your way in through the President's bathroom. Is that correct?" Halloway asked.

"Yes, ma'am," Geary said. "For now."

"What do you mean 'for now'?" Halloway asked quickly. "Are you considering other options?"

"No, ma'am," Geary told her. "We'll go with plan one. But if things suddenly change at the hostage site and we see a less risky opportunity to save the President, we'll take it."

Halloway didn't respond. She did not like a fly-by-the-seat-of-your-pants operation. She glanced at the expressions of the other council members. They were all stone-faced.

"Sometimes, ma'am," Geary went on, "unforeseeable events occur, and everything changes in a matter of seconds."

"Yeah," Toliver groused in a low voice. "Like the Mexican police suddenly showing up to protect a drug lord, and damn near ruining everything."

"Hold for a minute," Halloway said and pushed a button on the speakerphone. Then she gave Toliver a stern look. "Keep in mind we're amateurs when it comes to rescue attempts and they're professionals. So we'd better listen to every word they utter. They're our best and only hope."

Toliver slouched down in his chair, unconvinced and grumbling to himself, obviously not in favor of giving the Secret Service free rein. He glanced around the conference table, looking for supporters, but found none.

Halloway watched Martin Toliver sulk, detesting the man and his boorish behavior. Keeping her face even, she returned to the speakerphone. "Agent Geary, how far away are you from Los Angeles?"

"One hour and twenty-four minutes," Geary replied.

Halloway's eyes went to the digital clock on the wall. There were forty-eight minutes until the deadline. When the Secret Service plane landed they would be thirty-six minutes late. Two hostages were certain to have been executed. One at the deadline, a second thirty minutes later.

"Keep us informed." Halloway switched the phone off, then gazed around at the council and said with a sigh, "They'll never get back in time. And because of that, two innocent people are going to die."

"There's not much we can do about it," Walter Pierce said. "The plane is flying at top speed."

"Somehow we've got to buy another hour," Halloway urged.

"Our only choice is to release the Chechen prisoners," Alderman said, checking the clock. "If we hurry, there still may be time."

"What good would that do us?" Toliver challenged. "The Russians won't negotiate, and the terrorists won't go for half a pie."

Halloway jerked her head around. "How do you know that?"

"Know what?"

"That the terrorists won't go for half a pie."

Toliver shrugged. "They never do."

"I'm afraid Martin is right," Alderman interjected. "It's almost always all or nothing with these bastards."

"Let's find out for sure," Halloway said and signaled to the communications officer. "I need to talk with the commanding general at Guantanamo Bay."

"What are you planning to offer Aliev?' Alderman asked.

"Everything and nothing," Halloway said mysteriously.

She reached for the list of Chechen prisoners that had been faxed to the National Security Council. Somehow the terrorists had learned where every one of their fighters was imprisoned. There were twelve at Guantanamo Bay. None of the names were Arabic, but then Halloway knew that Chechens weren't Arabs. They were from the Northern Caucasus region of the Russian Federation. And the type of terrorists the Russians and everybody else feared the most. Homegrown terrorists who knew the people and the customs and the terrain. They melted in with the rest of the population—until the killing started.

The communications officer called out, "Ma'am, I have General Nichols on the line."

Halloway leaned forward and spoke into the phone. "General Nichols, this is Vice President Halloway."

"Yes, ma'am."

"General, I'm going to fax a list of Chechens we have imprisoned at Gitmo. There are twelve in all."

"I'm well aware of the Chechens, ma'am," Nichols said promptly.

"Do they have a leader?"

"Yes, ma'am," Nichols reported. "Give me a moment to get his file."

Halloway heard an order being issued, then the sound of papers being ruffled. She quickly organized the commands she was about to give.

Nichols' voice came over the speakerphone. "Their leader goes by the name of Shamil."

"Have him dressed and informed that he's about to be released," Halloway directed. "Then bring him to a room with a telephone. Tell him only that he is to speak with one of his Chechen brothers. Do you read me?"

"Yes, ma'am." There was a pause as Nichols cleared his throat. "Ma'am, meaning no disrespect, but are you acting under the President's orders?"

"I am," Halloway said firmly.

"Could I have that order faxed to me, please, ma'am?"

Halloway hesitated and stared down at the unsigned document that transferred the powers of the Presidency to her. It was time to activate the Twenty-Fifth Amendment. She reached for her pen.

The Chairman of the Joint Chiefs of Staff grabbed the speakerphone and spoke into it. "Paul, this is Walter Pierce. Do you recognize my voice?"

"Yes, sir."

"Then follow the Vice President's commands," Pierce said, his voice now rough as gravel. "We want that little bastard in a room with a phone in his ear, and we want him there within ten minutes. Got it?"

"Yes, sir."

The phone clicked off.

Pierce leaned back and apologized. "Sorry about that, ma'am. But you should know that Nichols is a top-flight officer. He was just being doubly careful."

"As we would expect him to be," Halloway said, nodding. "Have an order sent to him under my name."

"We'll need an interpreter to overhear the conversation," Alderman advised.

Halloway glanced around the Situation Room filled with staff and aides. Many were military, high-ranking and highly decorated. "Is anyone here fluent in Chechen?"

A middle-aged naval officer with a chest covered in ribbons stepped forward. "I am, Madam Vice President."

"And you are?"

"Admiral Robertson, Director of Naval Intelligence, ma'am."

"Stand by, Admiral."

"Aye, ma'am."

Halloway took another sip of lukewarm coffee, again thinking all they needed was another hour. An extra hour would save two lives and give the Secret Service enough time to activate their rescue plan. And she could get that hour if only the Russians would help. But they weren't going to budge. They weren't going to release their Chechen prisoners under any circumstances. That would be too—

An aide hurried over to Emmett Sanders and whispered an urgent message in his ear.

"Get it up on the video screen," Sanders ordered. "And show their projected course."

"What have we got?" Halloway asked, redirecting her thoughts.

"Trouble," Sanders said and walked over to the large video screen. "The Mexican fighter jets are now on a direct course to intercept the plane carrying the Secret Service Special Ops team."

Halloway asked quickly. "How near are they?"

Sanders pointed to the screen that showed four Mexican jets slowly closing in on Eagle Two. "They are three hundred and thirty miles due south. They'll make contact in twenty minutes."

Halloway strummed her fingers on the tabletop, thinking fast. "How far away is the *Reagan*?"

"Our Hornets can be there in twenty-eight minutes if we launch now," Sanders replied immediately.

"Damn it!" Halloway cursed at the thought of even more American lives being lost. "The Hornets will still be eight minutes late, and that exposes our plane for nearly the entire eight minutes. That's an eternity up there."

"Unless Eagle Two can somehow evade those Mexican jets," Sanders told her. "Otherwise they'll be forced to land or be shot down."

"Can you come up with some evasive maneuvers?" Halloway asked the former naval aviator.

"We can try," Sanders said and swiftly pointed to the four Mexican jets closing in on their target. "Madam Vice President, it's now or never. If we're to have any chance of getting that plane home safe, we have to act."

Without hesitating, Halloway gave the order. "Get those Hornets in the air!"

TWENTY-TWO

DAVID QUICKLY BEGAN THE fifth mini-transfusion, injecting another 50 ccs of whole blood into the President's IV line. Merrill was groaning and muttering through his stuporous condition. David's gaze went to the transparent nasogastric tube and to the cardiac monitor beyond it. The gastric juice coming up remained bright red. And the President was still in shock, despite having received over 200 ccs of David's blood. His blood pressure was 70/40, his pulse 140 beats per minute and thready.

"We're not making much headway," David said.

"At least he's got some blood pressure," Carolyn noted, filling the last of the syringes. "And he hasn't shown signs of a transfusion reaction."

"Which only means there's no ABO incompatibility," David told her, pushing blood in faster.

"Are you saying he could still have a bad reaction?" Carolyn asked.

"A really bad one," David replied. "Remember, they had a lot of problems cross-matching him earlier, and that tells us there's something in his plasma that doesn't like other people's blood."

"Jesus! This poor man doesn't seem to have anything going for him."

"Except a pretty good nurse and doctor looking after him," David said, checking the monitor again. The systolic pressure was still at seventy. "Pass me another syringe of blood."

Carolyn handed him the syringe. She was thinking that Merrill's survival was due far more to a good doctor than to a good nurse. How do you make a physician this good? Most doctors had difficulty dealing with a massive gastrointestinal hemorrhage, even when all the hospital's facilities were available. And David was keeping the President alive with virtually none of the medical center's resources. No blood bank. No endoscopist. No coagulation specialist. Every step, every treatment had to be improvised. Yet he never faltered, never lost his cool. She wondered if he had been a military doctor in combat. That would explain his nerve and quick wits under fire.

The President started mumbling again, the words indecipherable and jumbled.

Carolyn turned to David and asked, "Do you think the President suffered brain damage while he had no blood pressure?"

"Let's hope not," David said flatly. "Hand me another syringe."

As she passed the seventh syringe, her eyes drifted over to the President, who was moving his arms and legs. *Well, at least his motor function is intact*, she told herself. But he could still be mentally impaired. Carolyn had seen that happen before. A brilliant professor of archaeology at the university was admitted to the hospital in severe shock. When he left he was wearing diapers and babbling nonsense. But he could still move his arms and legs.

"The fluid in his nasogastric tube is turning a lighter red," David remarked, breaking into her thoughts.

Carolyn quickly looked over to the cardiac monitor. "And his pressure is up to 88 over 60."

"Good," David said and reached for the last two syringes of blood. "Now if we only had another half unit of blood, we could really get the President out of the woods."

"That's not going to happen," Carolyn said.

"Tell me about it," David pointed to a large syringe filled with water. "Would you connect that to his nasogastric tube and start lavaging his stomach again?"

Carolyn felt the syringe and commented, "It's lukewarm now."

"Make another ice slurry," David directed. "Keep stirring it until it's frigid enough to burn your fingertips. The colder the better."

Carolyn prepared the fresh ice slurry and hastily lavaged the President's stomach over and over. The gastric juice remained light red initially, then gradually turned pink, then yellowish brown. "I think the bleeding has stopped! The ice water must have done it."

"That and the Factor VIII in the blood he received," David said, showing little emotion. "But neither is going to last very long."

"Maybe it'll last until we get out of here."

"Don't bet on it."

The President moaned loudly, then twisted and turned in his bed and moaned again.

The terrorist standing by the door stepped inside to check out the origin of the sudden sounds. David pointed to the President, then to his mouth. The guard nodded and went back into the corridor.

"David," Carolyn said, motioning to the monitor, "his blood pressure is 96 over 70 and climbing."

"Excellent!" David said and placed the final syringe aside. Suddenly the weakness in his legs returned. The room began to sway. Hurriedly he reached for the night table and waited for his unsteadiness to pass. "It's doubly excellent, because we just ran out of blood."

Carolyn saw him holding on to the edge of the table and asked, "Are you all right?"

"Just my leg," David lied. "It's throbbing a little."

"Then go lie down on the couch for a few minutes," Carolyn urged.

"It's better," David said, knowing if he lay down his leg would stiffen and he'd have to drag it around like a limp appendage. As it was, he stood little chance against the terrorists. With a dead leg, he stood none.

"Let's try to awaken the President," he went on, changing the subject. "Pat his cheek a few times and see if you can get a response."

Carolyn gently struck Merrill's cheek and called out, "Mr. President! Mr. President! Can you hear me?"

Merrill groaned and moved his head away from the noise.

"Again," David directed.

Carolyn slapped Merrill's face with more force and cried into his ear, "Mr. President! Mr. President!"

Merrill's eyelids fluttered before they gradually opened. He blinked against the bright light. "Wh … where am I?"

"At University Hospital, Mr. President," Carolyn told him.

Merrill slowly nodded and said groggily, "Oh, yes. Yes. The hemorrhage. Did I pass out?"

"You just drifted off," Carolyn answered.

"Am I still bleeding?" Merrill asked through parched lips.

"No, sir. We've stopped it," Carolyn replied, relieved that the President was oriented and had suffered no apparent brain damage. "We had to give you another transfusion."

Merrill's eyelids began to close. "I'm so tired. I feel like I could sleep for a month."

"Go ahead and rest, Mr. President," Carolyn said soothingly. "We'll be nearby."

Merrill closed his eyes and drifted off.

Carolyn moved over to David and whispered, "I thought it best not to tell him he passed out."

"That wouldn't have helped anything," David agreed.

"Do you have any idea how long the blood transfusions will hold him in check?" Carolyn asked, keeping her voice low.

David shrugged. "I'd just be guessing."

"Then guess," Carolyn pressed.

"As soon as he's used up the Factor VIII in my blood, all hell is going to break loose."

"And how long will that take?"

"Not long at all, I'm afraid."

Aliev stomped into the suite and came to the bedside. He stared down at the sleeping President and studied him before asking, "Why is your President making those loud sounds?"

"He was bleeding again," David explained. "The blood was caught in his throat."

Aliev looked down at Merrill once more. "He seems to be all right now."

"That won't last," David said. "He could start hemorrhaging again in a matter of minutes."

"Then you can stop it again," Aliev responded, showing no concern.

"But we need more blood and plasma sent up to the Pavilion," David implored. "Without them the President will die."

"He looks fine to me," Aliev said, unimpressed.

"Don't you understand? He damn near died!"

"But he didn't. So just continue doing the same things you are doing."

"He desperately needs blood and plasma," David pleaded. "And we have no more to give him."

"Use your own, like you did before," Aliev said tonelessly, and walked out.

Carolyn watched him leave and hissed through her teeth, "What a cold bastard!"

And smart, David thought. The terrorists were so close to success. They weren't going to take any chances now. They would keep the area absolutely secure. Nobody in, nobody out, until their demands were met.

Aliev stuck his head back into the suite. "Doctor, you may receive the blood for your President sooner than you think. To be precise, in thirty-six minutes."

"Why thirty-six minutes?" David asked promptly.

"Because that is when the deadline comes to an end," Aliev explained. "If our Chechen fighters are released, the President will receive his blood. If the prisoners are not freed, your President can hemorrhage all day and all night. It won't bother us. You see, we will be busy killing hostages."

Aliev walked away, humming under his breath.

Carolyn shuddered at the terrorist's ruthlessness, and wondered who he would choose to kill first. Probably Sol Simcha, she guessed sadly. Not because the nice old man was of any value to them or to the outside world as a hostage. But because he was Jewish. And they would probably make him suffer, too. The bastards!

She moved in close to David and asked in a barely audible voice, "Where is that rescue team?"

David shrugged. "I don't know."

"But they will come, won't they?

"Eventually."

"To hell with eventually!" Carolyn blurted out. "I don't want to sit here like a lamb about to be slaughtered."

David took her hand and squeezed it gently. "We've got to play it smart and wait for our chance."

"Are you planning to grab one of their weapons?" Carolyn asked quickly.

David shook his head. "They've got us outnumbered and out-gunned. And even if we managed to bring down a few, the others would start shooting hostages until we surrendered. Grabbing a weapon won't get it done."

"How will you do it then?"

"It'll just happen," David said without inflection. "There'll be an opening, and they'll die without being aware of what hit them."

"How do you know so much about these things?"

"I read a lot."

"Ah-huh," Carolyn said, certain he was hiding something from his past. "Let's get back to the opening you spoke about. Can you really get to someone pointing a gun at you without them know-ing it?"

"There are ways," David said vaguely.

Carolyn thought for a moment, then a mischievous glint came to her eyes. "You mean, like zapping them with defibrillator paddles?"

David smiled thinly. "You think you could take out all five of the bastards that way?"

"Just fantasizing," Carolyn said. "But you never—"

John Merrill suddenly wheezed, with a loud rattle in his throat. He coughed hard to clear his airway and brought up bloody sputum that stuck to his lips before dripping off. Then more maroon-colored sputum came up.

Carolyn moaned. "Don't tell me he's bleeding into his lungs now."

"It looks like it," David said, lowering his voice to a whisper. "And if he really starts to hemorrhage into his bronchial tubes, he'll drown in his own blood."

"Can you do anything to stop it?"

"Not without more fresh plasma."

"But he'll suffocate to death, and he'll be awake and know it's happening."

David thought at length before saying, "The next time you're in the medicine room, grab a couple of vials of injectable Valium and syringes."

"What good will that do?" Carolyn asked.

"If necessary, I'll sedate him and suppress his cough so he won't be aware of what's happening," David told her, then added grimly, "And he won't struggle."

"But … but that'll be like killing him."

David shook his head. "It'll just be making his inevitable death easier."

Suddenly an alarm went off far down the corridor. Carolyn dashed to the door and listened carefully, then called back to David, "I think it's coming from Dr. Warren's room."

"Check it out," David called back. "I'll stay with the President."

As Carolyn hurried away, David leaned against the night table, his legs like heavy weights again. And his thigh wound was throbbing badly. He eased himself down on the side of the bed and rubbed at his wound. But his mind was elsewhere, now thinking about the alarm bell that continued to ring. If it was William Warren, the alarm probably signaled the return of a stubborn ventricular tachycardia that hadn't responded to lidocaine or bretylium. Bad news. Really bad news. Maybe the defibrillator would work. The throbbing in his thigh worsened, and he looked down at the dressing over his wound. Blood was soaking through. Shit. He hoped the sutures hadn't come apart.

Carolyn ran into the room, pausing briefly to catch her breath. "You'd better come quick! Marci is *in extremis!*"

David rose as quickly as he could manage, then hesitated. "Aliev is not going to let us run down that corridor again. He was mad as hell last time, and this time he might just shoot us."

"Maybe he won't," Carolyn urged, thinking fast. "Remember, he still needs us to keep the President alive."

"Aliev may figure we've done all we can and decide to take his chances," David countered. "And keep in mind they'll be making their break out of here very soon. At that point we become expendable. You and I will be like extra baggage."

"We still have to try," Carolyn pleaded.

David sighed resignedly. He knew Carolyn was right. He couldn't simply look away and make believe Marci didn't exist. And maybe they could ease her suffering a little. He moved to the door and peeked out. A guard was ten feet away, smoking a cigarette. Aliev was nowhere in sight. David came back to Carolyn and said, "Aliev is not in the corridor."

"I saw him and another terrorist stepping into the fire stairs," Carolyn recalled.

"Was the door left open?" David asked quickly.

Carolyn nodded. "And that chain-like device was next to it."

David knitted his brow, wondering if Aliev had gone to the roof to post a lookout. If he had, it was bad news. That would remove the roof as a point of entry for the Secret Service team. Shit!

"Maybe this is our chance," Carolyn prodded.

"Yeah, I guess," David said, knowing they were about to take a terrible risk. He peeked out into the corridor once more, and saw only a single terrorist. Hurriedly he turned to Carolyn.

"Okay. Here's what we'll do. You scoot down the corridor. If they stop you, tell them you're going into the treatment room for supplies. I'll wait a little, then be right behind you."

"They'll come after you," Carolyn warned.

"Not if I'm holding up a used plastic bag of blood," David improvised. "I'll tell them I'm coming to get you so we can refill it for the President."

"It's so dangerous," Carolyn breathed.

"I know," David said. "But we really don't have a choice, do we?"

Carolyn bit down on her lower lip and tried to steel her nerves. "Whoever thought the practice of medicine would come to this?"

"It's not just medicine," David growled. "It's the whole goddamn world. Now go!"

Carolyn turned for the door, then came back and kissed David hard on the lips. Twice.

"For double good luck," she said, and dashed out of the room.

———

From his vantage point on the roof of the hospital, Aliev could clearly hear Basagev's voice over the satellite cell phone. Once more they spoke in an unusual Middle Eastern dialect of Chechen.

"Everything is in order," Basagev reported.

"And you are on schedule?" Aliev asked.

"Actually we are somewhat ahead of time," Basagev answered. "Because of a tailwind, we should touch down in Los Angeles earlier than expected. Would you like me to slow the plane?"

"No," Aliev said promptly. "Maintain your current speed."

There was a loud burst of static, then the reception gradually cleared.

"And the nuclear weapon has been armed, in the event Los Angeles becomes the target for our bomb," Basagev was saying.

"Good," Aliev said. "But it seems we will be traveling on to Russia."

"So the Americans are complying, eh?"

"Just as I predicted they would," Aliev went on. "The Russians, of course, are being bull-headed."

"Which is what you anticipated," Basagev said. "But soon enough they will pay a heavy price for their stubbornness and for their cruelty to our people."

"A price beyond measure," Aliev snarled. "The oil-rich part of Siberia, which they are so proud of, is about to turn into a vast radioactive wasteland."

"And instead of Chernobyl, the Russians will mourn over Siberia now," Basagev prophesied.

"Now and for a thousand years to come," Aliev added solemnly.

"And for those same thousand years, all of Chechnya will sing your praises."

"And yours as well."

"Peace be unto you, Aliev."

"And unto you, my brother."

TWENTY-THREE

ELLEN HALLOWAY SCOWLED AT the bad news coming from the speakerphone. The Chechen leader at Guantanamo Bay was refusing to talk.

"He believes it's some sort of trick," General Nichols reported. "And he won't speak to anyone over the phone."

Halloway looked up at the digital clock. In twenty-two minutes the terrorists would start killing hostages. "Did you tell him he'd be speaking with Aliev?"

"I did, ma'am. He just shrugged."

"Hold for a moment." Halloway quickly glanced around the conference table and asked, "Any suggestions?"

"We could point a gun at his head," Toliver proposed. "I'll bet that would open his mouth."

Halloway waved away the idea. "All he'd have to do is tell Aliev there was a gun at his head, and their conversation would be over. And so would the life of one of the hostages."

"What about a public address system?" Alderman asked.

Halloway considered the proposal, but it too had a big flaw. It was difficult to recognize a voice that was being blurted out over a PA system. And voice recognition was critical here. But still, there was a slim chance it might work. As she reached for the speaker-phone, Halloway stopped her hand in mid-air. Her eyes narrowed noticeably. "I think I know how to do it."

"How?" Alderman and Toliver asked almost simultaneously.

Halloway lost her train of thought for a moment. She had to strain to get it back. "B—by offering Aliev more and giving him less."

"Be careful," Alderman advised. "If he thinks he's being de-ceived, he might do something drastic."

"I'll have to take my chances." Halloway signaled over to the communications officer. "Keep Gitmo on hold and get me Aliev in the Pavilion."

She glanced up at the wall clocks once more. It was just after 4 a.m., 1 a.m. in California. Only twenty minutes until the dead-line. Every minute, every second, counted now. One mistake could cost so many lives. Hurriedly she organized her thoughts on how to deal with the terrorist. *Most importantly, don't threaten him. That would only agitate him. Okay, so I won't threaten him. Instead, I—*

Suddenly Halloway found herself yawning, as a wave of fatigue swept over her. The adrenaline surge that had kept her going was fading fast and being replaced by the weariness of sleep depriva-tion. She bit down on her lip to suppress another yawn, then gazed at the others sitting around the conference table. Their faces were tired and drawn, their bodies slumped in their chairs. The long, stressful hours were taking their toll on everyone. But it was the mental toll that concerned Halloway the most. *Our brains are be-coming sluggish at the worst possible time*, she thought gloomily. *It's bound to affect our decision-making, if it hasn't already.* Fighting her fatigue, Halloway reached for her coffee cup and drank the last of it, then asked aloud, "How is our coffee supply?"

"Running low," an aide reported.

"Better brew up another batch," she directed. "We're going to need it."

"Coffee won't help us out of this damn mess," Toliver grumbled, rising from his slouch. "The President is as good as dead and we may as well face up to it."

Halloway ignored his remark and concentrated her mind on Aliev. *Let him have his way*, she decided. *Allow him to think he's in control and dictating every move. Then ask, but not for too much. And have something in reserve to offer. Then hope to God it works.*

"Madam Vice President, I have Aliev for you," the communications officer called out.

Halloway cleared her throat and switched on the speakerphone. "Mr. Aliev, I have a Chechen prisoner at Guantanamo Bay ready to talk with you. His name is Shamil. Do you know him?"

"I have heard of him."

"Good," Halloway went on. "I would like you to inform him that his release is being arranged and that he and his men will shortly be on a plane out of Guantanamo. He may not respond, but he will hear your message."

"Why don't you tell him?"

"Because he would believe you far more than me."

Aliev asked suspiciously, "What assurance do I have that this is not a deception?"

"Once the plane is airborne, we will arrange for you to speak with him again," Halloway replied.

After a long pause, Aliev asked, "What about all the other Chechens being held in prisons around the world?"

"I can only speak for the prisoners that the United States holds," Halloway said, trying to keep her nervousness out of her voice. "We will release all those under our control, but we have no say in what the Russian government does." There was another long pause. Aliev did not respond.

"If we can reach an agreement," Halloway prodded gently, "I can have the Chechen prisoners at Guantanamo on a plane in a very short time. The others will take longer."

"How much longer?"

"I need the deadline extended by an hour."

"No," Aliev said firmly.

The spirits of those seated at the conference table sank. All eyes went to the digital clock. Eighteen minutes remaining. They all realized that hostages were certain to die soon, and one of them could be the President's daughter.

"We are freeing the Guantanamo prisoners as a gesture of goodwill," Halloway said. "We would expect a similar gesture on your part. Surely an extra hour won't matter that much."

Again there was a long pause that went on and on before Aliev came back on the line.

"Assuming I have proof that the twelve Chechen fighters are in the air, I will give you thirty minutes more to free the others."

"But we have Chechen prisoners scattered all over the—"

"Thirty minutes, and no more."

The phone clicked off.

Halloway quickly switched to the line connecting the Situation Room to the base at Guantanamo Bay. "General Nichols, listen carefully and follow my orders exactly. Ready?"

"Ready, ma'am."

"First, gather up the twelve Chechens on your list and tell them they're being released. Treat them a little more kindly than usual."

"Understood."

"Next, place them on a transport plane that has only a pilot and co-pilot aboard. There are to be no guards."

"Ma'am! Ma'am!" Nichols objected strongly. "These are cold-blooded killers. They'll slit one of our boys' throats once they're in the air, and be happy doing it. They'll figure that one pilot is enough to get them home."

"They won't do anything if they're shackled hand and foot," Halloway said icily. "And I mean tightly shackled."

"Yes, ma'am."

"And instruct the pilot to fly due east at a slow speed, but not slow enough to arouse suspicion."

"Got that, ma'am."

"I want them airborne ASAP. How long will it take?"

"Fifteen minutes."

Halloway glanced up at the digital clock. Fourteen minutes until the deadline. "You've got ten minutes to have them up in the air."

Before Halloway could sign off, Walter Pierce leaned into the speakerphone. "Paul, this is General Pierce."

"Yes, sir?"

"Keep those Chechens in their prison clothes and speed their butts out to the tarmac. Have a C-130 waiting, engines fired up."

"Will do."

"In ten minutes, we want to hear that pilot's voice—no ifs, ands, or buts."

"Yes, sir."

Pierce switched the phone off and leaned back.

Halloway nodded appreciatively to the Chairman of the Joint Chiefs for his direct, no-nonsense approach. "Do you think they'll make it?"

"It's going to be close," Pierce hedged.

"Those Chechens aren't going to like being shackled," Toliver told the group. "It'll make them feel like they're still prisoners."

"Tough!" Halloway said gruffly, her eyes watching the clock move to thirteen minutes. "We need a backup plan in case this fails. I'm open to suggestions."

There were no responses.

Alderman took out his pipe and chewed on it, now reconsidering the deal they had just made with Aliev. His face took on a worried look. Something was off. Something was wrong. The Chechen terrorist had given in when he didn't have to.

Halloway studied his expression and asked, "Is there a problem?"

Alderman nodded slowly. "Something is going on here that we don't understand."

"Such as?" Halloway queried immediately.

"Such as why did Aliev agree to accept half a pie when he might well have gotten the whole pie?" Alderman asked back. "Why would he do that?"

"Because he knew the Russians would never negotiate," Toliver answered.

Alderman shook his head. "That's an assumption. And terrorists like Aliev don't assume anything. They just start killing hostages, and see if they can change your mind. And that's what terrorists are good at—changing minds. A true terrorist would never have given in so easily."

"What do you think is behind all this?" Halloway asked, now wondering if she had been outwitted by Aliev.

"It isn't only twelve Chechen prisoners," Alderman replied thoughtfully. "I can guarantee you that."

Halloway grumbled under her breath. They weren't coming up with any answers, just more difficult questions. And the clock kept clicking. She now had the uneasy feeling that a terrible disaster was going to occur on her watch.

Out of the corner of her eye, Halloway noticed a plasma television screen that was tuned to a cable channel. A BREAKING NEWS headline was flashing, and beneath it a subtitle read PRESIDENT SUFFERS SETBACK. She quickly snapped her fingers at the screen. "Turn up the sound!"

A news anchor was reporting, "The bleeding is believed to have been serious and required two blood transfusions. According to several sources, the President was rushed from the emergency room to an undisclosed location at University Hospital."

"Christ!" Halloway growled. "This is the last thing we needed."

"You'll have to issue a statement," Alderman advised.

Halloway thought quickly. "Tell them the bleeding has been controlled, and that the President is resting comfortably."

Alderman nodded his approval, then added, "You realize, of course, that the news of the hostage situation will break very soon."

"We'll deal with that when it occurs," Halloway said tersely.

"They'll demand a press conference," Alderman went on. "The country will have to be informed."

"I know, I know." Halloway felt like she was juggling hot potatoes. A public announcement would only complicate matters more. The press and leaders around the world would insist on being told who was in charge. The Twenty-Fifth Amendment would have to be activated. The shock waves would reverberate to every corner of the earth. Halloway took a deep breath and calmed herself. *You wanted to be President. Well, you're about to get your wish.*

A naval officer rushed into the room and came over to Emmett Sanders. He whispered a short message, then motioned to the large video screen. Four Mexican fighter-interceptors were closing in on Eagle Two. They seemed to be almost touching the American plane.

Sanders stood and hurried to the screen. "The Mexican jets are only twelve minutes away, and closing fast."

"And our Hornets?" Halloway asked quickly.

"Nineteen minutes away." Sanders pointed to a squadron of ten fighter jets moving in from the west. "And they're at top speed, ma'am."

"So our Secret Service plane will be exposed for a full seven minutes," Halloway calculated unhappily.

"And totally defenseless," Sanders noted.

"Is there anything we can do?"

"We can try to buy them some time."

"How?"

"By telling Eagle Two to hug the coastline and drop down to three hundred feet," Sanders explained. "That should put them below Mexican radar. It will appear as if our plane crashed."

Halloway squinted an eye. "But the Mexicans won't turn around because of that. They'll go in to investigate."

"Exactly right, ma'am," Sanders agreed. "But they'll want to search the area, so they'll come in slower at cruising speed, which is approximately five hundred miles per hour. And that just might give our Hornets enough time to get into position."

Halloway took a long breath, hesitating. She knew she was out of her depth. "How dangerous is this maneuver?"

"Very, ma'am," Sanders answered. "One wrong move, and they crash into the ocean and everybody dies. But Eagle Two has terrain-avoidance radar, which should help."

"But that's not foolproof, is it?"

"No, ma'am. Flying at such a low altitude is always risky business."

Halloway took another deep breath, watching as the Mexican jets moved even closer to Eagle Two. "Get them down to three hundred feet."

Sanders snapped his fingers to an aide and the order went out in an instant. Then he turned back to Halloway and spoke in a solemn voice. "Madam Vice President, there is a good chance our Hornets will engage the Mexican interceptors in under twenty minutes. If that occurs, we may have to bring those Mexican jets down. You should be fully aware of that."

Halloway hesitated, knowing she would be sanctioning an act of war. An out-and-out act of war, against a friendly neighbor.

"Ma'am?"

"Do whatever it takes," Halloway said bluntly. "Just get that Secret Service team home safe."

"Aye-aye, ma'am."

Suddenly Sanders' expression changed. Everybody in the room noticed it. Now he had on his war face.

TWENTY-FOUR

MARCI WAS FIGHTING FRANTICALLY for air. With every shallow inspiration she made a rasping, agonal sound. Her condition was so dire David thought her next breath would be her last.

"We've got to do something," Carolyn pleaded in a low voice, squeezing Marci's hand and trying to comfort her. "We've got to try!"

David shrugged helplessly. They had already tried increasing the flow of oxygen and more IV Solu-Medrol, but her symptoms had only worsened. "Without a long needle, there's nothing we can do."

"Can't you just use a regular needle to go through her chest wall and drain the effusion?"

David shook his head. "I could kill her doing that. At the very least, she'd end up with a collapsed lung, and then she couldn't breathe at all."

Carolyn patted Marci's hand and smiled, as if everything was going to turn out all right. But she could tell the young woman knew otherwise. Marci had that frightened look that said she realized death was coming. And soon.

Marci began panting for more oxygen, her skin color growing duskier. Between gasps she asked weakly, "Can . . . can you give me some medicine, please?"

"In a minute," Carolyn lied, then turned to David and hissed quietly, "Jesus! Do something!"

David hesitated briefly, then sighed and accepted the fact that what he was about to do could instantly kill Marci. "What's the longest eighteen-gauge needle you've got?"

"An inch and a half," Carolyn answered. "That's plenty long enough to go through Marci's chest wall."

And plenty big enough to cause a large pneumothorax in the process, David thought glumly. Then he'd have to put in a chest tube to re-expand the collapsed lung, but it would be too late. Marci would be dead before he could do it. Again he hesitated. "Don't you have a thoracentesis tray up here? That would have a longer needle."

"We don't keep any trays on the Pavilion," Carolyn informed. "We order them up as we need them."

David thought for a moment, then rapidly blinked. "Wait a minute! Didn't you order a paracentesis tray on Diana Dunn? You know, to remove some of her ascitic fluid?"

Carolyn shook her head. "That was canceled because she developed a fever and started acting strangely. The resident decided to do a lumbar puncture to rule out meningitis as a cause. So we ordered up a—" She stopped in mid-sentence, her eyes widening. "We ordered up an LP tray!"

"Which would have a very long needle," David said in a rush.

Carolyn nodded quickly. "Six inches worth."

"Is the tray up here?" David asked at once.

"I'm … I'm not sure," Carolyn stammered. "The lumbar puncture was put on hold because her fever subsided. The tray may have been sent back down."

"Find out," David urged. "If it's still here grab it, along with a 50-cc syringe."

Carolyn ran for the door. David leaned over and rapidly examined Marci. She continued to suck for air, her lips now a cyanotic color. And her neck veins were markedly distended because the pericardial effusion was so severe it was pressing on the heart and not allowing blood to flow in from the body's large veins. And there was a simple equation when it came to the heart. No blood in, no blood out. *How was this girl managing to stay alive?*

"Dr. Ballineau," Marci muttered softly, "are you going to get this fluid off my heart?"

"As soon as the nurse returns," David said, silently praying that the LP tray was still on the Pavilion. It was Marci's only chance.

"Will it hurt?" Marci gasped.

"A little," David replied. "But it will be worth it for you to breathe normally again, won't it?"

"Yeah," she said, her voice so weak it was barely audible. "No pain, no gain, huh?"

David smiled down at Marci, whom he had grown to really like. She was pretty and smart and full of life, despite her illness. She was a fighter. His gaze went to her face and as usual focused in on her doe-like eyes. He had seen those same eyes way back in the past. They reminded him of his wife, Marianne.

A hacking cough came from the doorway.

David glanced over and saw the balding terrorist looking in at them. He still seemed befuddled, just as he had been when David and Carolyn ran by him in the corridor earlier. And rather than shoot or shout at the pair, he simply followed them into Marci's room. He wasn't too bright, David decided. But that didn't make him any less deadly. On Aliev's command, he would happily kill a nurse and a doctor. And a President.

Marci began choking, her hands desperately clutching for her throat. Her lips were turning a deep blue.

It's the end, David thought sadly.

Carolyn dashed into the room, holding a cloth-bound tray. "Got it!"

A second terrorist suddenly appeared in the doorway. He yelled angrily in Chechen at the guard and shoved him down the corridor. Then he came back to David and Carolyn and motioned them to the door with his Uzi. "Out!"

"But this patient desperately needs our help," Carolyn pleaded, turning toward Marci. "Without us she'll—"

"Out!" The terrorist backhanded Carolyn across her forehead, and sent her flying into David's arms.

David was knocked off balance, but somehow managed to steady himself and hold onto Carolyn. Quickly, he asked her, "Are you all right?"

"More scared than hurt," she breathed, although a red welt was forming over her temple area.

"I will not say a third time," the terrorist threatened, now pointing his Uzi directly at them.

Supporting Carolyn, David headed for the door and asked the terrorist, "Where do you want us to go?"

"To roof, to see Aliev."

"For what?"

The terrorist smiled malevolently, then held his hand up high, cupped it, and slowly let it drop.

"Oh Jesus!" Carolyn whimpered. "I think he plans to throw us off the roof!"

"Yeah," David said tonelessly, knowing it was Carolyn who would most likely be killed. To Aliev, a doctor was all that was required to keep the President alive. The nurse was expendable.

"M … maybe we can reason him out of it," Carolyn hoped in a weak voice.

"Terrorists don't reason, they kill."

They walked across the corridor, which was silent and vacant, and entered the stairwell for the fire stairs. The terrorist nudged them toward the stairs with the barrel of his Uzi. "Nurse first," he ordered.

David hesitated and tried to think of a way to disarm the terrorist. And he had to do it before they started up the stairs. With his back to the terrorist he stood no chance.

"Go!" The terrorist demanded.

Suddenly, a flashback from a similar situation long ago came to David. But he needed a distraction for it to work again. A big distraction.

Moving slowly, David helped Carolyn up the first step and said under his breath, "Pretend you're going to throw up when your foot touches the next step."

On cue, Carolyn forced herself to gag, then abruptly leaned over the railing and began retching.

For a moment the terrorist's eyes went to Carolyn. When he brought his gaze back to David it was a second too late. David's kick was already in midair, heading directly for the terrorist's testicles. The man let out a muffled cry, then groped at his groin and fell onto the floor face first. David quickly pounced upon the terrorist. He held the man's head up by its hair and delivered a powerful, precise blow to the upper neck, crushing the second and third cervical vertebrae and severing the spinal cord beneath them. The terrorist's body convulsed, then went flaccid.

Carolyn stared at David, wide-eyed. "Did you kill …?"

David waved his hand, quieting her. "We've got to get rid of the body, or we'll both be dead."

Swallowing back her fear, Carolyn hurriedly collected herself and looked over to the staircase. "Let's throw him down the steps."

David peered down the stairs and saw the multiple tripwires and photoelectric sensors that were connected to explosives taped to the walls. "It's booby-trapped. The body will set off an explosion that will blow us to hell and back."

"So what should we do?" Carolyn asked anxiously.

David glanced around the stairwell, with its thick plaster walls that had neither ducts nor crawlspaces. There weren't any places to hide the dead terrorist, and it made no sense to drag the body across the corridor where it would surely be found. Shit! David grumbled silently, thinking they were trapped and bound to be discovered any moment now. Again, he surveyed the fire stairs, searching for a way out of the dilemma. Abruptly, his gaze stopped at the space between the staircases. He rapidly turned to Carolyn and said, "Help me pick him up."

"What are we going to do?" Carolyn asked.

"You'll see," David replied. "Grab his legs."

They lifted the body and moved it over to the railing, then rolled it over into the space between the staircases. The body fell straight down, then glanced off a rail and slammed into the landing on the floor below. It bounced up once and stayed within sight.

Carolyn asked, "Won't the terrorists see the body when they start searching for their missing man?"

David shook his head. "The Secret Service has the floor beneath us covered. Chances are they'll find the body and remove it."

"And if they don't?"

"Then we're in big trouble."

Carolyn pointed to the Uzi on the floor near the stairs. "Should we take his weapon?"

"No." David picked up the Uzi and tossed it over the railing. "If they find us anywhere near the weapon, they'll figure out what happened and we'll both be dead."

"Couldn't you have used it to shoot…"

David shook his head again, interrupting her. "There are too many of them. If just one of the terrorists is left standing, the President and his family will be carried out of here in body bags."

Hurriedly turning for the door, neither of them noticed the smear of blood on the floor that had come from the dead terrorist's mouth.

At the doorway, David peeked out into the corridor and saw a terrorist about to enter the nurses' lounge. He quickly jerked his head back in and waited several seconds before peeking out again. The corridor was now clear. Taking Carolyn's hand, he dashed across to Marci's room.

Marci was grasping for air with shallow, rapid respirations. Her entire face was now deeply cyanotic.

"Lower the bed!" David directed. "And pull her gown up well away from her abdomen!"

David hastily opened the lumbar puncture tray and painted Marci's abdomen and lower rib cage with an orange antiseptic. After slipping on latex gloves, he palpated the xiphoid process, the small cartilaginous structure at the very end of the sternum. Then he took a long needle and stuck it through the skin and muscle beneath the xiphoid process. Slowly he advanced it upward toward the heart, staying as close to the chest wall as possible. Be careful, he warned himself, trying to be even more deliberate. He didn't want to puncture the heart or tear a hole in it. *Goddamn it! I need an echocardiogram to guide me! I'm blind without it, and I don't know where I am anatomically.* He felt like he was practicing medicine in the Middle Ages.

Marci was gagging and choking, now unable to clear her airway. Her respirations sounded like squeals.

"David," Carolyn warned, "she's going out."

"I know. I know."

David pushed the needle up farther and felt the resistance of the diaphragm that separated the thoracic contents from the abdomen. He gave the long needle another thrust. The resistance vanished. But no fluid came out of the needle. *Oh, shit! I missed it! Am I inside the lung, or what?* The needle was in almost to the hub. Out of desperation he gave the needle a final push.

Clear fluid suddenly spurted from the end of the needle, gushing out in a steady stream. It slowed for a moment. Then the flow continued, pouring onto Marci's abdomen and sheet. David stared in awe at the volume of pericardial fluid being extracted. It had to be 200 ccs, or more. *My God! How did she stay alive with an effusion that size?*

The flow gradually diminished, until it was coming out in drops. David attached a large syringe to the needle and aspirated another 20 ccs.

"David! David!" Carolyn said excitedly. "You've got to see this!"

David looked over at Carolyn, who was motioning to Marci's face. The girl's cyanosis was disappearing right before their eyes, her lips and cheeks turning a rosy pink. And her neck veins were flattening to the point they were barely noticeable.

"Unbelievable!" Carolyn marveled.

"Oh," David swooned softly, enjoying the moment. *A life almost gone. A life brought back. It was one of medicine's magic moments.* With a nod of satisfaction, he removed the needle and bandaged the puncture site. *I was lucky,* he had to admit. *Just plain lucky.*

Blind man's luck on the first try. He put a smile on his face and gazed down at Marci, who was taking long, even breaths. "How are you doing, kiddo?"

"Better," Marci replied, taking another deep breath and savoring the air. "A lot better."

"So I can see."

"Thank you for helping me, Dr. Ballineau."

"You're welcome." David patted her shoulder and glanced up at her IV line. The plastic bag was nearly empty. He looked over to Carolyn and said, "Run a liter of saline into Marci. We've got to replace the fluid she's lost."

Carolyn hesitated. "Won't it just go back into her pericardial sac?"

"No, it'll stay in her intravascular space."

David pushed himself up from the bed. He abruptly reeled as his weakness returned and the room started to sway. He grabbed Carolyn's arm and tried to steady himself, but the wavering persisted.

"Are you okay?" Carolyn asked, alarmed.

"You'd better help me to the couch," David said, leaning heavily on her.

Carolyn placed her arm around his waist and led him to the couch, where he plopped down. She sat beside him and said, "I think all that blood you lost is taking its toll. You're the one who is going to need a transfusion."

David shook his head. "It's not anemia from blood loss. It's volume depletion. A liter of saline will take care of it."

Carolyn asked quickly, "Do you want me to start an IV on you?"

David nodded. "Pronto. And while you're getting the IV set up, check on the President and see if he's bleeding again."

"Okay," Carolyn said, rising to her feet. "But you stay put! Don't you move off of this couch, and I mean it. I can't get through this mess without you."

"I'm not going anywhere," David assured her.

"You stay put!" Carolyn ordered again, and hurried out of the room.

David leaned back, weak and now bone-weary as well. He felt his eyes closing and had to fight to keep them open. *Don't sleep,* he commanded himself. *Because if you do, you'll sleep deeply and lose valuable time, and your leg will stiffen and you'll be worthless in combat. And people will die because your brain was muddled by a little sleep, but not nearly enough. So stay awake!* He stretched out his leg and the throbbing pain came back. Good! That would keep his mind occupied on something other than sleep.

He looked over to Marci, who now had a white washcloth covering her forehead. It accentuated her eyes and nose and cheeks, making them appear far more prominent than they really were. Part of the washcloth was draped down along the side of her face and when she turned, it moved, like the end of a turban blowing in the wind…

Oh, God! David groaned as a flashback came into his mind. *Not here! Not now!*

But the images sharpened and the memories flooded back. A screaming mob of African terrorists were running toward him, yelling at the top of their lungs, the ends of their white turbans flying in the air. They were old and young—some boys, some men, all filled with hate and showing no fear. Then came the gunfire and explosions. The dead were everywhere, some without arms or legs or heads. Yet more came, their numbers endless. The Special Forces unit was surrounded with no way out. The mob was howling for their necks.

David jerked his consciousness back to the present. Sweat was pouring off him, his hands shaking so badly they flapped. And he couldn't catch his breath. With effort he clasped his hands together and forced himself to inhale. As air went into his bronchi, David heard a wheezing noise. *Shit! Oh, shit! I sound like an asthmatic.* He had to strain even harder to expand his lungs. Ever so slowly, his breathing eased and the other symptoms of his panic attack subsided.

David lay back heavily and gathered himself. The attacks had never come this close together. And they couldn't have come at a worse time. *Goddamn it! I'm turning into an invalid, just when I need every ounce of my strength to survive!*

He stiffened suddenly, as he heard footsteps coming down the corridor. They were heavy footsteps, accompanied by a rattling sound he didn't recognize. David hoped it wasn't Aliev, but braced himself in case it was.

Carolyn rushed back into the suite, dragging an IV pole behind her. "The President is doing okay."

"What's the color of his gastric juice?" David asked.

"Light pink with no clots," Carolyn replied, as she applied a tourniquet and rubbed alcohol over a vein in David's forearm.

"He may still be oozing blood," David worried.

"That beats the hell out of hemorrhaging, doesn't it?" Carolyn expertly started an IV and taped the needle into place. "How fast do you want it to run?"

"Wide open."

Carolyn adjusted the IV flow, then sat down next to David and sighed wearily. "This reminds me of my days as a flight nurse."

David looked over quickly. "You rode an ER helicopter?"

"For five years, before I decided to work on the Beaumont Pavilion," Carolyn answered, smiling weakly at the memory. "I miss it. There's something about zooming around in a helicopter that gives you a real adrenaline rush."

"It can be addictive," David recalled.

"Do you miss it, too?" Carolyn asked.

"The copter rides—yeah," David said wistfully. "But not the hell that came after."

"Well, it looks like that hell is catching up with you again."

"And with you."

Carolyn stared out into space briefly, then said candidly, "I just hope I don't fall apart when hell comes."

"It's already here," David said, reaching over to gently squeeze her hand. "And you're doing great."

"You're the one doing great. Only God knows how you've been able to hold things together up here."

"Just dumb luck."

"Baloney! You're not some ordinary academician. If you were, you'd be in a corner, shaking in your boots at this moment."

David shrugged and looked up at the IV streaming into his arm. He wished it was a unit of whole blood. That would surely set things straight.

"Right?" Carolyn persisted.

David shrugged again.

"Don't you clam up on me," Carolyn said bluntly. "I've got some important questions about you, and I want answers."

David had to smile at her directness. "Fire away."

"You were a doctor in the military. Right?" Carolyn asked.

David shook his head. "I became a doctor after my military service."

"Which branch were you in?"

"Special Forces."

"Really?" Carolyn said, taken by surprise. But then she nodded, thinking that would explain a lot. "What kind of missions did you go on?"

"You don't want to know," David muttered, his face tightening. He hated talking about the past. Hated it. Because it always brought back the bad memories. "Ask me about something else."

"Okay," Carolyn said, now seeing an opening she'd been waiting for. "How come a good-looking doctor like you isn't married?"

"I was," David replied, looking up at the IV bag, which was still three-quarters full. He wished the whole liter was already in so he could stand and walk out. "A long time ago."

"And?" Carolyn pressed on.

"Marianne was a nurse at Walter Reed, where they restructured my chin after the helicopter crash that ended my military career," David said neutrally. "She got me through a bad time. We fell in love. We married. I went back to college and got into medical school, and we planned for a wonderful future together. I graduated, did an ER residency, and was offered a faculty position at University Hospital. I rose up through the ranks and became Chief of the Service. Life was great. It couldn't have been better. We had a big house and a beautiful baby daughter. Then one day Marianne had a sudden nosebleed that wouldn't stop and was seen by our family physician. She was diagnosed with acute myeloblastic leukemia, and died eight months later."

"Oh," Carolyn said softly, and looked away. "I'm so sorry."

"Don't sweat it."

Carolyn flicked her wrists, unhappy with herself. "Sometimes I talk too much."

"You're doing fine," David said, pushing Marianne's face from his mind. But the sound of her voice—that warm, wonderful voice—stayed for a moment longer. It was always the last part of

283

the memory to leave. "What about you? I'd guess that someone as pretty as you has been married before."

"No such luck."

"Not even close?"

"Once I was close. Or so I thought. He was a handsome neurosurgeon who was separated from his wife and promised me everything. Marriage. Children. The big house. A vacation home ..." She let her voice trail off, her mind drifting for a moment.

"And?"

"And he went back to his wife," Carolyn said without bitterness. "And I went back to dating uninteresting men, with a few meaningless flings here and there." She sighed heavily to herself before adding, "None of them worth talking about."

"And then?"

"Then you find yourself in your late thirties, and even the uninteresting men aren't around anymore. So you resign yourself to staying single."

"No interesting men at all?" David asked.

"Only one," Carolyn said and smiled thinly at him. "And he just came into my life."

David squeezed her hand a little tighter. "Have you always been this subtle?"

"Always."

David reached for her chin and guided her lips to his. He kissed her softly, feeling her warmth and her pleasant shiver. "Do you usually sweep men off their feet like this?"

"Only the special ones," Carolyn said as she kissed him back.

"Where's an empty linen closet when you need one?"

"Almost halfway down the hall," she said, smiling slyly and kissing him again. "Do you know what I wish for right now?"

"What?"

"For the whole world to disappear for a while, except for you and me."

"It just did," David said softly and drew her even closer.

They heard footsteps rapidly approaching. Two terrorists were grumbling loudly to one another.

"Can you make out what they're saying?" Carolyn asked quietly.

David shook his head. "They're speaking Chechen, but I can tell from the sound of their voices that they're pissed off about something."

"Jesus! What now?"

"Who knows? Just be very careful what you say. Remember, they can understand every word you utter."

"Chances are they'll ask about the guard."

"If they do, play dumb."

The footsteps were now just outside the door, the voices even angrier.

David and Carolyn quickly moved apart.

Aliev hurried into the room, and glared at David and the IV running into his arm. "What are you doing in here?"

"He was about to pass out from fluid loss," Carolyn answered hastily. "He needed an IV."

"We tried the treatment room," David lied easily. "But there was no IV pole in there."

"And there was an extra one in Marci's room," Carolyn added to the lie.

Aliev's expression turned into a snarl. He waved away the explanation, either not believing it or not caring. "You were told to stay, and you disobeyed."

"But he needed the fluid," Carolyn argued. "He was about to—"

"Enough!" Aliev cut her off. "If this happens again, you won't have to worry about fluids, because you will both be dead. Do you understand?"

"Yes," Carolyn said submissively. Then she swallowed hard and requested. "May we finish the infusion?"

"No!" Aliev snapped. "The IV is to be stopped at once."

"Why?" Carolyn protested mildly. "It's only a saline solution. It can't—"

Aliev viciously slapped at the IV line, jerking the needle out of David's vein. Saline sprayed onto Carolyn and across the room. Some of it reached Marci. The girl choked back a scream.

David clenched his fists, resisting the urge to kick Aliev in his testicles and grab the Uzi. The Chechen was close enough for David to do it. But it would also be a death wish, because he and Carolyn would end up dead, killed by the balding terrorist in the doorway.

Aliev glowered down at David. "Do you have something to say?"

David shook his head and looked away.

Aliev's eyes suddenly narrowed. He quickly glanced around the suite before asking, "Where is the man who was guarding you?"

David shrugged. "He stepped outside a few minutes ago."

Aliev turned to the terrorist in the doorway and barked out orders in Chechen. The balding terrorist hollered down the corridor, then waited for a response. Moments later two voices answered. The terrorist looked back to Aliev and shook his head.

Aliev glared at David, saying, "We had better find our man or someone up here will pay a terrible price."

David was about to suggest that the missing man may have defected, but held his tongue. The last thing he wanted to do was agitate Aliev further.

Aliev growled under his breath, obviously upset with the turn of events. He checked under Marci's bed and in the bathroom for the missing terrorist, then came back to David and Carolyn. "When the guard left the room, which way did he go?"

David shrugged again. "I didn't notice."

"Why do I have the feeling that you are lying to me?" Aliev glowered.

"We didn't see the direction he went," Carolyn reaffirmed. "He just walked…"

There was a sudden commotion in the corridor, with loud yells and racing footsteps. The balding terrorist stuck his head into the room and blurted out a long sentence in Chechen.

Aliev clenched his jaw as his face turned a deep red. He grabbed David by the collar and jerked him up to his feet. Then he motioned to Carolyn with his Uzi. "Both of you, outside."

In the corridor, Aliev shoved David and Carolyn into the stairwell for the fire stairs, where a terrorist was pointing to a smear of blood on the white concrete floor next to the staircase. Aliev put his index finger on the smear and noted that the blood was fresh. Stepping back, he quickly scanned the solid walls of the enclosure, then peered down the stairs and into the space between the staircases. Finally, he checked the underside of the stairs going up.

"I think the American Secret Service has taken him prisoner," Aliev deduced, now speaking Chechen. "And they must have killed my cousin in the kitchen as well. It seems they have found their way around our booby traps."

"But how?" the balding terrorist asked.

"That I do not know," Aliev said and hurriedly snapped his fingers at a third terrorist. "Use your cell phone and connect me to the Vice President."

"Should I tell them why?"

"No," Aliev told him, then brought his attention back to David and Carolyn and switched to English. "Did you hear sounds of a struggle?"

"None," David answered. "But remember, we were busy caring for a very ill patient."

"And what about you?" Aliev asked Carolyn.

Carolyn shook her head.

Aliev stared at the couple, looking for signs that would indicate they were lying.

The terrorist next to Aliev handed over the cell phone, saying, "The Vice President is ready for you."

Aliev continued to stare at David and Carolyn as he spoke into the cell.

"Listen very carefully, Lady Vice President. One of my men is missing and I know he has been captured by your Secret Service. If he is not returned to me within two minutes I will kill a hostage." Aliev paused and listened closely to the response. "Yes. I will stay on the line."

Aliev waited patiently, now looking down through the space between the staircases and listening for any activity. Everything remained still and quiet. Once again he inspected the tripwires on the stairs going down. All appeared intact. Glimpsing at his watch, he said into the phone, "You have ninety seconds."

David tried to keep his face impassive, but he knew an innocent hostage would shortly be executed and he was responsible for it. *Goddamn it! My fault! I killed a terrorist, and someone was going to die for it. But I had no choice. It was either kill or be killed. Goddamn it*, he growled again to himself, still feeling guilt and wondering who would be chosen to die. Probably Sol Simcha, who Aliev had earlier threatened to push off the roof in his wheelchair.

David shivered involuntarily at the thought of the nice old man falling ten stories to his death.

Aliev saw David's shiver and asked, "Are you frightened, doctor?"

"Yes," David lied, gazing around at the three terrorists and knowing there was no way he could take out more than two and survive.

Aliev pressed the cell phone to his ear and listened carefully, then cried out, "He what?... You think he must have slipped! Is that what your Secret Service told you to say? Do you expect me to believe that nonsense?" There was a long pause before Aliev spoke again. "Oh! You will send the body up! That is so kind of you." Aliev curled his lips into a snarl, then said, "I would like you to stay on the line."

Aliev turned to the balding terrorist and issued a set of orders in Chechen. The terrorist nodded and smiled, exposing metal-lined front teeth. Then he hurried away.

David glanced over at the two terrorists remaining in the fire stairs, thinking he could probably kill both, but that would still leave two terrorists who, with their Uzis and grenades, could easily slaughter the First Family and most of the other hostages. Yet, without Aliev, the terrorists might...

A high-pitched shriek came from the corridor. It was a woman's voice, crying and screaming and begging.

Aliev held the cell phone up to the sound, then spoke into it. "Do you hear that, Lady Vice President?"

Then there were even more screams, louder this time. Then more begging.

The balding terrorist appeared at the door and pushed Diana Dunn into the stairwell for the fire stairs. "*Leela!*"—Move!

Diana Dunn gazed frantically around the group. "Why … why am I here?"

"To set an example," Aliev said simply.

He grabbed her by the back of her hospital gown and shoved her over to the railing that overlooked the space between the staircases. "What do you see?"

"I don't see anything," she said, her voice trembling.

"Well then, let me give you a closer look."

Aliev pushed the frail woman over the rail and watched her fall. She screamed at the top of her lungs until her head smashed into the rock-hard landing one floor down.

"Did you hear that, Lady Vice President?" Aliev asked into the cell phone. "Like my man, it seems that one of the patients slipped and fell to her death."

Aliev nodded to himself. "Ah! You did hear. Now hear this as well. If any more of my men disappear I will kill two hostages. And one of them will be from the First Family. Am I understood?… Good."

Aliev handed the cell phone back to the terrorist and instructed him in English to have the hostages lined up outside their rooms.

"All of them?" the terrorist asked. "Even the very sick ones?"

"All, except for the President," Aliev replied.

"Some are too ill to stand," David reminded him.

"One of them won't have to stand for long," Aliev responded, checking his watch. "Because he will soon be dead."

"These are innocent people," Carolyn pleaded.

"So was my dead wife," Aliev said icily, and stepped toward Carolyn. He poked her in the side with the barrel of his Uzi. "Now you will come with me."

"Wh … why?" Carolyn asked fearfully. "What do you want with me?"

"I'm going to give you the honor," Aliev said cruelly.

"What honor?"

"You will choose which hostage is the next to die," Aliev said, and pushed her out the door.

TWENTY-FIVE

EAGLE TWO SKIMMED ALONG the coastline in total darkness, at 560 miles per hour. There were no stars or moon visible, only faint flashes that came and went in the distance.

Special Agent Jake Anderson, the pilot of the Gulfstream turbojet, pointed ahead. "Those lights are coming from the Mexican interceptors."

"Are they closing in?" Joe Geary asked.

"It's hard to tell," Anderson answered. "But they sure as hell aren't any farther away."

"Do you think they're just trying to scare us?"

"For now."

Geary peered at the radar screen in the panel before him and asked, "How many interceptors can you make out?"

"Four," Anderson reported. "And that's three more than they need."

"Will this instrument panel tell us if they've got their missiles locked in on us?"

"No."

The turbojet hit a small air pocket and dipped slightly, then regained altitude. Both men glanced out at the flashes in the blackness again. The Mexican interceptors were definitely closer now.

"Do some fancy flying and get us out of this mess," Geary urged.

"We've just about used up all of our tricks," Anderson told him. "If those Navy jets don't get here soon, we're toast."

Geary grumbled under his breath. Everything that could go wrong was going wrong. Their chances of success were slipping away. He turned on a penlight and restudied the diagram of the Beaumont Pavilion and the plan to rescue the President. *It should work*, he kept trying to convince himself. If they could get back to Los Angeles in one piece, and if their timing was good and if the terrorists were in place, it should work. But all it would take was one mistake and there'd be a firefight with the President and his family in the middle of it. He sighed inwardly, wishing they still had a man on the inside they could communicate with. That would give them the edge they needed. But Ballineau was either dead or captured. He was no longer of use to them.

The radio crackled loudly before an accented voice came on. "Aircraft number N-Four-Three-Four-Two-P, this is Mexican Air Force jet flight leader. You must turn right to zero-two-zero and follow us to a nearby air base. Do you read? Over."

"Ignore him again," Geary said at once.

"We're going to really piss them off," Anderson warned.

Geary shrugged. "That happens in our line of business."

They flew on in the blackness, their gazes alternating between the outside and the instrument panel in front of them. One of the screens provided a heads-up display of the exterior terrain and beyond. It showed the sea and open air. No incoming jets were discernible.

Another twenty seconds passed before the Mexican flight leader spoke again. "Do you read, N-Four-Three-Four-Two-P? You are requested to acknowledge."

"Keep going!" Geary directed. "Maybe he'll think our radio is screwed."

"That won't last for long," Anderson said hoarsely.

"We don't need long." Geary checked his watch. The terrorists' deadline was rapidly approaching. "How close is the U.S. border?"

"Twenty-two minutes."

"They're not going to let us reach it."

"Tell me about it!"

Suddenly a Mexican jet zoomed overhead, producing a deafening roar. It was so close the Gulfstream shook violently and rattled in its wake.

"Holy shit!" Geary blurted out.

Anderson struggled with the controls and righted the turbojet. "That was to get our attention."

Ahead the Mexican interceptor slowed and leveled off, then began tilting its wings from side to side.

"And that's the international call sign for 'Follow me,'" Anderson went on. "We can't make believe we didn't see it."

"They've got us boxed in, haven't they?" Geary asked, steadying his nerves.

"And some," Anderson replied. "What do you want to do?"

Geary was sweating through his thick combat fatigues, trying desperately to think of a maneuver to reach the border with his team intact. He concentrated his mind and searched for an answer, but he kept coming up with the same conclusion. They were trapped with no way out. And landing on a Mexican airstrip was out of the question. They'd not only be delayed, they'd be put in jail. "Do you really believe they'd blow us out of the sky?"

"Oh, yeah!" Anderson said without hesitation. "To them, we're just a rogue plane carrying people who shot up a Mexican town."

Geary glanced to his right and left. He could see the lights of Mexican interceptors off both wings. *Christ! They're making a sandwich out of us!* Again he tried to come up with a way to buy time. "Do you think these Mexican pilots have ever seen combat?"

"No way," Anderson replied. "The closest they ever got to it was in some training exercise."

"So in all likelihood they'd be either gun-shy or trigger-happy."

"I guess gun-shy, real gun-shy."

"Me, too," Geary said with a firm nod. "I want you to call them and say we're a United States plane."

"What!"

"Just do it."

Anderson switched on his radio and said, "Mexican Air Force flight leader, this is N-Four-Three-Four-Two-P. We are a United States government plane. Do you read me? Over."

There was no response.

"Tell them we're authorized to be in Mexican airspace," Geary added quickly.

Anderson repeated the lie, and waited.

Still there was no response.

Seconds ticked by in the silence. Then the Mexican jets on their wings peeled off into the darkness.

"What do you think they're doing?" Anderson asked.

"Probably checking with their higher-ups," Geary said, looking out for the telltale flashes of the Mexican interceptors. He saw only blackness. "That should take a little while."

"I only need nineteen more minutes and I can get this baby to San Diego."

"They won't be having that long of a conversation."

Eagle Two flew on in the dark night, maintaining an altitude of three hundred feet and a speed of 560 miles per hour. The only sound inside the cockpit was the loud hum of the plane's two Rolls-Royce engines. A few minutes passed without the interceptors reappearing. There was no activity on radar or on the night vision screen.

"Do you think they've gone home?" Anderson asked, swallowing back his fear.

"Nah!" Geary replied absently. "They're just waiting for instructions."

"I've got a bad feeling here."

"Me, too."

"Maybe we should call Washington and see if they can clear a flight path for us," Anderson suggested. "You know, some kind of diplomatic bullshit."

"That's not going to happen," Geary said. "We're all on our own up here."

A missile suddenly streaked by the Gulfstream's cockpit. It came so close its trail of fire lighted up the cabin and blinded the agents for a moment. The turbojet abruptly dipped as one of its Rolls-Royce engines began to sputter.

"Jesus Christ!" Anderson bellowed. "Those bastards are going to kill us!"

"Where are those Navy jets?" Geary cried out. "Where the hell are they?"

TWENTY-SIX

ALIEV PARADED CAROLYN BACK and forth between the rows of hostages. They walked at a slow, deliberate pace, as if measuring each captive for execution. The selection process went on and on in silence. With each passing second the tension mounted. The male hostages tried to stand tall, but the fear showed on their faces. The women cowered and looked away.

Aliev stopped abruptly in front of the Russian Foreign Minister and spoke in English. "I notice your hands are shaking, Valerenkov."

Alexi Valerenkov clenched his fists and glared back. "I hope I live long enough to see you hanged."

"You won't," Aliev snarled, and turned back to Carolyn. "Now you must choose who will die."

"I can't," Carolyn begged off.

"Make the choice," Aliev demanded, "or I will kill two hostages instead of one."

"I'm a nurse," Carolyn pleaded. "You can't ask me to ..."

"Then it will be two."

They were standing by the nurses' station, looking down the corridor. All of the hostages, except for the President, were outside the doors to their suites. Some were so weak they had to lean against the wall to support their weight. A few were sitting on the floor. Terrorists with Uzis watched their every move.

"So let us begin," Aliev said casually. "We will choose one from this end and one from the other."

"Please don't!" Carolyn implored.

Aliev shoved her down the corridor in front of him. The phone at the nurses' station began to ring. He ignored it.

"We should answer the phone," Carolyn said quickly, hoping to spare people a little longer. "It'll only take a minute."

"We attend to business first," Aliev growled, and pushed her on.

They came to the Russian president and his wife. Dimitri Suslev looked beat and defeated, his face drawn, his head hanging down as if it was too heavy to carry.

"Ah, the powerful President of Russia," Aliev taunted in Russian. "Do you feel like ordering your planes out today to bomb Chechnya? Maybe you could kill a few hundred more innocent women and children, eh?"

Suslev didn't answer.

Aliev used the barrel of his Uzi to lift up Suslev's chin. "I should blow your brains out now. But I have other uses for you and your ugly wife."

They moved on, passing Ivana Suslev, who was seated on the floor and still gagging with nausea. Her blond hair was disheveled, her lipstick smeared, the makeup on her face cracked and peeling. She smelled strongly of vomit.

"Ugh!" Aliev said theatrically, dragging Carolyn along behind him.

They walked slowly up to the Secretary of State and his wife. The couple were holding hands and straining to maintain their dignity. Aliev paused to inspect them, like they were mannequins on display.

"Are you ready to die, Mr. Secretary?" Aliev asked.

"There are worse things," the Secretary replied evenly.

"Yes, I know," Aliev answered. "I have experienced them."

At the end of the corridor, they approached Lucy and Jamie Merrill. The First Lady was standing beside her daughter, her eyes glued on Aliev and the weapon he was pointing at them. If she was frightened, she didn't show it.

"Ah, the First Lady and the First Daughter, two of our most valuable hostages," Aliev remarked. "You would agree with me, no?"

Lucy Merrill didn't reply.

"And killing the First Daughter would make a very strong impression," Aliev continued on. "Certainly you would agree to that."

"You leave her alone!" Lucy snapped, hurriedly placing herself between Aliev and Jamie. Pushing her fear aside, she glowered at the terrorist and added, "Only cowards go after children."

"Oh, yes," Aliev said, nodding to himself. "The mother bear protecting the baby bear."

"You touch her, and you'll get nothing," Lucy warned.

"What if I just point a gun at her head?" Aliev wondered aloud. "In front of the President, of course."

"Bastard!" Lucy spat out.

"Yes. And a bastard who knows how to obtain the things he wants."

Aliev turned sharply and headed back down the corridor, shoving Carolyn in front of him. "So you've picked the Secretary of State to die first," he said, raising his voice for everyone to hear. "A good choice."

Carolyn quickly looked over to the Secretary and shook her head and gestured with her hands.

The Secretary nodded back. He understood.

Ahead of them, the door to the lounge opened and a wounded terrorist ran into the corridor. "Aliev! Aliev!" he called out, pointing to the blood-soaked bandage on his shoulder.

Aliev quickly pulled the dressing off and exposed a gaping wound that was filled with blood clots. At the edges were pieces of dirty cotton. He motioned Carolyn over and said, "You will attend to this."

Carolyn examined the shredded deltoid muscle, which was still oozing blood. She knew immediately that it was a through-and-through gunshot wound. "It has to be cleaned and he'll need antibiotics."

"Do it," Aliev ordered and steered the pair into the treatment room.

As Carolyn reached for a bottle of sterile saline, she had an almost overwhelming impulse to put dirt in the wound and start a virulent infection. But she just couldn't do it. Even a terrorist deserved humane medical care.

"What are you doing?" Aliev asked, moving in for a closer look.

"Irrigating the wound." Carolyn poured saline into the open muscle and carefully removed the blood clots and debris. The bleeding began to increase, particularly at the base of the gash.

"How do you stop the bleeding?" Aliev inquired.

"With a pressure dressing," Carolyn replied. She placed a thick gauze atop the wound and wrapped it tightly with an Ace bandage. "Now I'll give him a shot of antibiotics."

She hurried out into the corridor, through the nurses' station and into the medicine room. Aliev was only a step behind her. He crowded into the small room and peered over her shoulder, watching her every move.

"What is this antibiotic?" Aliev asked.

"It's called Cefobid."

Aliev eyed her suspiciously. "How do I know you are telling me the truth?"

"Here." Carolyn handed him the insert from the packaged antibiotic. "You can see for yourself."

The printing on the insert was small, and Aliev had to step out into the brighter light of the nurses' station to read it.

Carolyn took out the vial of Cefobid, which came as a powder and had to be dissolved in a diluent. Preparing the solution for injection, Carolyn suddenly stopped and smiled to herself. *Let's see if I can put another terrorist out of commission.* She reached up for a handful of Valium vials that David had requested. Quickly she removed two ccs from a vial and mixed it in with the solution of Cefobid. *That's ten milligrams of Valium—not enough to knock him out, but plenty enough to make him drowsy.*

"Okay," Aliev approved. "You may give it."

They went back into the corridor where the hostages were still standing. The President of Russia had slumped to the floor, obviously defecating in his pants. The stench was awful.

Aliev grinned at the spectacle, seeming to enjoy it.

What a bastard! Carolyn thought to herself, wishing it was Aliev who would be receiving the shot of Valium. A sedated Aliev would be easier to kill. Carolyn had never hoped for someone to die before—until she met up with Aliev. She would happily dance on his grave.

Aliev called the wounded terrorist into the corridor where Carolyn administered the injection of Cefobid and Valium. The terrorist stared at her without even a hint of gratitude. All she saw was hatred in his eyes.

The terrorist growled menacingly and spat at her feet.

You animal! Carolyn seethed and glared back at him, her temper almost boiling over. She clenched her jaw and resisted the urge to rip his bandage off and start the wound bleeding again. With effort she controlled her anger and silently said to him, *Let's see how tough you are when the Valium soaks into your brain.*

"All right," Alive announced, "we must return to our selection process."

"These people are so ill," Carolyn beseeched. "They have to be allowed to get back into their beds."

"They will," Aliev promised. "As soon as you've chosen the second hostage to die."

"Please don't—"

"You've already chosen the Secretary of State," Aliev cut her off. "So we need only one more."

At the nurses' station, the phone continued to ring. Aliev motioned to one of the terrorists to answer it. "Whoever it is, tell them we're busy with an execution."

They came to Sol Simcha, who was sitting in a wheelchair outside his room. He was reading from a Hebrew prayer book. He quietly recited a final verse before closing the book and looking up. His face was serene.

"Your God can't help you now," Aliev jeered.

"I wasn't asking for help," Simcha replied.

"What were you asking for?"

"That's between Him and me."

Aliev shrugged and pointed his Uzi at Simcha's head. "Whatever it was, it doesn't matter. Because shortly you will be a dead man."

"So will you," Simcha said without inflection. "They'll shoot you like they would a mad dog in the street."

"Say your last words, Jew!"

"No!" Carolyn screamed. "Let him alone!"

"Only if you pick someone to take his place," Aliev snarled.

"I can't do that!" Carolyn protested.

"Then the old Jew dies."

Simcha closed his eyes and thought back to the dreary day he and his family arrived at Auschwitz. He could still recall the exact moment his mother and father and little brother were pulled away from him and taken to the gas chambers. *Oh, how I would love to see them again! Dear God, I've tried to live a good and decent life. So in your infinite mercy, grant me one final wish. Let me see my family once again. Let me kiss my mother and father and little brother Yakov. Please, dear God!* Then Simcha began reciting the oldest of Jewish prayers, proclaiming there is one God and only one God. "*Shema Yisrael Adonai ...*"

A terrorist yelled down the corridor. "Aliev! It is Shamil on the phone! It is Shamil!"

Simcha felt the barrel of the Uzi still on his head. He continued to recite the *Shema*.

TWENTY-SEVEN

ONE OF EAGLE TWO'S engines continued to sputter and lose power, causing the plane to slow. It was now traveling at 490 miles per hour.

"We'd better pray the other engine doesn't go, eh?" Geary asked, with a mix of bravado and concern.

"Yeah," Anderson replied absently, his eyes fixed on the instrument panel.

"If we do have a total engine failure, is there any way to land this plane on the beach?" Geary asked.

Anderson shook his head. "If that happens, you can kiss your ass goodbye. We'd drop like a pancake from this altitude."

"And they could ship us home in boxes."

"Assuming they could find enough pieces."

Anderson tried to pick up the Mexican interceptors on the radar screen, but it stayed blank. *They are probably above and behind us,* he thought gloomily. They've got us up in their sights and are waiting for the order to push the button. And this time they won't miss. He turned his attention back to the night outside, and saw only blackness.

The Gulfstream's radio came to life.

"N-Four-Three-Four-Two-P, this is your last warning. If you do not ascend to two thousand feet and follow me, we have orders to open fire. Do you read?"

Anderson turned quickly to Geary. "What do you want to do?"

Geary hesitated, thinking fast. "Try to stall him."

"How?"

"Tell him we'll ascend to two thousand feet but we need to know where he's leading us."

"He'll just say for us to follow him in."

"Screw him! Tell him we need to know."

The radio crackled loudly.

"This is Mexican Air Force jet flight leader. You have thirty seconds to acknowledge our warning."

"We read you," Anderson said hastily. "We will climb to two thousand feet. We must know where we're headed. Over."

"You are to follow us."

"Flight leader, we *must* have a specific location. Over."

After a pause, the Mexican pilot said, "You will land at El Ciprés Air Base."

"Roger that. We are beginning our ascent." Anderson looked over to Geary and said, "Here goes! Let's hope those guys on the ground understand our Spanish."

"Yeah," Geary muttered miserably, then cursed to himself. God*damn* it! Being caught by the Mexican authorities was bad enough. But they were leaving the President in a dangerous lurch that could cost him his life.

Eagle Two slowly ascended to two thousand feet, still on a northerly heading. In the distance they could see the twinkling lights of Ensenada. Which was only a skip and a jump from the border. *So near*, both men were thinking, *so damn near*.

The radio crackled again.

"I wonder what the Mexes want now," Geary asked irritably.

"Who the hell knows?" Anderson replied, looking for the Mexican jets but not seeing them.

"Howdy, Eagle Two," an American voice came on. "This is Easy Rider from the USS *Ronald Reagan*, coming to take you home."

Anderson breathed a long, deep sigh of relief. "A big howdy back to you, Easy Rider. Over."

"Now you level off at two thousand and stay on your previous course," Easy Rider instructed in a Texas drawl. "Me and the posse here will take care of the bogeymen for you. Over."

"Thank you, Navy," Anderson said. "And you have a nice night."

Geary and Anderson leaned back and waited for their racing pulses to slow down. Both knew how near to death and disaster they'd come. Had the Mexican's pilot's aim been just a little off with his initial missile, eight Secret Service agents would now be stone-cold dead, their bodies at the bottom of the sea and unrecoverable. Had they been captured, they would have spent a long, long time in some flea-infested Mexican prison.

"Close, eh?" Anderson said finally.

"*Too* damn close," Geary replied, the back of his combat fatigues now drenched with perspiration. He reached behind and peeled the uniform away from his skin. His gaze went to the electronic flight instrument panel. A squadron of U.S. Navy jets suddenly appeared on the radar screen. Geary relaxed but kept his eyes glued in the darkness outside. "Are we going to see a dogfight?"

"No way," Anderson told him, thinking back to his days as a Marine aviator. He had trained with Mexican pilots at a naval flight school outside San Diego. He remembered the jets they brought with them. F-5 Freedom Fighters. Those planes were good interceptors, but no match for the F-18s. "The Mexicans will run for their lives when they see those Hornets."

"And what if they don't?"

"Then they'll die here and now," Anderson replied, pointing to a screen on his left. "We're talking about *ten* Hornets, any pair of which could blast those Mexican interceptors to hell and back."

"The Hornets are that powerful, eh?"

Anderson nodded. "And our pilots a hundred times more skilled. Along with the Israelis, they're the best in the world. You don't want to screw around with them."

The radio came back on. "Eagle Two, this is Easy Rider. Our Mexican *compadres* have decided to take a little siesta. We're going to cozy up alongside and escort you right back into the good old U.S. of A."

"Thanks, Navy."

"Any time, partner."

Eagle Two flew on in the darkness. Directly ahead were the lights of Tijuana, and just beyond that the glitter of San Diego.

"If you want to go over your rescue plans with the others one last time, you'd better get to it," Anderson said. "We'll have our wheels down in twelve minutes."

TWENTY-EIGHT

ONLY NOW WAS SOL Simcha feeling the awful fright. Although he was back in his room and the terrorists nowhere in sight, his hands were trembling. He had reacted the same way when he had been threatened by the Nazis at Auschwitz, Simcha recalled. At the moment one truly faced death, there was a calmness, an inner sense of acceptance. But later on, after the terrible threat had passed, one realized how good life was, even under the worst of conditions. And that's when the shaking started. Then came the dreadful waiting, knowing the executioners would return, but not knowing when.

Simcha sat in his wheelchair close to the door that was cracked open. He listened carefully to the conversation between terrorists in the corridor, hoping to glean new information on his fate. The young terrorists were speaking loudly and freely in Chechen, believing that none of the hostages could understand them. But Sol Simcha did. He was born in Ukraine where Russian was his mother tongue, and the language that the terrorists were now speaking sounded more like Russian than Chechen. As a result of the long and profound colonization of Chechnya by the Russians, the Chechen language had undergone so many transformations and was mixed with Russian to such an extent that it was often difficult to tell whether the younger Chechens were talking in Chechen or Russian. And to make matters even easier for Simcha, the Russian words the terrorists were uttering had a Ukrainian ring to them. Sol Simcha had no problem understanding their conversation.

"The old Jew tried to look brave," a terrorist was saying. "But did you see how tightly he held his prayer book? He was shitting in his pants."

"And he will shit even more when Aliev comes for him again," a fellow terrorist said.

"Jews!" the first terrorist spat out disgustedly. "They cause trouble wherever they go."

"*Nazis!*" Simcha growled under his breath. There were still plenty of them around, and they came in all shapes, sizes, and colors.

"Maybe there will be a lot of Jews at the place we detonate the bomb," the terrorist went on. "That would be a bonus."

"That would be a blessing," his fellow terrorist agreed.

"Aliev says the destruction will be unimaginable. He predicts thousands and thousands will die."

"And nobody will be allowed in the area for years to come, because of the intense radioactivity."

Simcha couldn't believe his ears. *Oh, my God! They're talking about an atomic bomb! They're going to drop an atomic bomb on this city! It will be like 9/11 a thousand times over!*

He moved closer to the door and concentrated his hearing. Now the terrorists were talking about a plane.

"Is the plane that large?"

"Oh, yes. It must be. We will be taking many hostages with us all the way back."

"And it will carry the bomb too, eh?"

"Without a problem. It's a big cargo plane that Aliev chartered. It can come up to us in a few hours from Mexico on Aliev's command."

"The plan is so perfect."

"It is better than perfect. After we drop the bomb, the plane will take us home, where we can watch the disaster unfold on television."

A voice called out from down the corridor.

"Coming!" a terrorist called back.

The conversation was over.

Simcha pushed his wheelchair away from the door, still stunned by the viciousness of the Chechens. Not only did they want to free their prisoners, they also wanted to inflict as much damage as possible on innocent people. In a crowded city like Los Angeles, they could kill hundreds of thousands, and seriously injure millions more. *And they can't be stopped!* Simcha knew he would be the next to die, and their secret would die with him unless he did something. But what?

Think, old man! Think! You thought your way out of a Nazi concentration camp. Think your way out of this!

Somehow I've got to tell the others. But how do I do it away from the terrorists? How? They watch every move I—

Suddenly, Simcha's eyes lit up. He quickly moved his wheelchair over to the nurse call button on his bed and pressed down on it.

There was no response.

He pushed the button again and again until Carolyn's voice finally came over the intercom. "What is it, Sol?"

"I'm having chest pain," Simcha gasped. "You'd better come right now!"

He tried to stand, but he was too weak. Instead he placed his head on the bed and allowed his arms to dangle by his sides. It gave the appearance he had passed out. He heard footsteps coming down the corridor, along with the rumble of a machine on wheels.

The door flew open and Carolyn rushed in, pushing an EKG machine in front of her. Aliev was a step behind, breathing heavily from having to run after her. He grabbed her by the arm.

"What are you doing in here?" he demanded.

"Sol is having a heart attack," Carolyn answered hastily.

"So what?"

"He'll die."

"Then let him die."

"We … we should try to save him," Carolyn said, desperately trying to think of a reason for the terrorist to allow her to treat Sol.

"Why should I care if the old Jew lives or dies?" Aliev said with a shrug. He motioned with his Uzi to the corridor. "Now go back to the nurses' station, obtain the drugs you need for the President, and look after his bleeding stomach."

Carolyn blinked. *Bleeding stomach! Blood!* She had a reason for Aliev to want Sol Simcha to live. "The President will shortly need more blood, or he'll die."

"Then give him more blood from the doctor," Aliev said.

"We can't. He's already weak from giving too much," she explained, then pointed to Sol Simcha. "But we could probably use his. His blood type is AB negative, the same as the President's."

Aliev remained expressionless, but he was thinking it was a good idea to keep the old man breathing to serve as a source of blood for the President. The people in Washington might insist on speaking to John Merrill again to make sure he was still alive. "Okay, treat him."

"I'll need Dr. Ballineau's help."

"Go get him."

Carolyn dashed out of the room and ran full speed down the corridor. As she passed William Warren's suite, she glanced in and saw the cardiac crash cart, and she briefly considered grabbing it for Sol. *No. Wait until David confirms the diagnosis of myocardial infarction, then come back for the cart if it's needed. Jesus Christ! Two M.I.s and a G.I. bleeder on the same floor, and only one doctor and one nurse to tend to them.*

Carolyn hurried into the President's room, and rushed to the bedside. David was flushing Merrill's nasogastric tube. Its contents were pink, with small clots in it.

"David! David!" she cried out and quickly described what was happening to Sol Simcha, and the story she had told about his blood type and how they might use his blood for the President.

"Is he really AB negative?" David asked quickly.

"Who the hell knows?" Carolyn said. "But that will keep him alive for now because Aliev thinks he is."

David nodded. "Were you able to take Sol's vital signs?"

Carolyn shook her head. "Aliev wouldn't let me near him."

"And what makes you think he'll deal with me any differently?"

"Because I convinced him we needed you to treat Sol and keep him alive."

David grabbed his stethoscope and said, "Let's go!"

They sprinted down the corridor, now joined by two terrorists, their Uzis at the ready. David glanced to the side and noticed the fire-stairs door was closed again, with the chain-like locking device back in place. *Aliev didn't go to the roof to post a lookout,* David deduced grimly, *or he wouldn't have chained the door shut.* More likely the terrorist planted another bomb up there. The bastard was making sure the explosion would kill everybody.

Now they were passing the nurses' station. David's heart dropped. Jarrin Smith and the Russian security agent were tied securely to their chairs. Jarrin caught David's eye and shrugged futilely. *Goddamn it!* David thought miserably. The ward clerk hadn't been able to contact the hospital operator. Somehow the terrorists must have discovered him trying. That's why he was tied up.

They raced into Sol Simcha's room, and hurried to his bedside. Simcha was slumped down in his wheelchair, his eyelids closed, his chest barely moving.

Carolyn leaned over Simcha and searched for a carotid pulse. "Sol! Sol!"

Simcha opened his eyes and said weakly, "Help me into bed, please."

Carolyn and David gently lifted the elderly man from his wheelchair and eased him onto his mattress. Carolyn slapped EKG leads across Simcha's chest as David reached for a blood pressure cuff.

Out of the corner of his eye Simcha glanced over to the doorway. A terrorist was standing there, watching everything.

"Where is your chest pain located?" David asked urgently.

Simcha mumbled an answer.

"Where?" David asked again, putting his ear by Simcha's mouth.

"I'm not having a heart attack," Simcha whispered in a barely audible voice. "But make believe I am, because there is something I must tell you."

"What?" David whispered back.

"They've got an atomic bomb," Simcha said quietly.

"What did you say?" David asked, wondering if he'd heard the old man correctly.

"An atomic bomb," Simcha repeated in a low voice. "I heard them talking about it in a Russian dialect outside my door. They didn't think I could hear or understand them."

David looked at Simcha skeptically. "Are you sure? Is your Russian that good?"

"It's as good as theirs," Simcha replied. "It was one mother tongue, growing up in Ukraine. Believe me, there is a bomb and they're going to drop it."

David pumped up the blood pressure cuff to make a covering noise. He motioned to Carolyn and said, "Start tearing off EKG strips and listen to what Sol has to say." Then he came back to Simcha. "Tell us about this atomic bomb."

"What!" Carolyn uttered too loud.

"Shhh!" David hushed her and again pumped up the blood pressure cuff. "Go ahead, Sol. Give us details."

"There's a chartered cargo plane on the ground somewhere in Mexico. It'll come up here in a few hours on Aliev's command. That's how they will escape."

David nodded at the strategy. That was the smart move. Have your own plane and pilot. Less could go wrong. "Do they plan to take hostages with them?"

"Yes," Simcha replied. "Then they'll drop the bomb from it."

"How do you know it's an atomic bomb?"

"Because they said the radioactivity will be so bad that nobody will be allowed in for years."

"Jesus!" David hissed under his breath. *An atomic bomb!* he thought, appalled, realizing that the explosives the terrorists were talking about earlier wasn't a bomb on the Beaumont Pavilion. They were talking about an atomic bomb.

Carolyn pretended to show David the EKG, and leaned over to Simcha. "Sol, are you sure they weren't just making this up to scare you?"

Simcha shook his head. "I'm scared enough as it is, and they know it. What they said wasn't meant for my ears. It was meant only for theirs. Believe me, I've had a lot of experience with this."

Simcha's mind went back briefly to a Nazi guard who enjoyed tormenting prisoners by misinforming them about their date of execution.

"Anyhow," he continued on, "I'll be the next to die, and I don't want the secret to die with me. Maybe you'll survive, and if you do you can notify the authorities."

"Don't give up," David said, patting Simcha's bony shoulder. "You may get out of here yet."

"Oh?" Simcha asked, and tried to read David's face. "What do you mean by that?"

"Just hang tough."

David led the way out into the corridor. Once past the guard, he turned to Carolyn and said, "Give Sol a placebo and make it appear that he's had a heart attack. Maybe that will cause Aliev to back off."

"Don't bet on it," Carolyn grumbled and glanced down the corridor. Aliev was hurrying toward them. "Here comes the cold-hearted bastard now."

"Let me handle this," David said rapidly, and began studying an EKG strip for effect.

Aliev came up to them and peered into Sol Simcha's room. "What has happened?"

"Mr. Simcha has had a heart attack," David said gravely.

"You must keep him alive," Aliev ordered. "After he's given his blood, it wouldn't do for me to shoot a dead man in the head. That would have no effect at all."

"Have you no sense of decency?" Carolyn screeched.

"Be careful!" Aliev warned menacingly. "You may be the next to die, after the old Jew."

David saw a flash of anger on Aliev's face, but it quickly vanished. The terrorist was mean as a snake but under control, and that made him twice as dangerous. Be very careful in his presence, David cautioned himself. He took a deep breath and resisted the urge to spin Aliev around and snap his neck. It would be over in seconds. But even if he succeeded and grabbed the Uzi, there wouldn't be time to use it. The other terrorists would mow him down. And Carolyn, too. David reached for Carolyn's arm and pulled her down the corridor, saying, "We have to go look after the President."

When they were out of earshot, Carolyn said in a low voice, "That was a stupid move on my part."

"Yeah," David agreed. "Don't tempt him again. He's ready to kill somebody, and I don't think it matters much who."

"It sounds to me like he's ready to kill a whole bunch of people," Carolyn said, then swallowed nervously. "Do you really think they'd drop an atomic bomb on this city?"

"Without giving it a second thought."

"Somehow we've got to let the people on the outside know about it," Carolyn said.

"Just tell me how to do it," David said. "I'm open to suggestions."

"I don't have the slightest idea."

"Me, neither."

Carolyn abruptly turned to David. "If the rescue attempt succeeds, we can tell them then."

"And what if the attempt fails?"

Carolyn shivered to herself. "I don't even want to think about it."

They entered the President's room on tiptoes. Merrill was dozing fitfully, twisting and turning and mumbling under his breath. His vital signs were stable, but the fluid in his nasogastric tube was now deep pink, with small blood clots floating in it.

"He's starting to bleed again," Carolyn said quietly.

David nodded. "And we have no more blood or plasma to give him."

"Is there anything we can do?"

"We ran out of options an hour ago."

David sighed heavily to himself, thinking that University Hospital was about to become even more famous for the wrong reason. Like Parkland Memorial Hospital in Dallas, where John F. Kennedy was pronounced dead, University Hospital in Los Angeles would now be remembered as the place where another charismatic American president died at the hands of others. And what was done and not done would be second-guessed for decades to come. David gazed over at the President and the blood-tinged fluid coming out of his stomach. It was only a matter of time now.

The stillness in the room was suddenly broken by a loud wheeze coming from the ceiling.

There was another wheeze, then another, followed by a raspy cough.

The panel above them slid open and Karen lowered her head out of the ceiling crawlspace.

"David!" Karen gasped and tried to suck air into her lungs. "I need an inhaler!"

David hesitated, wanting her to wheeze and choke for being part of a terrorist group. But his professional code of conduct gnawed at his conscience. He couldn't let anybody with a treatable medical condition suffer. He just couldn't. He turned to Carolyn. "Hand me one of the epinephrine syringes."

Carolyn reached into her pocket and held out the syringe.

At that moment Aliev burst into the room and stared at David and Carolyn. He didn't see the ceiling panel move back into place.

Everything went silent except for the soft clicks coming from the President's monitors.

"Why all the noise?" Aliev demanded.

"The President had a coughing spell," David answered.

Aliev glanced around the room suspiciously, then tilted his head back as if sampling the air. Gradually his eyes drifted down to Carolyn and the syringe she was holding.

"What is in the syringe?" he asked hoarsely.

"Epinephrine," Carolyn replied.

"What is it used for?"

Carolyn thought quickly, and said, "For cardiac problems."

"Is the President having this?"

"His heart beat is becoming weaker," Carolyn lied.

"See that he stays alive."

Aliev spun around and headed for the door. Just before he reached the corridor a loud wheeze sounded from the ceiling. Then another came, louder yet and more prolonged.

Aliev hurried back into the room and pointed his Uzi at the ceiling. Without emotion he squeezed the trigger, firing round after round until the panels above were peppered with bullet holes. Then he stopped and listened.

There were several seconds of silence before a weak female voice cried out, "Help me! Please help!"

Aliev yelled orders in Chechen to the two terrorists who were standing in the doorway. One of the men jumped up on the President's bed and hurriedly removed ceiling panels. With a grunt he reached into the crawlspace and pulled Karen's blood-spattered white blouse into view. The second terrorist helped him lower Karen onto the floor.

In a split second David was at her side. He ripped open her Oxford blouse and saw a sucking chest wound. With each inspiration, air was being sucked into the pleural space, putting pressure on the nearby lung and causing it to collapse. Karen was gasping for air, her skin becoming cyanotic.

David hurriedly turned to Carolyn. "Do we have a chest tube on the ward?"

"No," Carolyn replied. "And nothing that will substitute for one either."

David looked up at Aliev. "She needs a chest tube, which we don't have on the Pavilion, or she'll die."

"Then she dies," Aliev said, not caring. He motioned one of the terrorists. "Put her in the bathroom out of the way."

As Karen was being dragged away, Carolyn reached unnoticed into a nearby medicine cart and retrieved a pack of Vaseline gauze.

"So no one else was in the ceiling with you, eh?" Aliev spat at David.

"I never saw her," David said evenly. "She must have been hiding."

"Do you expect me to believe that?"

David shrugged. "It's the truth."

"One more truth like that and you'll find yourself dead."

Aliev signaled to the other terrorists and barked an order in Chechen. They followed him out of the room.

David dashed into the bathroom, with Carolyn a step behind. Karen's sucking chest wound was now shrouded with frothy blood. Her skin was growing even darker as she struggled for air.

David placed his hand over the wound and turned to Carolyn. "We need some sort of patch."

"Like this?" Carolyn asked and handed him a packet of Vaseline gauze, along with a roll of electrical tape.

"Perfect!"

David quickly covered the wound with a thick layer of Vaseline gauze, then began to tape it in place.

"Don't forget to leave one end open to act as a valve," Carolyn advised.

David smiled at her. "Where did you learn so much about treating a pneumothorax?"

"As a flight nurse on a MedEvac helicopter," Carolyn replied before injecting Karen with epinephrine to abate the asthma attack. "We saw at least one case a week."

With the patch in place and the epinephrine starting to work, Karen's breathing and color improved. She slowly took long, deep breaths, savoring each one.

"Better?" David asked.

"Much," Karen said, grimacing with pain. "And thanks for saving my life—again."

David's face hardened. "If it had been the Secret Service rather than me, they'd have let you die."

"You can't be serious."

"Oh yeah," David went on. "They know you're part of the terrorist group."

Karen's eyes bulged. "What!"

David repeated the accusation, then gave her details. "They know you worked in Chechnya, that you contributed to the Chechen charity that's a known terrorist front, and that you switched your on-call date so you would be in the hospital the night the terrorists attacked."

"That's insane!" Karen argued vehemently, despite the discomfort in her chest. "Of course I worked in Chechnya. So did dozens of other foreign doctors. And everybody contributed to that relief fund. We were told it was the quickest and surest way to get money to the hospitals." She coughed briefly and this worsened her chest pain. Clenching her jaw, she went on, "If you had seen the torture and rape victims and the little children with their limbs blown off, you would have written checks, too."

"And what about the switch in the on-call schedule?" David asked pointedly.

"I didn't request that," Karen said without hesitation. "Harry Summers did. It was his twentieth wedding anniversary and he had a special dinner planned for his wife. They can check that out with Harry."

David nodded slowly, thinking that all the evidence against Karen had been circumstantial and easily explained away. "It seems like they really had you pegged wrong."

"I'll say." Karen winced as another sharp pain shot through her chest. "If I don't make it and you do, make sure you clear my name."

"I'll take care of it," David promised.

"And one last thing," Karen told him. "I've got some pre-filled syringes of Propofol in my blouse pocket. I was going to use it as a general anesthetic for the President's endoscopy."

"So?"

"So, if you're able to subdue any more of the terrorists, you can inject them intravenously with the Propofol. They'll be out for hours."

"Won't I have to dilute it?"

"Fuck 'em!" Karen spewed. "If the concentrate makes them go too deep, it'll be a bonus."

David grinned at the unexpected profanity and patted her shoulder reassuringly. He fetched the syringes of Propofol from her blouse and hurried back into the President's room. There was a guard at the door, but his back was to them.

David leaned over to Carolyn and said, "She's not out of danger by any means. If that seal doesn't hold, she could die in minutes."

"I'll keep an eye on her," Carolyn whispered, then lowered her voice even more. "David, you'll have a hard time injecting Propofol into a vein if the terrorist is squirming around."

"It'll be easier to stick it into an artery," David whispered back. "That may kill him, but who the hell cares?"

Carolyn looked toward the bathroom, still keeping her voice down. "I never really believed Karen Kellerman was a traitor."

"I did," David said honestly. "But I'm glad she's not."

Behind them the President groaned loudly. They looked over and watched him continue to twist and turn, but now he was awake. Their gaze went to the fluid in the nasogastric tube. It was filling up with poorly formed blood clots. All hell was about to break loose.

TWENTY-NINE

THE FLUID IN THE President's nasogastric tube rapidly turned bright red in an instant. His bleeding was coming back with a vengeance.

"How are you doing, Mr. President?" David asked.

"Not as well as I'd like," Merrill complained mildly. "And this tube in my nose is bothering the hell out of me. Is there any chance we can remove it?"

"No, sir," David said. "We need it to lavage your stomach."

Merrill's face grew concerned. "Am I bleeding again?"

David nodded but downplayed it. "Oozing is a better description."

"Christ," Merrill muttered.

David motioned over to Carolyn to restart the ice-water lavage, then glanced at the cardiac monitor. The President's blood pressure remained borderline low at 98/60, which meant he was still volume depleted. And now he was bleeding more.

"What are those terrorists doing?" Merrill asked around his nasogastric tube.

"They haven't killed any of the hostages so far," David replied. "If that's what you want to know."

"But you think they will?"

"I know they will," David said bluntly. "Unless their demands are met."

Merrill sighed to himself, wondering how far negotiations had gone with the terrorists. "Has there been any talk of releasing those Chechen prisoners?"

"It sounds as if some have been flown out of Guantanamo Bay," David answered.

But to where, and for how long? Merrill asked himself. Flying prisoners out and releasing them altogether were two different things. He couldn't be sure if an exchange was underway, or if the move was just a stalling tactic. "If there's to be some sort of prisoner swap, I want my wife and daughter to be the first ones out. Understood?"

"Understood, Mr. President."

"David," Carolyn called over and pointed to a syringe filled with gastric juice. It was redder yet and now contained only a few small blood clots.

David and Carolyn gave each other knowing glances. Things were going sour again, and quickly. Merrill's condition would soon become critical if he didn't receive blood or an infusion of Factor VIII. Since neither was going to happen, it was only a matter of time before the President bled out and died.

David's gaze went back to the monitor. The President's blood pressure was unchanged, but his pulse was rapidly increasing. It was up to 112 per minute. A bad sign.

The President urgently needed another transfusion, David told himself. *Somehow I've got to get him fresh blood, and fast. But how do I do it? The terrorists won't let anybody or anything come up to the Pavilion. And I'm too weak to give any more of my blood.* David groaned inwardly. He was out of therapeutic options, and he knew it.

"David," Carolyn broke into his thoughts and gestured to Merrill's nasogastric tube. Now pure blood was flowing up through it.

"Crush up some ice and flush out his stomach with small pieces of it," David ordered out of desperation. "And let the ice chips remain in his stomach longer."

Carolyn tried the maneuver over and over, with only a modicum of success. The President's gastric juice was just a little less red than before. "I think the bleeding is slowing some, but not by much."

"Keep the lavage going," David directed. "Hopefully, we can stop him from really bursting loose."

"I don't think we—"

"Shhh!" David quieted her, now picking up the sound of helicopters in the distance. There were at least two of them. They seemed to be coming and going, like they were circling the medical center. David pricked his ears and concentrated on the distinctive put-put noise. *They were Black Hawks! Attack helicopters! It had to be the Secret Service team! The rescue attempt was starting! Good! Good!*

David felt the adrenaline rushing through his system, all senses suddenly heightened and alerted. Quickly he cleared his mind and pondered what he could do to assist. He was the man on the inside, and that was worth three coming through the front door. But he could only help if he knew what they were going to do. He had to know their plan. Most importantly, he had to know if his earlier message had gotten through. Was it to be like Mogadishu? Or had they chosen another way in? *I've got to know! Then I could give the President some protection!*

David hurriedly glanced around for a means to communicate. The suite's phone had been ripped from the wall, and his personal cell phone was long gone. *What about breaking a window and sending down a message in a bottle?* he asked himself. No good. The terrorist at the door would hear the glass shattering. And even if he didn't, no one would notice a small bottle dropping down at 1:45 a.m. in the black, misty air. The Secret Service might have their eyes glued on the President's window, but they'd never see—

David suddenly blinked.

In a flash the answer came to him. He leaned closer to Carolyn and whispered softly, "I'm going to walk over to the window. When I get there, I want you to place yourself between me and the guard at the door. Block his line of vision as much as possible."

"Why?" Carolyn whispered back.

"Just do it," David urged.

He ambled over to the window and waited for Carolyn to move into position. Then he reached for his pocket flashlight and quickly put his hand under the blanket covering the window. When the sound of the Black Hawks grew louder again, he began sending a message in Morse code, using his flashlight.

N-E-E-D   T-O   K-N-O-W

M-O-G-A-D-I-S-H-U   O-R   N-O-T

David peeked around the edge of the blanket and searched for a response. He saw only blackness. Perspiration started trickling from his neck and down his back. His pulse began to race as the guard standing in the doorway turned sideways. David hurriedly peeked out again and scanned the darkness. There was still no answer.

Come on, goddamn it! he growled inwardly, and sent out the message once more.

The sound of the helicopters faded as David's spirits sank. *My phone message to the Secret Service didn't get through! They don't know what the hell I'm talking about, and I don't know which way they're coming in. Not via the roof again,* he hoped. *That would be suicide for the agents, and for a lot of the hostages.*

The guard at the door barked loudly in Chechen at David. Then he repeated the order and waved his Uzi toward the President's bed.

David saw the look of displeasure on the terrorist's face. The guard didn't like him standing by the window. David pulled at his collar as if he were warm and getting a breath of air.

The guard grunted his disapproval, then reached into his back pocket for a plastic bottle of water. He took a big gulp and gave David another stern look. But before he could bark out another order, a loud yell in Chechen came from down the corridor. The guard hastily placed the plastic bottle on a chair just inside the door and rushed out of the room.

David watched the terrorist disappear from sight, then quickly glanced out into the heavy mist. He couldn't see the helicopters, but he could hear their sounds. They were closer now. An attack had to be imminent! But where and how? And how could he help without drawing the terrorists' attention? Just stepping out into the hall could get him killed. His eyes went to the door. The guard was still gone, but that wouldn't last for long. David's gaze dropped down to the guard's bottle of water sitting on a chair beside the door. It was open. No top. He thought of a way to better the chances of the rescue team.

David hurried over to Carolyn and asked, "Did you get those vials of Valium for the President?"

"Yes," Carolyn answered, then told him about the injection she'd given the wounded terrorist. "He got ten milligrams of Valium intramuscularly."

"Perfect," David praised. "How many vials do you have left?"

"Two."

"What's the dose in each vial?"

"Fifty milligrams of Valium in ten ccs."

"Draw up ten ccs in a syringe for me."

While he waited, David looked out into the black night again. And again he heard the helicopters but couldn't see them. Now they appeared to be circling the medical center.

"Here you are," Carolyn said, handing him a syringe filled with liquid Valium. "What's it for?"

"You'll see." David dashed over to the open bottle of water and estimated its contents. It was a 500-cc bottle that was a quarter full, and that meant it held approximately 125 ccs. Quickly David squirted the Valium solution into the bottle, swirled it around, and placed it down on the chair.

"Did you put the whole vial in?" Carolyn asked.

"Every drop."

"It has a preservative in it," Carolyn warned. "He might taste it."

"That's a chance we'll have to take."

Carolyn smiled slyly. "If he drinks the whole damn thing, he'll sleep for days."

"Or longer."

David raced back to the window and peered around the edge of the blanket, searching and hoping for a response from the helicopters. He saw only darkness. *Come on, damn it!* He desperately tried to think of another message to send to the Secret Service. In it he would have to identify himself and ask about their planned point of entry. *Jesus! How can I do that and keep the message short?*

In the distance he heard the sound of an approaching helicopter. It grew louder and louder, then seemed to hold its position. David pulled the blanket back a little more and scanned the night. A light began to flash intermittently in the darkness. They were answering his message! It read:

M-O-G-A-D-I-S-H-U

0-2-0-0

"Yes," David hissed softly, his spirits soaring. He glanced over his shoulder at the door. The guard still hadn't returned, but now there were footsteps in the corridor. David hurriedly turned back to the window and tried to come up with a way to warn the Secret Service of an impending nuclear attack. And tell them how the weapon was going to be delivered. *How do I do that? How? Just say it, goddamn it!* He rapidly flashed out a final message.

N-U-K-E   O-N   P-L-A-N-E

A rapid reply came from the helicopter.

R-E-P-E-A-T

David flashed the message again, and added two words.

B-I-G   C-H-E-R-N-O-B-Y-L

David closed the blanket over the window and checked his watch. 1:50 a.m. Ten minutes to go! Quickly he collected his thoughts and walked over to Carolyn.

He leaned in very close to her, his lips almost touching her ear. "Do exactly as I tell you, and don't ask any questions."

"O-okay," Carolyn said hesitantly, struck by the gravity in his voice.

"When I give you the signal, I want you to walk into the President's daughter's room and make like you're checking on her. Tell her to wait until you leave, then to count to sixty in her mind. That should be approximately one minute. Got it?"

"Got it."

"Then tell her when she reaches sixty she is to go into her bathroom and climb into the bathtub and stay there, curled on her side and protecting her head."

Carolyn's mouth flew open. "Is this—?"

David brought his index finger up and pressed it against her lips, quieting her. "Do the same with the First Lady. Say only what I told you to say. Get in and get out. But make certain they understand their lives depend on doing exactly what they're told."

Carolyn nodded quickly. "After I have them squared away, what do you want me to do?"

"Come back in here," David instructed. "You're going to help me move the President."

The guard suddenly reappeared and carefully eyed the presidential suite. He stared at David, then at the blanket covering the window, then came back to David. Satisfied, he picked up his bottle of water and took a generous swallow.

Good, David thought. *Drink it all, you son of a bitch. It'll save us the trouble of killing you later.*

THIRTY

"OF COURSE, YOU COULD always turn the plane around," Aliev was saying to the National Security Council over the speakerphone. "We have to ensure that you do not do this."

"We don't intend to," Halloway lied, keeping her eye on the digital clock. In eight minutes the new deadline would be reached, and another hostage's life put on the line. "The plane from Guantanamo is on a direct course to the Azores, where it will refuel, as you instructed."

"What about the other Chechen prisoners under your control?" Aliev demanded.

"Those at Bagram are preparing to take off," Halloway told him.

"If they are not in the air when the deadline arrives, a hostage will die," Aliev threatened.

"There's no need for that," Halloway exhorted. "We are living up to our end of the agreement. We expect you to do the same."

"You have a deadline, and so do we," Aliev said, not budging. "All prisoners are to be in the air, or a hostage will be executed."

"We are working as fast as we can," Halloway said. "You must believe that."

"I will believe it when I hear the voices of my countrymen on those planes," Aliev snapped.

"And then the President and the other hostages will be released. Right?"

"Oh, we should not go so fast," Aliev said, his voice softening a bit. "You might suddenly decide to return those planes to their bases. Maybe that is why you are keeping Shamil and his men in shackles. So to be absolutely sure this does not happen, we will take the political hostages with us. We—"

"With you?" Halloway interrupted. "That was not part of our agreement."

"It is now," Aliev went on. "We have a plane that will shortly be taking off from a Mexican airport. When all the Chechens are freed, I will give you the identification number of the plane so you can clear a flight path into LAX. Once it has landed, you will arrange for a large helicopter to come to the roof of the medical center. One of my men will pilot it and the hostages back to LAX, where we will board the cargo—" He stopped abruptly to correct himself. "—where we will board the transport plane, which will take us to Elmendorf Air Base in Alaska. The trip will take nearly six hours. By then all the Chechens should be safely home. We will release your President and his family, and fly on to Moscow, where Dimitri Suslev can beg for his life on television. Perhaps the Russians will reconsider their refusal to negotiate, no?"

The phone line crackled, then became silent.

Halloway and Alderman exchanged worried glances, both thinking, *Oh, God. What if the rescue attempt fails?*

Halloway quickly leaned toward the speakerphone. "We can't allow the President to leave the hospital. He's too—"

"You will have no choice in this matter," Aliev cut her off. "So stop wasting time, and get my Chechens in the air."

The phone line went dead.

The Situation Room stayed silent for a moment as the council tried to quickly gather their thoughts. Everyone was concerned about Aliev's plan to take the President out of the hospital. John Merrill's condition was too precarious. The move could cost him his life.

"We can't let them remove the President from the hospital," Halloway said resolutely.

"He'd no doubt die on that plane," Alderman agreed. Then he added darkly, "And once they were safely in the air, the signal could be given to drop the bomb."

Again the room became quiet. The image of a nuclear mushroom cloud abruptly came to everybody's mind. The last message from their man in the Beaumont Pavilion had repeated the word *NUKE* twice. There was no question about its meaning. And its consequences. A catastrophe was about to happen.

"How the hell did they get a nuclear bomb?" Toliver asked, breaking the silence.

"From any number of sources," Alderman answered. "At the top of the list would be North Korea, Pakistan, or some poorly guarded Russian facility."

"And it could be a hydrogen bomb."

"Could be."

"And it's heading our way."

"So it would seem."

"And beyond any doubt," Pierce interjected, "the plane coming up for the hostages is the one carrying the nuke."

"How can you be so sure?" Halloway asked at once. "Maybe there's a second plane Aliev will tell us about later."

Pierce shook his head decisively. "I don't think so, Madam Vice President. The key word here is *cargo*. Aliev was about to say cargo plane, but changed it to transport plane. He didn't want us to know it was a cargo plane."

Halloway looked at him quizzically. "I'm not following you."

"If he was only interested in transporting hostages, a passenger plane like a Boeing 757 would do fine. But you can't deliver a nuclear weapon from that aircraft. I guess you could get it aboard, but getting it off and detonating it would present huge problems. With a big cargo plane, you just open the back bay and slide it out."

"And onto the people of Los Angeles," Halloway added gloomily.

"I'm not at all sure that Los Angeles is the target," Alderman said.

"Why not?" Halloway asked, her eyes going to the digital clock. Five minutes to the deadline. And five minutes to the rescue attempt. "Give me quick answers. Time is running out."

"Because it doesn't make sense," Alderman said in a rush. "If Aliev drops a nuclear weapon on Los Angeles, he accomplishes none of his goals. All of the Chechen prisoners would be returned to prison, and he and his men would be as good as dead. Once they land in Alaska, they'll never be allowed to leave. Aliev would know these outcomes."

"Maybe he plans to die with the hostages," Halloway countered. "You know, dying with very important infidels in a jihad."

"Why die when you can accomplish your goals and live?" Alderman argued back.

"So what do you think he intends to do?"

"Drop the bomb somewhere else."

"In America?"

"No. I believe he wants to reach Alaska where he can be assured all of his fellow Chechens have landed and are free. Then he'll fly off and detonate the nuclear device."

"Why bomb Alaska?" Toliver asked promptly. "Hell! It's mostly snow and ice up there."

"It won't be Alaska," Alderman predicted. "It will be somewhere in Russia."

"Moscow!" Halloway exclaimed. "They know the Russians won't negotiate, so the Chechens mean to inflict as much damage as possible on their civilian population. God knows, the Chechens hate the Russians enough to do it."

Toliver nodded in agreement. "Kind of like a payback for what Russia did to Chechnya."

"Perhaps," Alderman said, unconvinced. "But the Russians aren't stupid. They may not be thinking about a nuclear explosion, but they'll be wondering if the Chechens plan to crash the plane into Moscow, like the 9/11 terrorists did to Manhattan and D.C. Believe me when I tell you the Russian Air Force won't let that plane within a hundred miles of Moscow. And Aliev knows this."

"So what the hell is going on?" Halloway demanded.

"I think he's going to try to create another Chernobyl," Alderman replied.

"Do you mean blow up a big nuclear reactor?"

"Oh, it's something far more important than a reactor," Alderman said and walked over to a map on the large video screen. With his index finger he pointed to Alaska and moved it across the vastness of Russia. "If one draws a line from Anchorage to Moscow, it goes through the heart of the Siberian plains and its natural resources."

"The Russian oil fields!" Halloway gasped.

Alderman nodded. "That's why the message from our man in the Beaumont Pavilion used the term 'Big Chernobyl.' The bomb's main purpose is to contaminate, not kill. A really dirty bomb would spew out a massive cloud of radioactive cesium and strontium and iodine. That entire area would become uninhabitable for decades. At ground zero, it would remain highly contaminated for a hundred years or more. For Russia, it would be an economic catastrophe. For OPEC, it would be a godsend. They and the Muslims would again control the world's oil market."

Halloway gazed at the map on the large screen and asked, "Are you saying the prisoner release may have just been camouflage for what they really intended to do?"

"Quite possibly," Alderman answered. "After all, they must have realized the Russians would never negotiate."

"And that we would," Halloway grumbled, her eyes still on the map of the Siberian plains. "How large an area of contamination are we talking about?"

"The Chernobyl disaster ruined three thousand square miles," Alderman replied. "A powerful nuclear explosion could easily double that number."

"Six thousand square miles," Halloway breathed.

"At least."

Halloway looked over to the digital clock again. Three minutes until the deadline. "What should we do about the plane?"

"I say shoot it down if it comes close to the United States," Pierce said forcefully. "We can't be sure it's going to Russia."

"We could be signing the President's death warrant if we do that," Alderman cautioned.

"We could blame the Mexicans," Pierce thought aloud.

"The Chechens would never buy that," Alderman said.

"I think we should allow the plane to come to Los Angeles and pick up the President," Toliver voted.

"We'd be taking one hell of a chance, Mr. Secretary," Pierce disagreed.

"Let me ask you this," Toliver said coolly. "Do you think Aliev plans to drop that bomb on Los Angeles or Russia?"

"Russia," Pierce said without hesitation. "But there's still—"

Toliver raised his hand, interrupting. "I think Russia, too. As a matter of fact, I'm convinced of it. With that in mind, I say let the plane fly on because I care a million times more about my President than I do about some damn Russian oil field."

After a moment's pause, everyone at the table began to slowly nod. Except Halloway. She stared straight ahead. She knew Toliver's plan was very risky. If he was wrong, it would cost countless numbers of Americans their lives. It would be 9/11 a thousand times over.

Alderman studied Halloway's face and asked, "What do you think, Madam Vice President?"

"I think we'd better pray the rescue attempt succeeds," Halloway said softly.

"We'll need a backup plan in case it doesn't," Alderman pressed.

"I'm aware of that," Halloway replied, still thinking about 9/11 magnified a thousand times. It was horror beyond imagination. But if she had the plane shot down, the terrorists would realize they had no way out. And at that point they would happily kill themselves, taking the President and all the other hostages with them.

"Well?"

Halloway's eyes went to the digital clock. Two minutes to the deadline. "We'll allow the plane into Los Angeles."

———

Aliev heard the helicopter coming closer. For a moment it seemed to be directly above him. Then the distinctive put-put noise began to fade. He pricked up his ears and waited for the sound to return, now wondering if the helicopter was circling. It wasn't, he decided, as the sound vanished altogether.

Aliev walked rapidly to the nurses' station and stared down at Jarrin Smith. "Go use the bathroom."

"I … I don't have to," Jarrin said hesitantly.

"This will be your last chance for a long time," Aliev threatened. "If you have to relieve yourself later, you will do it in your pants in front of the others."

"I'd better go while I can," Jarrin said, and waited to be untied before getting to his feet.

Aliev motioned to the wounded terrorist to accompany Jarrin into the nurses' lounge. He kept his eyes on them until they disappeared from sight, then checked the corridor to make certain no hostages were within earshot. Hurriedly he leaned down to the Russian security agent and whispered in Chechen, "What do you think about the helicopter, Yudenko?"

"It was a large one," Yudenko answered in a low voice. "You could tell from the noise and the vibration it caused."

"Do you believe they are doing aerial reconnaissance?" Aliev asked.

"Maybe," Yudenko replied carefully. "But why use such a big helicopter to just take a look?"

"That I do not know," Aliev replied and gave the matter more thought. "The only other reason for them to come and go like that would be to drop off men."

"Yes, yes," Yudenko agreed at once. "It must be a rescue team."

"But how would they attempt to enter?" Aliev asked, more to himself than to the agent.

Yudenko shrugged. "Perhaps through the roof again."

Aliev shook his head. "They are not that stupid. They know we would hear them."

"Not if they used an acetylene torch, like they did before," Yudenko contended.

"Maybe you are right," Aliev said. But he remained unconvinced. "To be on the safe side, I will have one of our men with his head in the crawlspace at all times."

"Tell him to be alert for a burning smell," Yudenko urged. "That will be the initial indication they are coming through."

"But our enemies would realize this, too," Aliev said uneasily. "And they would know we will be watching the crawlspace very closely after their failed attempt."

Yudenko knitted his brow, concentrating. "Perhaps it was only reconnaissance, after all."

Aliev shook his head. "I believe our first conclusion is correct. They have dropped men onto the roof. It is a rescue attempt."

"But why such a large helicopter?" Yudenko persisted. "They don't require that many men for a rescue mission."

"Perhaps to cover the sound of a smaller one that landed," Aliev conjectured. "But how will they try to enter? How?"

"Not via the roof, eh?"

"No," Aliev said and began pacing the floor, concentrating on possible points of entry. Not through the dumbwaiter, which they would assume was booby-trapped. Or down the crawlspace, which was too dangerous. Or up the elevators that were stuck in place, with their doors jammed shut. That left only one way in. He stopped in his tracks and turned to Yudenko. "They will come down the fire stairs."

"But they will think we have planted explosives in its staircase and on its door," Yudenko argued.

Aliev shook his head. "Only a fool would booby-trap his escape exit."

"Then surely they will know we have it heavily fortified," Yudenko argued on.

"They will storm their way in," Aliev insisted.

"But they will take such large casualties."

"That will not deter them," Aliev said with certainty. "Believe me when I tell you they have no intention of allowing us to leave the Pavilion, whatever the cost."

"But their President will die."

"They realize he dies either way."

Yudenko's face lost color, but he recovered quickly. "So here is where we make our final jihad."

"Yes," Aliev said and untied the Russian agent. "Tell the others to prepare."

Aliev hurried into the chart room and stepped over dead bodies to reach the far wall. He smashed out the window with the butt of his Uzi, knowing his satellite phone would not function in an enclosed room. For a satellite phone to work properly, one needed a clear view of the sky, which Aliev no longer had. And he couldn't return to the roof, not with the Secret Service rescue team now in place.

Aliev stuck his head and neck out of the window and dialed Basagev's number. He heard his second-in-command answer, but the static was intense and difficult to hear through.

"Basagev! Basagev!" Aliev yelled, then spoke in the Middle Eastern dialect of Chechen. "It is Aliev!"

"Al...cannot...your voice," Basagev replied.

"The Americans are about to launch a rescue attempt!" Aliev shouted.

For a brief moment the reception improved. "But I thought the Americans were negotiating," Basagev said.

"They were," Aliev told him. "But it was only a ruse to gain time while they planned a rescue."

The static came back and gradually grew louder.

"Perhaps … they … not succeed," Basagev said.

"No, my brother," Aliev hollered through the static. "Like us, they will fight to the death, and eventually their numbers will overcome us."

"So … what … we do?"

"We shall die gloriously!" Aliev elated. "You are to detonate the nuclear bomb over Los Angeles. I will switch on the homing device to pinpoint exactly where to drop the bomb. Do you hear me?"

"Nuc … over … Angeles," Basagev replied.

"Yes!" Aliev called back, overjoyed his message was received. He pushed the button on his satellite phone to activate the homing device. "Can you pick up the homing signal?"

"We … very weak … fading …" Basagev said, his voice almost impossible to hear through the static.

"If you can't detect my signal," Aliev screamed into the phone, "use the landing lights at LAX as a detonation point. Do you read me?"

"Lan … lights … LAX," Basagev replied before the static drowned out his voice completely.

Aliev switched off the satellite phone and stared out into the heavy mist. Yes, he thought, pleased with himself, the lights at LAX should work well. The airport was located on the west side of the city, and all planes landed from the east. So Basagev will have a good view of … Aliev's mind stopped in mid-thought, now aware of the gaping flaw in his plan. *The weather! The weather, you fool! The dense fog advancing in from the sea would obscure the landing lights at LAX and may well shut down the airport altogether. Then all incoming flights would be diverted to other destinations. If that were to occur, just a minor miscalculation by Basagev and the bomb would end up being detonated in the ocean off the coast of California, where its effect would be greatly muted.*

There were too many variables, Aliev thought sourly. Too many chances for things to go wrong. He concentrated on the problem and tried to think of an alternative landmark to guide Basagev. But what? Where? It had to be something visible from the cockpit. *The cockpit! Of course!* He slapped an open palm against his forehead. *Idiot! The new cargo plane's cockpit should have a Global Positioning System. It was the perfect homing device!*

Aliev quickly redialed Basagev's number. But all he heard was loud static.

Suddenly from above came the roar of an approaching helicopter, its lights a blur in the heavy mist. The chart room began to vibrate as the helicopter grew closer and closer. A stiff wind from its rotors blew in through the window and pushed Aliev back. He reached for his Uzi, but the wind and shaking floor made it impossible to aim the weapon. Grabbing the windowsill, he tried to steady himself enough to fire off a burst, but the vibrations became even stronger. Abruptly, an intense beam of light broke through the mist and flooded into the chart room.

Aliev spun away from the blinding light and, jumping over dead bodies, raced for the corridor.

THIRTY-ONE

"Just do it!" Carolyn instructed the First Daughter. "Do exactly as I told you."

Jamie stared at the nurse, wide-eyed and becoming unnerved. "Sh ... should I close the front door to my room, too?"

"No," Carolyn replied hastily. "That will just make the guard suspicious. Do only what I told you to do."

Jamie's lower lip began to tremble. Then the tears came.

"Dry those eyes," Carolyn ordered, in a stern voice. "First Daughters don't cry at times like this."

"This one does," Jamie said, her voice quivering with fright.

"Not in here, and not now." Carolyn reached for a Kleenex, and handed it to her. "I want you to sniff back those tears and start counting."

Jamie dabbed at her cheeks and began to silently mouth numbers.

One ... two ... three ... four ...

Carolyn hurried into the corridor and checked her watch. She was already thirty seconds behind. *Damn it!* She gave the guard a fake smile, and dashed into the First Lady's room. Lucy Merrill was lying on her bed, with a damp washcloth draped across her forehead.

Carolyn squeezed her hand and waited for her to open her eyes. "Listen very closely to me, Mrs. Merrill, and do exactly as I say."

"Wh … what is …?"

"Shhh!" Carolyn quieted her. "Just do exactly as I say. When I leave your room, count to thirty. Then get out of bed, and walk into your bathroom. Close the door behind you and climb into the bathtub. Lie on your side and curl up into a ball, protecting your face. And stay there."

Lucy sat up abruptly, now fully awake. "Does this mean what I think it means?"

Carolyn smiled thinly. "Don't forget to cover your head."

"What about my husband?" Lucy asked quickly. "Who will help him?"

"The doctor who has kept him alive through all this," Carolyn said.

"No, no! I mean in a non-medical sense."

"So do I. Now start counting."

Carolyn left the room and walked past the guard, keeping her gait even, so she wouldn't appear to be rushing. She yawned for effect as she entered the President's suite. Then she darted to his bedside. David was again lavaging Merrill's stomach with ice water and ice chips. The gastric juice was still bright red. And so was the blood dripping from David's leg wound onto the floor.

"All set?" David asked.

"All set," Carolyn replied and moved in for a closer inspection. "I think your wound has reopened."

David glanced down at the blood on his ankle and shoe. "Don't worry about it."

"I could wrap it for you," Carolyn offered.

"We don't have time," David said, glancing at his watch. *It was 1:58 a.m. Two minutes until zero hour!* He leaned down for the President. "Carolyn, you have to do two things very quickly. First, clamp off the nasogastric tube and tape it in place. Secondly, grab the IV pole and follow me."

The alarm on a cardiac monitor suddenly went off across the corridor. David and Carolyn stopped in their tracks and concentrated their hearing to determine where the alarm was coming from. It was near. Very near.

"It's Dr. Warren's room," Carolyn said.

"Oh Christ!" David groaned. "Not now!"

They raced out of the door and down the corridor. The terrorist guarding the President stayed put, but another terrorist followed the pair into Warren's room. The elderly physician was gasping for air, his hand clutching his chest in pain.

David hurriedly turned on the EKG machine and studied the strip it produced. William Warren was having runs of ventricular tachycardia.

David called over to Carolyn who was setting up the defibrillator on the other side of the bed. "Can you administer a shock while holding the paddles?"

"No problem," Carolyn told him. "This defibrillator has a manual override. All I have to do is press down simultaneously on the red buttons at the top of the handles and the machine will deliver an electric shock. How strong do you want it?"

"Two hundred joules," David replied, his eyes glued to the EKG strip. "Get ready!"

Carolyn applied the paddles on Warren's chest and moved her thumbs toward the red buttons. "Say when."

"Now!" David ordered.

Carolyn pressed down on the buttons. Warren's body tensed and briefly lifted off the bed.

David watched the moving EKG strip. Warren was still having runs of ventricular tachycardia. "Increase the setting to four hundred!"

Carolyn quickly adjusted the voltage and delivered a second shock. Again Warren's body jerked and lifted, then settled back on the mattress. The alarm on the cardiac monitor abruptly quieted.

David gave Carolyn a thumbs-up signal. "We've got a sinus rhythm."

Carolyn smiled down at Warren and said, "Welcome back."

Warren nodded gratefully, his chest pain eased, his breathing near normal.

David reached up to IV bag containing bretylium and increased the flow rate to two milligrams per minute. "Hopefully this will keep his rhythm regular," he said hastily. "Now let's get back to …"

Outside in the corridor a commotion suddenly started. There were yells and commands, followed by running footsteps.

David stiffened. *Oh shit! They must know the rescue attempt is coming! Somehow they found out!* He quickly checked his watch. It was 2:00 a.m! Zero hour! He grabbed Carolyn's hand and headed for the door.

The guard stepped in front of their path and motioned them back with his Uzi. When they didn't budge, he uttered a menacing growl and aimed his submachine gun at them.

"He's not going to let us leave," Carolyn whispered nervously.

"We've got to get back to the President, or he'll die in the rescue attempt," David said out of the corner of his mouth. "We've got to move him."

The guard forcefully jabbed the barrel of his Uzi into David's ribs, causing him to double over in pain. Then the terrorist shoved David back and pushed him up against the bed. With a smirk on his face, he raised his Uzi and pointed it at David's head.

Carolyn was petrified with fright. *Oh my God! He's going to shoot David! He's going to kill him!* her brain screamed. Acting on impulse, she lunged at the terrorist and pressed the defibrillator paddles against his back. Before he could react, she pushed the red buttons on the handles. The terrorist shook violently, stunned senseless momentarily by the strong electric current surging through his body. His Uzi dangled from his hand, its barrel pointing downward.

David moved in quickly. He spun the terrorist around and, with a powerful jerk, tried to snap the man's cervical spine. But the terrorist's neck was thick and muscular and difficult to grasp. David tightened his grip and forcefully jerked at the spine again. There was a loud pop just before the terrorist went limp and sank to the floor. For a moment he appeared lifeless, but then his left arm convulsed and he began to gurgle loudly. David reached for a pre-filled syringe of Propofol and hurriedly palpated the terrorist's bulky neck, searching for a carotid pulse. He found it on the second try and injected the entire contents of the syringe directly into the artery. It took the terrorist less than twenty seconds to die.

"Is he dead?" Carolyn asked, feeling a strong surge of adrenaline. "Good and dead?"

David nodded and quickly looked to the door to see if the disturbance had alerted the other guard. It hadn't. He reached down for the terrorist's Uzi and spare clip of ammunition, then turned back to Carolyn.

"They know the rescue attempt is about to happen! That's why he tried to keep us in the room at gunpoint. They wanted clear shots at the commandos coming in."

"Should we just wait here, then?"

"We can't," David told her. "We've got to move the President or he'll die in the rescue."

"But the guards in the corridor aren't going to let us leave this room," Carolyn argued promptly. "They'll shoot us on sight."

"And if we remain here, what happens when the terrorists spot the body on the floor?"

"They'll kill us."

"Damn right they will," David said, hurriedly checking his watch. It was 2:05. Five minutes past the zero hour! The President was living on borrowed time. "So we'll have to take our chances," he went on in a rush. "Listen carefully and do exactly as I say. You stay put while I clear the corridor. When I yell 'Go!' you run like hell for the President's room. Then disconnect him from his tubes and drag him into the bathroom. Try to get into the bathtub or as far away from the door as possible. Got it?"

"Got it," Carolyn said, bracing herself.

David tiptoed silently to the door and peeked out. The guard outside the President's room was yawning deeply and shaking his head, as if to clear it. *The Valium was taking effect,* David thought. *The man's reflexes would be slowed.* David crept into the corridor, his Uzi at the ready. The terrorist suddenly saw motion in his peripheral vision and began to raise his weapon, but it was too late. David fired off a quick burst into the man's chest, killing him instantly. Spinning around, David dropped to a prone position and scanned the length of the hallway. It was clear.

348

"Go, Carolyn! Go!"

Carolyn dashed out of the door and was almost to the President's room when a terrorist appeared from behind the nurses' station. David opened up with another burst of gunfire, hitting the man in his legs and lower abdomen. The terrorist fell heavily to the floor, face first.

Four terrorists down, David counted, with only Aliev left standing. He kept low, with his Uzi pointed in the direction of the nurses' station, and whispered a silent message to Aliev. *Come on, you murdering bastard. Show yourself. Just a little bit of your head. That's all I need.* Beads of perspiration popped out on David's brow and dripped down into his eyes. He hastily wiped them away, waiting and watching, his weapon steady. In the distance, he saw a foot stepping out of the treatment room. It must be Aliev! David started to squeeze the trigger of his Uzi.

There was a sudden blast of explosions. David was thrown across the corridor by the force of the detonations. He bounced off a door, then landed hard on the carpeted floor. It took him several seconds to recover and regain his balance. The air in the corridor was now filled with dust and floating debris. David couldn't see anything through the haze, but he could hear Secret Service agents rappelling down from the roof and entering the suites through large windows that had been blown open by carefully placed explosives. David crawled backwards until he reached the President's room and entered. He kept his head and body close to the floor, now hearing footsteps across the suite.

A voice in the dimness called out, "Mr. President! Mr. President! Can you hear me?"

"We're in the bathroom," Carolyn shouted back. "The President is okay. But there are terrorists in the corridor."

"Stay where you are," Geary ordered, then asked, "Is Ballineau with you?"

"Over here," David yelled, still keeping low. The dust in the air began to settle and David could make out two black-clad agents wearing night-vision goggles. He sprang to his feet and walked over. "Are you Geary?"

"Yeah."

"Let me fill you in," David went on quickly. "The corridor is clear down to the nurses' station, and four of the five terrorists are dead."

"How do you know they're dead?" Geary asked at once.

"Because I killed them," David replied matter-of-factly. "The only one left is their leader, Aliev, and he's the most dangerous of the bunch. He'll be heavily armed and ready to kill every one of the hostages he holds. We've got to take him out, *now*."

"Let us handle it," Geary said, giving rapid hand signals to the other agent in the room.

David removed his used clip of ammunition and expertly inserted a fresh one. "If you want to get to Aliev quickly, you're going to need me. I know the floor better than you, and better than him. I shift the odds in your favor."

"Are you sure you want in on this, doc?" Gear asked gravely. "All hell is about to break loose."

David ignored the warning and double-checked his weapon to make sure the new clip of ammunition was firmly in place. "We've got to get to him before he starts killing hostages."

"Okay," Geary told him turning for the corridor. "We're going in fast and low. You stick by me and follow my lead."

As they approached the door, Geary abruptly stopped and listened to a message coming into his earphone. "Yes, ma'am," he replied. "The President and his family are secure."

There were loud cheers in the background, which the Vice President had to shout over. "Do we have any further information on the plane carrying the nuclear weapon? In particular, the plane's ID, where it will cross the border, and what its final destination is."

"I'll ask," Geary said and passed the questions over to David, who shook his head.

"No luck, ma'am." Geary reported. "But we'll—"

David interrupted, saying, "They did mention intense radioactivity that would contaminate some area for years to come. We assumed they were talking about Los Angeles."

Geary transmitted the new information, then listened intently before responding, "No, ma'am. There was no mention of Russian oil fields."

As the phone conversation ended, David asked, "What's so important about the Russian oil fields?"

"That's where our intel people believe they're going to drop the nuke," Geary answered and pushed up his night-vision goggles. "Are you ready to kick some ass?"

"Ready," David replied and spat for good luck, just as he'd always done in Special Forces.

Geary gave final instructions via his microphone to agents across the corridor, then cried out, "Go!"

Geary and David rolled their bodies into the corridor and opened fire, blazing away from prone positions. Three more agents appeared at their side, shooting at will and strafing the far end of the hallway. David and the agents reloaded and opened up again, spraying the entire area from side to side. Then they held their fire.

They waited for several seconds in the dust-filled corridor, expecting return gunfire. None came.

"What do you think?" Geary whispered low.

"He's waiting for us," David whispered back. "And we can't stay here much longer."

"Why not?"

"Because we're in the open and he's got hand grenades."

"Oh, shit!" Geary groaned. He quickly signaled the other agents and yelled out, "Go!"

The group of five pushed themselves up and ran for the nurses' station. They were almost there when the terrorists opened fire. Two agents crumpled to the floor. One was hit in the abdomen, the other in the head. More bullets whizzed by.

At the nurses' station, David dove in head first. Another burst of gunfire caught a third agent in the shoulder. He rolled over to the elevators, clutching his bleeding wound.

David pressed up against the wall and hurriedly collected himself. Four of the enemy were dead, which meant there should be only Aliev remaining. But the return gunfire had been too intense for just one man. Maybe Aliev had another Chechen hidden away somewhere. David glanced over to the chairs at the front desk. Jarrin Smith was crouching down behind one of them, his hands still tied. But the Russian security agent was gone. Where the hell was he?

Geary called out to the wounded agent by the elevator, "Evans, are you okay?"

"I'll live," Evans called back and tried to reload his weapon. But his right arm was useless.

"Can you get those elevator doors opened?" Geary asked, lowering his voice.

"I don't think so, "Evans answered quietly. "It looks like they've got the doors jammed with metal spikes."

"Try to pry them loose with the barrel of your weapon."

Evans attempted the maneuver, but he had only one good hand and the weapon kept slipping.

Geary considered rolling across the corridor to assist Evans but quickly decided against it. He'd be a sitting duck and dead before he got halfway to the elevators. Geary turned to David and whispered, "That was a hell of a lot of gunfire for only one terrorist."

"I had the same thought," David whispered back. "Let's make them show their hand so we can see how many they've got."

"How are you going to do that?"

"Watch."

David reached over for a large medicine cart and shoved it with all his might. The cart sped across the corridor and crashed against the wall.

The terrorists blasted away, shredding the metal cart to pieces.

David waited for the barrage to stop. Then he carefully peeked out, using the corner of one eye. He saw the Russian security agent, Yudenko, standing half-exposed in a doorway.

"Get down!" David whispered loudly to him. "Get down!"

The agent brought up his Uzi and opened fire at David. Instinctively, David ducked low as a stream of bullets whizzed by him. The agent took out a fresh clip of ammunition but briefly fumbled with it. That extra moment gave David his chance. He squeezed off a short burst. The Russian agent clutched at his chest and staggered out of the doorway. A second blast ripped into him just above the bridge of his nose. He was dead before he hit the floor.

"Jesus Christ!" David growled, catching his breath and again pressing himself against a wall in the nurses' station. "It was the Russian security agent! He was one of them!"

Geary nodded gravely. "And he must have been their inside man. We knew they had to have one to pull this off."

And the bastard no doubt tipped off Aliev about the plan for Jarrin to contact the hospital operator, David seethed inwardly. "How the hell did they let a Chechen in their secret service?"

"Who knows?" Geary took a quick look into the corridor and came back. "I saw two bodies."

"And I can guarantee you there are three others I know are dead."

"Which leaves only Aliev."

The Pavilion became quiet. There were no sounds at all, not even the noise of movement.

"Do you think he's dead, or wounded?" Geary asked, keeping his voice down.

"I wouldn't count on it," David said, and concentrated his hearing. All he heard was the sound of his own breathing and the blood pumping in his ears.

Slowly the air cleared as the dust settled. Seconds ticked by in the stillness. Then more seconds passed.

The silence was abruptly broken by the noise of a wheelchair being pushed into the corridor.

"If anyone comes close, I promise you I will shoot," Aliev called out.

There was no response to his threat.

"I mean it," Aliev said gruffly, now appearing beside the wheelchair. "Do as I say, or the old man dies!"

"It's Sol!" Carolyn said, looking up from the wounded agent she was attending to in the corridor. "He's got Sol!"

Aliev ignored her. "You will drop your weapons onto the floor."

"Go screw yourself!" Geary called back.

Aliev aimed his Uzi at Simcha's head. "Let us see how brave you are when his blood begins to spurt out."

Carolyn resisted the powerful urge to go to the aid of the elderly patient who was slumped over in his wheelchair. "Please don't hurt him!"

"If you want to help the old Jew," Aliev said kindly, "you may do so. I won't harm you."

Carolyn hesitated, then slowly walked forward, her fear mounting. Her heart pounded in her chest as she wondered if Sol was already dead. He wasn't moving.

"Don't go, Carolyn!" David pleaded with her. "It's a trap!"

She disregarded his warning, and walked on. Her fright was almost paralyzing now. She had to force herself to put one foot in front of the other. Finally she arrived at the wheelchair and checked Simcha's pulse. It was thready and erratic.

"Sol?" Carolyn asked softly. "Can you hear me?

Aliev smiled thinly and nudged Carolyn with his Uzi. "Ah, an even better hostage now! So two will die if my instructions aren't followed."

Simcha raised his head to Carolyn and said weakly, "You are such a sweet girl."

"Oh, Sol!" Carolyn moaned.

"Have a happy life," he wished her.

Suddenly, Simcha felt strength coming into his arms. It wasn't a lot, but it was enough for him to do what he wanted to do. *Nazi bastard!* Simcha thought, his anger spilling over. *Die with me!* He grabbed the barrel of Aliev's Uzi and jerked it down toward the floor. "Run, Carolyn! Run!"

But before she could, Aliev pulled the weapon up and fired point-blank into Simcha's chest, sending the old man and his wheelchair crashing down. Blood gushed from Simcha's thorax and mouth. He coughed and choked, and more blood bubbled up. Then his head sagged and his lifeless eyes stayed wide open.

"No!" Carolyn screamed, horrified at the sight.

Aliev snatched Carolyn by the hair and dragged her across the corridor, using her as a human shield. She screamed again as he pulled her into the treatment room and slammed the door behind them.

Geary asked quickly, "Are there any exits from that room?"

"No, but he might try to blast an opening from the crawlspace to the roof with a grenade," David said, desperately searching his mind for a way to rescue Carolyn. One wrong move, and Aliev would kill her. "Who do you have up on the roof?"

"A helicopter pilot and a lookout."

"You'd better warn them, and tell them Aliev has a hostage."

"Will do." Geary spoke into his microphone and passed on the information. Then he listened to a message coming in over his earphone. "Good work," he said and came back to David. "We've got a sharpshooter up on the roof of an institute across from the hospital. He has a night-vision scope with a built-in infrared device."

"He'd better be careful," David cautioned. "If Aliev comes onto the roof, he'll have the barrel of his Uzi jammed into Carolyn's back. Even if your man gets off a head shot, Aliev could reflexively squeeze the trigger."

"Maybe, maybe not," Geary argued mildly. "But this might well be her best chance to survive."

"It'll more likely be her death warrant," David argued back.

A sudden noise came from the treatment room. It sounded like a metal tray hitting the floor and rattling around. Then quiet returned.

"Let's face it," Geary said somberly. "That nurse is already as good as dead."

"I guess," David muttered, knowing it was true but not wanting to accept it. He concentrated his mind, trying to think of ways to save Carolyn. To begin with, he'd need some sort of distraction. But what?

A nearly dead terrorist on the floor slowly reached for his Sig Sauer pistol and fired. Two bullets hissed by David's head and struck the wall behind him, sending plaster flying.

Geary reflexively blasted away, killing the terrorist before he could get off another round. The dead terrorist slumped forward into a pool of bright red blood.

David froze in place, his heart pounding so hard he could hear it. *Jesus Christ! So close! Another inch down and the top of my head would have been gone, and Kit would have been without a father.* A gruesome picture suddenly flashed into David's mind. He was in a casket, and Kit was walking toward him, crying, holding onto Juanita's hand. David groaned inwardly and shook his head to dispel the image.

"You okay?" Geary asked.

"I'm fine," David said, swallowing back his fear. He took a deep breath and waited for his pulse to slow. "I shot that bastard from a distance while we were running for the President's room. I should have made sure he was dead."

Geary nodded. "*Should have*s will get you killed in this business."

They heard the door to the treatment room creak open. Both men raised their weapons.

Aliev yelled out, "Any more gunfire and the nurse dies!"

"Let her go!" David shouted. "Take me as your hostage instead."

"Come in," Aliev encouraged. "Unarmed, with your hands in the air."

"No, David!" Carolyn cried. "Don't do it!"

David put his Uzi aside and slowly got to his knees, wondering what his next move should be.

Geary grabbed David's arm and pulled him back down. "Don't be stupid! He's using her for bait."

David shrugged off the hold. "We can't just leave her in there."

"Then it should be me that goes in, not you," Geary volunteered.

David shook his head. "He'll kill you the second you step into the room. He'll see your black outfit and night-vision goggles, and know you're a commando. And that makes you very dangerous to him. He thinks I'm just another doctor. I'd just be another good hostage."

Geary hesitated and carefully considered the plan. He didn't like using a civilian on such a risky mission, even one with Special Forces training. "What if I'm unarmed when I walk in?"

"It won't matter. He'll still see you as a threat and kill you," David said with certainty. "And keep in mind, the last thing we want to do is spook Aliev. He's trigger-happy enough as is."

Geary hesitated again before nodding. "If I hear any shots, I'm coming in after you."

David took a deep breath, steeling himself. "Remember to shoot high."

"And you remember to duck."

David got to his feet and kicked his weapon toward Geary. He knew that Aliev would never let Carolyn go. Two hostages were a lot better than one. Slowly he moved to the treatment room, with no plan in mind. He would have to act on instinct. And that was a big disadvantage when facing an armed terrorist. David's pulse began to race, but he willed it to stay steady. *Watch his head! It's always the head that moves first.*

David pushed the door open and entered the treatment room with his hands raised high. Carolyn was standing on the countertop, ready to climb up through an open panel into the crawlspace.

And just beyond her feet was a cell phone, its screen lighted and blinking.

Aliev pointed his Uzi at David. "Stupid move, doctor! I saw you handle that weapon. I know you are not just a physician. Better I kill you now, no?"

David quickly looked for a weak spot but found none. Any sudden move and he'd be a dead man long before he got to Aliev. He tried desperately to come up with a maneuver to save his life, but his mind was a blur. *Think, goddamn it! Think!*

"Well? Can you give me a reason why I should let you live?" Aliev asked. "You see, my plans will still work with only one hostage."

David's eyes went to Carolyn standing on the counter. Somehow he had to buy himself time to think. "Whatever your plans are, you're going to have to change them."

"Why?" Aliev demanded.

"Because you're surrounded on all sides," David said, keeping his voice even. "You have no place to go."

Aliev made a scornful sound. "What makes you think I have to go anywhere?"

"You can't stay here forever," David said, trying to prolong the conversation and gain more time.

"Don't be so sure," Aliev told him and reached for his satellite phone, all the while keeping his eyes on David. He pressed the redial button and listened intently for a response. After a few moments, he grumbled to himself and placed the phone down. Then he came back to David. "So, doctor-who-pretends-to-be-a-soldier," Aliev went on derisively, "can you give one good reason why I should allow you to live?"

David had no answer. He stared down the barrel of Aliev's Uzi and readied himself to make a final, desperate move. He loosened his foot inside his loafer, planning to kick the leather shoe at Aliev and throw the terrorist off balance. Then go for his eyes before he can recover. *Yeah, right*, David thought grimly, knowing his chance of success was near nil. But he had to try. Ever so slowly he began to flex to knee, his pulse now skipping beats. "I-I guess I'm a dead man," he said in an uneven voice.

"Not quite yet," Aliev said, glancing briefly at the wall phone. "You will live a little longer, because I have found a temporary use for you. You will follow my instructions to the letter or you will no longer have a head above your neck."

David quickly collected himself and shoved his foot back into his loafer, then asked, "What are these instructions?"

"When I say, you will go to the door and tell the Secret Service agent that I wish to speak with the pilot of an airplane that is en route to Los Angeles from Mexico. I will give you the pilot's phone number shortly. The call is to be patched through to the telephone in this room. Understood?"

"Understood," David replied, certain that Aliev was referring to the escape plane carrying a nuclear weapon. "But they'll never let you reach the airport, even with hostages. They'll never allow you to board that plane."

"I have no need to go to the plane," Aliev said, smiling thinly. "I will arrange for the plane and its cargo to come to me." The terrorist nodded to himself, obviously pleased, then glimpsed at his watch. "Yes, my plane will fly into the Los Angeles area within the hour."

David's jaw dropped. *Oh, my God! He's going to drop the nuke on Los Angeles, not the Russian oil fields! Aliev knows he can't escape, so he's decided to die here in a nuclear holocaust! And the plane carrying the bomb is only an hour away! They'll never find that damn plane in time! Never! They don't know its ID or flight plan or even where it will cross the extensive U.S.-Mexico border. They'll never locate that damn plane!* "Wh … what cargo?" David managed to ask.

"That's not your concern," Aliev snapped. "Now, if you wish to live, you will do exactly as you are told. Make one foolish move and it will be your last. Have no doubt, I will kill you without giving it a second thought. You are to do only the things I tell you to do. Understood?"

David nodded, straining to refocus his brain and think of a way to disarm Aliev. But how? How? One slip-up, and he and Carolyn were dead. And Kit was parentless and all alone in the world.

Carolyn shifted around on her feet and asked weakly, "M-may I please come down?"

"No," Aliev said sharply. "You will stay there. If the Secret Service refuses to follow my orders, you will help me blast a large hole in the roof with a grenade. This will give me a clear view of the sky and allow my satellite phone to work properly." He quickly came back to David and pointed the Uzi at his head. "And remember, one false move and I will kill you."

"You may not be able to," David said, staring up at Carolyn as a plan of action flashed into his mind. It was very risky and required split-second timing from Carolyn, but it was their only chance. David pushed his fear aside and willed his expression to stay neutral. "As a matter of fact, I'm certain you won't be able to kill me."

"Why not?" Aliev sneered.

"Because of the ceiling," David said, sending a subtle message to Carolyn by nodding to her. "It's about to fall down on you."

"Ha!" Aliev scoffed. "Do you expect me to look up?"

"No," David said and gave Carolyn another exaggerated nod. "I expect something to fall on you."

Carolyn got the message. She hesitated a moment to gather her courage, then dropped her full weight down on Aliev. They crumpled to the floor. Yet Aliev managed to hold on to his Uzi. He sprayed the room wildly, the bullets missing David but blowing out the large glass window.

David lunged for the Uzi and ripped it from Aliev's grasp. The submachine gun tumbled to the floor. Aliev tried to retrieve it, but David jerked him away and threw him against the counter. The terrorist went for his knife and held the blade like an experienced fighter. He slashed at David's chest twice, missing by inches. David backed up, his leg wound throbbing badly and bleeding more. Aliev slashed again, but this time David stepped inside the stroke and, grasping the terrorist's wrist, spun him around. Then David shoved him toward the blasted-out window, intending to push him through it. But Aliev broke free and came at David again, now circling and moving more deliberately. He held the knife in close and waited for an opening. His eyes came off David for a fraction of a second. He glanced over at Carolyn, then slowly began inching his way toward her.

David backed up, trying to keep himself between the terrorist and Carolyn, but his strength was fading rapidly. His legs felt weak and heavy again, and he knew they would soon give out. And that's when Aliev would make his move. The pain in David's leg abruptly intensified, as the large muscles surrounding his wound went into spasm. He grimaced and clutched at his bloody thigh, then dropped down to one knee. Aliev smiled malevolently and came in for the kill.

Get a weapon! David's brain yelled. *Any weapon!* He hurriedly reached for his stethoscope, planning to swing the metal end at Aliev's head. But his hand found the scalpel he had secreted away earlier. He grasped the blade and kept it in his pocket until Aliev was close enough to smell. Then David slashed at the terrorist's hand. The sharp edge cut through the flexor tendons to Aliev's fingers. He screamed in pain as his knife fell to the floor.

Struggling to his feet, David grabbed the back of Aliev's collar and pushed him toward the blasted-out window again.

"You'd better grow wings, you son of a bitch," David growled. "You're going to need them."

At the last moment, Aliev dug in his heels and tried to twist away. David pushed harder and slammed the terrorist down on the windowsill. Aliev's head went out the window, but his neck came down on the jagged edge of broken glass. A fountain of blood spurted out of his severed carotid arteries. He flailed his arms in a frantic attempt to disengage, but the more he tried the more he bled. His blood was everywhere, with most of it on the windowsill and adjacent wall.

David held the man down with his last bit of strength. It took Kuri Aliev less than a minute to become motionless. His breaths were now agonal, his arms simply dangling.

David limped over to the door and opened it. He gave the Secret Service agents in the corridor a thumbs-up "all clear" signal. Then he urgently motioned Joe Geary over. "The plane from Mexico is going to drop its nuke somewhere over Los Angeles! It's within an hour away!"

"It's only minutes away," Geary said hurriedly, all of his attention directed to the conversation coming in over his earphone. "And it's headed straight for us!"

"Jesus!" David breathed, his pulse racing again. He watched Geary anxiously and tried to read his expression, but the agent's face remained impassive. "What's happening now?"

"The grand finale," Geary told him, pressing in on his earpiece so as not to miss a word. "And the crazy bastard won't listen."

"Listen to what?"

"The repeated warnings from our interceptors," Geary answered. "We've shut down all the air corridors between the U.S. and Mexico. Planes approaching from the south have been instructed to go into a holding pattern while preparations are being made for them to land in Mexico. There's one plane that won't comply. He's making a break for the border, twenty-five miles south of San Diego. That's less than three minutes from U.S. soil."

Seconds ticked off. Then more seconds.

"Come on!" Geary urged, his face tightening. "Blow his ass out of the sky!"

More time passed. It seemed like an eternity to David as he envisioned the aircraft coming closer and closer to California. The plane was already near enough to detonate its bomb and cover San Diego with a blanket of deadly radioactivity. *And they can't even be certain they're tracking the right plane! It could be an innocent cargo jet with a malfunctioning radio. Or maybe the fleeing airplane was trying to evade the authorities because it was packed to the brim with cocaine and other illegal drugs. How can they determine if the plane they're zeroing in on has the nuclear bomb? Or do they just shoot it down and hope for the best?*

"Come on, damn it!" Geary implored, now with great urgency. "They're going to run out of time up there!"

If they haven't already, David thought miserably. That plane had to be at the U.S. border by now. Or across it.

Geary crooked his neck and listened intently to his earpiece, then let out a long sigh of relief. "Good riddance," he said before turning to David. "The terrorist plane is sitting on the bottom of the Pacific Ocean, compliments of the United States Navy."

"Are they sure it was the plane carrying the nuke?" David asked at once.

Geary nodded. "The pilot was yelling 'God is great!' and 'Death to America!' on his way down."

"That's good enough," David said and nodded back, then inquired, "What happens to the nuke now?"

"I suspect they're already making plans to fetch it with a deep-sea submersible." Geary glanced around David and peered into the treatment room. A Secret Service agent was carefully removing grenades from the terrorist's motionless body. "Is Aliev dead?"

"He's been neutralized," David said, using a term he hadn't used in over twenty years. But it still meant the same. Aliev was no longer a threat and would never be one again.

Geary's gaze went to the stunned nurse on the floor. "Is she hurt?"

David shook his head. "Just bruised."

As Geary relayed the new information to the Secret Service team, David spun around and rushed back to Carolyn's side. Helping her to her feet, he asked, "Are you okay?"

"Fi-fine," Carolyn stammered and gulped back her fright. She glanced over to Aliev's mangled body, and swallowed hard once more before adding, "I've never seen a man butchered like that before."

"Let's hope you never see it again," David said, and held her close. He took long, deep breaths to calm himself, but his pulse was still racing, his level of adrenaline sky high from his close calls with death. He looked over to Aliev and the pools of blood around him. It was poetic justice, David thought. Aliev was willing to let the President bleed to death. Instead, it was the terrorist who bled out.

Taking another deep breath, David brought his attention back to Carolyn. "You saved my life, you know. I owe you."

Carolyn smiled and brushed her lips against his. "I'll try to think of a way for you to repay me, David Ballineau."

A Secret Service agent stuck his head in the doorway. "The specialists are on their way up."

David nodded and took Carolyn's hand. "Let's go get the President and Karen squared away."

In the corridor, blankets had been placed over the two dead Secret Service agents. The dead terrorists were left uncovered. Circling flies were beginning to gather above their bodies.

David checked his watch. It was 2:30. It was just six hours since the President first arrived at the hospital. But it seemed like a lifetime.

Carolyn walked over to Sol Simcha, who was lying next to the overturned wheelchair. Beside him was a Hebrew prayer book that was opened to a page that contained the mourner's Kaddish—the prayer for the dead—that Sol must have been reading before he reached for Aliev's gun. She put the open book on Sol's chest and covered him with a blanket.

The door to the elevator suddenly opened. The gastrointestinal and hematology specialists hurried out, carrying bags of blood and fresh concentrates of Factor VIII. Two nurses from the ICU were a step behind them.

David pointed down the corridor. "The President is in suite one. And there's a doctor next to him with a pneumothorax."

As the group dashed down the corridor, Carolyn ran alongside and filled them in on the details. "His vital signs are a little shaky, but they're holding up. There's bright red blood in his nasogastric tube, but not as much …"

David leaned against the counter at the nurses' station and watched as Carolyn pushed aside the horror of what she'd been through, and went right back to nursing. Most people, man or woman, would have come apart. But she didn't. She never faltered. She really was some woman. And some nurse.

Joe Geary came up to him and said, "Doc, you might want to see this."

David followed the agent into the treatment room. Aliev was still impaled on the dagger-like slivers of the broken window. But now he was convulsing as his brain went totally anoxic. An occasional small spurt of blood came from his neck. Gradually the convulsions stopped, and so did the spurts.

"Nothing much we can do, huh?" Geary asked.

"Nothing at all," David said, and left the room.

In the corridor he looked down at the faces of the dead terrorists, now partially covered with buzzing flies that were feasting on fresh blood. Suddenly David's mind flashed back to Somalia, and to the stacks of bloody corpses and the swarming flies. The sounds and the smells all came back to him. Then the picture changed. Now he was searching a village in the bush, looking for Lewis Daly, the Tennessee sharpshooter the terrorists had caught and mutilated. *Oh, shit! Oh, shit!* David's brain wailed. He knew what was coming next.

But it wasn't a picture of Lewis's head. Instead, in his mind's eye he saw a crisp cold day at Arlington National Cemetery. The sky was blue, with only wisps of white clouds. David was standing at his best friend's headstone, and he heard Lewis's voice. "Let it go, David. Let it go. You've paid the price, and then some."

David blinked his eyes, and the picture and voice disappeared. He gazed down at his hands. There was only a slight tremor. And although his chest felt a little tight, he was moving air in and out with ease. David took a deep breath as he realized the new images had aborted the panic attack. He nodded to himself, remembering that the psychologist at Walter Reed had urged him to conjure up pleasant visions to ward off the attacks. Visions like small waves lapping gently against the shore, or floating butterflies. But those hadn't worked for him. The images at Arlington National Cemetery had. Yeah. Arlington. Where a ton of nightmares, and the men who endured them, had finally come to rest.

Joe Geary came alongside and held out a cell phone. "Somebody wants to talk with you, Doc."

"Who is it?"

"Somebody important."

David took the phone and said, "This is David Ballineau."

"Dr. Ballineau, this is Vice President Halloway. I want you to know how grateful we all are to you for saving the President's life. Goodness knows how you did it, but I thank God you were there."

"I'm glad I was able to help, Ms. Vice President."

"Oh, according to Agent Geary you did much more than help."

"I think he's giving me too much credit."

"We don't, and I'm certain the President doesn't," Halloway told him. "When things have settled down a bit, I'm sure the President will invite you to the White House, where he can honor your heroism."

"That's really not necessary, ma'am."

"Ah, but it is," the Vice President insisted. "And you couldn't very well refuse such an invitation, could you?"

"No, ma'am," David answered. "But there's someone else you should also invite."

"Who?"

"The nurse who kept the President alive all by herself while I was stuck in that crawlspace. Without her, the President would have never made it."

"Her name?"

"Carolyn Ross."

"She'll be on that list."

"Thank you, ma'am," David said. "I'll look forward to the visit."

"As shall we," the Vice President said. "And again, Dr. Ballineau, thank you for saving the President's life. The nation owes you a deep debt of gratitude."

The phone line went dead.

So I'm going back to Washington once more, David thought. *But not to Walter Reed, and not to Arlington. I've been there too many times already. Let those memories stay where they lie.*

Handing the cell phone back to Geary, he suddenly remembered another name that had to be added to the invitation list. He smiled to himself as a picture of Kit came into his mind. She'd be sound asleep now, hugging her favorite teddy bear and thankfully unaware of how close she had come to losing her father. "Would you tell them I'll be bringing my eleven-year-old daughter with me to the White House?"

Geary nodded. "I'll pass it along."

"Thanks," David said. "And thanks for taking out that terrorist who almost blew my head off."

Geary shrugged. "He was in the way."

The men exchanged brief grins as another team of Secret Service agents rushed onto the Pavilion and secured every room and exit.

David walked on, his pace quickening. He wanted to see how the President was doing. And he wanted to take Carolyn out to breakfast. With a lot of coffee, and a lot of conversation. After what they'd been through with Patient One, she undoubtedly had plenty of things she wanted to ask him, and he had plenty of things he wanted to tell her.

THE END

© Dennis Trantham

ABOUT THE AUTHOR

Leonard Goldberg is the internationally bestselling author of the Joanna Blalock series of medical thrillers. His novels, acclaimed by critics as well as fellow authors, have been translated into a dozen languages and have sold more than a million copies worldwide. Leonard Goldberg is himself a consulting physician affiliated with the UCLA Medical Center, where he holds an appointment as Clinical Professor of Medicine. A highly sought-after expert witness in medical malpractice trials, he is board certified in internal medicine, hematology, and rheumatology, and has published over a hundred scientific studies in peer-reviewed journals.

Leonard Goldberg's writing career began with a clinical interest in blood disorders. While involved in a research project at UCLA, he encountered a most unusual blood type. The patient's red blood cells were O-Rh null, indicating they were totally deficient in A, B, and Rh factors and could be administered to virtually anyone without fear of a transfusion reaction. In essence, the patient was the proverbial "universal" blood donor. This finding spurred the idea for a story in which an individual was born without a tissue type, making that person's organs transplantable into anyone without worry of rejection. His first novel, *Transplant*, revolved around a young woman who is discovered to be a universal organ donor and is hounded by a wealthy, powerful man in desperate need of a new kidney. The book quickly went through multiple printings and was optioned by a major Hollywood studio.

On the strength of the critical and popular reception of *Transplant*, Leonard Goldberg was off to the races as an author of medical thrillers. He began writing a series of new books, with a continuing main character named Joanna Blalock. The Joanna Blalock series features a forensic pathologist at a prestigious university medical center who has a Holmesian knack for solving murders. These books include *Deadly Medicine*, *A Deadly Practice*, *Deadly Care*, *Deadly Harvest*, *Deadly Exposure*, *Lethal Measures*, *Fatal Care*, *Brainwaves*, and *Fever Cell*.

Leonard Goldberg's novels have been selections of the Book of the Month Club, French and Czech book clubs, and The Mystery Guild. They have been featured as *People* magazine's "Page-Turner of the Week," as well as at the International Book Fair in Budapest. The series has been optioned on several occasions for development as a motion picture or television project.

Please visit his website, at www.leonardgoldberg.com.

Critics across the country have praised his novels as:
- "Fascinating … devilish" (*People* magazine)
- "Cool cuttings by a sure hand … scalpel-edged" (*Kirkus*)
- "Imaginative, murderous … captures the top shelf in the mystery world" (*Kansas City Star*)
- "Compelling and suspenseful" (Associated Press)
- "Diabolical" (*Virginian Pilot*)

- "A medical thriller — with uniquely ghastly murders" (*Los Angeles Times Book Review*)
- "Bone-chilling and provocative" (*Tulsa World*)
- "Fascinating and fast-moving" (*Booklist*)
- "Rushes along at a brisk clip" (*Chicago Tribune*)
- "A page-turner with medical realism and characters who command our sympathies" (*Charleston Post and Courier*)
- "Outstanding specimens of suspense" (*Knoxville News-Sentinel*)
- "The stuff of nightmares" (*Library Journal*)

His best-selling novels have also been praised by fellow writers as:

- "Loaded with suspense and believable characters" (T. Jefferson Parker)
- "Medical suspense at its best" (Michael Palmer)

Dr. Goldberg is a native of Charleston (with the accent to prove it) and a longtime California resident. He currently divides his time between Los Angeles and an island off the coast of South Carolina.